A Dance of Lies

A Dance of Lies

❖⋯❖

BRITTNEY ARENA

BLOOMSBURY
LONDON · OXFORD · NEW YORK · NEW DELHI · SYDNEY

BLOOMSBURY PUBLISHING
Bloomsbury Publishing Plc
50 Bedford Square, London, WC1B 3DP, UK
29 Earlsfort Terrace, Dublin 2, Ireland

BLOOMSBURY, BLOOMSBURY PUBLISHING and the Diana logo are trademarks of
Bloomsbury Publishing Plc

First published in 2025 in the US by Del Rey, an imprint of Penguin Random House
First published in Great Britain 2025

Copyright © Brittney Arena, 2025

Brittney Arena is identified as the author of this work in accordance with the Copyright,
Designs and Patents Act 1988.

This advance reading copy is printed from uncorrected proof pages and is not for resale. This
does not represent the final text and should not be quoted without reference to the final printed
book.

This is a work of fiction. Names and characters are the product of the author's imagination and
any resemblance to actual persons, living or dead, is entirely coincidental

All rights reserved. No part of this publication may be reproduced or transmitted in any form or
by any means, electronic or mechanical, including photocopying, recording, or any information
storage or retrieval system, without prior permission in writing from the publishers

Bloomsbury Publishing Plc does not have any control over, or responsibility for, any third-party
websites referred to in this book. All internet addresses given in this book were correct at the
time of going to press. The author and publisher regret any inconvenience caused if addresses
have changed or sites have ceased to exist, but can accept no responsibility for any such
changes

A catalogue record for this book is available from the British Library

ISBN: HB: 978-1-5266-8140-9; TPB: 978-1-5266-8139-3; eBook: 978-1-5266-8145-4; ePDF:
978-1-5266-8143-0

2 4 6 8 10 9 7 5 3 1

Typeset by [insert typesetter name]
Printed and bound in Great Britain by CPI Group (UK) Ltd, Croydon CR0 4YY

MIX
Paper | Supporting
responsible forestry
FSC
www.fsc.org   FSC® C013604

To find out more about our authors and books visit www.bloomsbury.com and sign up for our
newsletters

This advance reading copy is printed from uncorrected proof pages. This
does not represent the final text and should not be quoted without
reference to the final printed book.
No part of this publication may be used in any way for the training of
artificial intelligence technologies.

To Jeff, my everything.

And to those who feel invisible in their pain.

Author's Note

Dear Reader:
    This book began not as a mirror of my own experiences but as an escape from them. Yet as stories often do, it took an unexpected turn.

Fantasy has always been dear to me, offering a window to another world when I needed it most. I've always yearned for daring, fantastical adventures. And in my twenties, while battling illness that left me bedridden more often than not, I sought to write a story that would remind me what it felt like to be alive during a time where I felt more like a corpse.

What I didn't know I needed, however, was proof that someone like me—with all my pain and physical limitations—was enough to take center stage in such a tale. We often read about powerful heroines wielding mighty swords, but where were the ones who struggled to function, let alone fight?

Vasalie became my answer to that question. While her disability stems from long-term imprisonment, mine is a result of my struggle with POTS (postural orthostatic tachycardia syndrome), MCAS (mast cell activation syndrome), EDS (Ehlers-Danlos syndrome), dysautonomia, ME/CFS (chronic fatigue syndrome),

Lyme disease, and more. Writing her story was my declaration that our limitations do not define our worth or limit our ability to live wonderfully romantic and impactful lives.

I suspect many of you know pain on an intimate level. While I wish I could take that away, I hope I can at least make you feel seen—and remind you of how very valuable you are. Your pain, invisible or not, is never wasted. Your words matter. Your story matters. You are deserving of a main character slot.

—Brittney Arena

Trigger Warnings

Emotional abuse, physical abuse, alcoholism, PTSD, panic attacks, trauma, violence against children, sexual themes, graphic death, chronic illness, disability, and sexism.

The Crown's Syndicate

- SIRA
- KURST
- SERAI
- KARITHIAN ISLANDS
- LOREWOOD FOREST
- IRIVAN
- CENTRAL MIRIDRAN
- GALAN
- WEST MIRIDRAN
- MIRIDRAN

Map Labels

- BRISENDALE
- ZAR
- KASIM
- ISLE OF ANELL
- PHILAM
- VERIA
- RAZAM
- ANSA
- EAST MIRIDRAN
- MOUNT CARAPET

PART ONE

King of Lies

Chapter One

Voices speak to me in the endless dark.
    Sometimes, it's my own voice. An incessant humming.
Then it warps. Fragments.

Becomes ten, twenty. A choir. People I used to know, calling my name. *Vasalie. Vah-sah-leee.* They sing to me. They recount my failures. They tell me all is hopeless, that I am lost to this prison.

Only today, they are silenced by a long, winding screech.

Blades of torchlight cut into my cell, falling across my skin in stripes.

I shift from the onslaught of light, but clamps of steel dig into the raw skin of my wrists, fettering me in place. I narrow my gaze toward the window inset into the cell door. It never opens—never ever—save the rare occasions when the warden opts to ensure I'm still breathing. Which he did yesterday.

I think.

Still, I await the passing of a profile. The closing squeal of those shutters.

For the dark to swarm in once more.

My eyes have long since adjusted to it, after all. There is only ever the soft, taunting flicker from underneath the door.

Too exposed.

Far too *bright*.

I turn my gaze from the legs poking out from beneath my scratchy linen shift, unable to look at them for long. I count the rats instead. So many of them, huddling in the corners, gnawing on whatever they can find. Their razor-edged teeth are as familiar to me as the dirt and grime that coats my skin.

I am little more than a husk. A corpse. A set of bones, waiting to be buried.

I'm not sure my heart beats anymore.

I'm not sure I want it to.

Still, the window does not shut.

Then the groan of metal shakes the very foundation of this place—the outer door to the prison. Footfalls echo, echo, *echo*, a thundering pulse.

I lift my head.

Moments later, silhouettes crowd around my window, blotting out the light. The sound of keys rustle from just outside.

"Morta's teeth. That *smell*," someone says.

"If you take her out, I'll polish your armor for a week."

A weak pulse flutters within my chest.

"A week? You can't be serious. I wouldn't touch her with a ten-foot lance."

Have they come to carry out my execution? Metal bites into my forearms as I lean forward. I would beg for it, for that sweet moment of release. For a chance to stand on my own two legs and fill my lungs with the warm western breeze, if only for a moment before a blade strikes me down.

"I can't believe King Illian wants to see her like this. Can't imagine any amount of scrubbing would do any good."

King Illian.

Like the swing of an axe, his face cleaves into my mind.

The sharp, marble cut of his jaw.

The sleek sheen of dark curls.

The endless black of his eyes, and the way they always glittered when they beheld me, save for that last time.

That last time.

Illian.

His name is like the stab of a nail, straight into the cavity of my chest. I pull in a breath, feeling the ghost of a puncture in my lungs.

Part of me has begun to wonder if he was a dream. A wonderful one, then a terrible one. A phantom I cannot shake.

He's sent for me. *Why?*

I remember . . .

What do I remember?

That I was to live out my days in isolation, half mad, until I finally succumbed to the horrors of this fates-forsaken place. But . . . perhaps they need the cell? Perhaps I am too expensive a prisoner?

No. If the king wants me, it isn't to spare a cell.

"The hair will smell the worst. Throw this over her head," one of them says. "At least until she's back within the palace walls."

The cell door jerks open, smearing a fan of dirt across the flagstones. Armored boots come into view between my snarled, honey-brown strands.

One guard blocks the doorway as if I could run, while the other reaches for my arm with a gauntleted hand. A click, and my shackles separate from the main chain. A frisson of fear sets my limbs to trembling. I press my back against the jagged wall, but he wrenches me up with merciless intent.

Sudden dizziness tilts my equilibrium. But I'm held upright, a sack shoved over my head.

Daggers of pain embed themselves into my joints. My knees give way as I'm forced forward. My palms meet stone, my brittle bones quivering as though they might fracture. A cry hisses from between my teeth, my voice scraped raw.

"Let's go," says one of the men, hauling me up again. With a sigh, he gives me a moment to stabilize, to figure out how to balance once more.

Some weeks ago, or perhaps months—time has lost all meaning now—the warden reset my shackles. Until then, I was able to move around. A comfort I took for granted. I could stretch, lie down on the plank I used for a bed. I could feel around my cell, keep myself somewhat tethered to reality. Then came the warden, grumbling about the constant, annoying clank of my chains.

He tightened them after that. Removed several links, so that I could barely shift at all. Gone was the ability to stand.

Cool air stipples my skin as we slowly, painfully traverse the prison halls. Alarm ripples through me at the severity of the pain.

It's as if my weathered body can no longer hold what little weight I have left.

My muscles have atrophied. My strength is nonexistent. Eventually, my legs go numb save for a relentless, itching tingle, the pain like the stab of a thousand pins.

I've lost the body I'd earned, crafted through years of dancing, and now I struggle to remain upright. It is by the guards' strength alone that I make it up the stairs, both men heaving me upward from beneath my armpits.

Again, that grind and screech of metal, this time much closer. Then light washes over me like a warm breeze; even the sack over my head glows orange.

Warmth.

A sudden, unexpected tear tracks a line down to my chin. For so long, I've felt nothing but a gaping, cold hollow, both outside and in.

And I realize I cannot go back. Not ever. Whatever the king wants from me, I will *not* return to that cell.

Commotion whistles past as I'm dragged through cobbled squares. Every step is a negotiation, pleading with my body to obey. Even so, dizziness sends me toppling more than once. The guards wait with impatient huffs, not wanting to touch me more than necessary. All the while, sounds crowd my ears in a disorienting rush.

The trot of horses, the clatter of carriage wheels. I collect gossip, an endless trail of whispers.

Fates above, who is *that?*

More like, what *is it?*

But it takes all my focus just to keep my feet moving.

I'm hefted up yet another set of steps. And though I can't sense where I'm being led, recognition comes as my feet slip against cool marble, the ambience changing once more.

A frigid, echoing space. I have reached the palace after all, it seems. A few long corridors later and the sack is finally ripped from my head.

I blink, my eyes struggling to adjust to the light, even dim as it is. Familiar smooth beige stones make up the walls, floors, and vaulted ceilings. Sconces are set at intervals, light spangling across a pool for bathing on the far end. Rich incense laced with myrrh clouds my lungs, so different from the ever-present miasma of urine and sweat in the prison.

I clutch my abdomen, swaying with a wave of nausea.

A trio of women enter, encircling me as the guards step back, and all at once I'm being stripped, my shackles removed, and led into the pool—

Rags and sponges scrub soap across every inch of my bared flesh. Water is dumped over my head, over and over and over.

I feel as if I'm drowning. Or jerking awake from a long, terrible dream.

Flint razors and stones graze up and down my legs and under my arms, leaving my flesh smooth but red. When I'm led from the bath, perfumed oils are rubbed into my skin. Combs attack my hair, ripping their way through the tangles. And all I can think now is—

The king.

The king.

The *king*.

I have been here before, in this very chamber.

I have worn these perfumes before.

I have been prepared before.

Before...

Before the day my life was upended. Fragmented as my memories may be, that night is the one recollection time has not stretched thin. Here and now, it comes into even sharper relief—the jab of fingers into the tender flesh of my upper arms as I was dragged sleepily from my room in the dead of night; the way the king watched me from the shadows, even as his diadem betrayed him, snagging a glimmer of torchlight.

The way he took his time stepping forward, even as I was thrown before him.

The prod of rough hands as his men searched for weapons—as if I could hide one in my whisper-thin negligée.

My arms bound tightly in ropes like they were chaining some untamed beast.

A body I hadn't even known was there, pulled from my room.

The shouts. The accusations. The *interrogations*—

The slam of the guard's fists when I tried to run.

A small cry slips through my teeth as the memory crowds in—a horror I've yet to understand no matter how many times I turn it over in my mind. He *knew* I couldn't have murdered his adviser. I had been in his company the very hour the man supposedly died.

He knew I was innocent, yet he did nothing.

It was the first time he had allowed anyone to touch me. He was a jealous man, and that jealousy spread across his soul like a wick doused in oil—especially where I was concerned. So much as an ember, and he would combust.

But his jealousy was my shield. He was my protector. No one—no matter how highborn—touched me, and those who tried to get close to me paid for it with their livelihoods, their titles, and sometimes even their heads. Yet he had allowed those guards to put their hands on me—something he hadn't even done himself. Not once. Not even when I felt his yearning the way a man craves an ale after a grueling day's work.

Then, when I was sprawled on the floor like a puppet unstrung, he flicked his wrist so subtly I almost missed it, and his guards heaved me away. A reminder that no amount of hard work, wealth, or status can protect you from the wrath of a king. It didn't matter that I was his most esteemed dancer, his prime performer, his choice—*always* his choice—of entertainment.

The King's Jewel, they called me.

But that girl was someone else entirely. And like a mirage in a desert, I question if she ever existed at all.

And yet he sent for me.

The attendants give nothing away, going as far as to avoid my gaze. My arms and legs are shoved into clean garb: this one a shift of plain white cotton that reaches my knees, cinched at the waist by a rope.

I try not to look at my reflection in the pool, and fail.

I feel numb as I gaze at the unrecognizable waif before me. She barely looks alive, her eyes sunken, her frail form hunched like a hag as the attendants wrestle her frayed, waist-long locks into a pitiful braid.

When I'm deemed acceptable, the guards reenter. I hadn't even known they had left. Their grip on my arms is punishing now.

Before they lead me away, a new woman strides inside the chamber. She's middle-aged and fitted in a high-collared gray velvet dress that washes out her pale skin, her red-brown tresses tucked into a chignon.

It startles me when she looks directly into my eyes.

Like I hadn't spent the last however long in prison—and for murder, no less.

"I'm Brigitte," she says, matter-of-fact. "Have they given you something to eat?"

"We were instructed to take her directly to King Illian," says a guard, hooking the shackles back around my wrists. "We cannot delay."

"Fates above, look at her! She can barely stand," Brigitte says, noting my wobbling legs. "The least you could have done was had something simple prepared. Can't think for yourself, the lot of you," she harumphs before spinning on her heels and following us out.

I'm pulled into a vast hallway and led to yet another achingly familiar set of ornate double doors, these guarded by no less than ten armored men.

They swing wide at our approach.

Three wings unfold beyond expansive archways. The center is for private entertaining—where I'd spent most of my days. The far right is for his personal guard and staff, where I had dwelled in a small but gilded apartment that overlooked the gardens. Even now, a painful recollection paints itself in the canvas of my mind—ivory plasterwork filigreed in gold, a tall bay window, flashes of cherry red roses dancing in the breeze just outside.

My haven.

All over again, I feel the loss of it like a melody I can no longer hum.

But it's the third arch, far on the left, that we enter.

A knot of pain hitches up my throat, each encroaching memory more devastating than the last. These are King Illian's personal quarters, where we lounged for hours after his soirées, night after night, battling it out over chess, sampling cheeses, fruits, wines, usually in his study—

With a start, I realize that's where we are now, right outside his office.

"Wait here," says Brigitte, entering alone—no doubt to announce my presence.

The sound of birdsong pulls my gaze to my left, where a wide, arched window is open to reveal the vast forest sprawling beneath the palace and the hazed, blue crescents of the Galan Mountains in the distance. Clouds have swept in since I was released, bringing with them a fresh shower of rain. A few magpies dip underneath the eaves for shelter.

They play, and it looks like dancing.

It looks like *joy*.

The sight sends another spear of longing through me, and for once, my knees want to buckle for a reason other than pain.

I'd forgotten what real beauty was. What really existed beyond the walls of that prison.

I'd forgotten the simple things, like the scent of rain, the feel of water, the sound of wind.

The artistry of nature.

The breadth of it.

I'd forgotten what it was to use all my senses at once.

To see everything at once.

Feel everything at once.

Tears burn the backs of my eyes.

I'd forgotten what it was to want to be *alive*.

A breeze slips through the window, stippling gooseflesh along my arms and legs. And as I breathe the crisp, wet scent of petrichor, I vow to myself that no, I will *not* return to my cell.

Even if I must steal a guard's weapon.

Even if I must run Illian through myself.

Chapter Two

The King of West Miridran lounges at his gilded desk, its thick, four-pronged legs digging into the carpet like claws.

He does not bother to glance up. Not even as I'm ushered inside and Brigitte turns to leave, the door clicking shut behind her.

His brows are furrowed, his black quill gliding against parchment in smooth, steady strokes.

I take the moment to study him.

He is just as I remember. Young, nearing thirty. Only a handful of years older than I am. Strong shoulders, jaw still angular and sharp as a scythe, though his dark curls are shorter now, trimmed over his ears.

I draw in an uneasy breath, a spark of anger simmering in my belly.

There he is—my defender, my protector. The king who'd gaze upon me as if I were his most precious gem. The savior who'd offered me the world, so long as I came and danced only for him.

The liar who'd promised me refuge and opulence in the comfort of his court, only to abandon me to the rats.

I still can't understand why it happened, why he had punished me for a murder he knows I didn't—couldn't—commit. Had he grown bored with me? Had I done something wrong? Or had he discovered who I really was or where I came from? But no, that couldn't be; I'd left my old life behind with no tracks.

Over time, I'd realized the answer didn't matter. He could simply do whatever he wanted.

I'd thought I was special to him, but what is a single jewel to a king who has thousands?

I drag my gaze away, allowing my eyes to drift over the room. Low-hanging lanterns throw fragmented light across the walls, the ceiling, the ominous statue behind his desk.

The Fate of Morta.

Courtesan of Death, Reaper of Souls.

She stands tall, crafted from gold-threaded marble. An intricate hood shrouds her eyes, her nose, revealing only her famous full-lipped smirk. Her hair, long and flowing, drips down her gown like oil. King Illian always found her fascinating—perhaps because he's obsessed with beauty.

Lore tells us she offers every soul a chance to return to their life among the living, but she's so beautiful that no one can resist her, so alluring that refusing death is impossible. Some say she changes forms, or perhaps your perception, because everyone takes her hand.

Everyone accepts their death and is led willingly to Morta's Lair. *Death's* Lair. Everyone but me, because I never had the chance.

I waited and waited, but she never came.

King Illian releases a sigh, finally dropping his quill. Then his attention drifts up, slowly, as if time lags in his presence. His eyes crawl over me, pausing at my legs, my waist, my shoulders, before meeting my gaze. I want to shrink away. I feel like a fallen star— a once glittering gem now dragged through the mud.

He is still so elegant and I . . . I have withered away.

"Vasalie Moran," he says, his onyx gaze holding mine. "The past two years have not been kind to you."

I don't answer, though a retort climbs to my lips. *You did this to me, you lying swine.* But then his words hit me like a blow. *Two years.* I hadn't known how long. I'd lost track.

The king studies me, his lips pulling into a frown. I hope he remembers everything—the color of my blood, the pitch of my screams. I will him to see it in my eyes.

I hope he sees a ghost come to haunt him.

He blows out another exhale. "You wonder why I've brought you here, no doubt."

At my silence, he eases back, his long fingers twining around the arms of his chair. "I am merciful," he says, almost wistful. "I always have been—especially to you. I allowed you to live, after all, despite your horrendous crime." I tighten my jaw, but he continues. "And here you are, out of prison. So relax, my Vasalie; fortune has smiled upon you once more. Follow my commands, and you will never see your cell again."

My Vasalie. His property, as always—though a kernel of hope unfolds within my chest. *Follow my commands, and you will never see your cell again.*

But I know him. I've learned the taste of his lies. Whatever he says next will be tempting, like a gown strung with rubies and pearls, the flashy gems hiding the steel-boned corset underneath. Another cage.

"The reward," he says, "will be your exoneration."

"Exoneration . . ." The word escapes before I realize I said it aloud. It shatters on my lips, rough and broken, pitiful even to my own ears.

His lips peel upward into a knowing smirk—the same smirk he showcased at the end of my performances. "I want you to join the entertainment on the Isle of Anell during the Crowns' Gathering," he says. "As my informant, so to speak—though you'll be so much more. Of course, I can only guarantee you an audition. You must impress the Master of Revels to be granted a performer's spot. Succeed, however, and after . . ."

I sway and lose my balance, almost fall, but the guard behind me clamps my shoulder.

The Crowns' Gathering. My mind reels as memories return. It's a monthlong conclave for the united northern nations—also known as the Crowns' Syndicate—hosted by Miridran's three kings. It occurs every three years as a way to renew trade agreements and keep the peace among once warring nations.

An invitation to perform at the Crowns' Gathering is an honor, one any serious entertainer would kill for. Such a coveted position would bring as much fame as it would riches.

Despite being hosted on an island in East Miridran just a few days' ride from here, King Illian has never allowed me to audition before. It didn't matter how much I pleaded. And now, after all this time, after what he's done to me . . .

"Vasalie?" he prods. Impatience spreads across his face.

Anger flushes my cheeks and my voice cracks in what sounds like shock. Is this a joke? "Look at me, Your Majesty."

"I am looking."

My eyes drop to the floor—to my bony feet, my thin legs, no longer padded with muscle. Scars pucker the skin around my ankles and wrists, visible beneath my shackles. "I am in no condition to dance. I haven't been for a long time." *Thanks to you.* But my voice sounds frail, lacking the bite I wish I could muster.

"You will be," he says. "We have two months to prepare for your audition. But I won't sit here and convince you, Vasalie. Refuse my order, and you can go back to your dungeon and rot."

He can see it on my face; I'll do anything to avoid going back.

I'm on a hook, and all he has to do is reel.

"What will be required of me should I make it in?" I ask, almost a whisper.

"As an entertainer, you will be allowed access to places my other informants cannot go. You will act as my spy, reporting to me on everything I wish to know. And once the Gathering ends, you will be released with a full pardon. I'll return your title, your apartment, whatever you wish. Ask for it, and it will be yours."

Whatever I wish.

Back in my cell, I spent countless hours wondering what that was. What I would have done differently; what I would do if, by some miracle, I escaped. That was before hopelessness set in, absorbed like ink into the fibers of my being.

Whatever you wish. Ask for it, and it will be yours.

For the longest time, I thought it was revenge. I wanted revenge against the man before me, who threw me away without half a thought. I imagined all the ways I wanted to hurt him, and I don't deny that rage still exists. I still want revenge.

But more than that, I want to be free. I want to forget my past, my pain, and disappear. I want to pretend I never came here. I want to forget everything.

I want to forget *him*.

I look at Illian. "My name will be cleared?"

"Yes," he says.

"Then I want permission to leave West Miridran."

He opens his mouth, pauses. It was bold, I know, but I've realized something. He must need me, and only me, or he would have chosen a dancer who doesn't loathe the carpet on which he stands.

But . . . *why?*

"If you wish," he finally says.

"I want it in writing. Stamped with your seal."

"Fine, Vasalie," he drawls, scribbling on a document before snatching his seal. Once he finishes, he holds it out so that I can see. "But I will hold on to this until the Gathering has concluded."

I study him. If there is a lie there, it's hidden beneath the surface of his dark, hooded eyes. But . . . "Why? What is it you wish to discover?"

King Illian gives me a sour look. "To you, it matters not."

I swallow, threading my fingers together. Whatever he intends to uncover at the Crowns' Gathering, it is no small thing. Not when the whole of the Crowns' Syndicate will be in attendance. Not when he's offering me whatever I wish if I obey. There's something he isn't telling me, some hidden agenda. But if the cost of my freedom is lies and deception, I'll pay it.

I dip my chin, just once, in acceptance, even as I strain to keep my spine straight.

A smile creeps over his lips. "My Vasalie, returned to me at last."

My stomach turns inside out at the possessiveness once again coating his words. He motions toward the door, and a guard allows Brigitte inside once more. He juts his chin toward me, addressing her. "Take her from here. Do whatever is necessary to ensure she is ready, but she is not to leave my personal corridor."

Brigitte offers her arm, and I need her strength more than ever. I lean on her as she turns, leading me toward the door.

"And Vasalie," King Illian calls after me.

We halt.

"I have eyes and ears everywhere on the Isle of Anell," he says. "If you run, I will find you. If you speak ill of my name, I will hear of it. If you betray me, I won't only revoke your reward . . ." He pauses, and his eyes go cold. "I will kill you myself."

And just like that, new shackles bind my wrists, hewn from promises and carved from threats. But with them comes a second chance, and I won't take it for granted.

Muscles spasm in my back and legs the moment Brigitte and I emerge from the king's office, and I collapse, doubling over in a heap.

I expect the guards to yank me up. Instead, I hear Brigitte ordering them to fetch the physician and the meal she fussed at them about earlier.

"Foolish, the lot of them," she grumbles as their footsteps recede.

I feel her arm around me next.

She stays that way until the physician arrives.

She remains by my side even after, when I'm carted away on a stretcher into the physician's ward, when the physician examines me from head to toe with his dainty, pale hands, wrinkled with age.

She watches him like a hawk, and all the while, I fade in and out of consciousness.

Surely this was what she was instructed to do. Except it also feels somewhat like kindness, and I don't understand why. Illian no doubt told her who I am.

Hadn't he?

I don't recognize her from before. She wouldn't recognize me, either, considering she must be new. Besides, I was kept away from the public, save for when I was in full costume, with paints and cosmetics layered on my face like a mask. And even then, it was only for a select audience, chosen by King Illian himself, that I performed.

I break my silence when the physician leaves the room. "You know the reason for my isolation, don't you?"

Because others would talk if I were let loose and recognized in the palace. They might even do more than that. Lord Sarden, who I was framed for killing, was beloved—especially among the staff.

Until King Illian absolves me of guilt, no one can know who I am.

Brigitte takes a moment, folding her hands in her lap, the only hint of her discomfort thus far. "I am sworn to secrecy, so you needn't worry. But yes, Vasalie Moran, I know who you are and what you are said to have done."

What you are *said* to have done?

Does she not believe her king?

The physician returns. He makes me stand, sit, stand, measuring my pulse; I faint more than once. He pours tonics down my throat, with Brigitte's help. He concocts salves. He stretches my muscles, wriggles my joints, notating every spasm and wince of pain.

It takes him three days to give us a diagnosis—or lack thereof.

"Two years with such limited movement; it's a wonder she can walk at all," he says. "She may never get her full range of motion back. Nerve damage, if I had to guess. Muscle damage, too. And then there's the issue with her heart . . ."

I stiffen. "My heart?"

"A syndrome of sorts, I suppose," he says. "Nothing like I've ever seen. Your heart rate is too rapid—far more than it should be at times. But I can't seem to find a rhythm or reason for it. I suspect the triggers are quick movement, exertion, and heat, but even then, it is not consistent."

Brigitte asks what I can't. "Will she recover?"

"I don't know the severity of it. Conditions like these are unpredictable and often chronic." He sighs, giving me a pitying glance. "Whether you will recover or not, I cannot say. A routine of exercise and stretching may help, along with better nutrition. The pain and the fatigue, however . . ." He trails off. "I suggest you learn to live with it. Make the best of it."

The fight I'd felt upon seeing Illian vanishes, leaving me empty and hollow. Little more than a shell. It felt good for a time, but now I realize he has tasked me with the impossible.

For him to taunt me with exoneration—freedom, even—was heartless.

I curl into my cot and will the world to disappear.

Chapter Three

Three weeks pass and I'm still not convinced I've escaped.

There was nothing more the physician could do for me, so after another day of sleep, I was given a room in Illian's private wing, one floor below his apartments. It's quiet, secluded. The only other resident is Brigitte, whose room is just a few doors down.

My own room is modest and altogether too bright. White walls, stark against the dark swathes of curtains, the windows always open to let in the first rays of dawn.

This morning is like any other. Brigitte, who I've learned is Illian's chief attendant, sets aside my morning tonic, then wrestles my nightgown over my head, carting me to the adjoining bathing chamber where additional attendants wait. I'm scrubbed until my skin is pruned and raw. I soak for long minutes, and then I'm lifted out, dried, and handed back to Brigitte, who lathers expensive salves over my lingering scars.

"They'll get better," she tells me. "Time is a great healer."

I almost hope they don't. I want King Illian to see the reminders every time he looks at me.

After the ablutions, Brigitte joins me for breakfast and tea at a small table nested against the window. Too slowly, I am adjusting to regular food again, but I rarely handle it well. More than once, I've doubled over, spilling the contents of my stomach across the floor, her dress, my clothes. They've learned the hard way that I cannot touch a slab of dried meat, can't stomach so much as a ration of rye, even—the foods that barely sustained me in that fates-forsaken cell.

Now, I pry apart a pastry, letting my stomach settle between each bite.

"He asks after your progress," Brigitte says, regarding me through a ribbon of steam.

I haven't seen the king since the day he had me dragged from my cell, though I've sensed him in the shadows. A presence beyond the doorway, eager to look in.

"And?" I ask dryly. Surely she's told him the truth. That after two years in that cell, my muscles have warped and deteriorated, and even after everything they've tried to speed up my recovery—all the stretching and exercising the physician prescribed—I haven't been able to dance. Not really. Not aside from basic routines fit for a child.

A simple spin.

A pitiful leap.

It had taken me a week to even walk a straight line for more than a few seconds without my heart jittering, the world spinning beneath my feet. Another week to twirl without toppling halfway through. Even now, I can't move without the rush of dizziness, the currents of pain that extend from my waist down to my toes.

How hopeless I must seem. Perhaps she's ready to give up on me. This deal, this supposed second chance, is nothing but a cruel joke.

Brigitte looks out the window, a furrow crumpling her middle-aged face. Her knuckles turn white as she clutches her cup. "I tell him to be patient. Nevertheless, you must perform for him before you leave for Anell, and that time is soon, my dear. Not five weeks away."

And if I fail to prove that I'm capable of performing at the Gathering, he will send me back to that cell. I swallow against the bile creeping up my throat.

Brigitte tilts the teacup to her lips.

I crash mine into its saucer. "Why me?"

Why now, and why like this?

It startles us both, and Brigitte throws a hand over her chest, taking a breath before meeting my gaze. I know she can't tell me; I know Illian has a tight grip on everyone in his service. Still, I survey her expression, the strain in her eyes, until—finally—she says, "I don't know, child. I wish that I did."

There must be some twisted reason he's going through the trouble to prepare *me* instead of another dancer. But then I think of my desperation to escape his dungeon. He knows I won't risk my freedom, and I have learned the price of his displeasure. He thinks he has sculpted me into his ideal instrument, each crack deliberately crafted.

"What is he planning?"

She takes a breath. Wood creaks outside the door, and her mouth snaps shut. Still, she manages a shake of her head. She doesn't know. Of course she doesn't—and if she did, she wouldn't reveal it. But another question addles my mind. A pointless, ridiculous question, but I can't help but wonder. Who replaced me?

Who has become his new Jewel?

Someone lovely, I'm sure. Someone he doesn't want to tarnish with whatever task he plans for me. Still, I want to know. I want to see her, question her.

Does he look at her the way he looked at me?

Does he promenade with her in the gardens under the silvering moon like we used to? Do they spend hours talking, laughing, gossiping? Does he confide in her the way he used to confide in me?

Has he shared his plans with her?

An idea knits together in my mind.

My appetite only allows for a few bites. After choking them down along with another herbal tonic stocked with nutrients, I push away the tray and climb back into bed, ignoring the exhale from the other end of the table. Only when Brigitte leaves the room do I rise, gingerly slipping from the sheets. Once the lightheadedness eases just enough, I pull on my leggings and tunic, gather my curls into a loose plait, and exit my room.

This wing of the palace is quiet, but the halls have eyes. Guards are everywhere, observing me each time I stagger from my room. They witness every stumble, every pause, the way I often halt after several steps until the dizziness passes, all while pretending I don't exist.

But I'm no fool. I know they report my actions to Illian, and any one of them would strike me down at his slightest whim. Just like before.

I wonder, then, if he'll order them to punish me for what I'm about to do.

Ruby curtains cascade down the walls in tufts, spilling onto the checkered floor. Alcoves in mahogany panels reveal more statues like the one in Illian's office: depictions of the Fate of Morta or her supposed prophets, sunlight pooling in their open palms, quartz glimmering in their too-bright eyes.

The sheer extravagance of this palace brings back a rush of feelings I'm not prepared for. I'd always had an appreciation for it—the vaulted, frescoed ceilings like those found in a cathedral, the jewel-encrusted garniture and drapery, as if diamonds were as cheap as quarry rocks. It was a promise of what I might take for myself, what I could earn from my hard work.

Now, it's a stark reminder that underneath all the beauty prowls a beast.

Chimes signal the end of a court session, where an arch opens into another wing. I peer around the corner. A multitude of courtiers, advisers, and the like spill from the Order Hall to my left—some wandering in my direction, perhaps headed to Illian's offices, and others away to the main vestibule. I use the distraction, blending into the throng. The guards won't lose me for long, but I only need a few seconds.

I slip down a narrow hall devoid of windows.

I ache from my morning exercises but ignore the pain and glide down the corridor, hand brushing the paneling for support. This path I know by heart. My feet know the exact number of steps. And when I pass through the narrow archway, my skin recognizes the feel of this place, like a welcome from an old friend.

A single maid trails down the hall, a duster in hand. She startles when I step in her path, but her head remains downcast, as required of her station. "Who does this hall belong to now?" I ask.

"No one, my lady. Save for His Majesty, of course."

"But surely another dancer has charge of it, as the King's Jewel. Where might I find her?"

"My lady," she says, "there was only ever one. He has not appointed another Jewel." At my hesitation, she curtsies nervously and flits away, scurrying down the hall.

But her words remain, hovering where she stood.

He has not appointed another Jewel.

He did not replace me.

I turn, the breath stuck in my chest, my ears ringing as I approach a set of slender double doors. My fingers trail the molding before reaching for a rose-shaped knob. It's cool against my hands, and when I turn it, the squeak of dry hinges echoes along the corridor.

I step inside.

Dust sifts through the air, swirling against the plume of my breath.

The curtains are open along all the windows, and sunlight lacquers the dark wooden floor. Above hangs an unlit glass chandelier shaped like a rose in bloom—a present from King Anton, Illian's younger brother, once the renovations on this palace were complete. A palace that, while dating back decades, was a mere winter getaway before Illian took up residence.

But this rose is the only trace of either of Illian's brothers in this place, and I suspect it's why Illian abandoned this room for years before he gave it to me. He has no love for either, but especially King Anton, who reigns over Miridran's eastern territory.

Because Illian was supposed to inherit all of Miridran, not just the third he did.

It was the one subject he never broached with me—a sore spot, from what I could tell. But I'd gleaned snippets of the story during my time in the palace. Illian had always been primed, as crown prince, to rule Miridran as its sole king. For a reason I never discerned, King Estienne, Illian's older brother, was set to abdicate the throne long before either of the princes were crowned.

Then, twelve years ago, King Junien, Illian's father, decided to split his kingdom into three distinct territories and divide these among his sons instead. Each territory would be responsible for its own trade and economy, while the army would act as one unit rather than three. He announced it at a Gathering before the Crowns' Syndicate on Estienne's name day—and crowned him on the spot. Estienne was gifted with Miridran's central territory, leaving the western territory for Illian once he came of age two years later.

And the east, which Illian loved most, was reserved for Anton.

More than once, I overheard Illian complaining about his youngest brother, namely his arrogance, his debauchery, and, most of all, his greed. That so many adored Miridran's youngest king, and his hedonism, disgusted Illian. *The multitudes who overlook his vices only do so because he keeps their chalices full.*

I assume relations between them are still tense. If I make it into the Gathering, I suppose I'll see firsthand.

Still, it was here, under this rose, that I practiced. Rehearsed. Orchestrated steps and planned my shows. It was here that I dreamed. This small, abandoned ballroom at the end of a quiet hall was a gift from Illian after a long night spent impressing two dignitaries from foreign lands—all the while ignoring their jabs and jeers, the comments labeling me his pleasure princess, and a pitiful replacement for his former favored dancer. In addition, he gifted me a title he hadn't yet offered to anyone else.

His Jewel.

But I'd earned my place without entering his bed.

For enduring their cruelty with grace, Illian escorted me here the next morning. He had it cleaned and swept free of dust, the mirrors polished, the floors cleared. *For you,* he'd said, as I gawked at a space so drenched in light it felt almost ethereal. *And one day, I'll give you so much more.*

Like the lonely, gullible girl I was, I believed him. It was so easy back then. He made me feel adored. Just enough attention, the right amount of praise, that I always craved more. And it was a craving he often fulfilled in the most lavish of ways. Diamonds for my ears. Gold quatra snuck into the pockets of my costumes. A bracelet, engraved with my name.

Whispered promises that layered onto one another—a currency in themselves. *I will give you more.*

Anger swells inside me and, with it, determination. Pushing back against the ache in my ribs, I straighten and walk to the center of the room. There I settle onto the floor and stretch, following my old routine. The one I tried to do in my cell, even as my body deteriorated. First my feet, then my calves—

A loose board shifts beneath my weight.

It can't still be here, can it? I move aside, hesitantly sliding my fingernails underneath the wood. Splinters needle my flesh, but I pry until it comes loose.

Inside, a tiny lump of white velvet and fur sleeps right where I left it.

I lift the fabric, then cradle it against my cheek. I run it along my nose, my lips, covering the hitch of my breath.

It still smells like her.

It was the only thing of Emilia's I couldn't bring myself to sell—this one, single glove. Both had been in the bag she'd packed for me, but one had gone missing, and no matter how hard I had searched for it, it never surfaced. I had been devastated, because—oh, I loved them so. She had worn them the first time I met her, a lifetime ago. A girl no more than twenty-five, lost in fur and dripping with pearls, my father's diamond engulfing her finger. At eight years old,

I had been determined to hate her. I hadn't even wanted to meet her. *I don't need a new mother,* I'd told her. And she'd answered, *I know, but how about a friend?*

Emilia.

Emilia.

My chest tightens. "I'm sorry," I tell her—my chorus throughout the years. "I'm so sorry." I repeat it now in broken whispers until I'm starved for air. I'd hidden her glove there years ago to remind me why I was here—why I worked and strived and danced until my muscles tore and swelled. Why I ignored the comments and glares. The jealous courtiers. Their husbands and the way they cornered me when Illian wasn't looking.

It was all for Emilia, once.

But then I was swept away by glitter and gold and the promise of more, more, more. Just a little more, I thought, and then I'd be done. I would return to the home I'd fled and face my father. I'd drag him before a court to face the crimes only Emilia and I had witnessed. I wasn't a helpless child any longer.

But I was never ready. My life grew intoxicating, and I chugged it like wine. Even now, a small, traitorous part of me feels the pull. It wasn't until Illian threw me into the dark and left me there that I was forced to face the depths of my failure. Who I'd forgotten. Who else I let go free.

I forgot, because it was easier than remembering.

Eyes burning, I tuck the glove into the band binding my breasts, and as I slide the floorboard back in place, the soft lull of a violin teases my ears.

It's a familiar tune—so familiar it sends a pang through me. I trace the soft curves of the melody through the air. It fills my broken soul with a long-lost desire because this is a song I'd written. A gift.

For *him.*

He plays it now, probably knowing I'm nearby. The guards would have told him by now. Is it a taunt? Another joke? Or does it mean so little to him that it is but an idle tune, a harpist's choice for a mid-morning stroll? Perhaps he thinks nothing of it.

Slowly, I rise to my feet and tread down the hall.

The song heightens as I wander farther, and I pause behind the wide leaves of a potted fig tree. Before me is one of the king's preferred lounges. Scallops of velvet adorn the ceiling, suffused in the afternoon sun from skylights high on the walls. Chaises encircle the alabaster floor, each occupied by courtiers attired in their finest. King Illian himself lazes on a chaise near the center, sipping from a gold-hammered chalice, his dark green robe open at his chest and spilling onto the floor like ivy.

Brigitte tells me to put him out of my mind and focus on my recovery, but she doesn't understand. He is etched into the fabric of my being. Both his kindness and his cruelty are braided into a tangle of memories I can't escape. Even now, I see both versions of him: the man who gave me everything and the one who took it all away.

Two dancers perform a rendition of my *Illiuna* for him—a sultry song with sweeping movements, heavy arcs. I recognize them both: Marisol and Donatette. They were my students. I taught them this dance.

I'd loved them like sisters.

Donatette wears a creamy gossamer gown the same delicate pallor of her skin, while Marisol is resplendent in a lavender dress that flatters her deep, golden-brown complexion. They weave together effortlessly, a poise to their strides that opens yet another wound within my battered spirit.

I hadn't realized I would miss it so. Hadn't thought I'd long to move like that again. To see them dancing the way I used to, the gentle strength with which they pose . . .

Illian clearly made them a well-deserved offer similar to mine.

But why hasn't he made one of them his Jewel?

Donatette stretches her arms, and Marisol clasps her from behind, arching her back into a crescent. But before Marisol can slide underneath her partner, her eyes catch mine. She gasps and releases Donatette, who falls to the floor in a heap of silk and mortification.

The music ceases.

Marisol's lips shape my name.

I run, ignoring the way my muscles scream.

I can't bear to face them. Not when I fail to resemble even a shadow of who I once was. Not when they think I'm a *murderer*. I round a corner and slip back into my dance room, the bare wooden floors gleaming up at me. I settle my back against the wall, then slide to the floor.

Minutes pass, and no one comes for me. Instead, soft chords of melody arise; they've begun their performance once more. Marisol must think she imagined me. I let out a breath of relief, my eyes falling shut until my heart eases its pace.

As the music swells, I visualize the steps they take. I'd loved this dance. I'd spent months choreographing it.

I lift my arms, the rhythm as tangible as ribbons. It beckons me, and I listen. I rise from the floor. My arm glides over my neck then down, graceful like the dip of a wing. This feeling, this freedom to move, it was stolen from me. But I imagine the chains falling off, disintegrating like the late autumn leaves. I let the chords direct my steps, guide my pace. It's a whisper, a promise, a solace I'd missed for so long, and I hold on to it with all my strength. My throat aches with unshed tears. My muscles tremble, even as the music builds into a crescendo—

My breath whooshes from me in a painful lurch. I hit the floor with a thump, nerves aflame, feeling as if blades are dragging along my ribs. Water pools in my eyes, only to spill down my cheeks.

Because my body will never be the same. I will never reclaim what I lost. I am weak, frail. I could shatter as easily as glass.

The door swings wide and two guards rush in, jerking me up. Of course they followed me. Then Brigitte is there, her heavy eyes taking me in. The scene must be obvious—what I tried to do, how I failed. But she's swept aside like dust as the king enters. He pauses, jaw tight, then commands me to rise.

So I do. Immediately, stars smear my vision, the strength in my knees waning. Long moments pass as I gather my will. When the fog finally clears, I force my spine straight.

He steps before me then, assessing. I've gained some weight, a little muscle, but it isn't enough.

"Dance," he orders.

He wants to see my progress. He is tired of asking Brigitte.

I blink at him. "Without music?"

"Yes."

Even if I wanted to, the last of my strength has dissolved. "I . . . can't."

He steps forward, pushes my chin up with his chalice. "You will if I say you will."

His request isn't made by a king; it's a command from a puppeteer.

I still have five weeks. I shouldn't have to perform yet. Brigitte opens her mouth, but he whips up a hand in warning. She purses her lips at him before giving me a pitying glance.

My fingernails drive into the flesh of my palms. This man holds my life in his hands, but rage courses through me. He put me in that cell in the first place. And after two years of aching loneliness and pain, he drags me back out, expecting me to recover on his timeline. Hatred seeps through me, hot as lava. "Your Majesty," I say before I can think better of it. "I merely wish the time you promised me, so that I might prepare a performance befitting your *honorable* crown."

He catches the insult buried between the flattery. I tell him now, with my gaze, that I haven't forgotten. He knows I am innocent.

He says nothing, just watches me, silent for one breath, then two. He has never needed hands to touch me; his eyes prod my flesh as if it were clay. But then I realize the risk I've taken in angering him and curse myself inwardly. *Foolish.*

But when he doesn't chastise me or revoke our deal, I know for sure: whatever his plans, he must truly need me, and only me. He must not trust anyone else—perhaps because I'm the only dancer he has bound through unseen chains, tethered to him by desperation. Was that the reason he threw me in prison to begin with?

Or is it something more?

"Your Majesty," Brigitte says, attempting to smooth the tension, "she will be ready by the time we leave."

"Yes, she will be," he responds. "She will prove to me just how thankful she is for a second chance." He leans in, his wine-soaked breath clogging my ears. "Oh, yes, Vasalie," he whispers. "I see your little test. That streak of defiance never ceased to amuse me before, but know this: You are only here if you are valuable to me. A broken toy has no worth."

Broken toy.

No worth.

His words are blows, harsher than the guard's assaults. They burrow into my mind, sowing doubt and fear. I can't escape them, or the truth behind them: he broke me, and I am too fragmented to piece myself together again.

The certainty of it follows me, mocks me, as the days slip by.

Brigitte tends to me each day, pushing me through therapy, meals, treatments, practices. I retreat into the crevices of my mind. I float through the motions, drift through the hours.

At night, I leave the window open to the stars—to the rain, even—if only to remind me where I am, and where I am not. Even so, my sleep is fitful, nightmare-ridden, full of festering darkness, biting manacles. Shrieks and screams that echo throughout my dreams, so like the terrors that haunted my mind in that cell. I wake only to feel like I'm sleepwalking through the next day.

It is a brittle, absent existence.

"Vasalie," Brigitte scolds, tugging my arm from the window one morning. She's found me here more than once, in a trance, staring at the snow-crowned mountains in the distance. It's a reminder of the place I once called home—a place far away, separated by miles of sea. A place where the mountains are wholly covered in ice, so bright during winter you have to squint to see them. The place I ran from.

I wish I could run from here.

"You should be preparing," Brigitte says, scooting me toward the door. Normally, I'd have been in my training room hours ago. "You're to dance for King Illian tomorrow."

That's all I've done lately: train, practice, stretch, train. My muscles remember every dance I choreographed, every step I learned, but my body doesn't always obey. Even as I build my strength, the breadth of my movements . . .

My progress is not nearly enough.

Worse, my anxiety stacks into a fortress I can't navigate. I push myself and fail. I mourn what I lost. And when that timid thing inside me breaks—the last traces of determination and pride I desperately cling to—I crumble. I lie on the floor, heart rabbiting, lungs struggling for breath, needles of pain grating my skin like the jagged teeth of prison rats. *A broken toy has no worth.*

I have nothing to show but how destroyed I am. It reopens even more wounds from a time before Illian. *You'll never be more than a man's plaything.* My father's voice is so clear, I almost wonder if he's near. My father, who'd made a deal, who'd seen me as a token to trade with. Who offered me as a match for a man Emilia despised. It hadn't mattered that I was thirteen, that I hadn't even begun to bleed. *How could you deign to believe you'd be anything more?*

Plaything.

Broken toy.

"We both know it's a useless cause," I spit, wrenching my arm from Brigitte's grip. "Look at me." She can see it as plainly as I can. We both know I can't perform the way I need to. Not for King Illian, and certainly not for the elite environs of the Crowns' Gathering.

Freedom slips from my fingers like wax melting beneath a candle's flame.

But Brigitte grabs me roughly by the shoulders, shaking them as if to startle me from a nightmare. "You listen to me," she says, eyes so sharp I feel as if I'm being held at the tip of a blade. "I have a daughter your age. A scrawny thing like you. Life got the best of her, too. Her bastard of a father set fire to our house with us in it. He left us to burn. We escaped, Vasalie, with nothing but our lives. Our home, our land—it was all gone." She slides back her sleeves, revealing white ripples of scar tissue banding her arms. "Marian, my daughter, got the worst of it. Her whole body."

I stare at her, words caught in my throat like stones.

"She loved cooking," Brigitte continues. "Loved it so much it's all she could think about. Even after that—after being burned—she did not fear the fire. But no bakery would hire her. No one would even look into her eyes. I didn't earn much, but I took two jobs, then three, and with every quatra left over after our rent, I bought Marian a stove. Spices, ingredients, anything I could get my hands on, though it wasn't much. In our tiny corner of a kitchen, she baked. And baked. She had no training except what I could give her. But she had talent, brains, and swiftly discovered a method to refine millen into flour, and a fine one at that. Finer than any you have ever seen."

Impressive, I can admit. Millen grows plentifully in Miridran, but its tough stalk had once made it all but unusable.

"But when she went to the market to sell her samples and goods," Brigitte continued, "no one bought them. They avoided her, looked the other way. But still she went each day, determined.

"Then one day, a man from East Miridran sampled her scones. He liked them so much that he purchased her entire basket, then came back the next day after sharing it with his convoy, asking her what she used. When she told him about millen, he made her an offer. Turns out he was King Anton's closest friend, and now she works for a *king*. Not even King Illian can convince her to return, much less devise her process, and now he must settle for purchasing millen flour from the east in heftily priced trades. And my daughter? She lives in a palace. I'd be with her now if it weren't for . . ." She trails off, shaking her head. A pained breath leaves her lips. "She triumphed. That's what matters."

I don't know what to say, so I stare at her, my thumbs curling into my palms. It's quite the tale, but I still feel so numb.

"Your story is not a kind one," Brigitte says, kneading my hands softly between her own. "But though you've suffered your own fire, child, you won't always smell of smoke. And yes, it may have burned you," she tells me, and I lift my gaze. "But scars are powerful things, because they show your resilience. So rise from your ashes, my dear. Do not crumble alongside them."

With that, she leaves. But her words . . . They wash over me again and again until I fall to my knees and sink my head into my hands.

I thought I had made it. That I had escaped the horrors of my past. My father, his abuse. The man he planned to sell me to under the guise of marriage. I had escaped, because Emilia bought me that chance, and then I came here. Danced until my feet bled. I earned my place—and my peace. My hardships should have been over. Years of striving, almost starving, and I'd *made* it. I was King Illian's chosen.

Until everything was ripped away like a thatched roof in a heavy wind.

I think of Brigitte, of Marian. I'd give anything to have a mother. Or even a sister. Emilia, even if we weren't related, was the closest I had. Another hole opens within me, widening, fraying. I see Emilia's face again, and like a blow to my barely beating heart, I remember the pitch of her laughter, how it sounded like a song. The way I'd find her twirling in a pool of sunlight at the earliest hint of dawn.

Emilia had performed at the Gathering one year. It was the reason I had wanted to see it one day, if only to feel close to her once more. See what she told me so much about—the wonders of the palace, the splendor of such an event.

I tug the glove from where I'd hidden it under my mattress and graze it along my lips. "I failed you," I breathe. "I failed you so badly." But I know what she'd say. *Survive.* It's all she asked of me before I left. *Survive and be free, my darling girl.*

But the cost was losing you.

I press the glove against my eyes until it's soaked with my tears. My heart throbs painfully in my chest. Long minutes pass until the tears run dry, until the scent of cinnamon rises from the tray Brigitte left behind. A small scone like the one she described is nestled next to my cup of tea.

I take it, lift it to my lips, and pause.

Sugar. Flour. Cinnamon. This pastry, pressed and kneaded with an elaborate flourish, is made from simple components, and only when it is baked together does it form the scone in my hand. I pull it apart with my fingers. It breaks easily, flaking onto the tray like ash. It must be made from millen flour, Marian's creation. Light as air, thin as mist.

Rise from your ashes, my dear. Don't crumble alongside them.

An idea crafts itself in my head, small at first, but it grows like dough baked with yeast until it forms into something larger—

I pick myself up and race from the room.

Chapter Four

My first dance for the king comes at the break of dawn.

King Illian's guards lead me to a throne room in the entertainment wing. It's a small one, intimate, unlike the large one where he holds court, and this choice . . . it feels deliberate.

This was the location of my last performance.

It was the night before I was arrested. The night I thought everything would change—just not for the reason it did. Because after I had danced for King Illian and his courtiers, he asked me to do it all over again, except this time away from the crowd. In the privacy of this room. And he watched me with such ardency, such . . . *zeal,* that I thought he would break whatever it was that kept him from pursuing me.

"You are everything," he had told me, his hand planted on the doorframe above my head, just before he bid me good night and pushed away.

How close I had been to taking his hand. To pulling him back. If only to thank him, throw my arms around him. I was so enamored with him—not by lust but by gratitude. And even if it *had* led to more, I might have welcomed it.

The very thought curdles my insides, especially as I approach him now.

He reclines on his fretwork throne, gloved fingers drumming. Dark, embellished leather hugs him from head to toe; he's just come from a hunt. A small, dangerous smile bends his lips as his eyes flick to mine.

Around him lounge a handful of courtiers, each fitted in similar sable leather. I don't recognize them, but that's nothing new. He rotates his pawns with the season, never allowing anyone to burrow too close—save, once, me.

Even so, I expect their whispers. Their critical glares. Or has he not told them who I am or what this is about? That I am his former Jewel, and that my pardon hinges on my performance over the next few months? I had thought he would, considering their presence now.

Yet they do little more than appraise me with bored, half-lidded eyes.

And it's clear they don't expect much. I am thin, withered, my skin stretched too tight over delicate bones. I wear no makeup, no costume, nothing but black leggings and a thin band covering my breasts.

If the king is surprised, he doesn't show it, though he must wonder at my attire. Before, I was known for my artistry as well as my performances. I would sew my own costumes, craft my own props, paint my face until I was a siren, a goddess, an enchantress. Anything he desired.

Beauty was King Illian's weakness, so his weakness I became.

It's not even that I am particularly beautiful. It's simply that I learned how to *become*.

I glance toward the line of windows along the right wall, where Brigitte's maidservants await. At my signal, they release the tasseled strings on each curtain.

One by one, they drape shut, save for the last, where a lone, focused thread of light limns me from the side.

Dance is the purest form of expression, they say, but I can't express what I don't feel. I draw in a calming breath, allowing my mind to settle into silence. My bare feet press into the polished floor as I find my center of balance. Behind me, a violinist begins a haunting tune.

I rise to the tips of my toes, expand my rib cage with breath, then lean into my dance.

My movement and range may be stilted, but I find my poetry. I whirl, dip, pivot with grace and precision, sticking *only* to positions I know I can master.

It's a light sequence. Easy steps with soft, flowing movements. I've reached my serenity, and I hold on to it like I do my most cherished memories: the scent of earth as I play in the rain, with Emilia beside me; the kiss of silk as I stitched my first dress. I sway, sweep into arcs, and rise again.

But the king's unease reaches me like a foul odor. He rustles on his throne, no doubt wondering why I'm sticking to a basic routine. Soon, he'll grow bored.

I'm counting on it.

My fingers reach for the small black sack attached to my waist. I loosen the ties as I bend my knees, preparing for my moment. Flour seeps into my palms—just enough.

I come up in a spin, releasing it in a whirl as I pirouette. It billows around me like smoke, floating in my wake. My outfit is the canvas, the powder drizzling clusters of stars onto the black fabric as I twirl, bend, and twist into sensuous shapes—and with each step, I release more millen. Light dances through it, and with its cloak I disguise the bounds of my new constraints.

Millen is the distraction for what I can no longer do.

But it works. One look at my owl-eyed audience, at the white-knuckled fingers pressing into their chairs, and I know I have them. And when the flour finally drifts down, clouding around my heels like early morning fog, I slow with the music, lowering myself until

I am curled on the floor. The curtains ease shut, shrouding the room in shadow.

King Illian's slow clap beats in my head like a pulse. Carefully, I push upward as the curtains are swept open again, and then I am standing before him—and he before me.

"Clever, Vasalie," he says, eyes roaming over me with new interest. Dizziness blots my vision, and it takes everything in me not to sway.

Then he does something I do not expect. He bends and swipes a gloved finger along the floor, right where I'd been standing.

He inspects the flour, then raises it to his lips.

His eyes hold mine as he tastes it. Licks it right off his glove. "Millen flour, lighter than dust," he says, mouth curved to one side.

He edges closer and lifts his hand, as if to cup my jaw.

It hovers in the air between us, so close I can feel its heat.

The breath stills in my lungs.

He could have taken advantage of me so many times, but he never did. Even as lust darkened his eyes, even as wine filled his cups and the clocks ticked into early morning, not once did he lay a finger on me. I thought it was dignity. I respected him for it. But I am no longer his elite, his favored, the dancer his court admires.

With a wave of his hand, he dismisses his courtiers, and only when the room is empty does he whisper, softly, "My Vasalie."

I feel the ache of it. There's a longing in his gaze, one that sends a lick of unease down my spine—a reminder that there must be more to all this, more to why he pulled me out.

He wets his lips, watching my own. An uncomfortable warmth wreathes the space between us. But it's as if his pride keeps him from crossing that invisible barrier between us.

So what, then? Does he wish me to do it?

I won't—ever. I step back.

His mouth curls into a frown. "Tomorrow," he says, his husky tenor betraying him, "you will travel ahead of me to the Isle of

Anell. Once there, we will not associate with each other, as your guise places you from my brother Estienne's court. Remember, Vasalie, you are a tool through which I will work and nothing more. Do not pride yourself that you have earned this spot on your own merit."

The more I watch him, the more I don't believe him. If I were simply a tool, I wouldn't affect him so. Again, I wonder what his plans are. Fury smolders beneath his lashes, but I ignore it, my expression blank. "Yes, Your Majesty."

"Remember my warning," he says, stepping around me. "One wrong move, one act of defiance, and it's back to the cell with you. I am watching you, always."

"I would not wish to displease you," I lie.

"My instructions will be delivered to you. You need not seek me out."

All of this I know already, but his reminder whisks chills along my skin. I bow, the flour stirring around my toes.

Then he adds, "I'd like to give you your first one now. I want you to befriend the Gathering's Head of Staff. I hear he's a disgustingly kind fellow, so it shouldn't prove difficult."

I give him a curt nod, then hesitate. "Is there something you wish me to glean from him, Your Majesty?" It's difficult not to spit the words.

"His favor," Illian says. "He is well connected, having been around for years."

His command is vague, so I nod blankly, poised to turn away.

"And Vasalie," he says before I can retreat, "after your final task, you will return to me. Your last evening at the Gathering will be spent in the company of my court alone."

King Illian stands tall against the backdrop of his palace, watching my coach depart for the Isle of Anell. His figure shrinks as the traveler's coach glides away, but the warning in his eyes follows me through the twists and curves of the road as the drivers steer us into Lorewood Forest.

A cold shiver traces down my arms, but I focus instead on Brigitte's words before I left. After packing my bags, she drew me into a hug and whispered, "You're strong, just like my daughter. Strong where it counts."

She had heard Illian's words. I swallowed, pretending to believe her.

Still, I hope my brittle hug conveyed what words could not. She was patient with me, gentle, treating me not like a convict but someone worthy of being cared for. I wish I knew why she isn't with her daughter in East Miridran. I wish I had asked her more questions, but I will never forget her kindness.

My story for Anell will be simple, and not wholly untrue. It still places me as a dancer who once performed at the Melune—a small, albeit prestigious theater on the border of Central Miridran. There, however, I'm to say I snagged the attention of an adviser in King Estienne's court, who, after hiring me for a time, secured my audition for the Gathering. The adviser has, of course, been paid off by Illian.

But that story won't matter if I falter before the Master of Revels. My name might be on a list, but other performers will have twice the stamina, span of movement, and strength. Yet I'm auditioning as a solo dancer, which means twice the pressure.

If I don't impress him, I will not make it inside the Gathering.

A canopy of leaves hangs over the coach in shades of emerald and gold, filigreed by the glow of a warm, amber sun. It reminds me of the audience I'll entertain if I succeed: advisers, emissaries, heralds. Not to mention nobles, diplomats, and other court functionaries hailing from every shadow of the north—including the place I once called home. What if someone from my past were to recognize me? I've grown up since then, changed my name, but it's not impossible.

Worse, any one of the Crowns could order my head on a platter should I displease them, because I am not under King Illian's protection. I am not officially tied to him in any way.

Fear presses in on me as the sun shrinks behind the leaves, shadows fringing the coach like a veil of lace, and then the coach is too small, too enclosed, and suddenly I'm in my cell again, imprisoned by yawning darkness. Darkness with teeth, swelling with voices, *so many voices*—

Freedom never lasts. You're too damaged for this world.
Broken toy.
Plaything.

It took weeks for the nightmares to whittle down after my release; a month until I woke and understood where I was, why the ground had grown soft beneath me. That I wasn't falling, sinking into the earth and into some underworld below. That it wasn't the ground at all but a mattress. Longer, still, to grow comfortable existing once more in a world of daylight—a light that should make me feel comfortable, safe, but instead makes me feel exposed, my broken body on display for all to judge.

It seems I cannot exist in either: the light or the dark.

Here and now, I gulp in greedy breaths, pleading with my trembling body to relax. I push my head into my palms, drawing up that familiar anger, the rage that nearly had me ready to drive the point of a sword into Illian. I let it wrap around me, consume me, until I'm shaking for a different reason altogether.

I am still under Illian's control, trapped by his threats, but it won't always be this way. I make a promise to myself and chant it like a prayer—louder than the voices, louder than the grief. I will *not* go back to my cell. I will earn my freedom, no matter the cost.

My coach escapes the forest's hold, tree limbs stretching like spindly arms as we flee its reach. Dark clouds wend through the sky, then grow eerie with waning light—the grim transition from day to night. Central Miridran is wet with fog, spilling with rain every few hours. My back aches from sleeping in the cramped coach.

Three days feel like ten, until finally, we enter East Miridran along the coast.

While the art of glass is rooted in Miridran as a whole, East Miridran dominates the trade. At first glance, Philam's bustling port town would look like any other, its stacked buildings composed of dark wood and alabaster stone. Except each one is accented with glass, whether it be colorful windows, glistening cupolas, or luminescent steeples and spires. And with the morning sun now teasing the clouds, it's as if the town has been lit by a thousand prisms.

When we reach the port, the air is cool and brisk despite the flushing dawn. I'm handed my bags and loaded onto a curved wooden boat along with my silent escorts. Then the waves guide us to our destination: the Isle of Anell.

A thin, sandy shoreline graces the horizon, quickly swallowed by a scattering of trees that grow thicker farther inland.

I stare in wonder at Anell's seaside palace.

Rather than a single structure, it's a large network of white sandstone buildings capped with copper and glass cupolas and domes, sunlight glaring off them like liquid fire. Between them, bridges arc hundreds—maybe thousands—of feet off the ground, some enclosed in emerald-tinted sea glass, others open and shielded only with balustrades. Even the sides of the palace are decorated with large, ornate glass panels detailed with mahogany fretwork.

Then there's the waterfall spilling from its center in a cerulean ribbon, disappearing behind another bridge.

Based on how Illian once described it, I expected a gaudy structure, as pretentious as King Anton is said to be, considering he'd added his own extravagant touch to this place once he was handed the eastern territory.

But even I can't deny its magnificence.

Still, it makes me wonder just how different King Anton is from Illian. Does he look like him? Act like him? A libertine, I've heard, and not just from Illian. A philanderer obsessed with his own wealth and merrymaking. He was often spoken about at court by those who attended his many soirées, the rumors surrounding him more numerous than the other Crowns combined. Most notably, that he procures hundreds of women for his so-called Glory Court—forcing them to dedicate themselves to his pleasure alone.

Then there's King Estienne, the oldest of the three, who is whispered to be cruel and short-tempered. He's quick to behead anyone who offends him and enjoys it like he would a sport.

Perhaps I have them to thank for the vermin Illian has become.

As we drift closer, a bustling harbor splays before us, dockhands preparing for the arrival of larger ships. The docks themselves branch into stars, each reserved for the nations in attendance and marked by their own flag. The three at the center are clear: East, Central, and West Miridran. The flags are the same: a golden chalice against dark silk, the only difference signifying each territory engraved in the chalice itself. A diamond for West Miridran, a violet quartz for Central Miridran, and for the East, pearls and sea glass.

Then there's a dock marked by black flags fringed in colorful tassels for Serai, a large country separated from West Miridran by the sea. Following that, a dock for the Karithian islands to the north, and Zar to the east. The farthermost dock sends a jolt down my spine with its ice-white and blue flag centering a gold talon—a flag I once pledged to.

Brisendale.

Emilia would have walked that dock. Would have seen Anell for the first time from that vantage.

I swallow and turn my gaze, running it over a large, incoming ship with angular purple sails. Its bow is curved heavenward, capped in gold, and it docks underneath Razam's amaranthine flag. If the shouts are any indication, it's the first ship carrying foreign courtiers. Behind it looks to be an envoy of smaller ships from Kasim beneath yellow and sage flags.

A dockhand shuffles us off the boat, then points me toward a spherical structure made entirely of chromatic sea glass, arrayed by a copse of willows. From the outside, it reminds me of the music boxes Emilia used to collect.

The inside, while bare save for the ring of performers waiting to audition, is marbled in polychromic light from every direction. I skirt the edge of the room and set my bags on the floor, dazedly surveying the three girls pirouetting in sync in the center. Ribbons unspool alongside them, knotted along their wrists in shades of indigo and cerise that compliments their deep, golden-brown skin.

In tandem, they shift places, directions, and if I'm not mistaken, they're spelling words with their streamers. With their technique, I wonder if they might have studied in Razam or Zar, or even one of the island nations to the west. It's obvious from their precision that they've been formally trained, whether in an academy or private lessons, despite their age, for they can't be older than sixteen.

Next to me, someone whispers that they're triplets, the daughters of some renowned steward.

I wipe my sweat-slicked palms against my legs and shrink back against the wall. I've had some training, and Emilia taught me what she learned from her time as an actress. But not like this. I couldn't have afforded anything formal, not after fleeing my father with nothing but a small bag and Emilia's ring to purchase passage. My skills were developed through observation and practice in the theater I'd called home before Illian found me.

And here, now, I feel foolish and small, especially as I watch the trio. I may have the basics—like talent, flow, and a natural sense of rhythm—but even if that were enough, my new limitations will be clear.

All at once, the music ceases, and a nervous energy pulses through the air. Then a man standing to the side breezes into the center of the room, his flaxen hair swept neatly across his forehead, his toned arms bare against his loose vest and pants. And by that assuming stance alone, I gather he must be the Master of Revels.

I don't know what I'd expected, but he isn't much older than I am. Illian's age, perhaps, on the cusp of his thirties. And I would be remiss not to notice how well formed he is. Or the pale gold of his eyes and how stark they are against his darker lashes and brows—especially as that gilded gaze swings over the waiting crowd, settling on me for a breath, then two.

I feel as if I've been struck by lightning.

He is a study in angles, like a marble statue cut by lines of shadow and sun. I am no painter, but for him, my fingers itch for a brush.

I try and fail to read his lips as he speaks to the triplets in a low tone. Then he motions the next performer forward, and the next, and with each performance, my confidence dwindles more. He's testing them, gauging their ability.

I was prized, the Jewel of King Illian's court, yet now I wonder if it meant anything at all. Perhaps I simply moved in a way that pleased him and *only* him. And now, for a performance fit for royals, I have little to offer but a broken body and sack of flour.

The hours stretch on as performer after performer showcases their talents. I fight to keep air in my lungs, the sweat from my palms, until the clearing of a throat jolts me from my thoughts. The Master of Revels raises his brow at me, his pale eyes narrowing. "Reference?"

I quickly offer him my letter stamped with Central Miridran's seal, but he merely stares at me, uninterested. "We don't need another solo dancer."

I blink. "I've . . . been sanctioned by King Estienne's court." While it doesn't guarantee me a position, it does ensure my right to audition. I try to hand him the letter once more, but he crosses his arms.

"Regrettably," he says—unapologetically, "we only have room for one soloist, and the position is taken."

Taken? That can't be right. "You don't understand. I've come all this way—"

"As has everyone else."

"The recommendation comes from King Estienne's very own adviser..."

"Not from the king himself, then?"

"I—" I clamp my lip between my teeth, withholding a growl. "Surely you wouldn't want me to tell them you turned me away before I even had the chance to prove myself?"

He rolls his eyes, then scrubs a hand over his face. "Look, Miss..."

"Vasalie," I answer. "Vasalie Moran."

The truth. I was instructed to use my name, being that it's on the Miridranian registrar's list. At least no one will recognize it. My vocation as the King's Jewel kept my identity a secret during my time in King Illian's court.

"Miss Moran," he drawls, "I don't have time to waste on another performer who fancies ribbons or frills and a basic routine. Frankly, I've seen it all before, and so have the Crowns. I've even been requested by our kings to ensure this year's entertainment is a true showcase of Miridranian talent. Last time, one of our hotheaded soloists nearly got herself hanged after she was laughed off the stage, and I doubt you wish to share the same fate. So unless you can create wings and fly, I suggest you return to your ship." He pivots toward the harpist, who perches awkwardly on a stool in the corner, awaiting his dismissal.

"And if I can?" I say.

He angles back toward me, brow arching. "Can what?"

I level my chin, my glare a challenge. "Create wings and fly."

A bold claim, maybe. But if it's a little magic he wants, then it's magic I will serve him.

Chapter Five

The Master of Revels is far from amused.

"We don't do acrobats, Miss Moran, and we don't have the setup for aerialists here. Consider trying the circus—"

"You weren't serious, then? About the wings?"

He blinks at me, as if I'm mocking him.

I fold my arms. I'm not leaving, even if I have to sneak into the Gathering and poison the other soloist. A sprinkle of sassen powder and they'd be sick for at least a few days. Two years ago, I'd be ashamed for such a thought, but if I fail to get in, I'm of no use to Illian.

He rubs a thumb over his jaw, then blows out a sigh, suddenly weary. "You have two minutes of my time."

Before he can back away, I say, "Might I ask your name, Master Reveler?"

At that, he pauses. "For what reason?"

"You have mine. It seems only fair."

"Copelan, then."

"Copelan," I repeat. It's an old name with both Miridranian and Brisendali descent. I know this because my father had me study names and origins. "It means 'an abundance of passion.'"

In some contexts, it's closer to exuberance, but I don't tell him that.

Emilia once said that people loved to hear their name spoken aloud; it was her secret to garnering favor. For a glimpse, he appears puzzled—a reprieve from the severity of his gaze. I take it as a win.

Retrieving the mat from my bag, I unroll it across the floor. It draws a furrow from Copelan's brow, and more so as I unclasp the buttons on my coat, revealing snow-white gossamer that grazes the floor in feathery tufts. I'd sewn the skirt myself, with Brigitte's help. It's inexpensive, light, and flows weightlessly around me like dandelion fluff in a delicate breeze.

"'The Set Alune,' please," I request of the harpist. It's a common ballad, sung to children mostly: the story of a flightless bird who fashions wings from water. Yet another sigh reveals just how unimpressed Copelan is; I can almost hear his thoughts: *Too safe, too common.* But I won't doubt my decision.

I find my center of gravity and breathe.

The music commences in a flurry of rising chords. Dizziness sets in, but I take one step, two, then run until the seventh beat. On the eighth, I throw my momentum into a jump, arms splayed like a bird attempting to fly—

Only to tuck inward and allow myself to fall gracefully onto the ground. My head swirls, but I curl in on myself, palms flattened against the mat. Rising in a show of defeat, I give another halfhearted leap, and another, until I am down a final time.

I lie there, the anticipation building, then turn my attention to the ground around me. Rotating onto my back, I glide as if I'm floating through water. Tendrils of flour, now staining the rich blue of the sea, slip from my hand in ripples.

I gather my strength and pull to my feet, twirling onto the edge of the mat. Pain lances through my nerves, but I push it aside.

I wait for my moment, the harmony building into a finale. I stride forward, my secret already in my palms, and with every ounce of determination I possess, I spring upward. Arms spread, I release the flour, and with no short amount of satisfaction, I see the Master of Revel's expression drop into awe as my powder fans into large, billowing wings. And even as I land, the outline of my triumph lingers in midair a few beats before settling into a soft cloud around my feet.

I breathe out. My heartbeat stutters and my vision swims with stars, dizziness pitching against my mind for a long moment until it clears, but I feel something more that I haven't in years.

Pride.

I impressed him. Even more, I remembered what it's like to tell a story without words. It was something Emilia taught me from her time as an actress—something I implemented when Illian finally allowed me to coordinate my own routines. The first tale I danced into existence was of a white fox whose fur never grew the lovely golden brown and red hues of autumn, like his friends, and so he set forth to collect color from the Mystical Wood. Illian loved it so much, he asked that I teach it to a nearby arts academy, and since then, they perform it every autumn's solstice.

I remember wishing Emilia could've seen it. She would have clapped the loudest, would've dragged every acquaintance she ever made to a showing. Twice.

There was a time when I loved to dance because it made me feel close to her. It was under the lights of a stage that I kept her with me.

I exhale, turning the lock in my mind, the Master of Revels coming back into focus.

His lips tighten as he watches me. Then he bends, examining the powder.

"It will stain," I say.

"Then you've ruined your outfit."

"A story worth telling warrants a little destruction."

As soon as I say it, a bout of nausea grips me, nearly making me lurch as I recall a similar phrase that once left my father's lips. *A lesson worth learning surely warrants a little destruction.*

He'd said it after a banquet, when I hadn't eaten the delicacies the king's adviser had prepared. My father had been away for months at an encampment—souls, I'd missed him—and all the excitement and nervousness had stolen my appetite. But he'd been furious with me. It was an insult capable of jeopardizing his standing, he'd told me, as the newly appointed general of Brisendale's army. I hadn't understood, and so when we returned home, he'd taken my blue-crowned finch from its cage, placed it in my hands, and told me to squeeze, because the only way I'd learn was if I *felt* the consequences of my actions.

But I couldn't do it. Not with the ruffle of wings filling my palms or the tiny chirps slipping between the gaps of my fingers. So he did it for me. Grabbed my hand and mashed it with his own. I can almost feel it now—the soft crush of bones, like brittle twigs. The ooze that seeped onto my palm.

I curl my fists, trying not to sway.

"So this is the reason for the mat," Copelan remarks.

I nod, forcing my thoughts to the present.

"What exactly is this?" He dips the toe of his boot along the scattered flour.

"My own concoction." It isn't a lie. Before the journey, I experimented with it, adding powdered dye and finely ground crystals. "I call it '*Dust of the Moon.*'"

His brow lifts, disappearing into his hairline. "Moon dust?"

"I'll come up with a better name."

Unlikely.

Again, he stares at me, unsure of what to make of the wisp of a woman standing before him. But I see the shift as he rakes a hand through his hair. "Your movements were stilted. Have you an injury?"

"Something like that." I don't want to elaborate, and thankfully, I don't have to.

"You are untrained," he says. I'm not surprised he could tell. "Do you have experience in front of a crowd?"

"Festivals aplenty," I say. "And I danced at the Melune."

While that's true, I wasn't a tenured performer like he will assume.

After arriving on the shores of Miridran at age thirteen, I was alone, starving, and too young to rent a place to live. Emilia's ring bought me passage and only enough food to last a few months. During a particularly nasty storm, after the money had run out, I'd tucked myself under an alcove bracketed by two pillars that nestled into the side of the theater. The owner of the Melune took pity on me, hiring me as a seamstress and allowing me to make a home for myself among the rafters. There, I would watch each performance, every rehearsal, picking them apart until I knew every step. I memorized the criticism, jotting meticulous notes across scraps of parchment. I practiced until I was perfect, until they allowed me to join the performers onstage. And when an accident took out a star dancer, I jumped in and saved the performance.

That was the day Illian discovered me.

"The Melune," the harpist calls, the first I've heard from her. "Impressive."

Copelan paces a few steps, his gaze sliding along my figure. "Would you work with a partner if I requested it?"

"I don't know," I say honestly. "I haven't before." I probably shouldn't admit it, but he's made up his mind. I see it in the way his eyes glimmer, the way he now faces me fully, shoulders back, instead of angling away.

This is how I held the king's favor. By watching him, ascertaining what piqued his interest during my initial performance, and each one after that, whether it was me onstage or someone else. I read him like a book, memorized his tells. This man is no different. Men are predictable creatures, after all.

He approaches, corded arms crossed. "All right, Vasalie Moran," he says. "I am not your trainer, and I am not your nanny. I will not choreograph your dances; it's why we bring in only the best here.

But every performance is subject to my approval, and if the Crowns find you lacking, you will be removed from the isle. Am I clear?"

"As glass," I answer, ignoring the way my anxiety curdles within me. But . . . "What of the other solo dancer?"

"You'll alternate. Or perhaps," he says, a smirk inching upward, "I'll have you coordinate a routine together."

I'm not sure if he's mocking me, but I'm too tired to care. The energy I exerted leaves me shaky and weak, and I crave sleep. But King Illian's first task, however vague, sits in the back of my mind. *I want you to befriend the Gathering's Head of Staff.*

Thankfully, Copelan dismisses me with an assistant, who hands me a room key with instructions before snatching my bags, promising she'll deliver them to my room.

Outside, a cobblestone walkway winds toward the main palace. Sea-salted air coats my tongue and ruffles the ocean waves at my side, and despite my exhaustion, a new energy threads through my veins as I approach the entryway. And as I glide inside, I ponder whether I've slipped into slumber, because the sight before me is one only a dream could craft.

Everywhere I look is glass.

Glossy wisteria coils around a multitude of columns. Panes, gilded and stained with patterns of aquamarine and emerald, arc along the walls and vaulted ceiling. Ribbons of light pierce through, dappling a vibrant mosaic across the floor. Then there's the glass chandelier: a glimmering, upside-down willow, its branches cascading in tiers along the entryway, draping on either side of me like a veil.

A new addition, perhaps.

I wonder if this place outshines the Fates themselves.

Once more, my thoughts turn to Illian's younger brother and the stories I've heard—particularly the most unbelievable one—that he fell from Miridran's highest cliff when he was sixteen. Even now, his blood supposedly stains its rocks. Some believe the Fates sent a cloud to break his fall. Others say it was a hoax—a rumor meant to instill fear.

But there are witnesses who swear he died that day. *Actually* died. And that somehow, he returned to life without so much as a broken bone—as if he made a bargain with the Fate of Morta herself. But even I know she can't be bargained with.

Whatever the truth, King Anton wastes his second chance at life by making himself rich—richer than both his brothers—all so he can host lavish parties, revel in his Glory Court, and drown himself in expensive wine.

And as I traverse his palace, the evidence of his opulence surrounds me.

He supposedly made a great deal of his wealth by developing a more durable form of sea glass, made from sand and minerals off the eastern coast. No one knows the exact process by which it's formed. Not even Illian, who voiced his disapproval frequently. I don't blame him. King Anton's sea glass is supposedly stronger, more resilient, and ten times more versatile than regular glass. Yet he often uses it as mere decoration instead of discounting it across Miridran's other territories—when his is by far the wealthiest, no matter how many diamonds Illian pries from his mountains.

It's still an impressive feat, much as I loathe to admit it. The resources of the east were seemingly the least valuable, unlike those of his older brothers who trade rare gems, livestock, and ore. And now his territory's wealth is thanks not only to his innovations with glass but to tourism—some of which is no doubt drawn in from his ostentatious reputation alone.

Underneath another arch, the space widens even more. Glass stairs, like hardened ice, spiral off along the walls, with hallways opening between them. In the center, clear baubles dangle on strings of varying lengths, each enclosing a different flower: asters, crown imperials, hollies, and more.

I tap my finger against a globe. It swings, triggering an echoing chime. I startle like a thief caught stealing, but no one notices save for a frowning maid, who flits by with a stack of towels in her arms.

I call out before she can round a corner. "Excuse me, Miss..."

Pausing, she sweeps her gaze over her shoulder, meeting mine. It catches me off guard, because Illian's servants never dared. "The Head of Staff," I ask. "Where can I find him?"

She jerks her chin to my left. "A right at the end of the hall, last door."

"Thank you," I say, but she's already gone, another swarm of servants shuffling by in livery just like hers: loose linen tunics and pants underneath a beige apron, tied at the waist.

Following her directions, I step aside more than once as groups of guards pass by. They come from all over the northern continents, each donning armor and weapons unique to their nation. But it's King Anton's soldiers who capture my attention. Despite their sea-green cuirass and baldrics, they wear light-refracting masks, each clutching a large glass-edged halberd, not unlike a reaper's axe. Anton's particular contributions, I've heard, to spare the east from expensive metal, armor, and weapons imports.

The hallway quiets around the bend, allowing me a chance to catch my breath until the sound of voices slip underneath the farthest door.

"... and see to it the prophets are brought to me first."

"... won't arrive for another few days, if the correspondence is to be believed..."

The door itself towers above me, a framework of gold hexagons bordering fragmented cobalt glass, and the handle is an ornate sword. I wrap my hands around its hilt but pause, peering through the crack.

Two figures hover over a large desk. The first is hooded in a blue, threadbare cloak. The other is angled away from the door, his cream uniform reminiscent of the maid's, though blue and gold embroidery notates a higher rank. He must be the Head of Staff.

"Here're the last of the letters," he says, gathering a stack of envelopes. "On your way to Philam, then?"

"No time like the present," says the hooded one. "I'll dispatch them to my contacts in the north."

"I could always send someone on your behalf."

"Nonsense. I need the fresh air, and it's more urgent if it comes from me. Besides, I'll be discreet."

"With all due respect, you have not been discreet a day in your life."

"All the more reason to practice." With that, the man in the hood pulls the stack into his hands, then pivots toward the door.

Not wanting to be caught eavesdropping, I sweep back, but there's nowhere to hide. The door whips open, and there he is, pausing at the sight of me. Though I can't see his eyes, he has a regal air about him, a confident posture that feels almost overbearing. I can't help but bristle, more so as his lips quirk—a quirk that spreads into a saccharine smile as he calls over his shoulder, "Seems you have a guest, Laurent. And an interesting one at that." Then he ambles past, whistling, his cloak a whisper against the polished floor.

I remember too late that my skin is still dusted with blue millen.

"Don't be a stranger," the Head of Staff—Laurent—calls out. "Do come in."

Cheeks aflame, I ease into the office. Laurent is bent over his papers, organizing them into different piles. "What can I do for you?" he mumbles nonchalantly, then lifts his head, a warm smile on his lips.

Something about him puts me instantly at ease.

His eyes are silver yet soft as a cloud, a contrast to his cutting cheekbones and jawline. His hair is shaved, his skin smooth and deep brown, and if I had to guess, I'd place him in his late thirties. And despite his dignified, gold-threaded uniform, he has an eclectic presence about him that draws me in. A bronze ribbon coils up one arm, while a silver torque wraps his throat. Mismatching earrings decorate each ear, and I briefly think about how much Emilia would love them. She used to collect unique jewelry.

His brows climb as he surveys me. "I assume you're looking for the bathhouse?"

"Actually, sir, I had hoped to inquire about ordering supplies. I'm a performer, you see. A dancer, specifically." It's not entirely a lie. While I brought as much millen and dyes as I could, I will eventually need more.

But mostly, I needed an excuse to meet him.

"What sort of supplies?"

"Millen flour, primarily. I use it in my dance."

"Ah." He looks intrigued. "You must have just come from the auditions. Part of a troupe, I presume?"

"A soloist, actually."

"How'd you manage that? Copelan was intent on turning everyone away."

I suck my lips between my teeth. "I can be annoyingly persistent."

"I keep telling him to pull the stick from his ass, though I suspect if he does, he'll deflate."

I bark out a laugh, then touch a tentative hand to my cheek. My laugh, my smile—it's a small thing, but . . . I'd forgotten what it felt like.

When he returns my smile, I can't help but ask, "I take it you and Copelan aren't the best of friends?"

"Oh, he's decent," Laurent says. "But I find endless amusement in his glowering displeasure. As for your supplies, I would be happy to help, but you'll have to have it approved by him first—even given the nature of what you need. The way of things, unfortunately." He grabs a set of keys, then leads me into the hall. "Can I help you find your rooms?"

"I know where they are in theory," I say. "But this place is . . . rather overwhelming."

"To think this one was originally built as a mere summer getaway," Laurent says, shaking his head. "Miridran and its palaces."

"There are hundreds, aren't there?" Of course, many date back to before the War of Rites, before Miridran was consolidated into one nation. Half are in ruins still, while others were renovated into chapels, universities, and the like. "I wonder why they chose this one to host the Gathering?"

Guards skim our path as Laurent leads me down a broad hallway banking off the entrance. "An easy choice, I'd say. It's on its own island, disconnected from any landmass. I suppose that makes it feel safer. More . . . neutral, even if it's still considered part of East Miridran."

Laurent then ushers me into the palace's main hall—the sheer expanse of it even more spectacular than the entrance. Variegated glass wraps the room in its entirety, patterned to look like a forest at dusk. Fretwork columns partition the space, and between them, pathways spiral upward, soaring to multiple stories hundreds of feet high.

"Beautiful, no? Much of what you see here was built long ago, by our current kings' ancestors, such as the foundation, the columns, and floors. However, there are many new additions, thanks to His Majesty King Anton. Many of the mosaics, for instance. He spends much of his time here, adding to the construction, even between the Gatherings when the isle is empty."

Grinning at my expression, Laurent runs a hand over his shaved head, one of his glass earrings catching the light. "And if you think this is grand, you must not have seen his palace in Ansa."

Ansa, East Miridran's capital city.

"I haven't," I admit, rubbing my arm. Before, I couldn't imagine anything more audacious than Illian's palace. But now that I'm here, I feel a bit breathless.

"I hope you do one day," Laurent says. "It was once Queen Mercy's palace."

Queen Mercy—the first Miridranian queen.

Who, according to lore, later became the Fate of Morta.

A myriad of staff members whisk by, each enrobed in their nation's fashion. Several from Illian's court have already arrived, as have his guards, stationing themselves around the palace. Their gazes fix on me when I pass.

Laurent angles toward me. "West wing is that way. The fourth landing is reserved for performers. Don't forget to be in the dining hall by sundown." At my quizzical glance, he clarifies. "The welcome dinner for the performers is in the southern wing, third floor. I won't be there, but Copelan will. He'll be delivering his little speech before seeing how quickly he can vanish."

After bidding me good luck, Laurent is pulled away by a frantic maid, gesticulating wildly about a chamber pot disaster. He slides me an apologetic look before disappearing around a bend. At least I made a dent in my first task.

I stagger up endless stairs, my chest heaving. Stars pile in my periphery, and several times I'm forced to sit until I regain my vision.

Finally, I find my room nestled in a dark alcove at the end of the hall, almost as if they forgot it existed. I'm not complaining. It's quiet, and the view is unlike anything I've ever seen. The window overlooks a scattering of islands beyond the docks, and past them, the sea is nothing but mirrors and glass, capturing the pink glaze of the setting sun.

I take a deep breath, absorbing the calm before what will surely be a storm.

Chapter Six

The isle comes alive as more and more ships arrive.

Billowing sails pass behind the gauzy curtains of my window that evening: clusters of vessels finding their way to the docks as the sun sinks beneath the horizon.

A wind sweeps low, swirling the drapes around like tendrils of smoke, stirring the plants in the corner of my room. Briny air fills my lungs alongside a flitter of nerves.

My skin is red and flushed from the washbasin and my efforts to scrub the blue powder from my skin. Now, I organize my rolls of fabric and sewing tools on an empty desk, then sort my bags of flours, dyes, and a few other components I plan to experiment with as the last glow of sunset fades and stars dust the darkening sky. After tugging on my leggings, I grab a fresh tunic, twist my hair into a loose braid, and head to find the orientation dinner.

The moment I step outside, I bump into a maid, a stack of linens in her arms. "Miss," she says, dipping her head, "these are for you. May I?"

I step aside and allow her entrance. She places them on my bed, then tells me she will return each morning to collect what I've used. There's a saccharine quality to her—one that feels forced, especially when her eyes travel over the room, then me, to linger just a little too long before she leaves.

Illian.

How many has he paid off? How many are instructed to watch my every move?

Sconces bounce torchlight across the sandstone walls, lighting my path until I find the arc pass leading toward the southern wing. It's one of many I saw from the outside: a curved bridge enclosed in glass that connects various parts of the palace. As I step onto it, I'm so high above the world, it takes me a moment to orient. Beneath, wedges of glittering torchlight illuminate the grounds and docks. Servants shuffle around like ants, carrying trunks and carts of food. Not for the first time today, my eyes wander past the esplanade toward the western dock, my bunched fists relaxing when I ensure it's empty.

I'd known he wouldn't be here yet; the Crowns won't arrive for another week. Still, I'd wondered if he'd find a way to come early.

Even so, I know I'm not alone. But there's something about Illian's actual presence, as if he pulls a storm with him wherever he goes. As if at any moment, he'll shock me or drag me back into the dark, like the more frightening tales of Morta.

My protector is gone, revealed to be a monster. But I remind myself that I am not a damsel. I'm no princess bound within a tower.

I am a shadow.

I can be broken apart and put back together, like Brigitte says. I have endured cruelty, imprisonment, years of loneliness and pain. I might not be able to escape Illian, but I *can* clear my name and shape myself into something new. So here, in this serenity above the island, I repeat my promise: I will do as Illian asks and earn my freedom. I picture the deep, windy cliffs of Brisendale, the towns that lay beyond, folded into vales and carpeted in wildflowers. There, I could disappear. Live among the heather and birdsong and peaceful mountain air.

The brazen scent of fresh herbs and honeyed wine thickens at the end of the arc pass, drawing my stomach into twists as I descend the stairs. Chatter accompanies it, mingled with peals of laughter, the clank of silverware.

I take in a steadying breath, pausing at the precipice of the dining hall.

It's packed tight, the space elongated with narrow tables arrayed between pale sea-stone walls. I feel invisible as I slide onto the edge of a bench, taking in the multitude of other performers. Mostly musicians and dancers, I gather, several troupes all sitting together, but also bards and poets if their conversation is any indication. They grin cheekily as they jostle and tease each other, as if they share a lifetime of history. I slide my palms underneath my thighs, scanning for anyone who might be separate from the group. I'd hoped to determine who the other soloist might be.

A whistle pierces the chatter. Through an arched doorway, Copelan stalks into view. He looks refreshed, his bright hair swept back, a loose, flowing uniform similar to Laurent's hiding his sculpted form.

With a clap, he says, "Welcome, all, to the Crowns' Gathering," and glasses lift in recognition. "As you know, we're here for six weeks. That means forty-five nights of performances. Granted, we'll have only one signature performance a week for the entirety of our guests, but each night, we'll divvy you up to entertain smaller, more select groups. These are determined by request or assignment, so you will defer to me. As such, your role here affords you the unique privilege of spending time in each and every court present."

Every court. A reminder of why Illian needs a performer.

"There are rules you must adhere to. You are not to address our guests directly unless spoken to. You will accept no bribes, nor will you favor any audience member during a performance," he says, ticking off each regulation with his fingers. "We are bound by Miridranian law. If you are caught giving out any information pertaining to our land, resources, or leadership, you'll consider prison a blessing to the alternative. And if you're caught in a guest's quarters, you'll be suspended immediately. The same can be said if a guest is caught in yours."

An image of Lord Sarden's body the night he was found in my room slips into my mind—waxen, pruned flesh; a bulbous, watery wound. Rheumy eyes, lifeless yet accusing. Bile snakes up my throat. I hadn't known he was there, not until I was wrenched from bed and dragged from my room, sluggish from what I suspect was a tonic slipped into my drink. Guards pulled him out, cocooned in a bloodied sheet—someone must have snuck him in after I fell asleep. But he'd clearly been dead for some hours, and I'd been with Illian up until the hour previous . . .

"Through us, the most powerful presences in the Northern Kingdoms will bear witness to Miridranian talent and strength."

Cheers ring, chalices clink. I drag a hand over my face. I wonder if Copelan knows just how cunning, how vicious, the Crowns can be. Rules are no hindrance to them.

I wonder how many I'll have to break.

Copelan raises his glass with a forced smile. "Take tonight to get acquainted with your fellow performers. I expect everyone to retire at a reasonable time and fill the practice halls bright and early. We only have a few days before our first signature performance."

Food is served: fresh cod sauced in white wine over a bed of rice, presented in small stoneware dishes. After a few bites, I lay down my spoon, not wanting to be sick before this crowd. My eyes travel to Copelan. Like me, he's alone amid a room full of people and, like me, he seems to prefer solitude. A minute later, he rises from the table and slinks from the hall.

A slow, sneaking suspicion pulls me from my bench.

Wandering in the direction he left, I find another arc pass, this one higher than the last and overlooking the dome in the middle of the palace. It's quiet—so quiet my thoughts sound like voices. It drags me back to my time in Illian's prison, back to that dark, ever-present well in my mind. But I stave it off, repeating the promise I made to myself with each step, sealing it deep in the burrows of my heart.

On the other side, I come upon a wide turret ringed by ominous, amaranthine sea glass, in the center of which stands a large statue depicting a lover's embrace.

The tableau itself is a glossy marble, finely crafted, yet it looks as if it was cracked apart then glued together again. Veins of reflective glass mar its smoothness, shimmering under the moonlight.

A closer inspection reveals the figures aren't lovers after all. Not now that I recognize the hooded woman, the way her arm coils around the chiseled torso of a beautiful man. Her other hand grips a large, gilded mirror.

This tale I know well—a myth that ties back to the foundation of Miridran itself. Because the figure the Fate of Morta holds is Eremis, the only man to face her and live.

Eremis was the king's bastard well over a century ago. When he died, Morta held out her hand, but he did not take it, so enamored with his own beauty that he was not swayed by hers. He returned to his life on land, having cheated death.

This piece of art, however, shows Morta's revenge: the day she claimed him by holding up a mirror, capturing his reflection the next time he died.

He'd taken her hand, thinking it was his own.

A chill passes over me, bristling the hairs on my arms. Illian had images of Morta all over his palace, but here she feels close, somehow. A phantom in the shadows, the silence her song. Idly, I press the pad of my finger to her billowy lips, a faint ringing in my ear . . .

The sound of movement jerks me from my trance, drawing my attention to a nearby hall.

I ease past the sculpture and peek around the bend.

And there, in a wide, abandoned room, is Copelan.

Floor-to-ceiling mirrors encompass the space, reflecting his every angle, while sconces from the hall volley soft, fluttering light across the room. And he's dancing, sailing across the floor, a ribbon banding his eyes—

Blindfolded. He's *blindfolded*. Consumed in his own world. I can almost see it as he moves; he paints it for me with motion. There's no music, no beat, but I hear it in his steps. It flows from his leaps, his pirouettes, and I'm left breathless and gaping as he works up a sweat, his shirt clinging to his well-cut frame.

He is a harmony, a song. A melody made flesh. And despite his elegance, the graceful way he moves, he's powerful. A rare combination, and I have a difficult time keeping my mouth from falling open as he cuts into the air, lands on one foot, and spirals onto the other with perfect precision. Then, like a swan gliding across a lake, he drops to his knees, slides across the floor—

And lands right at my feet.

He must sense me, because he removes his blindfold.

For a moment, we simply stare at each other, unable to break away. He's kneeling before me like a man about to propose, his gaze roaming over my face.

Then he springs upward and airs out his shirt, seemingly unbothered. "Can I help you, Miss Moran?"

Heat lathers my cheeks, but I swallow the lump in my throat and decide on honesty. "You're . . . very good."

"You should be with the others. Conversing."

"I'm a soloist. I didn't see the point."

"A soloist unless I say otherwise," he reminds me, swiping strands of damp hair from his forehead.

I step past him and into the room, his eyes tracking mine in the mirror. "Will I meet the other soloist?"

"Perhaps if you had stayed—"

I twist to face him. "It's *you*, isn't it?"

A hint of a smile plays on his lips, and I have my answer. "I suppose I should be relieved. Fewer performances to handle on my own."

"You said something about performing together," I say.

His lips quirk. "I'd like to combine our efforts during the six signature performances. With all the Crowns in attendance, the pressure is high and cutting tension is vital. We control that atmosphere, see. Dance, like music, is transformative—an emotional experience they can share as one. Through it, we can unite, we can soothe, we can excite. And as soloists, we bear even more pressure. But..." His gaze rakes down my legs, then up again, deliberate. "This assumes we can actually work together."

"You think we can't?"

"In order to work with a partner, you must have two things: trust and abandon." He folds his arms. "Trust is established through time, but I worry, Miss Moran. Are you capable of it?"

My defense snaps into place. "Of course I am—"

"With your life? Truly."

I open my mouth, but his question digs into me, seeking cracks in the wall I've built. Is the person I've become capable of trust? Before, maybe, but when I think of the word now, my insides knot.

But how much trust would be expected of me for something so simple as a dance?

Before I can answer, he jerks his head. "Come here."

He isn't far, perhaps four steps away. I take three, despite the way my chest feels like it's caging a hundred fluttering birds.

A strand of white-gold hair dips into his gaze as he looks down the tip of his nose at me. "Stand straight. Lock your knees." I obey, and he taps my shoulders, swaying me to test my balance. I only just manage to resist tipping over.

Satisfied, he whispers, "Close your eyes."

My eyelids fall shut, my skin clammy. Whatever this test, I won't refuse it. He already saw my weakness. I must show him my resilience now.

Or perhaps I need to see it for myself.

"I visited the Carasian Mountains once," he says, slipping a band around my eyes. His blindfold.

Breathe.

Don't panic.

"It was a long time ago, during the great blizzard that lacquered ice across the roads in East Miridran for months," he goes on. "With nothing better to do, I climbed Mount Carapet—by myself."

The same mountain that King Anton fell from. Dizziness swirls over me, but I keep my feet rooted. I hear him circle me.

"There's no feeling quite like standing on the edge of a cliff, the world unspooling beneath you in waves," he says. I tilt my head, trying to discern his direction, but his voice is like wind, drifting from place to place.

Then he leans in, his breath stirring my hair. "Allow me to take you there."

A chill stipples my skin and I press my palms to my leggings.

"The mountain is your throne," he says from somewhere on my left. "The snow-laden grass a carpet beneath your feet. The trees are your soldiers, your white knights, standing at attention. The birds are your trumpets, your announcers, and when you level your gaze with the horizon, it feels as if you're flying alongside them."

I see it, this picture he draws for me. He stencils it word by word until I am there, my toes grazing the cliff's edge, the wind—his breath—cool on my skin. He tells me what I hear, what I smell, the taste on my tongue.

"You belong here," he says—a whisper, "with the world at your feet and leaves in your hair. You see the riverbed below, the wildlife. Deer prance freely, beckoning you to join them." He's to my right. Or in front of me, perhaps, but I am lost to the vision. "This is your kingdom after all; even the gale obeys your command. Go with them, Vasalie."

I'm tempted to step from my perch, the urge overwhelming. He chooses then to issue a simple command into my ear, so gentle I almost miss it. "Now fall."

He isn't behind me. Distantly, I know this, but still I let my weight plummet backward—

He doesn't catch me. My heart leaps into my throat, but then something light and soft—fabric?—lassos around my shoulders *inches* before I hit the ground, then lowers me until I'm flat on my back.

I rip the blindfold off.

An aerialist ribbon, it looks like. I scramble up, begrudgingly accepting the hand he offers me, dropping it once I'm steady. "I almost hit the ground!"

"But you didn't." His lips quirk, and he tosses the aerialist ribbon aside. "Well, Miss Moran, that certainly wasn't trust. But you're brave, and I can work with that. Abandon, however, is another matter."

Abandon.

"I'm not sure I understand," I say, a slight jitter still working its way through my limbs.

"It means giving up your freedom, your instincts, your boundaries." He narrows the space between us. "It means that you lend your partner a key to the areas you've locked away. It means you surrender everything you want, everything you are, in lieu of the dance."

"And you want me to prove it." Like his test of trust.

"Can you?" His smirk holds a dare.

I take my bottom lip between my teeth, then lean to grab the blindfold. "Not with words."

His hand twitches at his side. I summon my courage and wrap the blindfold around my eyes, and before I can change my mind, I close the remaining distance, my chest pressed against his.

I draw in air, feeling his breath rise and fall with mine.

He sets a palm on my lower back. Energy crackles like wildfire, and yet I can read it, somehow. I can read him, sense what he wants.

I dip backward, head lolling to expose my throat. He supports me until I'm upside-down, my back a perfect arch, tendrils of hair grazing the floor. Then he's over me, his breath hot on my neck, then my sternum, my stomach—

He wraps a hand around the back of my thigh.

Warmth skates over my skin as his fingers graze the soft skin behind my knee, lifting it to slide it over his shoulder. I take my weight onto my own hands, circling my other leg around his neck, and clutch my abdomen, preparing.

He swings me up in one quick motion.

Then I'm on his shoulders, his head against my stomach, and the air is thick, like fog.

I release the grip I have in his hair. He eases me down his chest until I'm sitting on his arms, my face in the crook of his neck.

For several seconds, we do not move.

Gently, he places me on my feet, steadying me when I sway. Then he unwinds my blindfold and stares at me. His mouth hangs open slightly, his locks splayed around his forehead. I've never done anything like that before. And his touch, the way it felt—

Heat licks my neck like the brush of a flame.

Until now, I hadn't realized how much I craved someone's touch. But I've been alone for so, so long. The only physical contact I've had since prison, besides Brigitte's fleeting comfort, was when the physician and Brigitte's attendants examined me with their rough, calloused hands. Even before, in Illian's court, no one laid a finger on me save for his guards on the night I was arrested. And this . . .

It's as if I've been sparked to life. As if I've awoken after years of slumber, feeling what I never thought I would again. I feel alive. Connected to my body. I feel every urgent beat of my pulse, a frenzy and passion that zings beneath my skin. In this moment, it's even more prominent than my pain.

I feel wild, and brave, as if I could indeed jump from that cliff and survive.

I wonder if Copelan feels it, too.

I watch him watch me.

Thoughts pass through his gaze like sifting sand, and I wish he would release the words gathering on his tongue.

I let my hand fall to his chest, if only to feel the thundering heart beneath. He shudders beneath my touch.

But then he shakes his head as if to snap from a trance, rubbing a hand over his neck. "I'll see you tomorrow, then. Practice rooms. Half past noon."

My heart is still galloping when finally I reach my room, and it takes me several tries to fit my key into the lock. My body still trembles, too, from weakness and exhilaration both. I can't erase the feel of Copelan's hands on my skin or the gentle, warm strength that radiates from his presence. I shudder out a breath, and that's when I notice it.

An envelope sits on my bed.

I trot over on sore feet. The air stills in my lungs as I collect it and tug out the soft parchment. It's in King Illian's hand, and my eyes dart to the docks beyond my window, only his ship still isn't there. I glance down, clamping my lip between my teeth as I read his words.

Rest well, Vasalie. You look like you need it.
I eagerly anticipate your first performance.

Chapter Seven

Copelan and I practice for several hours over the next week. We speak not with words but through gestures. Dance. It seems more is said this way.

I'm getting to know him by the way he moves.

He is respectful, patient, but never shy, and he expects the same of me. I rise to the occasion. I let him test me, evaluate me. He finds all the ways I can bend and shape and balance; I am a doll in his hands.

He might not say it, but I know I don't meet his expectations. Though I'm stronger than before, my strength doesn't return in full. We've cut our practice short more than once when it vanishes altogether, the exertion sapping my stamina embarrassingly fast. A thought hovers in the back of my mind like a phantom: I was broken apart, and now I wonder if, despite my earlier resolve, some things cannot be repaired. But I don't dare give voice to it. I want to believe that with enough work, enough practice, I can become again what I was.

But it's my ideas that Copelan craves, so I don't temper them. If my creativity can keep me in this game, I'll give it freely. He approves everything I ask for: crushed diamonds, gold flakes. Pots for steam. Rolls of taffeta, satin, tulle, and silk damask. Dyes—which Laurent orders, who seems to relish my ideas just as much. He spends any spare time he can with me and the seamstresses, sewing and planning.

It makes Illian's first task effortless. Laurent is as open and cheery as a bouquet of freshly bloomed daisies. If anything, he's become a friend, and despite my guilt, I let myself enjoy his company. Together, we craft everything from costumes to fans to crowns fashioned from dyed, painted coral until the day of the Welcoming arrives at last.

Each of the six signature performances will pay homage to the largest kingdoms in attendance save Miridran: Kasim, with its intricate, historical architecture and benevolent council; Razam, known for its fierce queen and notable developments in alchemy and astronomy; Serai, with its Sovereign Lord and colorful textile exports; and lastly, Zar, a country with lush farmlands and bountiful harvest.

Tonight's signature performance, however, will honor Brisendale, the northernmost country that spans the entire continent across the sea.

The Brisendali ships arrived late yesterday afternoon. There are six in total: four for their court and two for their king and his envoy. As soon as amber sunlight catches their sapphire flags, I turn from the window, a sharp, familiar pain sliding between my ribs. It was the Brisendali mountains I'd imagined during Copelan's test of faith. Those cliffs, verdant and ivory-frosted, farms and crofts nestled between their valleys—they were home.

I close my eyes, and for a moment I am back, perched on my rooftop balcony, that sapphire flag threading into the wind above my head. Emilia is next to me, her ash-blond hair piled atop her head in a mass of neatly pinned curls, her gown falling in velvet-soft pleats that match the gloves I love so much. She's ready to host one of my father's banquets, and I know she'll take me with her and show me what to do, how to act, not because she expects me to but because we'll suffer together, then share gossip late into the night, doing our impressions of every pompous, half-drunk noble. We'll laugh, and I'll think, not for the first time, that I'd give anything to be like her when I grow up.

Then I remember I'm grown, the vision isn't real, and this is what's become of me.

I force down a few bites of salted meat and olives, then lace my silver gown around me and fasten the ties, ignoring the queasy ripple of my stomach. Laurent's familiar knock comes a moment later—two raps in quick succession. I call him inside.

"Marvelous," he says, arms swinging wide as his smile.

"All thanks to you," I say, and mean it. Without him, my costume would not be half as grand. Tulle and lace, yes, but no pearl adornments, no silver embroidery. He's skilled with his hands, and he knows it; he's made an innuendo about it more than once.

"Nonsense! The costume is a mere ornament, a prelude to the talent beneath." He spins me this way and that. "If you were my type, love, I'd have dropped dead on sight."

That coaxes a small smile from my lips. He makes me feel as if I'm here by choice. "I think everyone will be too busy looking at you," I counter. "If I didn't know better, I'd peg you as royalty."

Especially now, with the sunset gilding his deep, burnished skin, his tall, lithe form well-showcased in a new outfit: a sleeveless garment scalloped in silver trim, matching the diamond shade of his eyes—which I notice are dusted beneath with gold.

He does a little shimmy at that. "Let's go charm the pants off some royals, then, shall we?"

I hold back a wince at the thought of attracting a Crown like Illian, or perhaps someone worse. Even so, I link my arms with his. "Only if you escort me. Perhaps I can scout for whoever might be your type?" In a courtier, that is.

"Ah, even if I could manage a dalliance around my schedule, I'd have to know what my type *is*. And I am still very much figuring that out." He pauses, head tilting. "I seem to think personality is what attracts me most, and it's usually a mischievous, troublesome one at that. But a set of dimples and a curvaceous form never fails to draw my eye, no matter who it is."

"One can admire aesthetics for many reasons," I say. "Ones that are not sexual, too, for that matter."

Not enough people acknowledge that, I think.

But as he ferries me down an ivory hall ornamented in mosaics, Laurent is pulled away. I continue on alone, missing his strength.

Twice, I pause on the arc pass, barely managing to keep the food in my stomach. It crawls with nerves and whatever else is wrong with me, and as I take in a shuddering breath, I let the fading sunlight ghost over my skin. I wonder what Emilia felt being here amid all this splendor.

She would have felt exhilarated, I imagine. Excited. I wish I could feel that, too.

Instead, sadness swells inside me like sickness.

I know I'm fortunate to be here, in a seaside palace that looks like a dream, a chance at freedom within my grasp. And so far, people here have been kind. But any friendships I form are built on lies. I am here because of Illian, who will be watching me, as he so zealously reminded me.

And whatever he asks of me, I will do.

The Dome Hall is unlike anything I've seen. The dome itself is stained sea glass, the columns and surrounding ceiling plastered and frescoed into a multi-dimensional a cloudscape. The floors are an alabaster stone, rough beneath my slippers, and there are no walls. Rather, open Palladian arches encircle the space, a fresh ocean breeze rustling the tablecloths anchored by large candles. The only exception is the double doors at the far end, hewed like the wings of a swan.

I linger on the other side, hidden by a divider backstage as the room crowds with an array of courtiers from every corner and crevice of the north. The expanse itself is arranged into sections, or lounges, with divans and chaises surrounding low-set tables, all set to face the open, clear center.

In minutes, the room will hold the most powerful figures in the Crowns' Syndicate.

Servants swerve between columns, delivering flutes of hibiscus-infused champagne. Musicians test their instruments—everything from bowed lyres to hammered dulcimers, flutes to cellos—and as the sun slumps beneath the horizon, they blend together as one.

Conversation dims.

The announcer takes his place.

And slowly, the winged double doors open.

First enters the Lord Sovereign of Serai—a tall, lithe man crowned in red stalagmites, his ebony skin a match to his woven regalia. He's escorted by two equally tall men swathed in colorful garments and beads, their faces veiled. They veer left, to where the Serain court reclines in the most vibrant assortment of colors. I'm not surprised; their widely sought after textile trade spans the whole world, including the discordant southern nations not a part of the Crowns' Syndicate.

After them, three other large processions sweep through, starting with Zar, an island that doesn't have a king, but instead a prince whose law dictates him too young to be crowned for another year. Kasim is next, whose ruling council enters together, consisting of their sultan and three ministers. And finally, the Karithian islands—a thriving archipelago of smaller nations northwest of Miridran, represented by several lieges.

The melody then shifts into an anthem I know all too well as King Rurik of Brisendale stalks inside.

I don't realize how tense I am until Copelan breaks my concentration with a hand on my waist, only to notice the way I've bunched my fists. He peels them apart, finding the welts I've created. "What's this?"

"Nerves," I answer, but it's only partly true.

He follows my gaze, to where King Rurik takes his place among the Brisendali court, and nods. "We'll especially want to please them."

It makes sense. Brisendale, commonly called the Beast of the North, is the largest and most influential nation next to Miridran. Not only do they supply ninety percent of the weapons across the northern nations thanks to rare metals found in their mountains—half the north is deeply indebted to them for it—but their army is unmatched. Twice the size of Miridran's, if not larger. At least they've kept to themselves despite the rumored appeals from the southern lands to encroach on Razam's territory.

But aside from slight tensions over Anton's weapons development freeing East Miridran from Brisendali dependence, Miridran and Brisendale have always been at peace. King Rurik was mentored by Illian's father, King Junien, before he died from scrofula.

I sneak another glance at King Rurik. I'd only seen him a handful of times before I left Brisendale. He was younger then, but he wears his age well. He could pass for thirty, though he's well past forty. Yet even now, I can't help but search his eyes. From here, I can't tell which, but one of them is fake. He'd lost it long ago thanks to a sparring accident, or so I was told. I remember noticing it the first time he visited my father at our home, before Emilia swept me away and out of sight.

Copelan watches him, too, his lip caught between his teeth. I wish I could pluck the thoughts from his head.

I wonder if, like me, he's working for someone.

I let my gaze fall over Copelan, now that his attention is elsewhere. Gone is the stiff-backed Master of Revels, and in his place is a figure from lore. A performer in every sense, from his tousled, flaxen locks to his gold silk tunic and ivory satin pants. His brows pull into a dark slash, such a contrast to the citrine flash of his eyes.

I force myself to look away.

Another twist of melody brings in the Queen of Razam, her deep amber skin flawless in her golden gown, her night-dark locks woven through with ribbons. Seven men flank her, each garbed in black, with a sun emblem sewn onto their shoulders. Vicious tulwars crisscross on their backs.

"Her sons," Copelan tells me, his breath skimming my ear, but I can't tear my eyes from the queen. I envy her poise, the way her chin is lifted, her hard obsidian eyes raking across the room as if measuring her prey.

"It's a miracle she's here," Copelan murmurs. "I heard she almost didn't come."

I heard that, too, though it's unsurprising. During my time at the Melune, Razam and Miridran were well on their way to war if relations weren't repaired—something about the queen vehemently rejecting Illian's aid against the threats from the south. It was all anyone talked about: whose children would volunteer for the army, what the draft age might be if it was implemented. Rumors stirred of Razami soldiers gathering along the edge of East Miridran.

But then King Anton traveled across the border with only two of his soldiers, supposedly as a show of peace—or foolishness. He met with Queen Sadira, and not only convinced her to cease the brewing war but to open trade with Miridran.

To this day, no one knows what he said to her.

Even now, I've heard she refuses to so much as speak to Illian. I bet it's because she can see straight through him.

A lyre joins with the stringed instruments and I stifle a breath, knowing what's coming.

The three kings of Miridran.

It should come as no surprise when Illian steps through the portal first, magnificently appareled in a midnight brocade with diamonds up to the collar, lest anyone forget his trade. His eyes are dark, vast, a slight, arrogant grin tucked into the corner of his lips—something only I might notice. Even so, the atmosphere itself seems to shift, even the light chatter ceasing.

My stomach turns as he strolls farther into the room—alone, unlike the other Crowns. No courtiers, no generals. Not even an adviser. A small assemblage of his court awaits—his seasonal selections, who will no doubt be discarded like I will be soon enough.

He selects a seat directly in my line of sight—the only member of the audience who can see a sliver of backstage.

And when he smiles, a chill snakes down my spine, because that smile isn't for those around him, no.

It's for me.

His eyes lock onto mine like a hook, even as an announcer from Central Miridran gives his condolences; King Estienne, Illian's older brother, was delayed in his journey and hasn't yet arrived. It strikes me as odd, but I can't focus on it, not when King Illian's gaze still holds mine. He slides his hand to his belt and pats it twice, then raises a brow, and it takes me a moment before I understand. I move my hand to the ribbon around my waist, and there, next to my satchel of millen, I feel it. A small, rolled parchment tucked into the silk.

I glance about, but no one aside from Copelan is nearby. And he couldn't be under Illian's employ—not after the test he put me through.

Hiding the parchment from Copelan's view, I unspool it near my waist and skim the letter. It's written in Illian's hand, just like the first note I received.

Tonight, pay my brother Anton special attention. Secure an invitation to his private dinner tomorrow evening as his entertainment by whatever means necessary.

As I roll the parchment up and hide it within the folds of my skirt, cheers erupt from the crowd. King Illian's mouth flattens into a line, and I drift my gaze toward the door where a young man stands with quite possibly the brightest smile I've ever seen.

My lips part without my consent.

King Anton of East Miridran looks nothing like his brother.

Unlike Illian, with his colorless garb and oppressive demeanor, his younger brother is vibrant in a verdant, double-breasted jerkin capped with gilded shoulder seams, the center of it parting to reveal a silken tunic beneath. Then there's the ostentatious belt, the boots paneled with jeweled buckles. His dark hair is wavy, like a wind-blown sea, his kohl-lined eyes a startling green beneath thick, shapely brows.

But it's his dashing grin that lights the room, rivaling even the stacks of rings glinting from his fingers.

It's apparent just how popular he is despite his well-known debauchery. People always did love a good show, and I must admit he delivers. The whole ensemble, but especially that crown. Glass protrudes from its golden base, stained with shards of aqua and emerald, like a garland of gilded leaves.

And it's *crooked*.

He soaks in the adulation before parading through the archway, women crowding him on either side, chins tilted up as if they're royalty right along with him.

I see now why people believe that he cheated death. He looks otherworldly, like he indeed has the power to deny his own mortality.

As he sinks into his divan, more wine is served, along with platters of roasted boar—thick haunches of steaming pink meat decorated with rosemary—followed by fruits indigenous to each country. I recognize pink mangoes and plump, aromatic ambarella fruit from Razam, pears and russet plums from Brisendale—Emilia's favorite, I remember with a pang—and apricots and grapes the size of my fist from Zar.

No one notices the potted trees being carted in, placed at intervals in the center of the room, not even as the candles and wall sconces wink out, one by one.

A strum silences the Gathering, quick as a whip.

Then the melody turns, shifting into something darker, more mysterious, accented with the soft beat of a drum. A ripple of nervous panic whisks over me as I prepare for my moment, as I beg my body to cooperate. The pain is compounded now after long days of practice and exertion, but I recall what Brigitte had told me once, something I had ignored until now. *Use all your senses when the pain is at its worst.* Taste, touch, scent. I peel off my slippers, focus on the cold of the stone beneath my toes, the tinge of brine on my tongue.

Fog drifts across the floor, blown by performers robed in diaphanous, azure gossamer. Each stands before a pot of dyed, steaming water, wafting it about with large, crescent fans.

I slide into the indigo cloud, curtained by its haze, and position myself on the floor.

A vocalist begins our tale, her voice soft yet resonate, carrying above the breeze.

Wake, woodlands; here comes your king.
Wake, forest, hear him sing.

The fog rises, and I am revealed.

My back, flat against the floor, arches upward. I am the frost king, waking from his slumber, ready to take revenge on the Sun who put me to sleep. My body curls in, then out, toes pointed, before a deep yawn stretches me to my feet in one graceful sweep.

In the snow, he steps.
Barren sun, you must now set.

The folktale is common, even outside Brisendale. The frost king is cursed, banished for five months out of the year. I show this while I move. As the music ebbs and flows, I make my urgency clear. His time, *my* time, will run out fast.

Frost king, go your course.
Frost king, our world is yours.

I glide across the floor, releasing my frost. Shimmering silver pours from my fingertips like snow, thanks to a component mixed into the flour. As I dance, it swirls around me, glimmering in the air, coating my skin, my dress, the trees and plants that set our stage. I bend into shapes I know I can achieve, and then Illian's task surfaces in my mind: *Pay my brother special attention.*

Through my movements, I find King Anton's eyes, gleaming even in the dark. My heart catapults, but this is my chance. I tread to him in a plume of silvery light.

The curve of his smile ticks upward at my approach. Two of his guards step into my path, but he waves them off.

Forest, quick, hide your light.
For the sun intends to plight.

I don't think about the ramifications of what I'm about to do. I don't think about how daring to touch a Crown is forbidden, even without the mess of silver dusting my hands. I don't think about how I'm about to pull a Miridranian king into a Brisendali dance—an offense in itself—or how Copelan warned us against involving the audience. All I can see is King Illian's handwriting, his instructions, and I act.

Don't be deceived, oh king, for the sun comes with golden rings.

This was meant to be Copelan's role.

I grasp King Anton's fingers and tug him up.

Amusement dances in those kohl-lined eyes, and for a moment, I am lost. Such a striking shade of green, somewhere between peridot and jade. But I snap from my trance and ferry him into the center of the floor, ignoring the bevy of gasps and whispers. He follows me with easy grace, as if he, too, were made for the dance. And, as if sensing my trepidation, he gives my hand a reassuring squeeze.

A bit of boldness returns.

I relish it, sliding my fingers along the sharp angle of his jaw, leaving a trail of silver. I feel the room tense around us, holding its breath.

My heart is a thunderous thing.

But then he grins, and I know I've made the right choice. I release his hand and circle him, arms raised, millen spilling until we are blanketed in a dense, pearlescent veil. Quickly, I slip a small sack of dust into his palm, subtly guiding his thumb to the release string. I whisper my request into his ear. He gives me a flash of brilliant white teeth. I can't help but smile back, elation swelling in my chest like a whorl of incense.

The cloud falls into a nebula that wafts about our feet. I arch backward, his hand supporting my lower back, the other hovering over me as if casting a curse. I let my head loll. He lowers me to the floor, then frees a large, billowing halo of golden dust that explodes outward—the warmth of the sun, the frost king's curse.

Before it settles to the floor, I dash behind the divider and out of sight, leaving King Anton standing before the crowd, plated in gold like the sun itself.

Chapter Eight

Only after I use the washbasin in my room to scrub the millen from my skin do I return to the Dome Hall.

This time, a black tulle skirt wraps my waist, a simple, laced chemise tucked inside—leftovers from costumes we decided not to use. Despite my efforts, a slight sheen of silver still shimmers against my skin, especially along my eyes and cheeks, where I tried to leave my makeup intact. Tonight, the talent is to join the after-party, and according to Copelan's rules, we're allowed to converse with anyone who approaches us. The opposite, of course, is forbidden.

But I haven't yet completed my task.

The weight of my actions squeezes my lungs, shortening my breath. I could have found another way. I should have waited until after the dance, captured his attention here at the party somehow. Anything would've been better than pulling *him*, a Miridranian king, into a foreign country's dance. And Brisendale, of all nations, whose king is notoriously short-tempered and very likely to take offense.

Then there's the fact that I robbed Copelan of his role.

Thankfully, by the time I slip back into the throng, the tension has evaporated, the atmosphere wreathed in a cheerful, inebriated sort of merriment. I'd left after our opening act, as a vocal ensemble wove through a myriad of Brisendali ballads while the millen was cleaned. After that, another troupe was to perform. Now, upon my return, a harpist's melody strolls about, sweet as ripened lychee. Copious amounts of wine flow from decanters; trays of miniature scones flutter by. All the guests have intermingled—including the Crowns.

I pilfer a flute from a nearby server if only to have something in my hands. I couldn't imagine consuming it, what with my growing fatigue and the way my muscles quiver and burn. I'd never make it back to my room.

I keep to the edge of the Dome Hall. Even so, several eyes drift my way and linger. Then, my gaze snaps to Illian's, as if he's tugged on some invisible rope yoking us together. But he merely gives me a passing glance before turning to Princess Aesir, the Brisendali princess and King Rurik's daughter. She's reclining beside Illian on his divan, her chin poised, her white-blond plait draped over a pale, bare shoulder.

It's been ten years since I've seen her, and even then, it was only from a distance; though we were close in age, my father was too worried about my lack of decorum to let us interact. But she's recognizable all the same. Tall, regal. Lush red lips like a drop of blood against snow. Frost-blue eyes that mimic her father's. She, too, glances in my direction, then angles her chin back toward Illian. They share a peculiar smile before engaging in a lively debate with two Brisendali nobles. I take the chance and dip from view, escaping to the other side of the room. I must stay focused.

Couples thread together for a dance. I ease through them, aiming for the veranda where I locate King Anton alongside his courtiers, each one draping over him like vines on a trellis. A lazy smile shows just how much he's enjoying it.

A hand snags my arm.

I swing around to find Copelan's accusing glare, his copper-flecked gaze as hard as steel. His fingers tighten around my wrist, and with his other hand he plucks my flute from my fingers and clanks it on a nearby tray. "Do you have any idea what you've done? Morta's teeth, Vasalie, I should—" He bites his tongue, realizing the scene he might create, the unwanted attention. He yanks me into a dance—an excuse to draw me close enough to hiss, "I should send you packing *right now*." Unlike me, he's still in the costume I robbed him of performing in: the iridescent silk wrapping his torso, the gold headpiece banding his brow.

"I—" My words falter as I grapple for an excuse. His eyes rip into me, searching. "I'm sorry. I thought—" No, I *didn't* think. I acted rashly.

"You thought what?" He whirls me into a spin, then jerks me close again, breath hot against my ear. "You thought you could ignore my rules? Thought you could steal the show for your own glory? Is that it?" His grip tightens on my waist.

"No! That isn't—"

"And him of all Crowns, Vas. Do you not know how dangerous that was? He's the most likely to—"

A deep voice cuts into our quarrel, thick with a northern accent. "Master Reveler, is it? Pardon, but I'd like to steal a dance."

Copelan and I swivel.

My heart speeds when I find the King of Brisendale standing there, and it takes me a moment to remember to breathe. His right eye . . . From afar, it looks so incredibly real, but up close, it's a little too glossy, the pupil a saturated, winking blue, cut from genuine sapphire.

I force my stubborn muscles into a curtsey. Beside me, Copelan sinks into a bow.

Only when we rise do I remember King Rurik's request. I jolt and offer my hand, his grip a little too firm when he accepts it. He leads me away, only for Copelan to step in our path once more. "Your Majesty—the dance—I can explain—"

"Step aside, Master Reveler," he says, his tone edged in ice. "If I require your explanation, I will ask for it."

Sweat coats my palms. Without a choice, Copelan retreats.

King Rurik steers me toward the edge of the Dome Hall, drawing me into a slow waltz. A veranda fans out beside us, spreading over the island below, where a lambent moon teases the night-dark waves. It catches in his light hair, washing out his features—his pale beard, his frost-bitten gaze. A true frost king. He looks so much like his daughter who, at a glance, still sits with Illian.

Both of them watch us now.

"Quite an invigorating performance," King Rurik says, recapturing my attention. "But I wonder at your choice of . . . *prop*."

For a moment, I think he means my millen dust, but then he spins us, pointing his gaze in King Anton's direction.

Prop.

"Your Majesty, I'd hoped to spare you," I say with more confidence than I feel, thankful my own northern accent had faded long ago. "You are too fine to be sullied by dust."

"Perhaps," King Rurik says, that sapphire in his eye winking. The other pierces into me like a single, sharpened claw. "But my court is not. With such fine Brisendali men available to join you onstage for a dance meant to honor my country, you leave me to wonder, Miss . . ."

"Vasalie," I answer him. "Vasalie Moran."

"Miss Moran," he says, dropping my hands; this was never about dancing, anyway. "Perhaps you acted a fool, as so many young women do, but such a mistake is uncommon at the Gathering. What with the time and meticulous care put into planning our evenings, I've found that choices here are quite deliberate."

My heart stutters. "I assure you, Your Majesty, I meant no offense—"

"Who put you up to it?"

"You misunderstand—"

His voice is as cold as northern frost. "Never lie to a Crown, Miss Moran."

My throat dries. He could have me ripped from this room with a flick of his wrist, could have me questioned until I couldn't remember lies from truth. I swallow my rising dinner, scrounging every corner of my mind for an excuse.

"She's working for me."

My head whips around.

King Anton gives the Brisendali king an absurdly innocent smile, swishing the wine in his gaudy, sea-glass chalice. Gold still coats him like a second skin, though he's wiped the worst of it from his face. "Quite the spectacle, no?"

He doesn't spare me a glance, but recognition hits me swiftly when I hear the deep, lazy lilt of his voice. He was in the office with Laurent. He was the hooded figure.

King Rurik lifts a skeptical brow. "Surely you don't intend to make enemies our first night here, Anton?"

"Morta's teeth, I would never," King Anton returns, throwing a hand over his heart as if he's been wounded. "As I'm sure you know, dear friend, the sun is the *antagonist* of that story," he points out, and I want to kick myself for not thinking of it earlier. "We would never paint you, or your noble subjects, with such villainy. But surely if you'd have preferred otherwise . . ."

King Rurik holds up a hand, the cruel twist of his lips smoothing out. "I concede; I hadn't thought of it that way."

"The fault is mine," King Anton says dismissively. "I see now why the interpretation was misunderstood. Allow me to make it right. Join my court for a private breakfast tomorrow, and perhaps we can find a way to expedite those shipments of cassava. Maybe I'll throw in an extra crate or twelve as a gesture of our growing friendship."

I press my lips together to keep them from tipping open. But then, perhaps I shouldn't be surprised at the hint of diplomacy King Anton seems to so carefully wield, considering his feat with Queen Sadira.

King Rurik swings an unreadable glance my way, then relents

with a sigh. "Well enough, Anton; consider this matter forgotten." He lifts a flute from a passing tray. "To the future, and to a successful Gathering."

"To prosperity and peace and plenty of wine." King Anton mirrors him with his own chalice. He takes a swig, then places a warm hand on my lower back.

He is touching me.

During the performance, I had initiated it. It was part of the show. But he, a *Crown*, is touching me of his own free will—something Illian never did for reasons I still don't understand. I almost wonder if my flesh is poison to his skin.

Ignoring the way King Rurik takes notice, King Anton ferries me away.

I shiver from the heat from his palm, and from the gaze King Rurik burns onto the back of my neck. I wonder if he believes King Anton, or if he's merely stowing the offense for later. Perhaps that's the reason for the clench in King Anton's grip as his hand moves from my back to my wrist.

Finally, we breach the double doors and glide onto a secluded balcony. Hills spread below us, brushing against the edge of the glossy, black sea. Night bells chime along the docks in the distance.

King Anton doesn't let go. I tense, waiting for the moment he tightens his hold, maybe even snaps my fragile bones. A memory seizes me: my father, scowling down at me, lips thinning into a severe line when he noticed the juice spilled across his desk, soiling his military documents and maps. It was before Emilia came into our lives. I'd been six, maybe seven, and I'd wanted to play with the little soldier figurines he kept. He had held my tiny wrist in his hand, squeezing hard, harder—

Pop.

King Anton releases me.

It takes me a moment to realize he's done nothing. My father had broken my wrist, but now, it is whole. His Majesty didn't hurt me. Still, I hold it as if he had—until I remember myself and bob a curtsey. "I owe you my deepest gratitude, Sire—"

"Miss Moran, is it?" he asks. His lips, crafted for smirks, peel upward a degree. "Surely you must know that everything has a cost."

Fear slides down my spine and it's hard to keep my knees from wobbling, but he merely gives me a roguish grin before strolling away.

I stand there gaping, but only for a moment before chasing after him. "Your Majesty, might I inquire as to how I might repay you? A dance, perhaps, for your court?" My stomach churns as I say it, but I need him to invite me to that banquet.

The King of the East pauses, then spins on his heel to face me. "The dance. Was it your idea, or the Master of Revels's?" He clinks his rings against the rim of his chalice.

I take a breath, gaze dropping to my slippers, stalling as I arrange my thoughts. "I admit I wanted to catch your eye, but my method was foolish." That, at least, is true. "I had hoped it would impress you, and a compliment from a Crown could guarantee a permanent spot in any theater or court. Perhaps even one as esteemed as yours."

Amusement flickers in his gaze like a winking star. "And you believe I'll give such an endorsement?"

Again, I sort through my words, carefully selecting the next ones. "You make waves out of ripples, Your Majesty. Everyone knows of your legendary ambition in the arts."

And the way he marries it with innovation, to say the least.

King Illian might have a liking for dancers, but that's nothing in comparison to the extravaganza in King Anton's territory. There are said to be hundreds of theaters, the largest within his home palace in Ansa. It's rumored to have multiple levels of shifting stages and intricate backdrops of painted glass. Then there are the glass displays on the streets, the glasswork that spans across courtyards and wraps around entire buildings—a venture begun by his grandfather that he expanded tenfold by dumping an unrivaled amount of resources into since his coronation. And his exploits draw in not only hordes of tourists but the richest of them from throughout the north, including Crowns. Quite regularly.

I observe the king before me. He's one of the most influential men in the Northern Kingdoms, let alone the wealthiest, which no doubt affords him a very dangerous amount of power. And as I stand before him, the truth of that makes me sway. But I raise my chin, even as my hands tremble behind my back. "I merely wish to practice the same fortitude as you, Your Majesty."

His lips spread into a smile. "Such flattery."

"Is it working?" I hold his stare.

"A good speech, Miss Moran; you have captured my attention indeed. But so, too, have you given yourself away. I see now that you are far too clever to pull me into a Brisendali dance without understanding the repercussions." I open my mouth, but he taps a finger to my lips. The shock of it freezes me in place as he adds, "However, these Gatherings are dreadfully boring, and I quite enjoy a good sport. So I will play your game, Miss Moran. Whatever it is you hide, I suspect I'll take great pleasure in seeking it out."

He removes his finger, leaving a spark along my lips. "Join my banquet tomorrow evening," he says. "It's a small affair; only my little Eastern Court will be in attendance, save for a few friends."

Relief fills my chest, though it's tampered by the note in my pocket. King Illian must have known his brother would invite me so long as I managed to pique his interest. Was it really so easy?

"I would be honored," I say, even as unease contorts my stomach. Not just from the next command I know awaits me just around the bend, but because King Anton says he will find my secrets.

And I believe him.

The strength to stand dissipates as I reach my room, and my legs give way. The pain from exertion lances every nerve. I hitch in gulps of air, pushing back against the rising fear, but it grows until it fills my throat.

The evening might have been a success, but King Anton's words haunt me, as do Illian's threats should I fail. I've made a spectacle of myself—the girl who touched a Crown her first night here. I've drawn the attention of several courts, and I'll be watched—not just by Illian but by everyone.

One more misstep in anyone's eyes, and I am through.

I scoot myself toward the window, nudging it open. Cool air threads through my hair. I focus on breathing, on forcing myself to relax. Nothing works.

Senses. I plaster my hands on the floor, feeling the grit of stone beneath my palms—

My body goes rigid at the sound of a knock.

"Vasalie, open up."

Copelan.

I groan and rise from the floor, a flurry of stars crackling into my line of sight. I fumble with the knob and open the door, only for Copelan to take one look at me—at the kohl now smudged beneath my eyes like a bruise, the way I'm leaning against the precipice for balance—and frown. "You're drunk," he says. "Pathetic. Absolutely pathetic. I thought you'd have more sense than that."

I open my mouth to refute him, but what could I say? That I am weak because I spent the last two years of my life fettered and imprisoned—and for murder no less? That the only reason I am here is so that I can do whatever foul bidding King Illian foists upon me?

"Foolish girl," he spits, and something inside me sinks. My trembling body follows suit, and I slide to the floor.

See me, I plead silently—hopelessly. But I know he won't.

With what sounds like a growl, he stalks over to a small table with a pitcher of water, splashes it into a glass, then shoves it into my hands. "Drink."

His jaw is tight, pulsing. I grip the glass, the room tilting as I fight to remain upright enough for a sip.

"The whole thing," he adds, and when I obey, he pours a second. "Another."

Is it concern for my well-being? The guilt of leaving me here? I'm too disoriented to put it together.

I force down the second to appease him, humiliation heating my cheeks when a queasy ripple sends it back up my throat. It sprays from my lips, splattering across stone. I swipe away my sweat-drenched hair, shaking.

Two arms lift me gently from the floor and deposit me on my bed, voice fraying with still-apparent fury. "Sleep it off. Tomorrow, we're going to have a talk, and not a pleasant one."

I should fret over his words. I should beg his forgiveness. I should try to explain, find some excuse, because Copelan could send me packing and I would be finished—both here and everywhere else.

But exhaustion has turned my brain and body to mud. Tomorrow, I will face the consequences. Tomorrow, I will convince him to keep me on. Tomorrow, I will surely receive my next order from King Illian, and I will carry it out, no matter what—because without this chance, I have nothing.

So I stay silent as Copelan sets the glass beside me and shuts the door, enclosing me in darkness.

Chapter Nine

Breakfast presents itself in platters arranged along the narrow tables of the dining hall. I skip the fruit and head for the cheese, layering it on a small loaf of bread with Brisendali plum conserve, despite knowing I won't manage more than a few bites. But I can't resist. It reminds me of home. Of Emilia.

But before I can sit, Copelan catches my eye and jerks his head toward the door. I groan inwardly, abandoning my food to follow after him as he lopes down the hall until it empties into a secluded garden somewhere in the center of the palace.

Hyacinth vines lattice the outer walls, the petals so vivid they could make for a perfect dye. A fresh, cool breeze gathers their perfume, funneling it around us along with a flurry of petals and fallen leaves. The Dome Hall looms high above, its stained glass canopy diffusing the early sun into glitter.

Copelan halts in an alcove next to a trickling fountain, pushing a hand through his hair before spinning to face me.

"I should have you removed." An angry flush splotches his neck and cheeks. "You've given me not one, not two, but multiple reasons to throw you out."

He's right, of course. I dismissed his rules and involved a Crown, no less. I touched King Anton without permission, and I could have caused a grievous offense on Miridran's behalf toward Brisendale. Worse, Copelan found me in what he assumed was a stupor last night.

"I know," I admit. "You have every right, and you probably should."

He glares at me, hard, a ray of sun limning his eyes. "So you agree?"

It's more than anger, I realize. He's actually upset, and it startles me. I lean against a trellis, idly plucking a nearby leaf. It's not that we've grown close, exactly, but we opened up to each other in a way. I suppose it's hard to avoid when everything we do is physical, intimate in a way others wouldn't understand, our proximity demanding a level of vulnerability I hadn't expected. I've felt every hard plane of his body; he's touched every curve of mine. A strange kind of connection pulls taut between us, however new.

Still, I don't know him, not really. And he certainly doesn't know me.

But if I want to stay here, I have to offer him something real. So I hand him a partial truth steeped in the same vulnerability he expects of my dance. "I wanted to make an impression. I made the wrong one, but I saw an opportunity and I acted; it's the only way I know how to perform. Otherwise, I am lost. Forgotten. Swept aside for those who are more trained, more practiced. I only ever succeed when I take a risk."

A memory contours in my vision—the time I first performed for Illian. I was meant to dance in the background, a backdrop for Esmée Fontaine, the prodigy who everyone knew was his favorite for a time—until she lost her position for some unknown reason.

Wanting to reclaim her place, Esmée struck a deal with Odette, the owner of the Melune, to draw Illian back to the theater by way of a grand production. His presence alone would sell out the place, and Esmée might evoke his interest once more.

And draw him she did, but not before rehearsing with the Melune's dancers—which by then included me—in the weeks prior.

Next to Esmée, I'd never felt so small. Or so in awe. She reminded me of a lynx, all lithe poise and strength. Even the more experienced dancers were intimidated by her, keeping far away as if her proximity would reveal all their flaws.

On the evening of the performance, lines ringed our small theater. When the king himself arrived, he settled into a private loge carved just to the left of the stage, almost at eye level.

Like everyone else, he couldn't keep his eyes off Esmée.

Short hair dipped across one sultry eye, with a black fringe that matched the dark, sparkling dress short enough to reveal her thighs. She was powerful, graceful. A seductress claiming her ground. Even I couldn't divert my attention from all the ways she twisted and contorted into unfathomable shapes, the way clay bends beneath a sculptor's careful hands.

That is, until Esmée bent forward and took her weight on her hands, her chin level with the floor. With impressive strength, she hoisted her feet above her head, lowering her legs until her toes dangled above her eyes. I'd never seen anything like it—just like I'd never heard anything like it when her wrist snapped to the side.

The show came to a halt. A physician rushed onto the stage.

Odette would have lost a fortune that night refunding the tickets. Odette, who took me in, who permitted me to live there, free of charge. Odette, who allowed me onstage. That would have been reason enough for what I did. But selfishly, I'd known this was my chance, and if I ever wanted to emerge from the background, I had to seize it.

So I ran, gathered all my savings. Within minutes, I had thrust my satchel of quatra at the composer, along with my request to continue, while Esmée was carefully removed from the stage.

The curtains did not close.

I had only watched Esmée's rehearsals; I'd never practiced her choreography. I picked up where she left off regardless, expecting the king to have grown aggravated and left.

But when my eyes lifted to his box, I found him there, observing me with sparkling intensity. And it wasn't a frown on his lips—far from it. It was a smile, sharp and dangerous, all teeth. So I continued, praying the dancers would join in as if I were Esmée. A single shaft of light homed in on me, shadowing everyone but him.

Under his preening attention, I lost myself. My body moved as if pulled by a string while my mind placed me where it always did while I danced: in that small, elevated valley behind my home, guarded by emerald pines, the sweep of peaks setting my stage. If I glanced up, I'd see Emilia in the kitchen window, grinning. My own heart lifted with a smile.

I focused on that joy. Channeled it, until a collaborative hush drew me from my reverie, and I found King Illian himself standing mere feet away.

He was younger then, in his early twenties. His curls were loose, longer, and his frame thinner. But he had the same cutthroat eyes, piercing and depthless. That same head tilt whenever he saw something he liked. "You are bold," he'd said, "to presume you are fit to take Miss Fontaine's place."

An apology formed in my throat, but I caged it in. I would be proud.

Odette rushed onstage, fell into a bow, profuse apologies tumbling from her lips. But Illian merely lifted a hand, his eyes still gripping mine. "I like bold," he'd said.

He'd sauntered away after that, leaving us in a wake of confusion. The next morning, Odette delivered my invitation to the palace, and the day after, I found myself with an offer. The role was small at first; I would alternate with his other dancers. But the pay was twice what the performers at the Melune earned, and six times what I collected for helping Odette sew and mend their costumes.

I had chanced my savings, every coin I'd saved from hours of work, for a fool's shot at capturing Illian's attention. I'd risked not only my position at the Melune but in all West Miridran.

And I became something great.

A deep sigh pulls me from the past. Copelan rakes a hand through his flaxen locks yet again. "I went to clean up your mess," he says. "I met with both the Brisendali court and His Majesty, King Anton, who informed me he had graciously fixed it himself, for some unknown reason. So perhaps you found some excuse he bought, but it doesn't change the fact that you broke the rules and negated my role, risking not only your reputation but *mine*."

His words tumble over me like a rockslide, and my gaze dips to my hands. He is right; I hadn't thought about how it might affect him. I don't want him to have to pay for what I've done, even knowing I can't afford to care.

"Furthermore, King Anton has requested your presence tonight for his banquet," Copelan says, "and apparently I've no choice but to allow you to go. Consider yourself fortunate, Vasalie, that I cannot yet kick you out."

"Would you," I hedge, "if you could?"

He looks at me, exasperated. "I should."

With a fingernail, I sunder the leaf in my palm, prying it apart in strands. "Why did you really let me into the Crowns' Gathering? You didn't want another solo dancer."

The wind picks up, combing through the garden, feathering his hair. He runs a hand down his jaw, then angles away, as if the words are knotted inside him.

I rest a palm on his shoulder.

He tenses beneath my fingertips but does not shake me off.

Finally, he says, "I am calculated, precise. Cautious. And it limits me. But you . . . you are my opposite. You came to me injured, yet your determination hasn't faltered. I doubt other dancers have half your resilience. And there's something about the way you spin ideas, the way your mind works. It's contagious. *You're* contagious." He takes a breath, as if to say something more, only to release it again.

I'm so thrown off-kilter, I feel as if the world is a tide moving beneath my feet.

No one has ever said anything like that to me before. Compliments have been lavished on me in the past, but they were always tied to my physicality. My sensuality. Not my mind.

I can't help but notice the way Copelan's fingers flex, almost as if he might reach for me. And when he wets his lips, holding my gaze, the air stills in my lungs. The moment seems to freeze, like a petal caught in the air. I don't understand the admiration pinned in his amber-flecked gaze.

"I see something in you," he says, relaxing his hand. "Here, the pressure can feel insurmountable. Suffocating. I know my talent. I know how to put on a show. But I can't give the Crowns something they haven't seen before, not the way you can. The dust, the wings, the things you craft and the way you lure us into a story . . ." He shifts on his feet. "That is why I relented. You are the missing piece, the spark we needed."

Warmth blooms in my stomach. He believes that I'm resilient. Valuable. A *spark*.

I need him to believe it still.

"The trick is to be remembered." I take his hand, folding it in both of my own. This—it's familiar. Touch is our language. "My mistake last night was that I didn't consider the ramifications for you or anyone else here. I won't be so thoughtless next time." I want the words to be true, but guilt clings to my ribs, threatening to cave them. It's a promise I might not be able to keep. My next apology isn't for what I've done but for what I might do—and what it might cost him. "Copelan, I am sorry."

He swallows, his thumb running a path along my hands. Butterflies skate across my skin from his touch, my heartbeat fluttering with them as he says, "Last night, in your room . . ."

Voices trail into the garden from around the bend, breaking apart the moment.

"... the seal, which will ensure ..."

"... assuming we can retrieve ..."

They're meant to be hushed, but they bounce around the enclosure until I catch a glimpse of ivory locks swept up into a golden circlet.

Princess Aesir halts by the fountain, oblivious to our presence on the other side of the arbor. A slightly taller, broader figure accompanies her, and it isn't until I see the hand resting on her waist that every muscle of mine locks in place—

That ring.

I blink. I must be mistaken. I'd thought that here, at the Gathering, I might overhear a familiar name or two, just enough that I could ascertain the happenings at home in my absence. But I never thought ...

I shake my head. I'm seeing things.

Because it can't be.

Not him. Not here.

But the large star of that burnished brass ring is unmistakable, and I know what I would find should I look closer at its engraving: a hawk in flight, its talons clutching a strand of lupine.

Then the figure angles just so, the prominent jut of his chin unmistakable.

My body reacts before I can make sense of it, my pulse surging into a painful beat.

He wasn't at the Welcoming; I'd have seen him.

How ... *how* is he here? I shrink back into the vines, wishing they would swallow me.

"We should give them some privacy," Copelan says, until his eyes latch on to my trembling hands. "Vasalie?"

"Please," I beg him, voice low. "Please stay quiet and don't say my name." It isn't the same; I'd changed it, but I'd been so young. It's different, but not different enough.

Copelan darts a gaze back toward the princess, still deep in a conversation I can't make out. Then the softness I'd managed to pull from him shrinks as he turns that glare back on me. "If you want a second chance, you will tell me what's going on. The truth," he hisses.

I shake my head.

I can't possibly tell him that the man speaking with the princess is my father.

My *father*. He is here, at the Gathering. I need to leave, hide—

"Ah! Copelan, is that you?" Princess Aesir calls, her chipper voice startling us both. I squeeze my eyes shut.

"Your Highness," Copelan replies. "A pleasant surprise indeed."

Numbness spreads up my hands as the two of them near. Copelan flicks a glance toward me. I mouth the word *please*. He shoves out a clipped sigh, then angles himself, blocking sight of me between the arbor and his body.

She's close now, maybe five feet away. Just around the bend.

"Copelan, have you met General Stova?"

No—no. My chest constricts. My tunic is too tight.

He isn't supposed to be here. Generals are almost never in attendance. He might have attended a Gathering once, but it was only because Emilia—a citizen of both Miridran and Brisendale on account of her familial ties—was invited to perform just after they married.

"I haven't," says Copelan, stretching out a hand. "It's an honor, sir."

"Copelan is our Master of Revels," the princess muses. "He oversees all the entertainment, including the show last night. Impressive, was it not?"

And then I hear my father's voice, rough as boots dragging against stone. "It was the talk of the evening."

He offers nothing more.

"Goodness, and my father's expression was priceless, no? You should have seen it, Maksim. Copelan and I had a good laugh about it this morning."

Maksim.

Just how casual is he among his betters? But then—

Last night. Had he seen me? Would he have recognized me? I feel as if I've run a mile, my vision puckered with stars.

He should not be here.

My thoughts are frenzied, but then I note the way Princess Aesir's slender hand comes to squeeze Copelan's upper arm. I notice, too, how his shoulders tense the way they do when he lifts me, when he's expecting to hold weight.

"Princess," says the general, "it's best we head inside."

Yes, please go, I beg silently. And somehow, they do. After a short farewell, their footfalls recede, and Copelan and I are alone once more.

He glares at me. "Speak, or I will send you away."

My voice is mired in my throat—or perhaps it's a scream. I feel frozen, that familiar current of fear pummeling through my blood as yet another memory claws forth—roaring shouts, a loud, splitting crack—but Copelan snags my wrist, yanking me back into the present. "*Vasalie.*"

"Stova," I breathe. I haven't tasted my family name in years. I never wanted to say it again.

"General Stova?" Copelan says, trying to understand. "What about him?"

I want to laugh, a wild hysteria bubbling in my windpipe. He's the reason I had to flee. He is the reason I left home, alone, with no one to protect me. He is the reason Emilia isn't with me.

She was the sunlight in my dreary world, and he is the terror who seizes the night.

"I—" I swallow, force out a response. "I knew him, once. Long ago."

Copelan releases my wrist and folds his hands over my shoulders, his eyes meeting mine. But where I expect to see the same hardness evident in his voice, I find a hint of concern.

"Not here," I plead. Not where anyone could overhear, especially someone employed by Illian.

His lips thin, but he backs away. "I will find you tonight before your banquet. Until then, I expect you in the Dance Hall, practicing. What do you plan to perform?"

"Something simple," I say. "Whatever you wish. I will be careful."

He heaves a sigh. "I know, because otherwise, I *will* let you go."

Chapter Ten

My fingers twitch as I hold Illian's next letter. It was waiting for me when I returned to my room after a grueling practice and a hot soak in the bathing chambers. I'd worn myself out in an attempt to calm my nerves after seeing the man I once called father.

He's here.

Here.

But I need only avoid him. Keep my head down, my face coated in cosmetics. Nothing has changed. *Breathe.*

Even so, it had taken hours for me to wind down. But now my mind thrusts back into action, swimming with dread. Illian's letter seems to pulse in my hands.

My gaze dips to his writing. I know it by the haunting tilt of his strokes—long and sweeping with the promise of blood. It contains no instructions, only a name, and a threat.

Lord Bayard.

Refuse, and your time here is at an end.

I lick my lips and lift the vial that accompanied the letter. The substance inside is clear. It isn't sassen root, where a milky sheen turns the liquid pearlescent. When I sniff, I smell nothing. It must be bellamira. It's similar to nightshade, except that it has no taste or smell. The giveaway. And it only grows in the north, in my homeland.

It's lethal.

The vial itself is tear-shaped, about the size of my thumb, and because of its design, the moment I tip it, it will release the entirety of its contents at once.

He told me I would spy for him. Ascertain information.

Not *poison* someone.

My breakfast inches up my throat.

Lord Bayard. The name isn't familiar. One of King Anton's men, I assume, but a death at the Gathering would disrupt the whole event. Surely Illian wouldn't want to send the Crowns into an uproar so early.

A soft rap vibrates my door. Startled, I cram the vial underneath my pillow along with the note before opening the door. Laurent grins at me, presenting a large package festooned in ribbons. A dress box. "Hello, my sweet."

I offer him a meager smile and step aside, allowing him entrance. "What's this? I already have a costume for tonight." I'd planned on performing the *Illiuna,* like I did for Copelan that first day. Safe. Easy.

Unlike what I'm now expected to do.

"I haven't the faintest." Laurent shoves the box into my trembling hands, then glides into my room, nose wrinkling at my mess.

I bite my cheek before unwinding the strands of ribbons, then slide off the lid. Inside is a heap of silk, and when I pull it out, it ripples down in a wave of emerald and aquamarine, like liquid sea glass. "Who sent this?"

"Ah, yes. The card." He hands me a small, embossed sheet of parchment, its edges rimmed in silver. I expect to see Illian's handwriting again, except the script is elegant, flourished, a ridiculous amount of embellishments accenting each letter.

Dearest Vasalie,

Please do me the honor of gracing us with this gown along with your much anticipated presence.

I shouldn't be surprised to see King Anton's name penned extravagantly along the bottom.

"How, exactly, am I supposed to perform in this?" I ask. The gown is long and delicate, like a layer of seawater already slipping from my hands. "Millen would ruin it!" Not to mention, I'd trip on the length . . .

Laurent shrugs. "That would be his problem, sweet. But you can't very well turn him down. Let's see it on you."

He's right; I don't have a choice. Shoving thoughts of the poison away for the time being, I dip behind a divider and shrug from my robe as Laurent calls, "Consider yourself lucky. And he's not bad on the eyes, too."

"He's aware," I mumble.

"Why shouldn't he be? And you are a princess for the evening, at his request. Might as well enjoy it." He lowers his voice conspiratorially. "I would."

As if I can enjoy anything now.

But as the fabric tumbles down my legs, I realize Laurent is right. I feel like royalty. What I thought was silk is something even softer—a fabric I can't name. Almost like gossamer, the brush of a butter-soft petal, it ghosts my ribs and waist before trailing off in a swirl of colors at my feet.

But there's no way I can dance without ripping it straight up my backside. Despite its loveliness, a flare of annoyance simmers in my belly. How presumptuous of King Anton to tell me what I can perform in! But I dismiss the feeling. He's a Crown. He can do whatever he wants.

I emerge from behind the divider, angling to give Laurent access to the back of my dress. "Would you?"

He secures the ties with steady hands before spinning me around. He must notice my unease because he takes my hands, squeezing his reassurance.

I watch his face, then, as he sees my scars. As he takes them in, one by one.

They've continued to fade, thanks to the salves, but they're still there—ropes of raised flesh banding my wrists, evidence of the fetters that bound me. For the most part, I've been able to hide them with cosmetics, costumes, and bracelets. When Copelan noticed, I told him it was from a short, experimental time as an aerialist. He bought the lie.

I can tell Laurent itches to ask about them, but he doesn't, and I'm thankful.

"It is an honor," he finally says, "to be requested by the King of the East."

"What should I expect?" I ask, pushing my next task to the back of my mind. I'm hoping he's familiar with the youngest Miridranian king and his habits. Perhaps that's why Illian wanted me to befriend him, I remember with a pang of guilt.

A soft chuckle. "His Majesty is . . . an unpredictable force, ever causing a stir with his antics, and those parties of his."

So I've gathered, even from the staff. During the last Gathering, he hosted banquet after soirée after banquet. Kept half the palace awake until the wee hours of the morning, the other half slobbering-drunk along with him.

Yet this is the man who supposedly stopped the Razami war. Though, I'd peg it on bribery, if his actions last night with King Rurik are anything to go by, and only because he thought himself invincible, like the rumors claim.

"Even so, one must wonder if it's mere frill. Decoration, meant to distract," Laurent says. "Perhaps he merely invites others into his lair to study them. And you poked him, my sweet."

His words loop in my mind as I ponder my reflection, a bitter taste on my tongue. I belong in costumes, not gowns. This one isn't cheaply made, hastily sewn, rigged with pockets and ties. It fits like gloss over my imperfect flesh and I long to peel it off.

"Anything else?" I press Laurent, tussling with my errant curls, fitting them into a loose coiffure.

Behind me, he runs a hand down the length of his surcoat, idly fiddling with its brass buttons. "I was well into my twenties during his coronation, when he came of age. That was, ah . . ." He ticks off his fingers. "Eight years ago now, and I've spent considerable time with him since. He is a riddle even to me, and yet I can't help but admire him."

I pause. "You're from East Miridran?"

"For some time now, yes. Longer than I would have originally liked." At my curious glance, he explains. "I grew up in Serai, but my sister wanted to move here. She became a glass smith, apprenticing in Philam. Naturally, I couldn't leave her."

Philam, the port town just off the coast. We'd passed through it on our journey here.

"You have a sister?" I say, turning to face him.

"And two nephews and a niece, all of whom have threatened me within an inch of my life if I don't bring them some kind of artifact from the isle."

I spill a laugh at that, grateful for his distraction. I tell him I want to hear more about them, and he promises me he'll indulge me soon. But as we ready to leave, I can't help but ask, "The stories. Are they true? About His Majesty's death?"

Laurent stills, almost as if he's debating whether to answer.

And then he says, "It wouldn't be the first time someone came back to life, if you choose to believe the tales of old."

"Eremis and the Fate of Morta, you mean?"

"Indeed. You know the full story, then?"

"I'm not from the southern caves, Laurent," I say, perching by the vanity. "The tale is common enough."

"Sure, everyone knows the tale in its most basic form, but do you know how she got her revenge?" Laurent asks, giving me a sly grin.

I recall the sculpture I found in the turret, the Fate of Morta's arm coiled around Eremis like a lover set to kill. "She tricked him," I answer.

"More to it than that," Laurent says. "My niece is quite the scholar, see. After Eremis refused Morta's hand the first time, she sent three prophets to warn him that if he did not humble himself and return to her lair willingly, she would come to claim him."

The prophets of old; I remember them from Emilia's stories. Some were devoted to the true Fates, as they called them, refusing to believe the Fate of Morta was a Fate at all. Others dedicated themselves entirely to her service. But a thousand years have passed, and prophets are few and far between. In both Miridran and Brisendale, religion is sparse because of it—more a collection of tales rather than truths.

"Eremis ignored the prophets," Laurent says, spinning a seashell pin between his fingers before sliding it into my hair, "living as if he were as immortal as the Fate of Morta herself. He spent his days beneath the sheets of married courtiers, thieving valuables, instigating fights until his fists were bloodied stumps. Then he started a war, to no one's surprise—during which he was slain once more. But, knowing her beauty would not drag him under, the Fate of Morta held up that mirror because, you see, the prophets hadn't just been sent to warn Eremis but to observe his weaknesses."

"Are you trying to give me a lesson on vanity? I don't see what this has to do with King Anton."

A shrug. "Nothing, perhaps. Or maybe everything."

A shiver slips down my spine like a winter-chilled wind; even my bones seem to grow cold. But I shake my head. Emilia loved the stories, so I did, too; I even believed them, once. But if the Fates are real, they've lost interest and moved on. I owe them nothing, and certainly not my faith, much less my devotion.

They haven't walked my path. They don't know my pain. I am but a grain of sand; I matter to them as little as dust.

At that, Laurent flicks the lightest dusting of powder over my nose and tells me I should leave the rest of my face open and bright, but I can't take his advice. I feel too bare like this, too exposed—especially now that my father stalks these halls. So when he leaves my room with a kiss to my forehead and a wish for good luck, I draw heavy lines of kohl across my lids and sweep gold leaf along the planes of my cheeks.

I wait for Copelan, dreading the moment he walks in, but as the minutes tick by, I can delay no longer. I force myself to stand, a sudden, transient spell crowding my mind with stars. The thought of performing tonight makes me want to sink into the floor.

After slipping on my shoes, I exhale in front of the mirror. The girl peering back at me is neither the girl I used to be nor the girl who emerged from that prison. I don't recognize her as she slips the vial of poison into the folds of ribbon around her waist.

I don't know what she is willing to do.

Chapter Eleven

The Miridranian wing is at the other end of the palace, crowning the top of a cliff. The journey alone, which took me across multiple arc passes overlooking the whole of the island, left me weary, breathless. But once I cross its threshold, I find myself slowing for another reason.

This wing is by far the oldest and the most luxurious. Glass mosaics predating even King Junien bedizen every wall, floor to ceiling, each pane encased in copper. They tell stories from every generation of Miridranian Crowns. The most elaborate illustrates the story of Mercy, a healer from the Mirin clan before Miridran was formed. During the War of Rites, Mercy became a renowned medic on the battlefield, healing not only her Mirin allies but her enemies as well. She later became the first Miridranian queen.

Here, Mercy wears a robe and a crown, cloth bandages slung over one arm. She kneels at an altar open to the skies, tears pearling on her cheeks. After her coronation, she was plagued by nightmares about those she couldn't save, so tormented that she was often found weeping in the chapels.

On the mosaic, Mercy's story ends there. But Emilia once told me the rest.

The Fates took notice of Mercy's pure, wholesome heart and bestowed upon her the power to gift the mourning with eternal peace. But the more death she witnessed, the more her heart sickened and swelled, like rotting fruit. The Fates did nothing for the dead, and so Mercy, in her bitterness, convinced one to come near so they might experience what she felt.

But it was a trick. She seduced the single Fate that obliged her, thieving enough of his power to create a Realm of Souls. Some say she even killed him. Drained his soul until he was but a shell.

Many claim that the Fate of Morta, once known as Mercy, uses her stolen powers to tend to the souls of the dead, issuing her judgment to grant peace or peril. But as real as she feels here and now, I remind myself that she's just a myth, a tale fabricated from history and interpreted through art. Whatever truth her stories have, it matters not. Faith has dwindled. The Fates no longer speak.

And the monsters of this day and age wear flesh and bone.

I find one of them watching me.

I pause before his scene. It's a younger Illian, kneeling before his subjects. He smiles a plotter's smile while a priest positions a crown over his head. But it's his too-bright eyes that give me pause, seemingly lit from within.

It's as if he's truly looking at me.

I could almost *swear* he is.

After mosaics showing similar scenes for King Anton and King Estienne, the hallway branches in three directions—a newer addition, likely retrofitted from a singular one. A flag embedded into the limestone marks the two on the right as Illian and Estienne's corridors. I veer toward the left, halting before a set of double doors made entirely of sea glass.

I run my fingers along their granular surface.

While I've seen sea glass before, Illian's pride keeps him from making use of it, and even here, I've never studied it up close. While most sea glass is clear if not dyed, the doors before me are opalescent, frosted, as if someone smeared around fragments of sand inside to obscure whatever lies beyond.

Even so, a pair of guards sense my presence. The doors swing open from the inside to reveal the labyrinth beyond.

I stand there, unable to move, trying to make sense of the scene before me.

Beyond the quiet, marbled entrance are multiple arches, the largest of which opens to an amalgamation of twinkling lights and lively chatter. A vivacious melody dances about, intercut with peals of laughter. Strung crystals drip from a frescoed ceiling like shards of severed moonlight, and underneath, a long table is spread with copious heaps of food. I press my hand on the doorframe to steady myself, until a courtier swings past, pausing when he notices me.

"You must be Miss Moran," he says, a glimmer of teeth flashing between a broad yet gentle smile. "We are so honored to have you. Please, come with me!"

The courtier offers me an arm, and I stare at it a moment until I realize he means for me to take it.

I feel small the moment I do, next to his tall, willowy frame. Then he leans in, his kind, amber eyes brimming with excitement. "Consider me your biggest fan," he says. "We all saw you at the Welcoming, and I said to myself, 'Gustav, you have *never* seen a real show until this moment.' You have altered my very existence, you know."

I still at that, until I realize no lust gleams in his gaze as he beholds me. Not once do his eyes dip to my mouth or skim the curve of my neck or chest. Perhaps I am not his preference, except . . .

His compliment seems more innocent than that. Genuine, even as he ushers me along. I utter my thanks, unable to trust myself—unable to rein in my curiosity, too, as I study him. He must be higher nobility, if his waistcoat is any indication: a maroon silk ensemble cuffed in gold that favors his olive skin and dark head of curls.

"Have you ever been to a king's banquet, Miss Moran?"

"I haven't," I lie. I've been to more than I can count, though this feels different. So unlike the stiff formality of King Illian's court.

"Ah, see, you were supposed to say yes, so that I could then tell you why this one is far superior." He's grinning ear to ear, no doubt hoping I'll inquire further.

I can't help but indulge him. "All right, why's that?"

"May I call you Vasalie, my lady?"

"Oh, I'm not a lady—" I begin, but Gustav drops my arm and whistles. My throat constricts as an enormous heap of white fur slinks from the shadows, one claw-edged paw at a time. I shrink back, but Gustav puts a reassuring hand on my arm. "Vasalie, meet Ishu. Ishu, Vasalie. Don't worry, she's quite friendly."

I'm not sure if he's talking about me or the tiger.

Because that's what I'm gaping at, I realize. And a humongous one at that, shimmering white with soft brown stripes, a maw full of dagger-thin teeth and eyes as blue as lapis stone.

Gustav threads a hand through the beast's fur, proceeding to press a kiss to her head. "She's practically a large pillow. Don't be afraid," he says, scrunching her cheeks. "Come on, give her a pat."

Tentatively, I let my fingers graze the tip of Ishu's ears. She watches me languidly, her eyes half-lidded, and if I didn't know better, I'd think she's enjoying this.

Or perhaps it's that she isn't threatened by me, and why would she be? One swipe of a claw and I'd bleed out. But . . .

"How?" I breathe. Tigers are not indigenous to Miridran.

"A gift from Queen Sadira, from the first time His Majesty crossed the border. She was just a cub then, so cute. Though she was quite the terror, chasing the guardsmen around. She even took a chomp out of Anton's pants once, right in the bum," Gustav says, a laugh slipping out. "But now she's just lazy, aren't you, Ishu, dear?"

A gift from Queen Sadira, after King Anton talked her down from a war. What had he said to her? What had he promised? My mind scrambles, but I can't take my eyes off Ishu. "She's . . ."

"Breathtaking?" Gustav guesses.

"Yes, and so much more."

"She demands to greet each guest individually, you see. Otherwise, you would be an intruder. That's why she's here in the entryway. Royal watch kitten."

Ishu shoves her wet nose into my dress and nudges up against me, knocking me into Gustav's side. Panic seizes me. I worry she'll somehow sniff the vial I have hidden, but Gustav pushes her back. "Away, Ishu. Others want to greet Miss Moran as well."

Ishu retreats into her alcove obediently, albeit with a groan, plopping down on a pillow larger than my bed. Even so, she doesn't take her eyes off me.

Our foray into the dining room garners less attention.

I expect to find King Anton at the head of the table. Instead, he's lounging about in the center, relatively unassuming. A loose, dark tunic rests against his chest, gaping at the center to reveal a wedge of smooth, sun-bronzed skin. The top of his hair is gathered into a small knot, revealing just how sharp the sweep of his jaw is. And while a few ridiculous bangles adorn each arm, he hasn't bothered with a crown or waistcoat.

A small affair indeed, I scoff inwardly, because no less than twenty of his courtiers surround him. Or so I assume, until I take a closer look.

On his right sprawls the Queen of Razam herself, a flute balanced between her fingers, her head thrown back in a fit of laughter.

Here, there is nothing of the knife-edged woman from the Welcoming. She tilts her glass to her lips as King Anton leans in, whispering something into her ear. Then, to my bemusement, wine sprays from her lips at whatever he said.

I swear I even hear her *snort*.

They are friends, I realize. Likely more, though she's twice his age. And her sons, all seven of whom surround them, join in the revelry, springing upward to clink glasses from across the table.

The closest prince detects us when he sits, sneaking me a friendly wink. "Who have you brought us, Gustav?" His bangles clank on the edge of the chair as he twists to shake my hand, and I can't help but notice he rivals Anton in both embellishment and charm, his dark cotton kantha richly embroidered in azure and gold that matches the layers of necklaces gracing his neck and the gems piercing his lobes.

"No one for you to play with, Your Highness," Gustav chuckles. To me, he says, "Prince Sundar is Her Grace's oldest son." It's then that King Anton notices us.

"Lord Bayard," he calls, gesturing us toward two open seats directly across from him. "And my Lady Vasalie. Join us, won't you?"

My pulse jumps. *Lord Bayard?*

Illian means me to poison Gustav?

Gustav—another doe-eyed, sweet lord, just like Lord Sarden. The lord I was supposed to have murdered.

Lord Sarden, who was devoted to his young, pregnant wife, who always made a point to smile at those he passed. Who gave most of his earnings away. Illian and I learned as much firsthand when we visited his manor, when I performed at his wedding. When we spent hours at his after-party, conversing, a few weeks before his death. I'd even thought Illian had overlooked the way Lord Sarden had critiqued his stance on Razam and the almost war—an offense I should have known he'd never ignore.

He didn't perish by my hand, yet his death was blamed on me. But Gustav . . . His will be my fault. After all this time, my punishment will have been warranted. I will deserve worse. So much worse than what was done to me . . .

I jolt at the peculiar way King Anton is regarding me. I force a swallow, shoving my thoughts down with it. Gustav, being the gentleman that he is, tucks me into my seat and tells me about each prince while they engage in lively chatter. Next to Sundar is Mantrin, known for his military prowess alongside with his brother,

Veer. Then there's Arjuna, an expert archer, and Tara, whose tunic represents his achievements in astrology. Nakula is on the Queen's other side, and lastly, Karun, who I'm told is quiet but effortlessly wise and kind. More than once, I'm gifted a smile, even as I have little to add to their conversation.

And I don't understand. They are treating me as if I'm nobility, not the hired entertainment.

"When will I be performing?" I ask Gustav, biting back the other, more pressing question of how I'm going to perform in this souls-damned gown.

Or how I'm supposed to muster up the nerve to poison him.

King Anton beats him to a response, his cheek dimpling. "Miss Moran, you are here as my guest. There is no need to perform tonight."

I resist the urge to gape, but only just. Not dancing? A *guest*?

He chuckles at my expression. "Relax. Tonight is for revelry, not work," he decrees, waving a ring-clad hand.

He invites others into his lair to study them.

At that, Gustav passes me a hearty, golden stew that smells of fresh cloves and cardamom, even a hint of cinnamon and fennel, followed by a dollop of bread. "Courtesy of Her Majesty," he says, bowing in Queen Sadira's direction.

I spoon some into my bowl, dipping the bread before taking a bite. As I swallow, my eyes meet the queen's narrow, seemingly disapproving gaze, but then the spices melt together on my tongue, pulling an errant hum from my lips.

A hint of satisfaction flits across the queen's face before she turns away. My heart does a silly little leap; that almost-smile was pointed at me. Then to King Anton, she says, "Your older brother. Is he unwell?"

I'd almost forgotten about King Estienne, Illian's older brother. He'd missed the Welcoming, something about a delay, but I'd been too focused to wonder why.

King Anton merely shrugs, plucking a stem of grapes from a nearby tray. "Delayed is the word, but who knows?"

"Not enough room in his carriage for all his wardrobe?" Amusement glitters in the queen's eyes. "We all know how vain Miridranian kings are."

My breath hitches. Surely he won't allow such an open insult.

But he barks a laugh, bumping her shoulder. "We have so many charming qualities; it comes with the territory."

"Yards and yards of territory," she quips.

"You shouldn't complain, My Queen. If I didn't take such care of my appearance," he says, plopping his chin on his hand, "you and your sons would be deprived of such a view."

The meal stretches past sundown, with dishes I've never tasted before. I can't eat much more than a sample from each tray, but Gustav explains each dish, occasionally checking the queen's response to ensure his pronunciation is accurate. It never is, and laughter spills across the table like wine. It even catches between my teeth until I feel the warm tingle of the vial against my hip, a reminder of my task. I can't dip the poison into his glass here without being seen, and the delay is the only bit of comfort I have. Still, revulsion swims in the pit of my stomach, snaking up my throat like bile.

All the while, I notice the way King Anton's gaze lingers on me—more so than on anyone else. I can't help but think he's assessing me, like Laurent said. As if my movements, the way I breathe, could give something away.

As if he can sense the danger tucked against my side.

And the monster I'm about to become.

"A toast," he calls suddenly, springing from his seat. He hoists his flute heavenward, a signet ring half the size of his finger glinting like a star. It reminds me of Illian's, though Anton's is polyhedral in shape as if it was handcrafted, with a design etched onto its rim.

All at once, the room quiets; even the music dies away. Yet again,

King Anton's eyes lock on mine. My pulse skips a beat, but then he swings his head toward Gustav. "To Lord Bayard," he says, with no short amount of pageantry, "whom we honor tonight."

Cheers spread across the table. Sweat gathers along my brow and I try not to let my flexing fingers inch toward the vial hidden in my dress.

"It is because of his efforts that, as of this week, we have concluded the development of the most astounding invention of our time. In doing so, we have brought Miridran and Razam to a new level of not only friendship but also an abundant future for us all." A single gesture, and everyone rises, Queen Sadira included. I fumble upward, steadying myself against the table to keep from wavering.

"My friend," King Anton says, "you have altered the course of history, and Miridran is forever in your debt."

Invention. Altered history. I swing a glance toward Gustav, who smiles sheepishly, raising his glass in return.

Who *is* this man?

"Might I inquire as to the invention, my lord?" I ask while others applaud.

But it's King Anton who responds. "Ah, but we can't yet spoil the surprise. You will know by the Gathering's end, Miss Moran."

Vague as that is, I try to shape Illian's intent into something I can make sense of. Perhaps he wishes to stifle Gustav's invention or disrupt his brother's trade. Except doing so would harm West Miridran, considering a percentage of trade is taxed across each territory and funneled back into the Miridran army as a whole. Surely he wouldn't wish to weaken it.

"Nevertheless, we did not drag you here merely to sing your praises," the king says to his friend. He motions for everyone to sit. "I would not pull you away from your family without good reason."

As we settle in our seats, I tuck my hands underneath my thighs, sliding my gaze once more to Gustav. He must feel my question because he says, "My daughter. She's been ill for a long time."

"I'm sorry," I whisper, the apology fragmenting.

His eyes, glossy now, drop to his plate. "Encephalitis, they tell me. She may not last the year if it progresses further. It's the first time I've left home in years."

Guilt tightens my throat, thieving me of words. Encephalitis—inflammation of the brain.

My instinct is to comfort him, offer some modicum of hope, but my task sits on the edge of my tongue, rancid and heavy, eager to escape. I want to warn him to leave while he still can. I want to beg his forgiveness. I pull in a breath, unsure of what might slip out, until Queen Sadira rises from her seat.

Her deep-set gaze, winged with a sweep of kohl, drifts toward Gustav. Then, with the flick of her fingers, a servant breezes in, a corked bottle resting atop a pillow he carries. Inside is a syrupy, nacreous liquid—a tonic of some kind.

She grabs the bottle, long nails clinking. "Taheric, tusca milk, and a few other herbs indigenous to our region. It may help, perhaps even cure, your child. The concoction has worked miracles in my country thus far on many aggressive, inflammatory ailments. If you accept, I will have it sent to your family; my men will leave this very night. To show our gratitude for our accomplishments together."

Taheric—I've heard of it. It's rare, a root grown only in the southern lands, a single pearl-sized drop of it rumored to cost as much as a ship . . .

Gustav's gaze swivels between his king and Queen Sadira, his throat bobbing. At that, King Anton adds, "Take it, my friend. It is the least you deserve."

Gustav rasps his gratitude to the queen, his face awash with emotions. To his king, he just nods—a gesture that says more than words. King Anton's eyes shine as he beholds his friend, even as servants shuffle in with decanters, others clearing away dishes. The music resumes, a plucky tune dancing across a lyre. Wine is refreshed, topped off in each flute. Mine is filled from Gustav's personal bottle—at his request. "To making a new friend," he tells me. Prince Sundar, grinning cheekily, clanks his chalice against both of ours, and in a blink, everyone else joins in. Even Queen Sadira, who taps hers softly with mine, saying, "It is a pleasure to meet someone who wields talent so beautifully."

I'm so surprised my thanks comes out hoarse.

And then the meal comes to a close.

Anxiety sweeps over me like a chill, and my hands go numb.

The room empties, guests following King Anton one by one through a shroud of gossamer that obscures a lounge beyond.

Soon, I am alone.

And no one seems to notice. Gingerly, I dig the vial from my gown, cupping its shape in my palm. After all I just witnessed, my insides feel like water.

A breeze wends into the room, cold against my clammy skin.

I don't want to be the one who ends Gustav's life. How could I? More so, how could I deprive his daughter of her father? A father who loves her, cares for her, worries for her—a sentiment more precious than all of Miridran's gems combined. I'd have given anything for such a father.

What could Gustav possibly have invented?

But it doesn't matter. Either I walk from this place or he does, and I don't know him. Not really. I tell myself he would do the same if he were in my position. And who's to say his personality isn't a façade? Or this whole charade, for that matter? Besides, he's a nobleman. His life is abundant in wealth, in joy. In love.

I deserve a chance at the same.

My time is running out. Soon, they will realize I'm missing. They will also know that I was here, unaccompanied, with his glass. So I weave together a plan, the only one I have time to make, and with that I make a choice.

I don't pour the poison into the glass he left behind.

I pour it into mine.

Chapter Twelve

Gustav swings back inside the room, swathes of gossamer fluttering behind him. "Vasalie, won't you join us?"

I force out a timid smile. "Apologies, My Lord. This is all so . . . overwhelming."

He shakes his head. "Should be a more common occurrence, yes?" He swoops his glass from the table, then offers an arm to help me up.

I take it, my poisoned glass in hand. We ease through the curtains, but I halt on the steps, bracing myself against a column.

At first, I don't understand what I'm seeing. Colors splinter across every surface, dancing up the walls and bright as sunlight. It's as if I'm peering at the world through a prism. I reach out, letting shades of light and color play across my palm, glittering like dew.

I feel like I'm in a dream.

Below, large cushions are clustered across the floor, everyone lazing about and gazing upward, as if picking out constellations in the night sky.

"Rather stupendous, no?" someone says, voice skimming my ear. I startle, only to find King Anton leaning against the other side of the column.

"What exactly is it?" I ask, steadying myself so as not to spill the wine.

Despite the flakes of color and light, it's dark, and I can only vaguely make out his expression. "Look up. In the center," he says.

I follow his direction. Above, several panes of sea glass hang suspended like an enormous wind chime.

"It's refracting the light," Gustav says, joining us. He gestures toward the wall, where two brass tubes, lit inwardly by torches, focus beams of light toward the display.

"Is this the invention?" I whisper, but Gustav shakes his head.

"Shh, here comes the best part," King Anton says, teeth flashing.

It's then that I notice the figures beneath, holding strings connected to the blades of sea glass above. They twist, angle, and the sculpture above twirls with them. Light bends around and around, a tessellation of kaleidoscopic shapes—

A scene builds along the walls before my eyes. It's fuzzy at first, warped, but then it comes into focus until I can see it clearly: a range of mountains quilted in green, split by a curtain of water that pools at the base of a valley. Above, a swirl of clouds cuts into an iridescent moon. A breath looses from my lips.

Because this . . . it's impossible. An image created with *light*. I blink as if it might vanish, but it does not. The music swells, setting the scene, even as applause explodes around me.

"Come with me," King Anton whispers into my ear. He grabs my hand as freely as I took his during my dance, the band of his signet ring like ice against my palm.

"Your Majesty," I say, frantic, as he pulls me toward an archway at the far end of the room. I can't abandon my task, can't risk Gustav leaving. I had a plan, but—"I shouldn't leave. At least, not without offering my farewell—"

His eyes cut toward mine, brow arching. I soften my features, hoping to mask my panic.

"I won't keep you long," he says after a moment, then tugs me along.

I have no choice but to oblige. He leads me underneath the archway, ease in his posture. At some point, he'd donned a fine, pewter surcoat belted at the waist. His dark hair looks effortless, his jaw smooth and angular, as if shaped by a chisel. He's irrefutably beautiful in all the ways Illian is, which sets me even more on edge. Like a decorative cake, strung with pearls, layered in gold leaf. Inedible. Poison, should you try.

Poison.

Worry gnaws at my mind even more now. I don't know what King Anton intends, but I suspect it has something to do with the promise he made. He wants to unearth my secrets. I clutch the stem of my glass, aware that every step leads me farther from Gustav.

Breathe, I remind myself. *He might interrogate me, but perhaps I can learn something in return.*

He releases my free hand, but still I follow him, finding myself in a narrow hall hedged in glass, the night sky dripping with stars above. The floor is pure, hammered gold, reflecting the color of my dress like a ripple of water.

I can't help but compare Miridran with my home. Miridran showcases its wealth like a trophy, like each belonging is a prize meant for a pedestal. Illian's palace was proof, what with the diamond-encrusted garniture and artwork alone. And while his brother is certainly of a different variety, the extravagance of this place is overwhelming, exaggerated at every corner. Miridranians follow the examples set by their kings. They spend their lives hoarding as much as they can, measuring success with riches and the size of their vaults.

I fell into that trap. Before Illian shucked me off like a garment he soiled, I collected paintings, jewelry. Trinkets. Anything I found tempting. Yet, in the end, my belongings offered me nothing when it mattered most.

Brisendale values a different kind of wealth.

Wealth is the protection of tradition, values, and people. Back home, there are no lavishly gilded palaces or treasure rooms stocked full of jewels. We build fortresses. Barracks. Keeps. We craft weapons and armor and big thick walls. We make them with our strongest metals and stones until we're sure nothing can break through. The Beast of the North, they call us—and not just because of our numerous armies but because the whole of our land is wrought in steel and stone like a mythical dragon with scales of bone.

I pause, noticing the way King Anton's shoulders are shaking. A peculiar sound escapes him, almost like a wheeze before he clears his throat.

It takes me a moment to realize he's laughing.

At *me*.

And only when I resume my tread do I realize why. The wooden heels of my slippers clank against the golden floor like the clap of a gong. I'd been so lost in thought I hadn't noticed the music had faded away. A hot blush swarms my cheeks.

He is, of course, still grinning. "I'd pay for your thoughts just now."

"I was merely admiring the view, Your Majesty," I say, afraid of where he might be leading me.

"Ah, yes. I've been told I'm quite spectacular."

He pulls me through another arch before I can reply.

We're in a turret now, one open to the night. A gentle wind soughs through its columns, bearing the scent of sea and salt. At the edge is a cylindrical structure standing on wooden limbs, a tube at the top protruding eastward, toward the ocean. It almost looks like a spyglass, albeit much larger.

The king releases my hand. "There's an eyepiece on the narrow end of the tube. Give it a try."

Curiosity wins. Setting my glass on the ledge, I peer inside, only to find myself looking at . . . "The *heavens*," I breathe. "The stars, they're bright—bigger and bulbous. And the moon—"

"Here," he says, tilting the device down just so, to where the ocean fans out like crinkled silk. It comes into sharp focus, and I can see it up close. Sea-foam froths over the waves like lace, spumes shifting gently with the tide. Sprays of water gush over rocks. Night gulls flutter against its surface, dipping to wet their beaks.

"What . . . *is* this thing?"

"I haven't decided on a name yet. Nothing quite fits," he muses. "Gustav wants to call it a Looker. Gustav is bad at names."

"Even so, it's astounding," I say. "I've never seen anything like it."

"I feel similarly about your performance, Miss Moran."

And there it is, the reason he brought me here. I straighten, releasing the contraption. "Then why am I not performing this evening, Sire?"

"Oh, but you *are* performing." He folds his arms, gray velvet pulling tight against his shoulders. "Right now. Are you not?"

I bite my lip, angling back toward the device. I know what he's insinuating. But I say, "I'm meant to entertain through movement, not conversation."

"I disagree," he says, tossing me a lazy smile. "I think you're equally skilled at both. Modesty is unnecessary here."

"Is that why you invited me? So you could question me until you can fabricate answers where there are none?"

Bold. That was too bold.

"Answers? Of course I want them. Can you blame me? But I have other reasons as well."

"Such as . . . ?" I let my fingers slide along the tube. It's cool against my touch, sending shivers along my arms.

"You aren't from my court. I'd certainly know about you if you were." A shrug. "Thought you might enjoy a taste of the East."

"And this gown?" It must be expensive. Why bother?

"Carefully selected and paid for, just like you."

I lift my gaze.

He believes someone is paying me off. He had hinted as much after my dance.

He might as well be right.

His eyes are dark in the low light, shadowed, and here he looks so much like Illian that it unsettles me. It's in the arch of his brows, that all-seeing gaze, the way it feels as if he's raking hands over me, twisting and turning me without the barest touch. I don't dare let my gaze flick to my glass, there on the ledge.

But I can't appear as if I'm hiding something, so I unknot the lump in my throat and unclench my sweat-slicked fist. He misses nothing, eyes dipping to my hands.

I swipe them against my skirt, idly reaching for my glass. "Would anything convince you that I merely wished to impress you when I pulled you into that dance?"

He smiles, and any hint of Illian vanishes. "If I thought you'd tell me the truth, I would ask."

"Then we are at an impasse, Your Majesty."

"It was confirmation I sought, Miss Moran. My brother has been seeking an invitation to one of my receptions for some time now; souls, he's attempted with several others. Pretty cooks, half-dressed noblewomen, the like. But you . . . you are exceptional. I had a difficult time denying you."

His words splay between us, a truth I hadn't anticipated. My pulse careens—a bird taking flight.

He seems to notice that, too, and releases a soft laugh. "Easy, now. I have no proof that you are under his thumb, merely suspicion. But before you throw in your stake, Miss Moran, think carefully. Get to know your opponents. You may find you like them better than you do your allies." He sweeps his chin in the direction of the party. "Stay a while. Drink my wine. Get to know my friends. Think about them the next time you are asked to infiltrate my court."

Gustav's image unfurls in my mind. I understand King Anton's tactic now. He thinks he can appeal to me. Thinks that if I see the faces of those I could harm, I might not move against him. That I might reconsider.

He doesn't know how much it's working. The glass in my hand becomes heavy, weighted, as if the poison has turned to lead. I don't want any of this.

I hope he doesn't notice the way I haven't taken a sip.

I shake my head, regaining a bit of sense. Whatever he shows me, it's curated. Carefully selected. But I know the rumors, the whispers about his Glory Court and those he's lured inside. The fact that he's probably slept with and then discarded more women than I've met in my entire life. Does he really think I'll believe him to be some bastion of goodwill after the convivial show he put on tonight with the Razami court? I admit he's intelligent, that he's contributed to Miridran in his own deluded way, but I am no fool.

He says, "Speak freely, I bid you. I am not the type to take offense. Whatever it is you're refraining from saying, let it out."

He wants honesty? So be it. "You paint a pretty picture, Your Majesty—"

"Anton is fine."

"—but I've heard otherwise," I say.

"And you believe everything you hear?"

"Rumors are like threads. They unspool from a skein of truth, do they not?"

"Then let us get to the truth, shall we? The skein is here before you."

Perhaps it's because I feel cornered like a mouse, with little way out—but if I can turn this back on him, I will.

"The Glory Court," I say, dropping the accusation before him.

"Do you think I need to hire someone to sleep with me?" He gestures at his perfect face. My fingers yearn to smack his smirk right off, but it only grows when he sees my expression. "What have you heard, exactly?"

"That you stock it full of concubines. Nearly a hundred women at any given time, there at your disposal."

"And if it were true?" He steps closer, until he's towering over me. "Little Minnow, are you jealous?"

Minnow. A fish. *Really?* I glower at him, cheeks aflame. "They say those who reside there were forcibly abducted from their *homes*."

"That's quite the accusation."

"And the moment you tire of them, they are never seen or heard from again. Hundreds upon hundreds have disappeared." The mere thought makes my fists curl, my nails scoring into my flesh.

He leans down, meeting my gaze. A lock of hair falls softly over his cheek. If I was closer—if I wasn't disgusted with him—I'd itch to brush it back. "If you would like to know about my Glory Court, ask anyone who actually spends time there. I hear there are some around these very halls. And," he tacks on with no short amount of mirth, "there's room for you, should you find yourself tempted to join."

I stare at him, aghast. But I refuse to let him pry his way under my skin again. And yet . . . "Are you not going to defend yourself?"

"That seems like an awful lot of work."

"You aren't afraid of what they'll say?"

"Fear is not to my liking," he says. "Anything else?"

"You seduced the queen to stop a war. Or was it bribery?"

"Neither, but I am flattered."

"It was not a compliment."

"I have an innate ability to turn anything into a compliment. One of my favorite qualities. I assume there's more?"

Aggravation climbs up my throat. "The amount of hard-earned Miridranian funds you waste on your ridiculous parties, then. You have an entire port full of pleasure barges. Four vineyards to stock your palace . . ."

"Diplomacy is never a waste, Miss Moran."

"They say you set your own hall on fire during one of them. That you were playing with fireworks—*inside*—while drunk."

"The place needed a remodel anyway."

His casual air only serves to unnerve me. But there is one last question I have, albeit a risky one. Offensive. I could never—

"Ask," he dares.

"They say you fell off Mount Carapet ten years ago," I blurt. "That you couldn't have survived."

Again, that strange smile spreads across his cheeks.

"What?" I ask.

"You," he says, shaking his head. "You're so . . . I don't know. Serious. I find myself wondering what your smile looks like."

The fire on my cheeks intensifies; it's a struggle to keep my composure. Especially when he's so . . . amused. And so close. "My smiles are earned, Your Majesty," I tell him, shrinking back.

He watches me for a few uncomfortably long seconds before extending his arm. "I meant what I said earlier. Relax tonight. Enjoy yourself, for once. And by the Fates, call me Anton. Shall we?"

I don't miss the way he's skipped over my question about his supposed death, but it's just as well. It's likely a rumor devised to make him seem more like a god.

I take his arm only because I cannot refuse him, even if he acts otherwise.

About that. "Would I not be chastised for addressing you so informally?"

"Perhaps, though not if no one's around."

"I don't plan on being alone with you often."

"Don't worry; the intimidation will wear off."

I scowl. But he doesn't notice, an all-too-pleased grin on his perfect face. His appeal, I realize. How easy it must be for him to wrap his charm around someone like a sash and lure them into his Glory Court with ease.

At least he doesn't press me further. Even so, my insides tug and pull as we return to the lounge. Lights bounce across the room as the glass show continues, images scrawling about before dispersing into a smear. I don't pay attention to them, not this time. Instead, my gaze catches on Gustav, even from across the room. He lounges with Queen Sadira's sons, gesticulating, laughing. The king—*Anton*, rather—abandons me, slinking onto a divan next to them.

They drink, they laugh.

I watch.

I thought I could do it. I thought I could be as ruthless as King Illian was toward me. I thought I'd do whatever it took to survive, no matter the cost.

Gustav notices me and rises, inviting me to join them. I tell him I'd rather stand. Night-crisp air washes over me, my stomach roiling.

"Actually, I could use a few minutes to stretch my legs," he says, too kind to leave me alone.

I had counted on it.

"I hope if anything, you're enjoying the rosé," he says, bumping his glass against my poisoned one—a gesture that nearly makes me choke.

Hastily, I force a change of topic. "Are His Majesty and the queen..."

"Morta's teeth, no," he answers, barking a laugh. "The queen has no interest in men. Never has, never will. She'd sooner kiss Ishu."

I frown. "But her sons..."

"Adopted. Every last one," he says. "But all equal heirs."

"As in... they will split the kingdom when she passes?"

"The late King Junien took her advice rather literally. Her sons will rule as a joint council of sorts, along with whomever they marry."

"But they won't fight over the throne?" I ask. While I had heard something like this before—her sons are common knowledge at court—I suppose I hadn't fully grasped the concept. And most court gossip is nothing if not critical of Queen Sadira in every regard.

He shakes his head. "In Razam, power is not what one seeks for oneself; rather, it's found in numbers, like a chain on a necklace. The crown is merely a pendant. Decoration. What truly matters is what they do together as one." He pauses. "It's the reason Anton's father split Miridran among his sons, you see. He and the queen were once friends. He learned a great deal from her, and her mother before her—and Razami traditions and tales. And when he grew sick with scrofula, he was inspired by her methods of distributing power and came up with a solution to alleviate his mounting fears. It's why he issued the decree he hoped would strengthen Miridran by granting all his sons power rather than forcing the burden all onto one."

I think of Illian, of Anton, and the brother I have yet to see. "Too bad our kings have no love for each other," I say. Whatever the former Miridranian king's intention, it failed. And even if he hadn't split the kingdom in that way, I can't imagine they would work together in any sense.

"Indeed," Gustav responds softly. Sorrowful, even. "But it isn't for lack of trying."

I don't know what to believe any longer.

We fall into an easy silence. Ishu has been let loose and pads between the guests. She brushes past me once, her leathery snout nudging into my hip. I worry she'll sense the danger I possess, but then a nearby courtier dangles a small wedge of cheese, luring her away. A moment later, she settles in a heap next to Anton, her massive head in his lap.

Get to know your opponents. You may find you like them better than you do your allies.

Gustav tells me about his home, his wife, the way he met her on a trip to Serai. How he refused to leave without her, promising his life's earnings to her family in exchange for her hand. He talks about his daughter, her bouncy black curls. How her favorite food is leka fruit, and when she cooks with it, it stinks up the whole house. He asks me questions, too, but doesn't press when I offer vague answers. The music plays, darkly sweet, befitting my rising dread.

"Have you traveled much, Vasalie?"

"Not much beyond here and West Miridran."

It comes out before I realize what I've just said, the backstory I just fuddled. I jump to add, "And Central, of course—"

"Ah, the west," Gustav says, oblivious. "A friend of mine lives there. Perhaps you've heard of him? He was best known for funding the Academy of Arts in Galan. Eduard Sarden and his wife, Anita—"

My chest seizes, my breath sputtering out. Gustav does not notice. "He's been traveling on Crown business for a few years now, I've heard, but I was hoping he'd have made it back in time for the Gathering. I was so looking forward to seeing him," he's saying. But my hearing fogs.

Lord Sarden.

Lord Sarden, who is dead, except Gustav doesn't know, somehow. Thinks he's . . . traveling? And now Gustav is next in line for Illian's noose . . .

I focus on breathing. On standing, even.

A server offers us wine. My glass is full, untouched, but he refreshes Gustav's. Gustav claps him on the back, thanking him, and tips the cup to his lips. My pulse drums in my ears. King Anton's words swarm in my mind, but I keep to my decision.

I drink from my own glass.

The poison has no taste, but my tongue curls all the same. I finish half the glass, a spasm contorting my stomach a moment later, but I'm unsure if it is from the poison or the near-constant nausea that haunts me. Still, I feign a stumble. As intended, Gustav catches my arm. He collects my glass, worried it might spill, and places it on the table behind us along with his own.

I wish he was not playing into my hands.

"Here, let's find you a seat—" he says.

I shake my head. "I'm quite all right, My Lord. I merely drank too fast." I offer him a sheepish grin.

"You're quite certain?" He's wary.

"A dizzy spell," I say. "Not unusual for me." That, at least, is true. Even so, I feel the poison at work. My head swims giddily, my vision hazing. Nothing worse than usual. Yet.

I turn and select a flute, handing him the other. "I want to thank you—for everything. Tonight was easier by your side."

He bumps my shoulder softly. "I'm glad I could make you feel welcome."

"Another toast then? As you said." I lift my glass. "To a new friend indeed. And to your family's health."

His grin is as bright as the prisms around me. It reminds me of Laurent's—achingly pure. In short order, we finish the contents of our glasses, colors falling in front of us like rain. An overture, along with the music. It's as if we're standing in a summer shower, like those back in Miridran. It almost distracts me from the growing weakness in my limbs as my insides curdle more violently now.

I wonder what Gustav will feel—how much worse it will get.

The show drifts to a close.

The lights wink out.

Gustav's brows knit, confusion contorting his gaze, and guilt roils through me. He staggers on his feet, his gaze then sliding toward me. He opens his mouth—

And drops to his knees.

Chapter Thirteen

I fall with Gustav, strength leaving me in a similar *whoosh* as my knees slam against the limestone floor.

Mind whirling, I shout for help—though my tongue is growing thick and ungainly in my mouth. My heart is a hammer against my ribs. A blur of guests rush over. Gustav's eyes peel open, but they're foggy, like breath against glass. Then Anton is there, a commotion of shadows crowding around us. He drops to hold Gustav's face, then bellows, "Get my physician. And water—now!"

Gustav mumbles something. I pale as I notice his ashen face. I long to reassure him, to tell him that he will be all right, but I can't shape the words in my mouth—

Shouts scatter my thoughts. Anton, barking commands. A servant hastens over with a pitcher of water, only to stumble, trip. It sluices over the king. The servant apologizes profusely, whisking a large rag from his apron, dropping to pat the king dry while another rushes forward with more water. Again, a blinding pain knots beneath my ribs, and I find my gaze catching on the first servant. Long hair, bound at the nape, a mole underneath his left eye.

Blood freezes in my veins.

I've seen him in Illian's court. I know I have. He's one of Illian's attendants. With his rag, he dabs the king's chest, arms, but Anton is too distracted, too focused on Gustav.

I force myself to concentrate, and that's when I notice it. Something underneath the rag, though I can't see what. The king shakes him off. "Where in the souls-damned palace is Karis?"

"Here!"

A woman swathed in white breaks through the commotion. A physician, I think. She ambles to Gustav's side while the servant makes his escape. But before he leaves the room, our eyes lock.

There's a glint in his gaze, one I don't think I'm imagining as he tucks a ring-sized box into his pocket, discarding the rag.

Something just happened, something I should have caught, but my vision shuts down as he vanishes around a bend, the tumult of the room pulling my focus in a swirl—the effects of the poison overtaking me at last. King Illian's voice—no, it's his brother. He's saying my name, but I can't see anything, disoriented as I am—

Lights cloud into haze.

Haze fades to black.

Warm, buttery light caresses my cheeks.

I squirm, wiggling between soft sheets and softer pillows. Any minute now, I'll hear Emilia's voice demanding I rise *this instant* because my breakfast is getting cold and she spent all morning making my favorite almond cakes. Not to mention, I'm most definitely late for my lessons. Emilia will tell me she'll have no choice but to hire a governess if I can't be on time. I know it's a lie. She loves telling stories, which is what the lessons become anyway until she dozes off in her chair like the elderly.

But everything is quiet. No mountain birds chitter lovingly against the eaves; no singing trills from the gap underneath my door.

I crack open my eyes. The world around me is hazy but bright, as if I'm peering through sunlit clouds, like the ones that sometimes scalloped across my balcony back home, high as we were. But it isn't my stone-gray walls or the low-lit hearth across from my bed.

I bolt upright.

"Careful," cautions a voice, deep and soothing.

Laurent lifts a hand to my cheek. "How are you feeling?"

"What happened? Where am I?" My mind gallops, careening me back to the last moment I remember. Gustav on the floor, Anton shouting—

"It's all right," Laurent assures me. "You, my sweet, are in a guest room in King Anton's wing. The physician just left."

King Anton. His wing. I take in my surroundings: the bed, sage-green, quilted silk with feather-soft pillows. An azure velvet wing-back chair. Along the wall, gauzy curtains shift in a sea-kissed breeze. I press a palm to my pounding head. "Gustav—"

"Is *alive*," Laurent assures me. "But not well. Poisoned, we believe, and it looks like you were, too. It was in the wine." He swipes his knuckles against my forehead. "You've been battling a fever all night. We gave you a concoction, but it might not have taken effect yet—"

"Will he make it?"

"Gustav?" He lets out a breath. "He will be fine, as will you. But it may take a few days for the worst of it to pass. You'll notice yellow splotches on your skin here and there, but they will fade gradually over the next week or so as your body detoxes."

I let out a breath, though worry still clings. "May I see him?"

My plan was, in part, selfish, but I'd hoped . . . foolishly, I'd hoped that it would work twofold. If I drank a measure of the poison first, they wouldn't suspect me. But more important, I'd hoped it would save Gustav's life if he didn't consume the full dose. Bellamira works that way; unlike other poisons, it's quick to take effect but slow to cause real harm. With a lesser portion, your body has a fighting chance.

It was all I could think of to save him.

As for King Illian, I completed his task. I poisoned Gustav. He never said he had to die. And if he discovers I've been poisoned, too, I'll tell him it was to throw suspicion off me.

"I'm afraid not," Laurent responds. "No one can until we get to the bottom of this. King's orders."

I hide my fidgeting hands underneath the silk-lined sheets. "Who could have done this?"

"I don't know, though it seems Gustav was the mark, not you. Try not to fret."

A sour sort of relief pools within me. I should leave it alone. And yet—"Why would anyone want to harm him?"

"Could be anything. He's close to His Majesty, for one, and he governs all the glass exports."

I pull my lip between my teeth, recalling Anton's speech from last night. That strange device in his turret. Gustav is an inventor, like his king. An innovator. Perhaps even more.

"When you are well enough to leave, His Majesty asks that you not speak of the matter. Happenings such as this can send the entire Gathering into a panic, and we might never catch the culprit."

A memory blinks into my vision. The servant with the rag—a face I had recognized. I try to grasp onto it, but murkiness wraps around my mind, muting my thoughts.

Perhaps I had merely imagined it.

I press my palms to my eyes. I should be relieved; they think I'm innocent. But an uncomfortable feeling crawls over my skin, like an itch I can't scratch. Like I'm missing something.

"Vasalie," Laurent says, tugging my hands from my face and giving them a gentle squeeze. "I take care of my staff. No harm will befall you while I'm here."

His promise is so sweet my heart aches. I cling to his hands, then pull him into a hug. His scent—cloves and juniper—envelops me in a cocoon of comfort and warmth. I've forgotten what it feels like to have a friend. I haven't had one in a very long time.

Because Copelan isn't a friend. Time with him is like scaling a cliff, navigating rocky terrain in hopes of a rewarding view. And often I find it, high on his shoulders, his hands tight on my waist. But I don't understand the thing between us, the feeling I get when he's around—aside from his frustration and my fear and all the ways they tangle together.

I pull from Laurent's embrace, a reminder of why I'm here souring my stomach. Whatever friendship exists between us, it's a lie. I don't deserve him.

He hands me a lukewarm cup of tea, a slight grin on his lips. "Copelan has agreed to help watch over you. Just in case."

I choke on my tea.

That's the last thing I need. He's already upset with me, not to mention suspicious—especially after my behavior in the garden. "That isn't necessary," I say. "I—"

"I'm afraid I must insist," Laurent says.

I breathe out a sigh, pinching the bridge of my nose. "He won't be happy about this."

"I'm not."

I go rigid at the sound of Copelan's voice. And it should come as no surprise when I find him leaning against the doorframe, arms crossed, sporting that ever-present scowl.

Laurent chuckles at the terror on my face. "Do you feel well enough to walk?"

My hair is a mess of tangles. Swiping it back, I inhale steadily and try to rise, but it's like I spent the night with my head in a cup, drinking until my veins pumped wine.

Laurent steadies me. "Let her rest for a few days," he tells Copelan. "That's an order." I'm not sure which of them has more authority in my case, but with Laurent's tone, I doubt Copelan will argue.

"I'll take her to her room," Copelan says. His expression is stern, almost menacing.

I frown.

He isn't going to do what I think he is. Surely he isn't.

"I'll make it on my own," I start, but he leans down, scooping me into his arms. All at once, his scent overwhelms me—musk, sandalwood. I hate how comforting it is, now that I'm so accustomed to it. To him.

Even so, I protest his carrying me, which he ignores as he marches us through Anton's chambers. Voices fan out, and then the king himself is standing there, blocking the entryway, divvying instructions among his guards.

His eyes lock onto mine and my face blazes with heat, as if I've somehow been caught in a compromising position.

"She agrees to your terms, Sire," Copelan says, dipping us both in a quick bow. "She will keep silent. Won't you, Miss Moran?"

I don't miss the warning in his voice.

"Yes, Your Maj—"

Copelan sweeps me past the guards and through the doors, then through one arc pass and another. I feel like deadweight in his arms, but he parades on as if I'm as light as a wisp until finally we reach my room. He swings open my door, deposits me on my bed, then yells to someone outside. "Bring chamomile tea and bread, maybe some fruit."

But I just want to sleep.

The bed dips as he sits beside me. "Tell me this is a coincidence," he says, searching my face. "Tell me you had nothing to do with the poisoning."

I tense but cover it quickly by adjusting the quilt. "Why would you think that? *How* could you think that?"

"I don't know, Vasalie." He threads a hand through his now-mussed hair. "First, you cause a scene on the Welcoming night. You tell me it's because you needed to take a *risk*, and I want to believe you, but then, in the garden, you force me to hide you from a foreign general, no less, and refuse to tell me why."

"He has nothing to do with this!"

"What is it, Vas? Did you steal from him? Offend him? I should march you right to him and get the truth from his own lips. I will, if you don't talk!"

"Leave it alone," I warn, fingers curling into the sheets.

"There are no secrets here," he says, gesturing between us. "Not if we're partners. Not if you hope to convince me I should trust you enough to keep you here. You should already be gone."

My voice goes cold. "My past is *mine*. To share at my own discretion."

"Not when you were conveniently *beside* the man who was poisoned, for Fates' sake!"

I give him an incredulous look. "Was I not poisoned myself?"

"The ice beneath you is thin, Vasalie," he growls. "And it grows thinner still."

"Copelan, please—"

"*Speak*."

All the frustration and fear clogs my throat until it feels like I'm going to throw it all up. "He's my *father*!" I shout, dumping the words into the space between us like a pail of ice. I rise from the bed, using the window to steady me, but blood hurtles through my veins, fast as a riptide. My eyes swim with the threat of tears. "I ran away. I don't know what he'll do if he finds me, but I am *not* going back."

His voice. I hear it, even now, invading my thoughts. *Stop me, Emilia, and you will rue the day you set foot in my home . . .*

When I turn, Copelan tracks the line of my tears, one by one, his eyes wide.

I slump against the windowsill, then slide to the floor. "I didn't know he would be here."

Copelan approaches tentatively. He bends and gathers me into his arms once more, carrying me back to the bed, and it's such a tender gesture that I don't know what to say. I can only look at him when he places me upon it and eases next to me. "Would he harm you, Vas?"

He . . . *cares.*

I want to pull him closer, to curl into him and forget this whole conversation, because yes, my father would harm me; I don't know how, but he would.

When I don't reply, Copelan curses. "I can't allow you to stay if you're in danger."

My heart skids to a stop. I grab his hand, willing him to relent. "He won't recognize me. I was barely thirteen the last time he saw me, just a girl. Regardless, my costumes offer a suitable disguise. He merely caught me off guard."

"Even still—"

"You *can't* send me away," I plead. "This is everything. It's all I have. I have nowhere else to go."

Once more, he shoves his fingers through his hair. Seconds pass, each longer than the last. Then he startles me once more when his hand curls around my jaw, only to fall away.

"I had a partner my first year at the Gathering," he says.

His voice breaks over the last word, like a wave against a jut of rocks.

I glance up. He fiddles idly with a string on the edge of my quilt.

"The former Master of Revels hired both her and me as soloists that year, but we worked so well together, we decided to combine our efforts—much like you and I now. The Master of Revels wasn't pleased at first, but after that first night, we were the most requested performers. It was our idea to end each week with a performance to honor the attending nations, which garnered us heaps of favor. It's the reason the Master of Revels later recommended me as his replacement for the next Gathering once he was set to retire."

"What happened to her?" I ask softly.

"She . . ." He wipes a thumb across the bow of his lips. "She made a mistake. A naïve, foolish mistake, and it cost her her career. Deprived me of a partner."

I blink at him. "Mistake?"

He swipes a sharp gaze toward me. "She involved herself with a Crown. Sought after his attention and—" He pauses, shaking his head. "And I never saw her again."

It makes sense, now, the way he's been acting.

He snags my hand, rough at first, but then his grip softens. "You will understand why I am as careful as I am, especially with the company kept here at the Gathering. I don't want you to end up like her. All it takes is being in the wrong place at the wrong time. Trusting the wrong someone. You don't realize how easily that can happen."

Except I do.

"How long ago?" I say, voice frail.

"It was nine years ago. We were young, careless. Barely eighteen. Kids who thought we were in love." It looks like he wants to say something more, but his jaw tightens, as if he's screwing it shut.

Nine years. That was long before I came to Illian's court. I was sixteen and still working at the Melune while Copelan was here, performing at the Gathering and falling in love.

"I've never been in love." I don't know why I say it. Perhaps because it feels so far from reach.

Copelan releases my hands, and cold air washes over my palms. They feel empty, just like the heart that's being hollowed out in my chest. I may have found a way to save Gustav, but for how long? And what will Illian have me do next?

Knuckles brush my cheek, tenderly pulling me from the misery of my thoughts. When I glance at Copelan, my pain is there, reflected in his gaze.

But his expression shifts—subtly, like a darkening sky. He tucks an errant curl behind my ear. I pull in a breath. Half the time, he looks like he wants to shove me off the island, but now . . . now I go utterly still because he doesn't move his hand. He lets it linger by the shell of my ear.

It drops to my neck.

My throat bobs as his thumb grazes my jaw, my clavicle. It's calloused, but that roughness feels . . . good.

"Copelan," I breathe. It comes out hoarse.

His thumb lingers there for a moment before he lets it fall, like it pains him to remove it. He purses his lips before saying, almost reluctantly, "I'll send for a sleeping tonic. Take it after your meal. You should rest. Laurent will check on you this evening." He slides off the bed and draws my curtains to a close. "Recover with haste, Vasalie." A little smile curls his lips as he reaches the door.

"Wait."

He pauses, a hand on the frame. I shouldn't keep him; I know it. But I say it anyway. "Stay. Just for a little while."

Copelan hesitates. His eyes shift between mine, searching for something. He must find it, because he comes back, settling down next to me, careful not to shake the bed. He rests his large back against the headboard.

Tentatively, I take his hand. I examine it, twisting and turning it, running my nails along his palm. He lets me.

"Tell me more about you," he whispers.

"What do you mean?"

"Your family. Not your father, but the good things. Your childhood. What Brisendale is really like."

Home.

I reach back in my mind, searching for a time where I was happy.

And for the first time in so long, I let myself remember. The good, instead of the bad.

The first time I saw Emilia, not the last.

I'd been hiding in my mother's old closet. My father was downstairs. If he had known I was missing from his wedding reception—or that I had skipped the ceremony—he hadn't cared.

I don't remember my mother, but there was something about the smell of her gowns back then, familiar like a lullaby I knew by heart. So I stayed there, curled up in a heap in her closet, resolute, uncaring; I didn't need a stepmother, and certainly not the prissy, haughty actress my father met on his latest trip, or so my lady's maid had told me. Jealousy, I later realized.

But then a woman, no more than twenty-five, barreled into my hiding place, a vision of white velvet and fur, pearls dripping from her ears like snowdrops. *Can I hide here a while?* she'd asked, and when I nodded, she breathed a sigh of relief and climbed in with me. Then she pulled a basket of pastries from her skirt, telling me she'd liberated them from the reception. *You have to eat some of these,* she'd said. *Because if you don't, I'm going to eat them all, every last one. And then I'll feel awful, because I've already eaten two slices of cake and sugar doesn't exactly agree with me, because . . . look. Just look at my hands. I'm shaking like a wet dog.*

We ate until we made ourselves sick, our fingers sticky and dresses splattered in powdered sugar, and it wasn't until I heard my father shouting for his missing wife that I realized who she was.

I don't want a new mother, I'd said.

She'd answered, *I know, but how about a friend?*

A smile breaks out at the memory, so wide it hurts.

I think of the days we spent by the hearth, Emilia braiding pearls into my hair and telling me her favorite fairy tales.

I think of the ice-fringed pines, the snow that never melted in winter, even under the harsh, noonday sun, and how Emilia always played in it with me, despite her deep hatred for the cold, because she knew how much I loved it.

I think of the quilt I dragged with me everywhere I went, even outside, because Emilia had made it from her collection of costumes from her time as an actress.

I think of the scarves we fashioned into fortresses until my father forbade it—but even then, we'd simply wait until he left for his post.

I think of Emilia's smile, broad and freely given, and how when I was angry, she would pinch my cheeks until I laughed.

And I tell Copelan—all of it.

Chapter Fourteen

I dream of the Fate of Morta.

Only, unlike before, when her face was a mere void underneath a pitch-dark hood, I see her.

But it isn't the face I expect. Dimly, I recognize her, but I can't place her no matter how hard I try. Pale skin, soft eyes gray like the ocean at dusk. And she's so familiar, so close—why, *why* can't I remember her?

Though I sense this is a dream, I know where I am. I'm in my room on the Isle of Anell, my hands splayed on the window. It's as cold as ice against my fingertips, and through it, I see her like a reflection on the glass.

But she isn't a reflection. Her lips move independently from mine, forming words I cannot hear.

Has she come to claim me? Offer me death? Beyond her, a tempest stirs the sea like a pot of soup, heavy clouds pouring sheets of gray into the waves. Lightning crackles and pops. Thunder shakes the floor.

She becomes the thing you want most. Someone told me that, once upon a time. A time I can't recall. A voice I can't remember.

I try to discern what she's mouthing, but I can't understand. Is it a song? A lullaby? But her eyes tell a different story; they flash like the lightning outside.

And then I hear her. Audibly. Loudly. *Vasalie!*

I jolt, but then she speaks again, her voice a trumpet in my ears. *Open your eyes!*

My heart stampedes, thundering within my chest. I know I am asleep, but this feels so real, so visceral—

Open your eyes, she pleads again. But I don't. I can't. My eyelids are weighted like clamps of steel. They won't budge. The sleeping tonic—Laurent gave me one. It's locked me in a dream, like a coffin I can't escape.

Oh, Vastianna, my darling girl, please! Her eyes are frantic—

Frantic, like the time she pushed me into a closet.

Frantic, like the time she shoved a suitcase in my hands, pressed a ring into my palm, and told me never to return.

Frantic, like the last time I saw her alive.

"Emilia," I choke. She reaches for me. I see her now, so clearly. Emilia, who saved me. She's young, unbroken, so beautiful it cleaves my heart in two. My breath comes in short gasps. I throw my fists against the glass, pounding. If only I could shatter it, I could reach her, save her—

Lightning rends the bruise-colored sky. Thunder shakes the palace, fissuring the very walls.

Wake up, she tells me. *Now!*

I snap awake.

Lightning catches the sharp planes of King Illian's face.

I lurch, my pulse ratcheting.

He's lounging in the chair next to the bed, his fingers inches from my skin, hovering over my thigh. But he drops them like he's been caught. Almost as if here, under the shadow of night, he had nearly done something he'd never dared before.

Light flares once more against the smooth stone of my walls, offering me a better glimpse. He's shrouded in a black cloak, shadows pooling around his eyes, though his hair is still styled back from the day. A low growl hums then, from beyond the window, faint as the vestiges of my dream. The storm was real, it seems, but not nearly as violent.

I draw in a heavy breath.

Silence yawns.

Illian sighs, resting his hand next to my leg, just above my quilt. "Have you recovered? I heard you were ill, and I was worried."

He knows what I've done.

He has come to punish me.

Fear squeezes my lungs in a choke hold, but I manage, "Almost recovered, Your Majesty."

Two days have passed since I woke up in Anton's wing—two days spent in bed, healing from the effects of the poison, which kept me in a feverish ebb and flow until earlier in the night, when the fever broke for good.

Rivulets of rain drizzle down the pane of my window, thunder still rattling the outside air. For a breath, all I can see is the whites of his eyes.

His lips quirk. "Either you were foolish or brilliant."

I draw an uneasy breath. "Your Majesty?"

"Tell me, Vasalie. Did you realize what I gave you was cut by duskbane, making it safe for you to consume so that you might, too, play a victim? Or," he says, his fingers sprawling out like a spider, "did you mistake the poison for straight bellamira and try to spare the man by consuming half his dose?"

Duskbane. A rare root that tames the effects of bellamira. I only just resist loosing a breath and coat my response with frost. "I would *not* risk my freedom for a man I hardly know."

Only, that's exactly what I did.

Get to know your opponents. You may find you like them better than you do your allies.

I loathe Anton for those words, for the way they infected my thoughts. All I could think about was how I would be depriving a sick girl of her kind father—a rarity in this world.

But I had to find a way to complete my task. I *had* to.

Only, if Illian is to be believed, the poison wouldn't have killed him anyway—not if it was tempered by duskbane. Illian never intended him to perish. My effort was pointless, and now Illian has reason to doubt me.

I am of no use to him if he can't trust me.

Was this a test, then? For him to see what I might be willing to do? But that doesn't make sense, either.

"I want to believe you," he murmurs. A sigh, and then, "Regardless, it was a success, and I have what I need."

I have what I need.

If he didn't want Gustav dead, then what, exactly, *did* he need?

Again, I feel like I'm missing something. My mind spins through the events of the banquet, but I can't seem to focus under the intensity of his gaze.

Then I remember something else, something Gustav had said.

Perhaps you've heard of him? Eduard Sarden and his wife, Anita. He's been traveling on Crown business . . .

Wouldn't Gustav have heard about Lord Sarden's death, particularly if they were friends? The death of a lord is no small thing. And yet Gustav had said he was traveling.

I think of the time I spent in Illian's palace. Donatette's reaction. The attendants, too—not once did I hear a whisper about the crime I was supposed to have committed. Brigitte was the only one to mention it.

"No one knows what happened to Lord Sarden, do they?" I say. "No one knows he was murdered."

And there, a crack in his composure. It's in the twitch of his lips, the slight widening of his eyes.

But he quickly recovers, leaning back. "It wasn't politically expedient to reveal his death at the time, so I put out a rumor that he was traveling on kingdom business for the last two years. You should thank me for it."

Is that the real reason he kept me secluded in his wing once he pulled me from prison? Why he didn't let me wander around the palace? Not because others would wonder why he let a murderer out of prison, but because Illian didn't want me to find out that *no one knew*?

A cold sweat breaks across my forehead; I feel moments away from retching.

"Of course," Illian adds, too casually, "those two years will be coming to an end shortly, and rumors will start to fly if he does not return on schedule. Should you do as I command, people can easily be convinced that he met with some misfortune while abroad. But if you defy me . . ." He shrugs. "His body is preserved in the icy tundras of Brisendale, frozen and available should I send word to have it returned. And with him are all the letters you two exchanged during your little love affair, letters that will prove you were furious with him when he refused to leave his wife for you."

"Affair? Letters? I—I never touched him," I say, my hands numbing. "I never wanted him. I *never* wrote him letters . . ."

"Try to speak against me," Illian says, "and all I need to do is produce the body and its evidence. Do you think they will take the word of a king, or that of a dancer? The story is rather simple; it writes itself. You left my court of your own volition. Found him during his travels. What a nasty confrontation you had, the two of you, a few weeks before the Gathering. You thought you got away with it. You fled to Central Miridran thereafter, charmed an adviser into garnering you an audition, and here you are."

I shake my head.

How very prepared he is.

I defy him, and he publicly pins me with the murder, ruining my name before every country in the north.

But why?

Why?

He knows the story is false; he penned it himself. He imprisoned me to make it believable—even to me. And for what? So that I might come here and do his bidding?

Maybe it's that simple. He wanted Lord Sarden dead for his offense, and he needed a way to control me. Two birds, one stone—but to what end?

"But none of this is necessary," he adds, "should you be a willing participant. It would be much more pleasant for the both of us if you were. Perhaps we might even find a way to be friends once more. Perhaps," he says, wetting his lips, "there is an even greater reward at the end—one far more satisfying, if you come to accept your place in all this."

Is he really so deluded? I bark out a laugh. "Such irony, when I might have spied for you *willingly* once." Such lengths he went to, when I might have done anything for him without half a thought.

His hand stills atop the quilt.

And just like that, I am unable to restrain the barrage of emotions I feel for him—the rage, the hurt, the cavity of loss left gaping in my chest. Or perhaps it's because I am desperate to make him feel something, to make him remember what we could have had—that I would have gone to the ends of the earth for him, had he only hinted that he wanted me to.

"You were my *everything*."

I hadn't let myself fully accept it amid my devastation, but it's true. And my adoration might have even blossomed into something more. "I looked up to you. I was devoted to you. I could have even *loved* you one day," I go on. The secret smiles he gave only me, the gifts, the attention. The belief he had in me. I flourished under his appraisal. And more so, we had a bond.

Or so I had thought.

"Then you became someone I did not recognize. You ruined what I was. You ruined *me*." I can't help the hate steeped in that last admission.

His brows notch, and if I'm not mistaken, I see a hint of regret. It's in the way his lashes shudder against his cheeks, the way his chest rises and falls.

"I wouldn't expect you to understand," he says softly. "But one day, you will see that there is a reason for everything."

Almost an admission. The closest I'll get.

"A reason, you say." I glare until his eyes connect with mine once more. "Is it one you are too ashamed to admit? Or is it so vile a thing that words could not possibly convey it?"

His hand closes into a fist, but only for a moment. I wait for him to answer, to snap at me, even. He does not.

He just . . . watches me.

An uncomfortable feeling flits across my skin. I want to wrap the blanket tighter around myself, but I can't act like a sheep. I fear that if I do, he'll become even more the wolf.

"Your Majesty," I say, patience thinning. "I am still unwell. Are you going to inform me of my next task, or may I go back to sleep?"

He stands, folding his arms behind his back. "So charmingly short-tempered. I am pleased to see the Head of Staff spending so much time in your presence. Another job well done."

A sick feeling swarms beneath my skin, though I'd known this—whatever *this* is—was coming.

"He will find himself rather overwhelmed, what with the requests about to come in. Requests for performances, banquets, and so on—and of course you understand that, for him, it means arranging the entertainment, the food, the livery, the seating, the music. Even the decor, down to the last candlestick. And while he might handle most of it, he's understaffed in . . . certain areas." Illian cants his head toward me, a half smirk hugging the corner of his lips. "You, charming Vasalie, get to be his savior by offering him the services of a very special tailor friend of yours who can help—so long as he brings her in."

"But the restrictions," I say. No one can enter the isle after the

Gathering has begun unless they secure all the courts' permission. It's for everyone's protection. "He won't do it. And even if he would, he wouldn't hire just anyone—"

"Oh, I think he will. Just give him some sob story or another about her. Annais is her name. Do what it takes, Vasalie; I need her here. This is your next task."

"And even if I convince him to break the rules, what then? How would she get here?" The Gathering is nothing if not heavily guarded.

"I've made your job easy. She is already aboard my ship, waiting for you in my cabin. An easy fetch."

My insides twist. "We can't just waltz through the front entrance—"

"Laurent knows this palace as well as anyone. That is, in fact, the point." He strides toward the door, then pauses. "You have two days."

And then he's gone.

PART TWO

King of Glass

Chapter Fifteen

The next day, I find Laurent in the dining hall swarmed by stewards, cooks, sacristans, heralds, even performers—poets, bards, and dancers alike. Distress strains his features as he attempts to dole out orders, barely audible above the crowd.

It's just as Illian said.

After settling an argument between two cooks and firing directions to another group, Laurent is approached by the seamster on staff. He reviews a pattern for three dresses, one for each of the triplets I'd seen during the auditions. He marks it up, scratches out accessories they don't need—the train, the gems. "We don't have time," Laurent tells him.

I sit on a bench, an apple in hand. I work my way slowly through it amid the commotion. Convincing him might be easier than I'd anticipated.

It takes an hour for everyone to clear, each set in their tasks for the day, and finally, Laurent is alone. He turns to me, exasperated.

I force a chuckle. "What *was* all that?"

He sinks to the bench next to me. "A certain royally spoiled king has requested a *themed* performance to showcase all of our 'rich' Miridranian history, presented in musical form, to Brisendale during a private banquet that takes place across not one, not two, but *four* nights. That means new backdrops, meals, costumes, everything. We have three seamsters, and I'm one of them. I won't have time to eat, let alone sleep, and even *that* won't be enough." He swipes a hand over his forehead. "We require several days' notice for something of this caliber for this very reason, but I've been told that I either accommodate them or lose my position. I'll never be invited back." A laugh. "I should retire this instant out of spite."

"What would you do," I ask, "if you retired?"

As soon as the question leaves my lips, I regret it. I shouldn't want to know. I can't get even more attached. But he told me once he was offered the position by Anton himself after years of overseeing a theater in Ansa, East Miridran's capital city, so there's a part of me that's curious if he'd want to go back.

He sighs. "I couldn't. The salary I make here sustains my family for the next few years. My sister is still an apprentice, and my nephews and niece rely on me. And if I lose the position, I would be the talk of the north. No one would hire me." He buries his face in his palms, letting out a groan. "Fates have mercy. I'm going to end up a seamster to some old courtier who wants big, feathered hats and fancy britches. My nephews will call me Uncle Underthings."

"Laurent," I say, glancing about to ensure we're alone. "What if I could get you help?"

"Can you sprout extra arms?"

"You know I'll help, though I'm quite slow. The thing is . . ." I brush an errant hair off my forehead. "I know someone. A tailor. A good one, and perhaps—"

"Impossible." He shakes his head. "You know the rules."

"I know, I *know*. But . . . she's a friend. She's sewn hundreds of costumes before. And she's fast. We would keep her quiet. I'll even pay her from my own wages. I don't have family; I don't need the money, and she doesn't charge much." The lie is acid in my throat, but I ignore the burn. I can't let my guilt win out.

He clasps his hands together for a long minute, staring at them.

I put a hand on his shoulder. "I just want to help," I tell him again. "I know; I understand it's a risk."

"This woman," he says. "How long have you known her?"

"A long time. And"—I pause, swallowing—"she needs the money, and a place to escape. She's in a bad situation. Her husband, he . . ." I trail off, letting the insinuation play out, carving my nails into my palms as the seconds tick by, each one an accusation. *Liar, liar, liar.*

"Vasalie, no one comes here without a full registration. If she's caught, you and I would lose our positions, maybe more . . ."

"I know. But I . . . I trust her with my life." I squeeze his arm. "She needs this as much as we do."

I'm filth. Lower than filth.

But I have to do this to survive. I have to. I force the reasoning down my throat, but it keeps inching back up.

"And she's where?" he asks.

Dear heart, I beg. *Please grow cold.*

"Philam." It's the town closest to Anell, merely a boat ride away.

Laurent runs a hand over his face. "I suppose if she stays in your room . . ."

"We could keep her out of sight," I say. "And we will be careful. The only issue is . . . well, Copelan. Since he's keeping an eye on me and all."

"Copelan's as busy as I am at the moment, and he can't very well enter your room. And I . . ." He clenches his fist.

Then, like a man resigned, he relaxes it. "I suppose I could make it appear as if she's been here the whole time. I've done it once before for a friend in a . . . unique situation. I would have to forge paperwork, but with the palace as large and crowded as it is, I doubt anyone will notice a new face."

"And I can tell her what to say if questioned."

He scratches behind his ear. "There's a ferry that travels to and from Philam for supplies. Or you could take a rowboat after dark, so long as you skirt the isle on the west side."

"I can get her." I swallow down the urge to vomit. "But I would need a way to sneak her inside."

He bites his lip, a moment passing before he says, "There is a way." When I eye him, he scoots closer to me and lowers his voice. "Vasalie, what I'm about to tell you, you mustn't reveal to another soul."

Laurent, you trust too easily. "Of course."

He hesitates, and I offer him the best reassuring glance I can, squeezing his arm.

When finally he tells me, I wish to all the Fates he hadn't.

"There is a network of tunnels that run throughout the palace. They were built almost a century ago and had been completely forgotten about, but Anton rediscovered them."

Secret tunnels. A network of them. Is that how Illian reached my room? Or has he merely paid off enough staff to ignore his comings and goings?

"Only the Miridranian kings know of this?"

"Only His Majesty, King Anton," Laurent clarifies, "and his most trusted guards. He's since added to them, and he opted to keep them a secret should a precarious situation ever arise and he needed an escape." He pauses. "Just this once, you may use them to bring your friend in unseen. You'll find an entrance in the kitchen cellar. Follow the main tunnel. If you don't branch off, it will lead you underneath the guard's barracks and straight to the docks. Go after nightfall, and don't get caught."

I squeeze his hand again. "I can do it."

His fingers curl into mine. "I'm trusting you."

"I know," I whisper, heart bleeding. I wish I were actually helping him. I wish . . . I wish our friendship was genuine. That I deserved his trust.

After this, I won't deserve to look him in the eye.

I rise after that, but he wraps a hand around my wrist. "Vas?"

When I turn, his eyes go unfocused. "Be careful around the halls, yeah?"

"Of course," I say, something about his tone setting me on edge.

"Something big is happening. Something bad."

A thread of unease twines around me. "What do you mean?"

"I don't know, exactly. Last night, we were expecting the arrival of three prophets from the Temple of Mirin. We received a short but urgent correspondence, a mention of an augury, for which they demanded to be taken before all the Crowns. His Majesty charged me with ensuring their safe arrival, but word reached me that King Illian found them first. He sent them away, threatening them with arrest for attempting to incite chaos at the Gathering."

The Temple of Mirin dates back to the Mirin clan, and Queen Mercy. It's one of the few active temples in Miridran. Not only does the temple house all of Miridran's historical records, but its prophets are well respected. Authorities in the community. They teach at universities, attend local hearings, ensuring not only justice but grace to those who need it. They allocate taxes to help the needy.

To outright deny them an audience is not only a slight against the Fates, should they exist, but a dismissal of a valued Miridranian community.

"Can't someone track them down if it's so important?"

"We tried," Laurent says. "We couldn't find them. Then a page reported to me this morning that he witnessed King Illian issue orders to follow and quietly subdue them once they left—until the Gathering has concluded. It means, Vasalie, that whatever auspice they intended to deliver, King Illian wanted them silenced. Furthermore, he wanted the arrest to take place outside of Anell, in the hopes of it going unnoticed by the Syndicate."

"But there hasn't been a new prophecy in over a hundred years." It's yet another reason religion has dwindled. Aside from the prophets of Mirin, most prophets hole up in their near-abandoned chapels, studying the stars, translating their interpretations into poem and verse, waiting for the day their words are confirmed, while others have abandoned their faith, saying the Fates have abandoned *us*.

I once thought such prophecies were mere myth. My father drilled that into me. But Emilia had been obsessed with the Fates.

She collected old tales, poems, and various literature on them behind my father's back. She believed in them, believed that the only reason the Fates were distant was because they feared the Fate of Morta after she tricked one of them, stole his power, and obliterated his soul.

Even so, the more merciful Fates found ways to relay warnings amid tribulation to their dedicated servants through cosmic visions—from the movement of the very stars themselves—she had told me. Prophets and acolytes spent their lives learning how to translate the sky for this reason. And it's never an isolated event, meaning that if more than one transcribes such a message, it's likely the translation is correct.

But there still lies room for error. So it was rumored that, long ago—when the very first prophets were established and when a prophecy was at its most urgent—a coil of flame like an adder's tongue would spit from the mouth of the prophet who read it aloud.

"There hasn't been, meaning it's no small thing. What's more, guess where the prophets are being held?"

I shake my head, stomach turning.

"A Brisendali ship," he says. "Princess Aesir's, to be exact, and that ship is no longer here. And this isn't the first time King Illian and the princess have conspired, either. A dockhand overheard something about that ship being loaded with Brisendali weapons—ones that came from the princess's ship. Some bargain has been struck between them—something King Illian is trying to hide—and I believe the prophets were trying to warn the Crowns about it."

A bargain, between Aesir and Illian? I twist my fingers, pull at my knuckles. He had never spoken of her during my time as the Jewel. I hadn't known they were friends. Or maybe it's more than friendship.

Maybe it's only a matter of time before we learn of an engagement. But I'd heard that Aesir had been engaged multiple times before, only for her to spoil it in some manner—throwing fits, offending her betrothed—almost as if she were doing it deliberately.

Perhaps she and Illian deserve each other. But I let my mind retrace Laurent's words. The ships, the weapons . . .

"You suspect war," I say, tucking my hands underneath my thighs.

"I think," Laurent says, lowering his voice even more, "that Illian is funding a Brisendali war against Razam. He can't do it in the open; his brothers would never support such an allocation of Miridranian assets. But if a war begins"—he pauses, taking a breath—"all of Miridran will be forced to take sides. And King Estienne, as withdrawn as he may be, will never side with Razam. Not if it means going against the Beast of the North."

"Does Anton know of this?" Even if Laurent finds the youngest Miridranian king an enigma, he seems loyal to him all the same.

"Of course, though he can do little without proof. Even admitting such suspicions would provoke turmoil among the Crowns. Trying to save the world from war is the very thing that could start one."

But this doesn't add up. Brisendale might be built to withstand war, but they have never initiated it. King Rurik, for all his faults, is concerned only for himself and his land. He's too guarded, too greedy, to disrupt his coddled life. Unless . . .

My pulse goes cold.

Unless my father is influencing him.

Even so, Illian refuses to trust his own courtiers, let alone his brothers'. How could he deign to trust a foreign nation with such a plot as this?

But then I recall the way Princess Aesir leaned into him, a red smirk fixed on her lips like a bloodstain. I think of King Rurik and his sapphire eye, the way he watched Anton and me. I think of what I've seen so far: Illian poisoning Gustav, but not with the intent to kill. Illian demanding I sneak Annais into the palace. I try to fit together the pieces, to no avail.

At the banquet, Anton mentioned a new era of friendship and wealth between Razam and East Miridran, thanks to Gustav. Was that what Illian wanted to stop? If so, why not kill him?

Then my mind snags on something else, something that has been bothering me even more after last night.

What do I have to do with all this?

It's time I find out, because whatever it is, he's dragging me into it with him.

And I'm so very tired of being left in the dark.

After leaving Laurent, I seek out Copelan in the Dance Hall. He's watching the triplets rehearse, and I can't help but observe for a moment, too. Threads of harmony intertwine, accented by their swift, lithe movements. He appraises them with a knuckle under his chin, stopping to correct their posture once or twice.

I often find myself wanting to learn their names, to interact—and the same with the other performers—but my proximity to anyone puts them at risk.

When finally Copelan notices me, he tells them to continue without him. "We'll rehearse again this evening." With that, he guides me into a nearby empty room, a soft wind whistling past the open window.

"Our signature performance," I say, lacing my fingers together. I missed three days of practice, thanks to the poison. "We need to practice."

But he merely turns away, swiping a hand through his hair.

I brace myself. I thought we had made peace. The other night... was it only a tonic-induced dream?

Abruptly, he spins on his heel. "I've had constant requests for your presence," he says. "Constant, Vasalie. They beg me for the girl who sparked the first night with *magic*."

Magic. Or dust, rather. Mere millen. So simple a thing. I open my mouth, but he whips up a hand, pacing now. "I reassigned others to your post during your recovery, during which my performers were asked—no, harassed—about our upcoming performance. They want to know what big spectacle we have planned. You set a precedent that night, and they crave more. The artistry, the atmosphere, and Fates help me, the *controversy*. They ate it up."

"I'm sorry, I didn't realize this would—"

He silences me with a wave. "Last year, I kept it safe. They were bored. Apparently, it's a wonder I've been invited back. I've been considering what you said about risks. And as bruised as my ego might be, you were right."

"I . . . don't understand."

He faces me then, bouncing on his heels, a gleam in his eye I haven't yet seen. "Let's give it to them. Let's make this a Gathering to remember."

I blink back my surprise. A part of me stirs with anticipation, but I can't forget Laurent's warnings. Illian's plans, whatever they might be. And then my father . . .

The last thing I need to do is draw more attention to myself.

"I don't know, Copelan. I think you were right. The wrong spark could start a fire—one we might not be able to douse."

He surprises me further, collecting my hands in his own. "I'm telling you that I was wrong, Vas. I judged you too quickly." He rubs his thumbs across my knuckles, and it's hard not to get caught up in his excitement. It's a new side to him. "It's too late for the signature dance in two days, considering the time we've lost; but for the one after . . . let's do something bold."

Dread coils within me. "How bold, exactly?"

He tugs me toward him. "Trust me, Vas, you will love it. What do you say?"

The tightness in my chest has an iron grip; any tighter, and my lungs could collapse from the pressure. But Copelan looks like a little boy who's just been handed a flint and tinder.

And I still need this position. This, whatever *this* is . . . it's miles better than his anger.

So I don't let him see the fear weighing me down. I shove it behind me and force down a breath, letting a smile tease the edge of my lips. "Who are you, and what have you done with Copelan?"

"He just woke up," he says, and swings me into the air.

Chapter Sixteen

I wait until dark before seeking the tunnels, but the kitchens aren't empty upon my arrival. The staff lingers around a table, planning meals, sampling sauces, all in preparation for the next day. At least they're too preoccupied to notice me as I squeeze behind shelves stacked with crates of fresh produce.

I find a door behind another set of shelves at the end of the storage alcove. But the moment I wrap my fingers around the handle, a tap on my shoulder startles the breath from me. I snap around, only to find a kitchen girl offering me a sheepish smile. A hair net covers her apricot hair, her apron smeared with flour as pale as her skin.

"Vasalie?" she asks. I blink, then nod. She motions me to follow. "Over here."

I tread after her before I can think better of it, and she leads me down another narrow space too small to be called a hallway, then pauses before another door. "You almost went into the pantry," she whispers. "Cellar is this way."

I open my mouth, but she notes my confusion and clarifies, "Laurent asked me to make sure you find your way. Especially since they've put me in charge of the cellars for the Gathering." She reaches for the handle but slides it upward before swinging it open. "This way it won't creak and alert the others."

She guides us inside, lighting a small lantern beside the door. The space is dark and ovoid, large casks wedged together on one side, the other stocked with bottles. The moment the door shuts after us, I swing to face her. "I thought . . . I thought no one knew . . ."

She holds up a hand. "He told me only that he's helping you the way he once helped me. Your secret is safe."

He did tell me that he once forged paperwork for a friend. But then I notice her hand. The tattered skin, the way it branches up her arm and neck—

Burn marks.

I peer more closely at her face. The scars are less visible there, what with the smattering of freckles. Then there's her eyes, a matching amber, and so very familiar—

My heart stops in my chest.

"Marian. You're Marian."

It's her turn to look confused, but it confirms my suspicion. Brigitte's face is one I'll never forget, and the story she told me more so.

The story that ignited something in me. That pulled me to my feet when I needed it most, when I was ready—so ready—to stop trying.

Marian's story.

I shake my head. "You look just like her," I say. "Your mother."

She licks her lips. "You . . . know her?"

"I met her in West Miridran. During a . . . visit," I say.

The moment I say it, her eyes widen, sparkling with tears. She takes my hands. "When did you see her? How did she look?"

"She looked well," I tell her. "Truly." I wish I could tell her the whole of it, what it meant to me, and I vow to do just that once I'm free.

At least she relaxes. "She's the reason I'm here, the reason Laurent helped me. I live in East Miridran, but she's stuck in the west. King Illian won't release her from his service."

But Brigitte didn't seem trapped—at least, it appeared that way, until her words come back to me: *I'd be with her now if it weren't for* . . . Then she'd trailed off.

How could I have forgotten? I'd been too consumed in my own pain to notice hers.

But then I recall what else Brigitte had told me.

"He won't release her," I say, "because you refused to work for him."

Marian's eyes fall, and she tucks an errant curl behind her ear. "I should never have left her in the first place. And she does such a good job; she's made herself indispensable to him."

"It doesn't sound like your fault," I say, wishing I had something more to offer her. "If anything, it's his."

"I was hoping he'd bring her here to the Gathering, and then I could try to sneak her out." She pauses, taking a breath. "I can't have my name on the staff roster, not when Illian might recognize it. Laurent helped me forge documentation for that reason alone. I know it's wrong, but I refuse to abandon hope that he might one day bring her."

Brigitte, trapped. All that time, I'd assumed I was the prisoner, not her.

"I'm sorry," I breathe. I want to pull her close. To help, somehow. But being close to me could cause Marian more harm. Illian is the shadow that hovers behind me, my chains wrapped around his long, elegant fingers like the reins of a mare.

I settle for "She was good to me. I hope you find your way back together soon."

Marian smiles warmly, then tugs a bottle from its spot. She reaches inside the now-empty crevice and yanks something I can't see.

The rack shifts, opening like a door to reveal a deep, yawning pit of black.

Wind, cold as a crypt, brushes my shoulders. I wrap my arms around myself.

"The tunnels," Marian says. "Please keep these a secret. One of the reasons Laurent put me in charge of the cellars was to make sure they remained that way—though I know if Laurent told you, he did so for a reason. They will be empty, but be careful. Only use them when you must."

I swipe away a spiral of dust as I slip through the tunnels. Here, they're nothing but a wide expanse of dark, unpolished stone. The air is stale, dry, catching in my throat, though a cool breeze whistles through cracks and crevices every so often. Where it comes from, I cannot see. Only faint wisps of light from underneath the doors break up the syrupy dark; Marian advised me to leave the lantern behind. She also told me to head straight, which will take me outside, and to avoid the tunnels that branch off. She trusts me, like Laurent.

She shouldn't. I veer left.

Laurent's suspicions, the things he heard—I have to know if Illian is funding a Brisendali war. It would change everything. The Beast of the North's strength is matched by no one and nothing—not by steel, not by men, not even by the entirety of the other northern kingdoms. No one would survive them, should they decide to put their weapons to use. And when they win—because they *will* win—nothing would be out of my father's reach. His appetite for blood will drive him to push through more borders until none remain.

I'll have nowhere safe to disappear to.

It used to be idle talk. Slurred rants by the fireplace after he'd returned from his station, the scent of cognac sour on his breath. *All nations should follow our order,* he'd say. He'd speak of their avarice, their wretched ways. The absurdity of the last vestiges of piety some clung to—as if *he* were all-knowing.

And I might have bought into his reasonings, had it not been for Emilia. Yet it seems King Rurik may have caved under my father's influence.

If Brisendale is the Beast of the North, then my father is its fangs, already coated in blood. And if I am helping to enable his war—

I have to know.

I'm supposed to retrieve Annais by midnight, but this might be my only chance to seek answers. I'll just have to be quick.

Feeling faint, I use walls for support, jumping when something spindly crawls across my fingers. Adrenaline chases my heartbeat into a sprint, slowing only after a few long minutes of uninterrupted travel. Just when I'm about to turn around, the tunnels lift, taking me higher into the palace itself.

And then they narrow.

And darken.

Dark like my cell. Cloying darkness, stale and never-ending. Eternal.

Swathes of it. *Layers.*

A familiar panic hurtles through my chest. I press my hands to my heart as if I could push it back down, but it grows thicker until my lungs feel heavy, as if I'm gulping seawater. Sap. I slink against the wall, the ghost of my shackles weighing down my wrists. I can't seem to draw in air—

No. I can't let this happen. Not here, not now. I thrash around in my mind, fighting to regain the body slipping from my control—

Copelan.

His arms, the way it feels to be held by him. The way it feels to be touched, even if it takes me hours to recover from our rehearsals. And our last one was as exhilarating as it was exhausting. An escape—maybe the only thing holding me together.

Until I fail him.

Because I cannot balance the way I need to. I lack the strength or stamina required for many of the moves, forcing him to compensate with his own strength.

I never tell him how humiliated I feel.

A broken toy has no worth.

I am weak and brittle as century-old bone.

No—breathe. Please, breathe.

A glimmer catches my eye, just beyond the corner. I round it slowly, brushing dampened hair from my forehead to clear my vision.

Because surely my sight is deceiving me.

Shivers of prismatic light dance along the walls ahead like leaves in the wind, and it takes me several moments to understand.

The *mosaics*.

Or the backs of them, because I am on the other side.

And I can see straight through them.

Figures stride by, tapering the light as they pass. And not only that, I can even make out fragments of conversation.

"Anton," I say under my breath.

Instead of paintings, the palace is decorated with sea glass mosaics. They line every hallway, garnish every room, and from my brief explorations, I know they're opaque from the other side. But here, certain panes are thinner, near translucent. They must be the new additions to expand the tunnels Laurent spoke of. And it's brilliantly done. Being that they extend only slightly off the wall, who would know there's a walkway behind them?

He's made the entire place an illusion.

I don't know if I'm impressed or unnerved. Has he been spying on us? On *me*? Or are they merely an escape route, like Laurent said? My room is free of sea glass, perhaps because I am mere staff, but who's to say he hasn't been watching from the halls?

Chills spike the hairs on my arms. Is this why he suspects I'm working for his brother?

It was confirmation I sought, Miss Moran, he'd said. But then, if he had proof, he would have detained me by now.

I will have to be more careful.

I continue on, drifting past several more mosaic displays. There are small ones, clustered like jewels on the walls, and large ones, like the great tapestries in Illian's palace.

I find the Dome Hall next. It's above me now—a wide circular expanse, with a small mosaic designating the center of the floor. I use the mental mark and veer left, toward the Miridranian wing.

Crimson light teases a passageway ahead, and I find what I'm looking for: the mosaic of Illian's coronation. It's an older one, clearly predating Anton. Only, it's as if Anton had it moved out a few feet from its original place on the wall, narrowing the hall just fractionally. And though the glass is thicker than the new ones, it's still somewhat translucent.

A quiver passes over me as I recall his lucent eyes, the feeling of being watched. Perhaps I had been.

Further down, the next mosaic is the West Miridranian crest, just outside the tall, double doors of Illian's corridor. Two guards stand sentinel outside. I follow the bend until I reach another: a black and red diamond over a hearth. I peer through. It looks like an antechamber, and a plain one at that, with a few wingback chairs angled over a luxurious, crimson rug.

Until I notice the chandelier.

Like the rest, it's glass. It hangs unlit, crystalline, looking as if it was sculpted from ice. And it's massive. Hundreds of shards hang down like spears, each carved to a thin, fine point.

I shudder, tearing my eyes away, my gaze snagging on Illian's desk, just there in the corner. I recognize the seal stamped on scattered documents.

But he is nowhere to be found. I swallow my disappointment and press on, but even as I find more mosaics, the remaining rooms are dark and empty. Nothing.

I'm about to turn back when I reach the outer edge of Illian's wing. I don't have time to explore further, as much as I want to, and it's too much of a risk.

But then a flash of blue draws my eye.

A quick peek, I decide, and then I'll return. Only, this time, it isn't a mosaic I find but a crack in the wall.

No, not a crack. A door, set ajar. A quick glance tells me the space is empty, so I nudge the door a sliver more, enough that I might see what lies beyond.

My fingers rise to my lips.

There are images everywhere. Strange ones, blurry, as if I'm looking at them underwater, each one individually lit. Faces, trees, blooms. White-capped waves. They remind me of the ones I saw at Anton's banquet, but there's nothing to project them. No tubes, no torches.

What *is* this place?

It must be artwork of some kind, magnified by glass, extraordinary in detail.

Then one, brighter than the rest, pulls my eye, and the breath catches in my sternum. Because it's Anton, his virescent eyes sharp as a cutlass. And he looks so real, as if someone froze him in time. In fact, the longer I stare, the more I return to one detail.

His eyelids are mid-blink.

Odd, that an artist would capture that.

Unless they aren't paintings. At the banquet, I hadn't asked where the images came from. Art, I had assumed. But these aren't canvases laden with brushstrokes. They are different, more . . . immediate. I would almost think it magic if I dared.

But magic exists only in myths and tales of old, reserved for divinity and the Fate of Morta. But then, how is this possible?

A figure eclipses the doorway.

I lurch back, but it passes by. Voices crowd into the space, more entering from the far door.

I race down the hall, not willing to get caught. Nor can I keep Annais waiting any longer.

The tunnels feel longer, dimmer, but I retrace my steps, sure someone is following me, until finally the tunnels spill me back out onto the main one underneath the cellar. This one is dark, full of cobwebs and dust.

A bell signals ten minutes until midnight. I pick up my pace despite the patter of my heartbeat and the way it screams at me to rest, my steps beginning to waver and swerve.

It takes me longer than I expect to reach the outdoors. When finally I stumble out a discreet outer door that blends into the stone, the air is dense and humid from the storm, and the night suffocating and thick. The tunnels have led me underneath the barracks and disgorged me into a formation of rocks and sand dunes near the docks. Even still, a few patrols are scattered along them. I study their rotation, and when I see an opening, I make a run for it, damp sand crunching beneath my feet.

When my heel catches on a rock, I stumble.

A guard pauses his trek along the western dock, right near King Illian's ship. I don't move, praying the dune in front of me casts a bold enough shadow.

It doesn't. The guard walks my way.

I hear the puff of his breath as he draws near.

I have no weapon, nowhere to hide. But my eyes track a small hilt on the back of his boot. If I stay low, I can trip him and pilfer it—because I can't get caught. This *can't* be it. With quavering hands, I rip a strip of cloth from my tunic.

But when he stops a few feet away, the moon spotlights the emblem on his shoulder.

Illian's. He gives me a quick once-over then turns, approaching the closest group of guards. "Time to toss the pots, assholes," he says, drawing two flasks from his jacket. "The evening's plenty quiet."

He's distracting them.

Of course Illian wouldn't have risked it, not if there was a chance I'd fail.

I dash across the ramp and descend the stairs leading to the captain's quarters. My calves are screaming, but I knock softly against the door to Illian's cabin. It parts with a creak, and then I'm looking at a woman twice my age with large brown eyes and dark, ruddy tresses, her skin rosy and freckled like a sea of stars.

"Annais?" I prompt. I expect her to scold me for being late.

Instead, she seems dazed. Frightened, even, as I try her name once more.

Then, as if being ripped from a dream, she snaps from her trance. Offering me a curt nod, she slips out the door and awaits my lead.

"Does she talk?" Laurent asks me, his tall form propped against my door.

I want to know the same thing; I've yet to hear Annais speak. Even last night, as we traversed the tunnels and slipped back into my room; even as I offered her my bed and prepared myself a spot to sleep on the floor, cushioned by fabric; and even when I brought her breakfast the next morning, she didn't utter a word.

It wasn't for lack of trying. I asked questions. She met each one with the press of her lips. I wonder if she's meant to watch me. To report to Illian, after I frayed his trust at the banquet. Then, when I awoke this morning, I found her toying with the sewing kit, expertly mending a deep tear in my skirt.

That, at least, was a relief.

"She's suffered a great deal," I tell Laurent, dismissing the rising dread in my chest. "Just show her what you need her to do."

Laurent gives me a wary look, then relents with a sigh. "You're right. I suppose we all need time to heal, and a second chance." He gathers a pile of fabric into his hands. "I can take her to the sewing room."

I want to cry at his kindness. I don't deserve him. But this is a reminder that I don't know her past, the hold Illian might have over her. She might be as bound as I am.

Perhaps we aren't so different.

Chapter Seventeen

"Once again," I pant, racing after Laurent, "I beg you not to make me do this."

The past four days, Copelan and I have spent hours rehearsing—so much that collapsing becomes a regular occurrence, as does losing feeling in my feet for hours at a time. My fingers are pricked and calloused from sewing with Annais. Not to mention, Laurent and I have worked tirelessly on a stage environment.

The upcoming dance is meant to honor Razam, and I haven't forgotten the queen's words to me. I want to thank her in my own way. But I would never design to wrap myself in their garments and attempt to tell a tale only they should give voice to, so I had to be creative. How might we revere them when my king refuses to do just that? When he hopes to jerk her into a war?

Perhaps I have spite to thank, but an idea came together in my mind.

I just hadn't expected Laurent to like it so much. Hadn't expected him to make me do *this*.

Pulling a chain of keys from his tunic, Laurent halts in front of two double doors that stretch so high I can barely see the architrave above, embellished with gold-dusted plasterwork. A lone guard stands to the right, but he doesn't so much as acknowledge our presence.

"Your idea, your responsibility to ask. Besides, His Majesty made mention of just how *entertaining* he finds you," Laurent adds, waggling a brow. "I doubt he'd deny you anything."

My cheeks catch fire. "Morta's teeth, Laurent. That isn't—"

He jams the key into the lock, swings open the doors, and nudges me inside.

The moment I step through, he pulls them shut, abandoning me.

"Traitor," I mutter under my breath, but when I turn, I choke on a swallow.

I spin slowly, but the view doesn't change. Gold curtains fall in luxurious sheets between wide, gilded columns. The ceiling vaults hundreds of feet high, complete with a large, glasswork sun positioned like a chandelier, its spokes waving outward like ribbons in water, each one glowing under the skylights as if it were the real, noonday sun. And the floor—

It's moving.

No, not moving. It's water underneath stained, cobalt glass. I am standing above a *pool*.

My stomach sinks to my toes, causing me to sway.

How I'm going to dance on this, I have no idea. Nor do I know what I'm supposed to do next, because the room is empty. No sign of the smug, self-indulgent king who was supposed to be here.

A curtain to my left rustles slightly as if blown by a breeze. Except there's little airflow here. I approach warily. Then a sound— something that sounds suspiciously like a snore.

Surely I didn't just hear a *snore*.

But there it is again, ever so faint. I swipe back the shimmering gold curtain. It should come as no surprise when I find Anton there, lounging across a large marble throne as if it were a divan, bare feet pointed straight in the air. If that weren't enough, two women draped in delicate green silk—no doubt from his Glory Court, drat him—fan him lightly.

And they look all too pleased with their assignment, with no hint of distress. At their feet, Ishu sprawls on a wide cushion, paws outstretched. She slits open one eye at me, unconcerned—as are the women, one of whom has the nerve to shush me.

But then the other leans close to Anton's ear. "Your Glorious Majesty," she says softly.

He jolts awake, only to notice me and sag back into his throne, a ring-clad hand thrown across his forehead. "Morta's bum, what time is it?"

"Half past noon," I say bitterly, unable to restrain myself.

With a groan, he stretches and eases upward, his hair disheveled about his neck. Ishu mimics him with a stretch of her own as he says, "Ladies, you may retire." The women curtsey so low I roll my eyes. Then I realize I haven't done so myself. It feels too late now.

Once they leave, he dons his boots, lacing up each one before finally acknowledging me. "Please accept my most sincere apologies; the Council of Trades was such a bore, it put me right to sleep." He smooths his wrinkled jerkin before adjusting the sleeves. "I am at your service, Miss Moran."

"My apologies, Sire," I say, batting a hand where his attendants departed from, "for interrupting whatever *that* was."

I am not sorry.

"Perhaps you should have joined me. Running you ragged, are they? Or perhaps you are still recovering from my banquet?"

My pulse jumps at the mention, but I keep my voice steady. "It is my pleasure to serve the Crowns however I can."

For a moment, he merely studies me, a subtle curve to his lips—lips that contain a multitude of secrets. Ironic, now, because instead of him finding mine, I've found his. Only yesterday, I had been in his tunnels.

Leisurely, he descends the steps at the base of the throne. "What is it you've come to ask of me? Or is it the venue you wished to see?" He strolls toward me, forcing me to stagger backward.

Except he doesn't slow. My back hits a column, my breath ratcheting in my throat as he looms over me, arching a single brow. "Miss Moran," he says. "Pardon, if you please. You are blocking the rope."

My face goes hot. I sweep to the side, and he snags a tasseled rope from beside me. "Welcome to the Hall of Thrones, Minnow."

One by one, the curtains lift. Each reveals a large, high-backed throne protruding from the marble wall, and at their feet, rows of steps encircle the whole of the hall.

No, not steps, but benches, embedded with cushions for each seat.

Then there's the farthest throne, one that extends to the ceiling, its arms and legs coated in gold.

It makes Illian's throne look like a footstool.

"I assume that's yours," I say, jerking my chin in that direction. When I glance back at Anton, he's leaning against that column, a smirk as crooked as the crown set atop his sun-kissed face. Ishu plops down at his boots, bathing in a thin stream of sunlight.

"Ask what you will, Minnow," he says.

I think of Gustav but refrain. I make my formal request instead, relaying what I need him to do. All the while, he regards me steadily, his lips twisting in thought.

"Consider it done," he says, straightening. "There's little I would not do for Her Grace, Queen Sadira, and her people."

He says it like a warning.

Again, Laurent's suspicions loop in my mind. I slip my hands behind my back so he can't see the nervous fidget of my fingers. "Thank you, Sire."

"A favor for an answer. Do you enjoy it? The dancing?"

"I—" My brows notch. "Yes, Sire."

"Yes, yes of course. But what is it, specifically, that you enjoy? *Why* do you dance?"

So simple a question, and yet he paces around me, like I'm a fly caught in his web yet again.

Or perhaps it isn't so simple, now that I think of it. For so long, I told myself it was how I remembered her. Emilia.

But there's more to it—more than I want to admit aloud. My fingers run idly along the edge of my tunic as my thoughts slip back through time. Dancing was easy at the Melune. Convenient. I liked the art of it, but that wasn't what kept me practicing among the rafters or giving up all my earnings in hopes of making an impression. No, I kept going, kept pushing until I became the King's Jewel, and even then, I didn't stop. I told myself I was becoming powerful, influential. Untouchable, all so that if I ever saw *him* again, my father, he would look at me and the king by my side with every ounce of fear his cold heart could muster.

I liked how dancing made me feel, but passion didn't come until later. And even then, it was born from a selfish desire. I was building myself up so that I might feel strong.

But what I'd really done was build a wall. A fortress like those back home. And I barricaded myself behind it, not so that I might be strong enough to face him but so that I wouldn't have to. I enclosed myself between layers of stone so that I could pretend nothing outside of my little world existed. I could forget my past.

I succeeded.

And that's how I failed Emilia.

I inhale slowly, pain crumpling my insides. Tears threaten, but I stave them off.

I feel the king's gaze without looking up. He's paused his pacing, standing less than a foot away, so close I can smell bergamot and oranges, see the sweep of his lashes. The indent on his bottom lip.

The subtle bob of his throat as he evaluates me, yet again.

He makes me feel bare—of clothes, of skin, of bones. Like I'm as transparent as his glass, and he's searching for the components that bind me together.

I am saved when the door swings open. We both swivel to find Copelan stalking toward me. He sinks into a bow when he reaches us, turning his attention toward the king. "Your Majesty, I trust all is well? Laurent sent me in case I could be of help."

Yet Anton doesn't take his eyes off me. "Indeed, Master Reveler. Everything Miss Moran has requested will be done for her."

I bounce my gaze toward Copelan, who looks between us as he rises, a slight twitch in his jaw as he manages a nod. "We will leave you in peace, Sire." He takes my arm, tugging me rather forcefully toward the door.

Anton notices it, missing nothing. But all he says is, "Certainly. I'll see you two out."

By the time we return to the Dance Hall, the palace is dark from an afternoon storm, only a shimmer of torchlight illuminating the elongated room. I crack open a glass pane, letting in a cool wash of air.

When I turn, I feel Copelan's question before he asks it.

He folds his arms, his white tunic bunching at the chest. "What was that about?"

"What was what about?"

"The way he was looking at you. What did you say?"

Defensiveness kicks in, hardening my resolve. "I said nothing beyond my request, to which he agreed."

"He was practically standing on your toes."

"I can't control what he does," I say, unable to stifle an exasperated breath.

He shakes his head, scratching behind his neck. "Of course. I am sorry. It's just, that's the way, that's what . . ." He trails off, and I remember.

"Your partner," I whisper.

He heaves a breath, his eyes falling. He had told me she involved herself with a Crown. It had ruined her career.

"Who did she . . . ?" But I trail off.

I already know who she was involved with. I saw it in Copelan's stance, the clench of his jaw. Just now, I saw it.

And who else? Anton is charming. Deceptively so. And it's rather easy to pique his interest. He collects women like he does his jewelry, piled thick and waiting to be used, a bevy of them stashed away at his Glory Court. Illian might have a strange fascination with me at times, but it was always confined to just me. Souls know a hundred other courtiers vied for his attention.

I put a tentative hand on Copelan's strong shoulder, feeling the way it shudders beneath my touch. "Kings can take many things," I say, and he meets my gaze. "I'm sorry for what they've stolen from you, but they can't take moments like this one. They can't take ones they aren't here for unless you let them. So I think the greatest revenge," I tell him, "is creating as many as you can, while you can."

I would kill for another memory with Emilia. Just one, where I can sink into her quilt, soak up her laugh, flip through her memories. She used to say the greatest revenge is a smile. A smile for every harsh word, a smile for every moment of pain. *Fake it if you must, my darling; if wielded properly, it can be more effective than a blade.*

Fingertips skim the line of bared flesh above my leggings.

I understand what Copelan is saying. We don't need words; we rarely use them, after all.

A moment. This one. Maybe I need it, too.

My palms grow damp, but I grip his arms. He hoists me up.

We rehearse. And there's something a little furious, a little desperate in his movements, as if he's trying not to snap and break free—but from what, I don't know. I feel it in the way he holds me, the way he pushes the boundaries we've set. The way his fingers glide lower than they ought, the way they linger and splay.

The way mine do the same.

When we finish, I'm panting, and so is he. We stay that way, a hair's breadth apart, watching each other until our breathing settles and I'm ready to collapse. Only then does he lead me back to my room, a hand on the small of my back.

"It's only a few days away now," he says, standing outside my door. I pretend it doesn't affect me when he lifts a finger, twining it around a loose coil of hair. "Are you ready, Vas?"

"Sure," I lie. Because Illian isn't going to like it one bit.

Not when Copelan's hands are about to be all over me in front of the whole Gathering.

When he leaves, I try for a nap, though I'm interrupted when Annais slips into my room. I ask her if she needs anything, but she merely gives me a passing glance before settling down to stitch a worn costume.

That's when I notice what I hadn't before, nuzzled there against her breastbone.

A necklace with a single charm. It almost looks like a Miridranian birthstone etched into a coin. A four-pointed star in particular, which signifies a child born amid tribulation. And around the outer edge of the coin, there's an engraving. I can't quite make it out, but it almost looks like the age-old language from the time of the clans—clans that existed in these lands before Miridran itself. Like the one Queen Mercy hailed from.

"Annais," I try. There's a wariness to her gaze when she looks at me. I swallow, threading my fingers through my hair. "Do you have children?"

Her eyes fall shut, and I don't miss the way her fingers inch toward the necklace. But she drops them, fixing her gaze steadily on the needle in her hand.

And I'm not sure if I imagined it, or if it was merely the whisper of wind outside, but I could have sworn she answered me underneath her breath.

I could've sworn she said, "A son."

Chapter Eighteen

The few days before our next big performance blend together.

We haven't had much time to practice, Copelan and I, but we don't need it. Something about this next dance is visceral, as if my body knows the motions based on sense alone. Even so, nerves coil within me. Not only for our proximity, the response we might provoke, but also from the message I am about to relay, however subtle, in regard to Razam.

But my time to fret is limited. Each night, I'm sent to entertain small parties hosted by drunk dignitaries from across the Miridranian courts. It's common, Laurent tells me. Large families are spread between the three territories, and the Gathering is the only time they make an effort to see one another. So they kick back their chalices and carouse while I alternate with other troupes.

I find myself longing to know the other dancers, to interact, but I keep my distance. I am too dangerous a friend. So I fulfill my duty. I dance, and I hold my tongue.

Each night Anton is there—a familiar, recurring presence. He stays an hour, maybe two, entertaining the courts with his ridiculous tales, then retires not long after.

He never speaks to me, but I feel him watching me, scrutinizing me—especially when I dance.

It's worse than an interrogation, the way his eyes rake over me. It's as invasive as touching. Perhaps he is still suspicious—especially after the banquet. Or more so, because of it.

Yet I can't seem to put a pin on him, either, though I watch him as much as he watches me. It's become a game at this point, as if we're circling each other, waiting to see who might make the first move. I don't break his gaze until I'm forced to. He doesn't break mine until someone pulls him away. Whoever breaks first seems to lose something—though what, I don't know.

But I begin to notice things.

He smiles easily—much easier than Illian—and when he laughs, he laughs proudly, freely. He flirts in abundance, seemingly enjoying the challenge of charming anyone willing to indulge him. A new companion, or several, languish over him each night. They come from every court by the looks of it, each more eager than the last. They rub his chest, dangle on his arm, massage his neck, no doubt eager to unravel the enigmatic king. And he revels in it.

Yet he drinks like a man parched, and that tells me he's either unhappy or he's trying to forget something—something that haunts him from dreams to waking, the way my father now haunts me.

I long to know what it is.

Tonight unfolds like any other. After my performance, I retreat into the shadows bordering the room, anticipating my dismissal. However, an unexpected guest graces the soirée—Prince Raiden, the Prince of Zar. So engrossed is he in a game of marble joust that he's forsaken his customary silver headpiece, his dark curls falling freely. Courtiers lounge with the seventeen-year-old prince around a table, musicians stringing an idle tune in the background. They forget about me entirely.

It isn't until I back against a wall that I realize Anton is next to me instead of indulging in his usual proclivities.

"You have yet to answer my question," he says, fiddling with the brass buttons on his burnished gold velvet jacket—his gaudiest piece yet, bedazzled in rows of hematite stones. Even locks of his hair are strung back with them. "About why you dance."

"Why do you drink and flirt with anything that breathes?" I return, only to bite my tongue in regret.

Until he says, "Because I am exceedingly wonderful at both."

"I think flirting is your way of interrogating."

"I think you are scrumptious," he says with a grin, proving my point exactly. "Care to answer me *now*?"

"I can't imagine why you want to know so badly."

"Little is more revealing than one's passion. Or lack thereof." He glances at me pointedly.

"Are you always this presumptuous?"

"I am precisely the right amount of presumptuous."

I let out a huff. "What makes you believe that dancing is not a passion of mine?"

"It pains you in some way or another, does it not?"

So he's noticed that, too. "That hardly means it isn't a passion."

He swirls the liquid in his glass. "What I find most interesting about you, Minnow, is that sometimes you do seem to love it. You transform not only yourself but the room. You enchant us. We are spellbound to you, and you to your dance. Yet there are times you seem to loathe it, too."

I loathe that he's been watching me so closely.

Perhaps it's the exhaustion, but I have nothing in me to combat him further, so I relent, if only a little. "I dance because . . ."

Because I must, I almost say. *Because I am forced into it, now.*

I hate that my passion, my greatest joy, my way to remember Emilia, is now a weapon in Illian's hands.

"The first thing that comes to mind," he says, nudging me with his shoulder. "What is it?"

"Power," I blurt. "Because there's power in it." Power in commanding the attention of my audience, a power I lack in every other area of my life.

But that isn't the whole of it, either. And it's as if Anton knows, because he watches me steadily, waiting, and it makes me so angry, so *seen*, that I shove the rest at him, ready to be done with it. "And because it makes me feel less alone."

And now he will no doubt dissect every word. Heat crowds my cheeks, and I straighten, poised to walk away, when he says, "I drink because I cannot otherwise quiet my mind. Because I, too, feel alone. Because I want and wish for many things I cannot have, and that, Minnow, drives me absolutely wild."

The breadth of his answer startles me.

But I say, merely, "Another way of telling me you are spoiled, then."

Once again, my self-control has slipped.

He grins, leaning in. "Spoiled, pretentious, and far too wealthy. And devilishly fetching, I should add."

I barely resist an eye roll. "Then what, exactly, can you *not* have?"

His eyes travel over me at that, but then he merely frowns at his drink. "At the moment? More wine."

"Deflective."

Even so, I run his words through my mind again. He revealed more than I did, if only I could understand *how*.

"I am flattered by your curiosity," he says, chin inching up. "And by that adorable little blush."

I throw a hand to my cheek before I can stop it, a futile attempt to halt the rising warmth. It grates on my nerves even more. "I am *not* curious, and I'm merely overheated."

"You are blushing even more ardently now. Don't worry, Minnow. I take it only as the highest tier of compliments."

"With such dazzling confidence, Sire, I'm surprised you haven't constructed a statue or several in your honor."

"By the Fates, you're right. I should pose for one at once."

"Alongside your stacks of gold—"

"And preferably in the nude."

"—with a companion draped across your lap."

"Generous of you to offer," he says.

A growl travels up my throat, along with a score of insults. It takes all my willpower to clamp my tongue and walk away.

Especially as his chuckle skitters down my back as I do.

The day before our big performance, whispers haunt the halls. At long last, King Estienne, Illian's older brother, has arrived.

I'm told he's in a foul mood after his delay, when Copelan informs me that I will be entertaining him this evening.

Before retrieving the last-minute costume Annais is stitching, I stop by the kitchen to grab her lunch.

Marian is there.

She greets me with a hug, which I'm not prepared for. When I tell her what I'm looking for, and how much, she tells me to wait where I am. "I'll fetch a few platters I saved from a banquet."

The moment she disappears, the kitchen doors fly open and two Brisendali guards stalk in.

They are trailed by the general.

For a blink, terror roots me to the ground. But then my brain catches up and I slink behind a stack of crates.

My father is not a particularly tall man. He's average in height and build, but it's his carefully crafted tone, the sheer confidence he wields like a king would a scepter, that makes it feel like he's towering over the room.

"Who," he says, thrusting up a serving tray piled with haunches of meat, "is responsible for this?"

Even his voice, deadly calm as it is, projects.

The cooks, all eight of them, pause, knives mid-slice, pots boiling over.

And then I watch with mounting dread as Marian returns from the pantry. Unaware, she flits past him, a garnished platter in hand.

"You," he calls, halting her. "What is your position here?"

Marian blinks once, twice, before registering the emblem on his shoulder. "General," she says. "My apologies. I am in charge of the cellars, stocking and managing their contents."

"Then who is in charge of the food?"

His gaze rakes the kitchen, but no one answers, like prey frozen in the path of an arrow notched.

He whirls back on Marian. "Your name?"

My chest tightens, my heartbeat a hammer.

Don't tell him.

"Ma—" She stops abruptly, then says, "Maria, milord."

Because if she were to tell him her real name, and he were to investigate . . . I shudder.

"What seems to be the problem, milord?" she adds calmly, but I can see the tension in her hands, knuckles white from gripping the platter she arranged for me.

He studies her, and I wonder what he sees. She's my height, my age. We could be sisters. And her scars do not detract from her beauty. They merely serve to highlight the strength in her eyes.

Eyes that are golden-brown, just like mine.

Does he think of me, here and now?

I wonder, then, how long he searched for me. What havoc he might have wreaked once he realized I was gone. Did he cry for me, even once? Or am I nothing to him but a lost mare, good only for fetching a price?

"Come here, Maria."

Come here, Emilia.

Marian approaches as nervous whispers swarm the kitchen. My father shoves the meat-laden tray at a nearby guard, but not before grabbing a haunch. His weathered fingers pull at it, dig right into its dry flesh. "Do you see the problem, Maria?"

Do you see the problem, Emilia?

"Do you think my men are dogs?" He makes a sweeping gesture at them. "That they are capable of prying apart leather with teeth sharp as knives? Or perhaps that they might beg for any scrap you offer in this Fates-forsaken kitchen?" he says. "Or maybe you thought us incapable of distinguishing days-old hog meat from that of a fresh boar?"

Do you think I'm a fool, Emilia? Did you think I would not notice the closet empty of clothes? The missing jewelry? The coins that disappeared from my vault little by little?

A sound like wind rushes through my ears.

"No, milord, please," Marian says. "I can have a fresh meal prepared and served to your wing within the hour..."

My father's eyes glaze over, frenzied as they are, and I know...I know where he is.

Only you noticed too late, husband. She is gone, forever out of your reach. I've made certain of it.

Marian remains calm.

So had Emilia.

Oh, I do hope you're wrong, wife, as I will peel every strip of skin from your bones until you beg me for death, he had said. *You will return her to me.*

She did not.

Quick as a whip, my father's hand lashes out. Snakes around Marian's throat. And then he's shoving the haunch of meat through her teeth, down her throat, until she's choking, crying, clawing for air, the platter dropping from her hands—

The room blinks white.

And then I am in the foyer closet, watching Emilia, watching as my father clamps his hand over her throat—

I am there.

I am back.

Emilia brandishes a vase from the mantel behind her—my mother's vase. She smashes it over my father's head. Blood wells from the cut, beading along his brow, saturating his skin. He doesn't let go. He won't let go. Terror seizes my entire being.

Then he slams the crown of her head against the hearth.

Again—again.

Again, until she stops fighting, and her body goes limp.

He scoops her up, cradling her like the doll he thought she was, red soaking her curls and bleeding down the back of her dress as he shoves through the balcony doors. Even then, I had known what was about to happen. Silent sobs warped my vision, but I heard her voice in my head, her words from only minutes before. *I cannot go with you, my love. I need you to run, no matter what. If you love me, you will run. Go through the drain, take it into the next village. Sell this ring, and never, ever come back.*

With my father turned away, I took my chance. Grabbed my suitcase and crawled for the front door. Guilt tore at my soul, but a sickening fear pushed me onward. If I stayed, he would do the same thing to me.

I opened the door, poised to flee. Only I glanced back just in time to see him thrust her over the rail. Like a stale loaf he might toss away, throw to the birds.

Like she was nothing.

"Please, General, the fault was mine," I hear distantly, the head chef's high-pitched voice. "I overcooked it, an oversight that won't happen again—"

My eyes fly open as my father flings Marian to the ground. She's wheezing, her face patchy and red, tears streaming in rivulets down the length of her neck.

"There, you are correct," he says. "It won't happen again, will it?"

Only dimly do I register him leaving. I'm trembling so violently I can't see.

Minutes slide by, maybe more. I lose all sense of time. My hands have long since gone numb, but I cover my eyes with my palms. Dig my thumbs into my braid. Over and over, I see Emilia. The blood blossoming from her scalp. The shape of her figure plummeting off the balcony.

My lungs ache from trying to breathe.

At some point, Marian nudges me gently. I glance at her, unable to find words. Unable to move, even, when I should be the one comforting *her*. How despicable I am. How lowly, because I did not emerge from hiding. I could have stopped him, and I did not.

"Marian," I breathe.

I want to ask if she's all right, but of course she isn't. And what could she say? Looking at her now, a pained smile on her lips—she would tell me that she's fine.

So I say nothing as she arranges a new platter. She's quiet, too, but I don't miss the way her throat bobs, like she's trying to swallow. To recover. It must be on fire.

I am on fire. I feel it everywhere, scorching across my flesh. This happened because of me.

He will never stop hurting so long as he walks around like he's a king and we're the carpet upon which he treads.

I can't erase Emilia's death from my mind, can't stop seeing what he did to Marian, even as she squeezes my hand and releases me, walking away.

I could have stopped him long before he came here. I could have returned, told the world the truth of who he is. What he did. More so, I would have been under Illian's protection as his Jewel. And now it's too late. I'm but a puppet, like my father said I would be.

Unless—

Unless I clear my name. No one would believe the words of a convicted criminal, but once I'm free of Illian, the daughter of General Maksim Stova could tell the world the murderer he is. I'm the only one who knows the truth of Emilia's death, the only one who knows the demon he tries to hide. If I survive this Gathering, I could expose him.

Because he doesn't deserve death; that's too kind. No, I want him to rot in a cell like I did. I want him to think of me and Emilia every day for the rest of his life. I want our voices to taunt him in the dark.

This is what I should have been planning all along, ever since I was released. But I thought he was far out of reach. Instead, he's here, violent and cruel as ever—and the hounds master of the Beast of the North.

And he's been delivered straight to me. Or me to him.

No.

I will take everything from him.

I will ruin him.

Chapter Nineteen

Back in my room, I dig, frantically, through my half-unpacked bag. I leaf through clothes, face paints, and undergarments until I find it.

Emilia's glove.

I squeeze my eyes shut, pressing the pads of its fingers to my lips, and there I make a promise to do what I didn't before. I make it into a song, a prayer, a plea. I beseech any Fates who might listen, because I might be the only one who can wrench power from my father's grip.

This time, when I tuck away the glove, I tell Emilia that promise. I vow to take back what is rightfully ours.

Our home. My status. Everything she wanted for me. I will clear my name and reclaim my title, not as the King's Jewel, but as the heir to House Stova.

And I will banish her murderer into the never-ending dark.

Illian deserves a similar fate. But this would be a small revenge in itself, because if I'm right about my father pressuring King Rurik to ignite a war, Illian's plans might be thwarted with him gone.

It isn't much. But it's all I have because I need Illian. I need him to seal my release.

Laurent finds me while I'm assembling my costume for tonight. It's a stretch of black taffeta, belted with a braided silver band. As I fit myself into it, he helps me loop the intricate ribbons along the back while telling me about the raid on King Estienne's envoy.

"They say bandits attacked before he and his men reached the coastline in the dead of night. A huge number of them, too, enough to ransack every last carriage."

Laurent then tells me to be cautious. Nothing extravagant in my dance, no stunts with the audience. "Vasalie, King Estienne is one to be feared. Not only did he capture every last raider, hence the delay, but he brought them *here*. Sixty of them, imprisoned in his corridor. Not in the dungeons but his personal hall. My staff—they hear them. Screams, things from nightmares. Understand me when I say to get in, do your job, and leave. I loathe that Copelan is sending you in the first place, but everyone else is assigned to other posts."

Of Illian's two brothers, I've heard the least about King Estienne. Mere mentions between the bat of a fan. Mostly that he's a recluse, secluded in his own lair. But toy with him, and he's dangerous. Vicious, like a viper's strike. One of Illian's attendants who apprenticed in the Miridranian army alongside King Estienne once told me that, when they were young, their captain found sport in playing with the young prince—pissing in his tent, stealing his clothes, even letting his comrades knock him around. To thicken his skin, the captain claimed.

Until Estienne torched their camp, made it look like an accident, and killed fifty men in the process.

Cold settles against my bones as I enter his halls. It doesn't help that I'm particularly weak tonight, what with the overexertion of the last few days. And perhaps I am mistaken, but when I pass one of Illian's guards, I swear I see a frown crack her blank expression, as if she's surprised to find me headed in this direction. Even so, I keep onward until King Estienne's doors swing open and I'm permitted entrance into his nest.

Puddles of violet light hover high above from stained sea-glass sconces, limning the heads of the near-silhouetted guests. Aside from that, the room is as dark as the black basalt walls, and spherical, like a cavern. Like what I imagine Morta's Lair might look like. And the centerpiece—a throne of obsidian quartz—looms at the far end.

In it rests a figure in black velvet and leather, a foot propped up on one knee, a goblet resting idly in one hand as he partakes in a conversation to his right. A single red glow from a pendant chandelier above catches the ominous steel crown wrapping his brow, and only when my eyes adjust can I see him more clearly.

The King of Central Miridran looks almost nothing like his younger brothers. His eyes are dark and deep-set, like Illian's, though his face is covered with freckles that look like shells in the sand, the same hue as his deep, flaming locks. Even seated as he is, I can tell he'd tower over the room, his legs long and sprawling.

Something about him is familiar, however, though I can't figure out what.

Laurent told me they would call for me when I'm needed, but so far, I've gone unnoticed. Serving boys flit back and forth, ferrying bowls of blood-red grapes and trays of drinks between guests. A discordant melody winds around me, low and vibrating. Textured, like the brush of snakeskin. Like the hum of chapel bells during a storm, and there's no set tune.

Nor can I see where it's coming from.

A familiar voice dips into my ear then. "No matter what, do *not* look left."

An irresistible impulse urges me to do just that, but the tone of the warning stops me short. Instead, I track my gaze to my right, where Anton leans against the precipice, just over my shoulder. I bob a short curtsey.

He merely offers me a tight grin. "Evening, Minnow."

"Your Majesty," I say. Of course he would be here to greet his oldest brother on his arrival. Illian, on the contrary, is nowhere to be found.

"Why," I ask, "can I not look to my left?"

For the first time, perhaps ever, his smile drops, and it's then that I catalog the difference in his appearance. His dark hair isn't windswept; rather, it's tied back in a knot at the base of his neck, a few, purposeful strands waving loosely about. Every last button on his fine, soot-black, sleeveless jerkin is secured, his toned arms free of his usual stacks of bracelets. And he carries no chalice, his breath untainted with wine.

It's as if he's an alternative version of himself tonight, proper and refined.

"Vasalie," he says softly, "you should leave. I will call for the Master of Revels; he can perform tonight in your stead."

Vasalie.

Not Minnow, not Miss Moran. An uneasy feeling tightens my stomach, but I am not here by choice. "Your Majesty, I cannot refuse my post..."

He shakes his head. "You are leaving. *Now.*"

"But I—"

He takes hold of my wrist, pulling me with him. "I'm not giving you a choice." I've never seen him like this. The urgency, the concern...

Two guards slam the doors in our face.

Noise, music, chatter—it ceases.

"Leaving before the festivity starts, Anton? So unlike you."

King Estienne's voice is low, like Illian's, but harsher. Almost as if he spits his words.

All at once, Anton drops my arm and smooths the crease from his brow. His usual, relaxed smile snaps back in place as he pivots to face his brother. "Festivity?" He glances about, a single brow arched. "If you promise to start it, I promise to stay."

A thread of tension quivers in the air.

It breaks at the flash of teeth. "A fine point," King Estienne drawls. Then he spurs from his throne and stalks toward us.

I hear it, then. A slow drip, one splash after another, however faint. Like a leak in the ceiling, falling into a half-full pail. I angle my head, but Anton steps into my line of sight. "Don't look, Vasalie," he whispers, his gaze fixed ahead. "Not for my sake, but yours."

King Estienne takes notice of me then, slipping his hands into the pockets of his doublet. "Ah, the dancer I've heard so much about, no? They told me what she did, brother. I'd have loved to see it. You, a spectacle."

"I'm always a spectacle," Anton says, offended. He edges in front of me, almost as if he's trying to hide me. But his brother slinks around him easily.

"You were running off with my entertainment, weren't you? Tsk, tsk." He looks down his nose at me.

"Can you blame me?" Anton slings an arm over my shoulder. "I've always had a thing for dancers." With his other hand, he flicks my nose.

I bite the inside of my lip, resisting the urge to glower up at him for that.

King Estienne watches us, thoroughly unimpressed with me if the downward curl of his lips is any indication. "What is your name, dancer?"

"Vasalie, Your Majesty," I say, forcing the tremble from my voice. "Vasalie Moran."

I pray he doesn't ask where I'm from. I don't know the adviser Illian paid to recommend me, only that he's from Central Miridran. If King Estienne inquires further—

"Vasalie Moran, did you hear what happened to my envoy?"

I'm not sure if I'm supposed to know, but I don't think it wise to lie. "I did, Your Majesty. I am grieved to hear of your troubles."

He nods. "Tragic, I tell you, though I like to think every hindrance can be advantageous with the right outlook. Wise words from Father," he says, addressing Anton. He claps twice. "If it's entertainment you seek, I shall deliver. In fact, I've thought very carefully about this evening. I admit, I've been anticipating it a great deal, what with the gift I've prepared for my guests—including you, Vasalie." He holds out his arm. "Would you care to assist . . . ?"

Dread courses through me, but I place my hand atop his.

He whisks me to the center of the room. And when he snaps his fingers, it's like a jolt through my bones.

A heavy door behind the throne screeches open, then two guards come striding through.

And in each of their hands, the end of a large chain.

Clatter, clank.

Clatter, clank.

I hear them before I see them, the prisoners that emerge from the shadows.

"Bandits, every last one," King Estienne says from beside me.

Some are my age, others older, and some younger, near children. Most are women. They're fettered in manacles like the ones I used to wear. Maybe fifteen of them, their garb filthy, mud-caked. And yet their faces have been scrubbed clean.

"I know what you're thinking," says King Estienne, and I feel his eyes on me. "*These* are the outlaws who dared attack my men and postpone my journey? Hardly. It turns out, I find these ones in particular rather valuable. The rest," he says, cupping my shoulders, "well, let's just say they weren't so fortunate." He spins me back toward Anton, whose usual sun-kissed skin is now leeched of color.

No, not toward Anton.

Drip.

Drip.

I try not to look. I try to hold Anton's gaze the way he holds mine, but even then, I can't help it, the background bleeding slowly into focus.

Behind him, secured on the back wall—just to the left of where I'd stood—hangs a large metal board with long, crystalline pikes protruding outward like a bed of nails.

And every last spike pierces a neck, an abdomen, or the yawning mouth of a corpse.

Drip, drip. Like the swing of a pendulum. The click of a heel. The patter of rainwater, cool and slick.

Drip.

Metal goblets are scattered along the floor, each perfectly positioned so that it catches their blood.

I sway on my feet.

"As for you," King Estienne says, and a surge of panic floods my veins. "Instead of a performance, how about a less arduous role? You'd make a fine auctioneer, I think."

He digs a key from his belt and chucks it to a guard, who then unlocks the first prisoner from the main chain. When she looks up, the sight of her in shackles cleaves open a wound inside me—one that never healed, only scabbed.

Light curls, brown eyes. Small in stature, so like Emilia I have to heave in a breath. Her strong chin is notched upward in defiance, though she keeps her gaze leveled away from the horror ratcheted upon the wall. Even so, I note the bruise-colored bags underneath her eyes, the chills puckering her alabaster skin.

I wonder how many of them she knew. How many she loved.

I wonder if she watched them die.

And King Estienne is going to make me auction her off.

He can't do that, can he? Ownership of any kind—it is forbidden. Unless—

But of course. So long as she's judged a criminal, she can be stripped of all rights. Legally.

Sorrow burrows deep into my heart. Whatever she did, deserving or not, she will spend the rest of her life a prisoner, at the mercy of whoever purchases her.

"Let's start with ten quatra," the scum of a king beside me says. "Vasalie, if you please."

The woman's hands shake, like my own, but she does not cower.

I loathe myself as I step forward and call it out.

"Fifteen quatra," someone yells.

"Thirty-five quatra, and a ruby."

"Fifty!"

I don't even have to raise the price. The bids come fast.

"A hundred, and three pearls the size of my fist! She's a darling, that one."

"A hundred, and my wife!" The crowd erupts into laughter.

"Is she really worth it?" someone else calls. "A bit scrawny, no?"

My dinner swarms in my gut, threatening to rise. They pick apart her appearance. They joke about what she'll be good for, how she'll be used.

"Small hands. At least they look soft—"

"But those lips. Imagine—"

No, stop.

"Twenty thousand quatra and five chests of pearls. For all of them."

The bidding halts.

I swivel, horrified, and meet Anton's sparking eyes.

"Really, Anton," King Estienne drawls. "Glory Court running thin these days?"

Glory Court. Of course.

Hatred rises up my throat. I had hoped, foolishly, that Anton might not be as despicable as I'd thought. That he might have been protecting me, earlier. That everyone was wrong about him.

But this is a game to him. A sport. Everything is, and he's in it to win.

Anton takes a casual step forward, pilfering a half-empty glass from an unsuspecting noble. Downing it in a swig, he winks at the man before swaggering toward the throne, clapping the backs of two men he outbid. "Can anyone beat my offer? No?"

The prick has a bounce in his step.

King Estienne rolls his eyes and slaps the key into Anton's hands, mumbling a low, "You ruin everything."

Anton merely flashes a pleased smile. "A pleasure, as always."

With a curl of his fingers, Anton's guards swing forward from their positions along the wall, their glass-like helms reflecting glimmers of amaranthine torchlight. He relays his orders—something about letting the prisoners enjoy the revelry for a while. Come dawn, they will be loaded onto a ship and escorted to their *new home*.

Courtiers snicker throughout the room. Their amusement is like hot wax burning into my stomach. And then Anton tosses me a key, nodding his head toward the prisoner. "Vasalie, be a darling, would you?"

He wants me to lock her back into the main chain.

The music resumes, louder than before, this time from a trio of musicians who just arrived. At last, the attention is diverted off me, the party proceeding like there isn't flesh decaying mere feet away. As if the monstrosities here are of little consequence, barely worth so much as gossip.

I swallow, my stomach once again ready to yield my dinner, and turn back to the woman. She does not look at me.

My palms are sweating. The key, heavy as iron, nearly slips from my grasp.

Gently, I take her manacled hands, wincing at the raw, reddened skin where the shackles dig into her flesh. My own wrists throb at the memory.

And she's shaking.

There's a lockbox at the end of a smaller chain, which hooks into the shackles. I pick it up.

I can't . . . can't help her. Even if I slipped her this key, what could she do? The both of us would be caught.

I slant a glance over my shoulder, where King Estienne slouches back on his throne, a companion curling up with him. She is as tall as he, and equally as muscled. Another sweep of the crowd tells me no one's watching.

And I'm in the shadows. Even the guards holding the main

chains are laughing, conversing among themselves. They don't bother to stay alert, and why would they? No one would dare try anything here.

When I lock her into the main chain, I make the mistake of meeting her eyes. They're big, golden, soft as melted butter. I see the single, stubborn tear glossing her right eye, refusing to fall. She tightens her lips in resignation. There is no hope for her, and she knows it. I am well acquainted with the feeling.

Before I can think better of it, I pry a pin from my hair. She couldn't use it until she landed on the main shores, but—

No. I won't risk it—can't. Ever since my father, and Marian . . . my purpose has shifted. It's no longer about disappearing, no longer about a second chance, no.

It's about justice. Vengeance.

I'm about to pull away, to refuse her this chance, when Anton grabs my wrist. My breathing stifles. His fingers dig through mine. He finds the pin easily and wrestles it from me, then drags me along with him.

Fear pounds through my veins, pulses in my eyes.

I've been caught.

He will have me arrested.

What was I thinking? I've put myself at risk twice now. *Twice.*

Hate burns within me, like a flame set across oil, igniting at its flashpoint. I shake with it. Shake as it spreads into every vein, every capillary.

I hate all of them. The Crowns, the courtiers, their sickening cheer amid such atrocities. I hate my father. Emilia, for leaving me, when I could have just gone along with my father's plans and she would still be alive. Most of all, I hate myself for condemning this woman to her fate.

I am so angry that I don't notice the arm Anton has wrapped around me, as if I'm his souls-damned escort, until he ushers me into a shadowed alcove, sheltered from the two sconces above.

"Foolish Minnow," he says, holding up the pin. "Tampering with my winnings." He then slips it back into my hair, just above my ear. I ignore the tingle that runs along my scalp.

I can't find it in me to muster up an excuse. To defend myself. Even as he waits, his green-gold eyes like lanterns in the dark.

When finally his patience frays, he blows out a breath. "Vasalie, I will not report you for what you just attempted to do, but do not try it again. If my brother had seen you, you would not be standing here right now. You would be on that wall."

Drip.

Drip.

My fury liquefies, becomes *molten*. "You," I spit. "You dare to protect me, and in the same breath you purchase them? Merely to stock your despicable Glory Court?"

"*Yes.*"

I clamp my teeth over my lips, so hard I draw blood. A part of me had hoped—desperately, inanely—that he might set them free. He has the power to do what I cannot. But then I recall his arrogance during the banquet. He's proud of that vile, horrible court.

"I paid enough, didn't I? What, does that disgust you? Anger you? Are they not criminals?"

"Yes, but—"

"But what?"

I have no right to defend them after what I *didn't* do, and yet . . . "Some are practically children, others elderly! And souls, what if they were hungry? Desperate? What if they weren't all guilty? I don't know—I don't know!" My vision tunnels. Blurs. "Not all criminals are evil." I bet most aren't, in fact. "And none—*none*—deserve this."

"I shall be nothing if not a cordial host."

"A demanding one, you mean." Oh, the way rage boils within me, the way I long to shove my knee in his most tender spot . . .

"I am offended," he says, pointedly not. "I wine and dine my guests; rarely do they want for anything."

"Except freedom."

He takes my chin in his fingers, tilting it this way and that. "You would know a thing or two about that, I assume."

I open my mouth, then snap it shut.

He leans in. "Speechless? Yes, I tend to have that effect. Now leave, Vasalie. If Estienne calls for you, I will tell him I sent you away. Your *Master*," he drawls, "shouldn't have sent you here to begin with." Once again, he ushers me toward the door.

My Master.

The Master of Revels, he means.

I think.

After tearing off my gown, I retrieve the pin from my hair, watching the reflection of a flame lick along its golden surface.

My fingers close around it, squeezing until it scores a red mark against my skin.

I don't know how to process what happened this evening. I don't know what to do with the emotions that push and pull against my rib cage; I feel as if they're ripping me to shreds. I'm exhausted, ashamed. Relieved. And there's hatred still—for myself, for Estienne, for Illian. My father. The Crowns. The courtiers. *Anton*. He protected me. He stopped a war. The queen admires him, and yet he did *that*.

In this moment, I hate him the most.

Because I almost had faith in him.

Because I want, so badly, to believe he is different, and yet every encounter with him leaves me confused, frustrated. *Breathless*.

Because I don't know whether he's the safest of them all.

Or if he is, by far, the most dangerous.

Chapter Twenty

The morning of our second signature performance comes before I'm ready.

I take extra care in my preparations, gliding kohl along my eyes in heavy strokes, tapering it with a flourish at each crease. I shimmy into my costume. Annais helps me lace together the nude, satin bodice. The bones inside are thin, flexible, allowing me to move freely, and on top is a sheer gossamer, shimmering with azure stones, like beads of water pearling atop my skin.

The skirt has a similar effect, dark satin scrunching into ruffles on each of my hips, intended to look like storm clouds. It stops beneath my thighs, bare skin peeking through, and Annais ties another piece around my waist—tendrils of crystals that swish and dance like rain as I walk down the hall. Matching strands glitter against my half-pinned hair.

Down a narrow corridor, I find the back entrance to the Hall of Thrones. Inside, the usual array of Crowns and courtiers await, but outside, Laurent sections the performers into groups, each behind their own divider. There's a platter of plucked pomegranate seeds, sliced amlas, and a selection of cured meat, which I avoid, but at least I see Marian come and go, a smile on her face.

I don't know how she does it.

The triplets perform first. They mime a Razami children's tale while a storyteller narrates, though perhaps mime is too simple a word, what with their acrobatics. Through the curtained doorway, I catch glimpses of their act, but amid their performance, Copelan arrives.

Until now, I hadn't seen his costume. His eyelids shimmer with gold; his hair is swept elegantly off his face. Tan breeches hug his legs, his neck looped with a brass carcanet.

And he's shirtless.

Gold swirls around his chest, the design unfurling across his arms, neck, and shoulder blades. He doesn't notice me at first, but when his eyes find mine, they sweep over me like a sandstorm.

My mouth dries.

Last night, after everything, I had sought him out. Pulled him from another practice and thrown my arms around him, needing to feel safe, if only for a moment. Needing an escape from all my anger and fear, both of which feel lodged in my very heart. And he let me do it, stunned as he was, until I left without a word.

Now, it's a struggle to look away. But I drag my gaze back to the Hall of Thrones, only to find Illian in my line of sight. Like my first night, he's perfectly positioned so that he can see me—only he isn't looking at me.

He's watching Copelan.

I know that look. It's the look he's given a thousand men before when their proximity to me was too close. I think of all the ways Copelan is about to touch me, the ways I will touch him in return.

But this is the position Illian forced me into.

So I wipe it from my mind, checking the pouches sewn into my outfit, and breathe. Servants bring out decanters of wine. After another troupe finishes, sitar players thread into the crowd, distracting the audience from the bayans and tablas now being assembled across the space. Musicians take their place once more. Sconces are lit, enclosed by cerulean sea glass. They pitch a dim, bluish light across one crescent of the room, and on the other side, torches cast a scarlet haze.

Heat dips down my spine.

I pretend there isn't water beneath the floor.

I pretend Emilia is watching.

Our song begins with the resonant hum of a zither.

Copelan steps out, releasing a trail of sand behind him. He scatters it about in patterns, whorls, matching the tempo as he meanders slowly toward the center of the room—spinning, focused on his task, oblivious to the storm behind him—

The storm that is me.

Once a year, the infamous Brisendali storms from the north invade the Razami desert—angry winds and ice-chilled rain that stir its dunes into a maelstrom of fury.

I pirouette onto the dance floor at the strike of a bayan.

I spill millen like rain. It plumes around me in clouds—a new, deep blue mixture that billows outward, upward. Winds pour into the room, blown by fans brandished by every member of our audience—a gift we left on each seat, with instructions.

Copelan is the desert, the sand that is Razam, and he pivots, sensing my disturbance.

I kick up sand with my feet, sullying it with the rage of a tempest most foul. And though I don't look at Copelan, I feel his approach like a shift in the winds.

The drum slams down in a resounding *wham*.

He shoves me, quick as lightning. I exaggerate the movement, lurching forward before throwing myself back against him. Absorbing it, he bands my waist, tucks his head against my hip. We bend, jump, the momentum hoisting me into the air—

He catches me. Lifts me over him in a wide arc, spins—

Wham.

He tosses me away. By some miracle, I land on my feet.

I whip toward him. Our battle has begun.

Wham.

I run and leap. He catches me around the waist mid-arm. I'm curled in on myself, legs poised off the floor as he spins, both of us releasing our opposing forces—sand versus rain, ferocity versus control. His gold coats my hair, my blue shadows his skin. When my first pouch runs dry, I slip from his hold, ready to escape, but he snatches the sheer fabric of my sleeve and yanks.

It rips free.

Cool air kisses my skin and I'm left in only my low bodice and skirt.

Illian will be furious.

I am furious. At everyone. I ignore the rattle of my bones, the pain shooting fire along my nerves, and throw my fury into my dance.

Wham.

Bounding onto Copelan's shoulders, I burrow my hands into his hair. He bounces us both. I spring into the air, and once more, he cradles me in his arms before swinging me upright, my chest to his, our breath mingling. I wonder if he tastes my rage.

Wham.

I slide down him, slowly, slowly, his hands supporting me. My fingers find his jaw, his neck. The warm, smooth skin along his chest. I smudge the gold there, my hands coated in it.

His pupils dilate as he dips me into a split.

Wham.

I release him and fall backward, spine curved as I touch the ground. He slides over me, covering me with his body. His heart thunders with the bayan, just like mine.

He props himself on his arms, legs lifted in the air, chin just over mine.

His breath is hot on my lips.

We stare at each other.

Wham.

This dance, it feels feverish. I slide out from underneath him, rising. He rises, too, an eagerness to his stance. I raise my leg, poised to dart away. He grabs my foot. Uses it to circle me, rotate me, faster, *faster*, like a hand guiding a wheel while my other foot anchors on the ground.

It's as if I'm flying.

My curls drift around me as if I'm underwater, millen showering from my hands.

And Anton's favor comes to life.

A million raindrops made from light shatter across the walls and floor, little echoes of prisms carefully placed before a glow torch. Even from across the room, I manage to catch his smile, alongside Prince Sundar's.

And Copelan—

He's smiling, too.

Wham.

We are a torrent of rain and wind, sand and clouds.

I lower my foot as the beat changes pace. Copelan pries his fingers into the ribbon around my waist.

Wham.

He twists me around into the crook of his arm.

I fall back, draping across it.

Wham.

Featherlight, he uses the crook of his finger to skim my collarbone. Then it travels lower, gliding a path down the center of my chest—

Wham.

He whisks me up, hand threaded in my hair. Knotted in it.

Wham.

The song comes to a close, the desert's might overcoming the storm, the message I wonder if they'll ascertain. I'm ready to pirouette away, to draw back my force.

But Copelan doesn't release me, his chest heaving. His gaze tracks up my throat, hooks on my lips. And I don't have time to think, to back away, because one minute, he's staring at me, and the next—

He's gripping my neck and pulling my mouth to his.

My surroundings tunnel as his other hand fists my curls, drawing me closer. Waves of dizziness lave over me, from both the built-up tension, the fury—

He breaks away, fast as a snapped sitar string.

Everything goes still.

I don't think I imagine the intake of breath from the crowd or the loud barrage of his heart. It's all I can do to stay upright. My ears ring wildly. And he's gaping at me, his eyes molten.

Time stretches like a wrung-out cloth. I can't tell if he wants to yank me back or toss me away.

Then, as if returning from a trance, he grabs my hand and lifts it, sinking us into a bow.

Claps fill the audience. We break for the exit. But as we reach the divider, I turn back.

I don't see Illian's gaze, the press of his lips, no.

I see only his fist, clenched white at his side.

Back in my room, my hands shake ferociously as I scrub millen from my pores. I want to bury myself in blankets. I don't want to return. Not to mention, my muscles feel as though they've disjointed from my body, and even that doesn't compare to my addled mind.

After our dance, Copelan disappeared without a word. He left me outside the Hall of Thrones, panting, not knowing what to think or how to feel.

I should pretend it never happened. But the sting of it lingers like a barb under my skin. What he did was both a long time coming and something I never thought would happen. Something we both wanted and refused to do, because there was a line. I don't know how it was drawn, but we both felt it, both respected it. Then Copelan blazed right through it as if it were made of wet parchment. Copelan, who lives in constant fear of the Crowns. Copelan who, until recently, never broke the rules.

He smashed his lips to mine in front of the whole Gathering, then fled as if I'd burnt him.

I slide into a simple green gown, its satin grazing my ankles, then coil my hair into a loose chignon before gathering slippers for my throbbing feet.

I cannot have him.

I cannot want him.

He wouldn't want me if he knew my truths. Where I spent the last two years, what I've done, even here. What I still might do. How *angry* I am.

A rough knock rattles my door. Annais, perhaps, returning to assist me.

It isn't Annais who stands at the precipice of my door, but Copelan.

His hair is soaked, his skin scrubbed clean, yet he has the gall to say nothing. To stare, open-mouthed, like he did after that soulsforsaken performance. Anger curls my palms and tightens my fists. Has he come to tell me it was a mistake? Has he come to make it my fault? "What," I bite out, "could you possibly want?"

He lets out a breath, as if he has the right to be angry. But *he* did this to *me*. He smeared our line. "Well?" I hiss.

"I don't know, Vas!" he explodes, stepping toward me. "This is wrong. It's reckless, dangerous, but—" He brackets my face in his hands. "I can't get you out of my head. I can't wash you from my skin."

My throat feels thick as I swallow his words.

I shake my head, because no—I can't start this with him. I can't afford the cost of it. Not with a chance that I'll lose myself and my purpose between touches and silken sheets. "We can't."

He leans his forehead against mine, breathing me in.

I should push him off. But then his hands are once again in my hair, gliding down my aching back, whisper-light caresses like the press of satin. He sets his lips over my eyes, my cheeks. My jaw. "I don't know what to do with you," he says hoarsely, tugging on the ties of my dress. He doesn't feel the way I tremble. "You're too much trouble and yet . . . you, Vasalie, are my shackles. I can't seem to set myself free."

Shackles.

Illian.

I shove him, nearly losing my balance. "Leave," I croak. Illian could come looking for me. He might already be on his way, ready to punish me for Copelan's actions, and if he found him in my room . . . "You must go. You can't be here."

"Vasalie," Copelan says, stepping toward me, but I veer out of his reach.

"I—I can't do this, can't—"

"All right. Okay." His face is red, flushed, and he's looking at me like I slapped him. "I get it. I understand. It will not happen again."

"You don't understand," I try, but his jaw is locked tight as he whips around.

"Copelan," I breathe. "I'm sorry."

He doesn't hear me through the slam of my door.

An hour later, when I return to the Hall of Thrones, claps resound like the snapping of bones. At first, I don't realize it's for me, but then I see Copelan lingering in the center, a forced smile apparent on his lips. He extends an arm in my direction.

I can't get you out of my head. I can't wash you from my skin.

Dread twines through my already nauseated stomach. I shoulder through the crowd. Copelan's indifference cracks as I take his hand, but he fixes it quickly, draping an arm over me. I feel like I could collapse. As usual, adrenaline is the only thing keeping me upright.

Praise soaks over us until we're drenched from it.

Then the shouts begin.

"Are you courting? How long?"

"Kiss her again!"

"A love story in our midst!"

We're just another spectacle, a form of entertainment. Copelan politely tells them we're exhausted, but they grow rowdier, yipping around us like dogs begging for treats.

"Did you meet here?"

"Has he taken your virtue?"

"Give us a spin!" someone yells—a man in a crisp Kasami uniform with medals on his shoulder. Beside him, his partner, another handsome courtier, says, "Dip her!"

The room is a whorl of silk and sound. It's all happening so fast I can't think clearly, let alone respond. But the voices fade when I find King Illian skirting the edge of the crowd.

A dark velvet waistcoat hugs his chest, embroidered with red garnets along the hem. Black opals shine from his rings. He looks like a villain from one of Emilia's fairy tales: dark, sinister, yet surprisingly stoic, any trace of fury carefully veiled. Beside him, Princess Aesir of Brisendale whispers in his ear, but he isn't listening.

He's watching me.

"Please," I say over the furor. "Copelan and I are friends; it was merely part of the show. We're thrilled you enjoyed it."

A disappointed hum settles over the room, but only for a moment. People squeeze in, shoving more questions in our path as we try to escape: how we came up with the dance, what the powder is, who made our outfits. Copelan has the grace to steady me as I sway. "Let's not overwhelm Miss Moran."

Overwhelm is an understatement, when I'd sell my soul if only I could be left to sleep for a year straight.

We almost make it to the exit when Princess Aesir moseys into our path.

Tonight, her ivory locks are gathered to one side, and a red dress splits down to her navel like the cut of an unripened plum. "So then," she muses, a delighted grin spreading her lips, "that means you're free for the taking, no?"

Copelan and I both drop into a bow, after which he cuts me a cool glance. "Indeed, Your Highness."

She twists an errant lock of hair between her fingers. "Perhaps, then, I might steal you away? I have a list of . . . *requests* I'd like to present you."

I ignore the sultry dip in her tone, though my hands itch to pull Copelan away. Even if . . . even if I denied him and would deny him still.

It's selfish. But he's my comfort in this Fates-forsaken place.

It doesn't matter, though, because she's royalty and we are the sand beneath her feet. Neither of us can deny her anything.

"I'd be happy to oblige," Copelan says, but I'm already walking away, pushing through hordes of glittering nobles, my neck damp, my lungs starved for air. I can't seem to pull in a full breath.

The courtiers take notice of me. They grasp at my gown, my waist, my lower arms—a taste, a touch, whatever they can get in passing, bolder than those in Illian's court when he wasn't there to scare them off. Gossip trails my heels as I finally breach the exit, pilfering a glass of water as I go.

Out in the narrow hallway now, my legs turn leaden. I need to sit and rest. To collect myself, or collapse in peace, but my room feels miles away.

The last of my strength falters, my knees ready to fold. I grab for the first door I can find. Underneath, it's dark, so I pray it's empty. Turning the knob carefully, quietly, I slip inside.

Only it isn't a room, but a library. Small, about the length of the dining hall, and twice as ornate. Foiled leather tomes crammed together across mahogany shelves, the ceiling embellished in matching fretwork. At the far end, a circular chaise basks in front of a large hearth that kindles a too-small flame.

And facing those flames is a straight-backed silhouette. In his hand is a silver glass, and he twirls the liquid inside slowly, his face shadowed by the peak of his cap.

I know that cap. The way it creases in the center, curving to a subtle point near the crown of the head.

Fear locks my muscles—and my lungs.

General Stova.

I need to run. To hide. But my feet are like stakes, planted in the ground. Unresponsive. He witnessed my performance. He saw everything.

He saw *me*.

But I remind myself, ardently, that he wouldn't have recognized me. I'm not thirteen anymore.

Except I still feel as small. Smaller, even, than I used to.

Move, I beg myself. It isn't time. I'm not ready. But when he rolls his shoulders, his emblem catching the light, the past flashes before my eyes: a gown, pink as petals; blood, red as rubies. A crack, a cry. Then the sound of Marian choking, the finger-shaped bruises now gracing her neck. My stomach turns to water.

I feel the cold of the glass in my hands. *Break it*, something inside me whispers. *Break it; use it to slit his throat*. He deserves to rot in a cell like I did, yes, but what if I could kill him now? He is alone, vulnerable. It might be my only chance.

A tremor wracks my body.

I try to move but can't. He's too quick, too armed, too strong, and I'm a fool to think I'll ever be able to face him, a fool to assume I'll find the courage I need. *Never*, whispers that dark, familiar voice in my mind.

Any notion of justice or revenge was but a naïve girl's plea.

A shadow crawls along the floor. Another silhouette, tall and slender. I sense the presence hovering behind me, a thing of nightmares. The Fate of Morta, ready to claim me. Because my father will turn around, and he will find me, and she is here, waiting.

He angles his face, firelight teasing his jaw.

The glass slips from my fingers.

A hand snakes out from beside me, catching it before it hits the floor.

Chapter Twenty-One

Illian tucks the glass back in my palm, careful not to let our fingers brush, as always. "Miss Moran, is it? A pleasure to find you here." He tilts his head toward the fireplace, where my father stands. "Say, and who is this? Ah! General, have you met our soloist?"

An unusual panache for him, a cordiality he rarely displays. It would strike me as odd if I weren't struggling to keep my knees from buckling.

Slowly, General Stova angles our way.

The breath turns to sludge in my throat. I wait for the spark of recognition in his eyes, the moment his cool composure turns to fire.

But he merely gives me a dismissive once-over before bowing his head. "A pleasure, Your Majesty. Miss Moran. Pardon, but I must return to the party. My king awaits."

Hesitant relief tempts me to sag. He didn't recognize me; my disguise is intact.

"Do enjoy the party," Illian says, succeeding in emptying the room—his plan, no doubt.

My father leaves me alone with Illian.

I focus on the flames before me.

"You're shaking."

For the first time, his presence doesn't scare me as much as it should.

I release a trembling exhale, easing my grip on the glass. "A long performance. I'm tired." Artlessly, I dip into a half-hearted bow, then stride away as if he'd dismissed me, knowing, too, that he won't let me go.

"Vasalie."

I halt before the door.

He moves behind me, my phantom with chains. "I do hope you aren't getting attached."

Copelan. I can't let his name affect me here, when so much as a blink might turn Illian loose. I level my chin, hold fast to a mask of vacuity. "It was an act, meant for the performance." But the words feel brittle on my tongue.

A soft laugh escapes him. "Oh no, Vasalie, not him. You can keep your pup for now," he says over my shoulder. "If you manage to hang on to him, that is."

My heart lurches, once, twice.

"The Head of Staff," he says. "He's been rather accommodating so far, no?"

The word *no* forms on my lips. I won't hurt Laurent.

"A shame such kindness will be his downfall," Illian says.

Downfall? I don't stop to think. "Not him. Whatever it is, please, there must be another way—"

"You had to know it was coming."

"No," I repeat, pulse ripping through my veins. "Your Majesty, I can't. I won't do it."

Illian rounds in front of me, drawing so close I have to lean back to avoid brushing against him. So close I can see his lashes, the spokes of shadow they cast onto his cheeks.

"Don't you know," he hisses, "that you breathe because I allow it?" My chest is tight, aching with panic. He fans a breath across my lips. "Oh, Vasalie, do not force me to leave you in the dark once more."

Darkness, laughing.

Shadows, mocking.

Steel, cutting, digging, bruising.

My puppet strings go taut.

What a fool I was for thinking he wouldn't send me back so soon, that I might be sacrosanct, too valuable for him to discard. But here, under his shadow, the fumes of his breath, I feel it.

You breathe because I allow it.

How right he is.

If I wish to leave here alive, if I want to enact vengeance and reclaim my life, the life my father owes me, I cannot pull against my chains.

My eyes burn with my feeble response. "What do you need me to do?"

A serpent's smirk lifts the edge of his lips, and he whispers my next task into my ear, soft as a lover's caress.

My feet are heavy as stones. A cool, nighttime wind soughs past windows, loud as a scream. It numbs my cheeks, my fingers. I wish it would numb my heart.

With Illian close on my heels, I emerge once more into the Hall of Thrones, this time under the gilded architrave, the doors slung open to reveal the soirée beyond. But I feel his departure a moment later, just as I feel the pair of eyes that settle on me.

Not for the first time, Anton scrutinizes me with a gaze that sees too much. Even as courtiers congregate around him, vying for his attention.

Tonight, he is adorned in his usual frippery: a dark, velvet jerkin with mauve shoulder seams that arc like scythes, stacks of rings banding his fingers. Even the boots that reach up past his knees are embellished with threads of red and gold.

To his right, Gustav clanks his chalice with a woman in an intricately laced indigo gown that lays beautifully over her deep, amber-toned skin. "Aha! You see, Your Majesty; Lady Reila agrees." Grinning broadly, his gaze travels over his shoulder.

And catches sight of me.

"Miss Moran!" he shouts, ambling over. "How are you? You look well. And that performance! Once again, you have deprived us of words."

I hope my smile doesn't look strained. "I'm relieved to see that you're well," I tell him, and mean it.

He links his arm with mine, drawing me toward Anton and his company. "Come, let me introduce you around . . ."

"Oh, no—" I attempt, but he insists, unencumbered in his joy. My eyes skip around nervously. There's still no sign of Laurent, and my signal has not yet occurred. Even so, nerves stir in my chest like a swarm of wasps. It takes all my strength to stay upright, to not puke on my gown.

Inhale, exhale—I force the commands onto my body.

The light from our performance is unchanged; we remain bruised in shadow, a blue like that of the sea at dusk, while gold falls softly onto clusters of guests now indulging in a dance. It's there that I see Copelan, effortlessly guiding the princess into a waltz, the crowd forming a radius around them.

But there's no room in me left to care, so I force my gaze away.

"Miss Moran," Anton says by way of greeting, and only then do I realize I've missed the rest of Gustav's introductions. I sink into a bow, but Anton's already strolling off, a new escort on his arm, while Gustav and his friends pepper me with questions about the dance, our inspiration. Answers fall from my lips, but I barely consider them.

I find myself looking for Anton again, and too easily, I find him. He's not far, lingering by a pillar near Prince Sundar, who illustrates some tale or other before his brothers and the queen. Anton's escort laughs and whispers in his ear, but he merely peers off in the distance, seemingly at nothing.

But he feels my stare, his eyes gliding toward mine.

It's then that I notice just how tight his jaw is, how different he seems. How disturbed. Gone is the lazy grin. Gone is the spark in those dancing, viridescent eyes, and in its place, there's something dark, born of shadows. I can almost feel it from here.

Does he sense what I'm about to do?

In this moment, my instincts fall away, and I want him to. I don't care if he's good or not, I care only that he opposes Illian.

I want him to stop me.

Save me.

See me.

Gustav notices me staring and squeezes my arm gently. "It isn't you."

"Pardon?"

"His mood."

I pause, swinging my attention back to Gustav. "Is something wrong?"

He hesitates, then tugs me a few feet from his group. "Do you believe in prophecy, Vasalie?"

Emilia had—though only if they had been confirmed. And there hasn't been a confirmed prophecy in over a hundred years. Then I recall the prophets Laurent spoke of, the ones taken captive, and realization dawns. They must have found them. "There's been a prophecy. A confirmed one. Hasn't there?"

He nods solemnly. "Indeed, and it's rumored that—"

"Gustav," Anton murmurs, approaching. "Not here."

And I no longer believe Gustav; now that Anton's here, it's clear I'm the source of his glowering discontent.

His court, some of whom had drifted casually away, inch back when they notice the presence of their king. Gustav moves the conversation away from the prophecy, instead telling tales of Eremis's life. The lovers he took, the children he sired, the treasure he hid—a pietersite gem from Morta's Lair, though some argue it was her hardened heart. Half the room mills around us now, and I wrap my arms around myself, growing increasingly uncomfortable—

especially with the weight of my task pushing down on my shoulders.

My stomach plummets like a stone in water when the general appears.

I shuffle back, back, back until I'm deeper in shadow, though it can't hide me for long.

A tip to the general was all it took, Illian had told me. A tip to set the general on Gustav's tail, to announce the poisoning to the rest of the Gathering right when Illian wished it to be known.

I don't see Laurent yet, and I pray to anyone who will listen that he's far away.

Fast as a whip, my father seizes Gustav's arm and shoves up his sleeve, examining the swath of skin. "Who allowed this man entrance into the Hall of Thrones?" he clamors.

Anton doesn't miss a beat. "General, kindly remove your hand from my subject."

My father, undeterred, brandishes Gustav's arm high, letting us see for ourselves. "This," he shouts. "The yellow splotches here are symptoms of bellamira fever, brought about from a recent poisoning. Your Majesty, King Anton, am I wrong?"

Splotches. Like the ones I have. Sallow in tone, though my cosmetics cover them. Gustav is not so lucky.

Murmurs arise, the packed array now backing off, opening a spacious ring around Gustav and King Anton.

All over, I begin to tremble.

At a mere lift of Anton's hand, the bustle silences. "I did not wish to raise alarm until we knew more," he says coolly. "Lord Bayard was indeed poisoned, though as you can see, he is quite well. Our investigation was better orchestrated in private. My physicians have alleviated any concerns of contagion, so you need not be worried—"

"You mean to tell us there was a poisoning here at the Gathering, and you kept it a secret?" King Rurik pushes through the horde. "Anton, you've put us all in danger."

A deep chuckle slithers from the shadows. "I shouldn't be surprised to find you've incited such chaos in my absence," King Estienne says, his dark form propped against a column to my right. "It's so like you."

"Be that as it may," Anton responds, "everything is quite under control." But the uproar has begun, voices competing against one another.

"Your Majesty, how could you have kept this from us?"

"How can we feel safe here?"

Prince Raiden, the young prince of Zar, stalks over, his brown skin almost glowing in his silver jacket. "The culprit," he says. "Have you detained them?"

Illian selects this moment to slink forward. "Please," he calls over the chaos. "Calm yourselves." The commotion dies down, a temporary hush. He rests a hand on Anton's shoulder. "My little brother has the best intentions, I am certain. Let us allow him the chance to speak. Please, Anton, tell us what happened, from the beginning."

Anton, unamused by Illian's act, clasps his hands together behind his back, surprisingly stoic amid the turmoil. He recounts the night of the banquet, including the meal that was served, the timing of events, and lastly, the guests in attendance.

He does not mention me.

"Just to confirm, Your Majesty," my father cuts in, "you said it was your most trusted nobles alongside the Razami court, yes? Would you vouch, then, on your honor as a Miridranian Crown, for every attendant that night?"

I hold my breath, fingers carving into my palms. My father is trying to get Anton to admit he doubts either his own court or Razam's.

But it was me.

Me.

Anton senses the trap. "Every last one, General."

I understand why he can't hesitate. If he questioned them, it could lead to accusations against Razam.

Then it hits me, Illian's intent. *Razam.*

Laurent believes Illian is funding King Rurik's future war against Razam, and I wonder if this is their first move. The first knight slid in a board of chess, because if they can incriminate Razam before the Crowns, they can get support. Allies. More funding. I flick my gaze toward King Rurik. His pale features are contorted, wrought with rage.

An act. A role, like the one my father plays now.

"Right then," my father says, circling Anton as if he can make him prey. "If it was the wine that was poisoned, let us examine the wine itself. Where did it come from? Was it grown here? An import? A gift from Her Grace?"

Again, the insinuation is clear, but Anton is swift. "Every ounce of food and drink brought inside these halls is examined first and accounted for. Her Grace brought no wine with her. Check the records yourself if you wish to confirm it. In fact, the contaminated bottle was brought in by Lord Bayard himself."

Out of the corner of my eye, I notice Prince Sundar standing protectively in front of his mother, while Gustav looks like he's seconds from fainting.

"Then let us focus on the sequence of events," my father says. "Was it or was it not served from a fresh decanter?"

"It was," Anton says, the first hint of annoyance slipping through. In any other case, a general would never be permitted to question a king, but in the presence of other royals, he has no choice but to pacify them and respond.

A trap, so perfectly set.

"Then let the Head of Staff answer for this."

For one heart-seizing moment, I think—hope—Laurent might have retired early. That he might be far enough away. But when he shoulders through an assemblage of courtiers, warm torchlight falling across the planes of his cheeks, my eyes fall shut.

Don't speak, I silently beg him.

"Your Majesties," Laurent addresses both Illian and Anton, bowing stiffly, an arm reverently tucked against his ribs. "The wine served that evening was stored in King Anton's cellar. As previously stated, it was from Lord Bayard's personal collection."

"Then it's simple," my father says. "One of your staff is to blame. Whoever opened and poured the bottle into the decanter—which would have been done in the cellar itself—would have ample opportunity to slip bellamira inside without being seen."

"With all due respect, General, no one in my kitchen would dare." Laurent says it ardently, perhaps too much so, and I recall his vow to always protect his staff. "No one would have motive for such an act."

Just then, another figure is dragged into the room.

Air rushes through my ears.

"The cellar wench, Majesties," says a guard, his hand latched around Marian's upper arm. He releases her beside Laurent. "She would have poured the wine."

I freeze. Laurent's eyes widen in horror. Marian, somehow composed, rights herself then bows.

"The Crowns are constantly burdened by threats," says the general, striding around them with slow, deliberate steps. "Perhaps she was paid off. An ample sum for a quick job. The motive matters not."

"With respect, I beg to differ," Laurent says. "Every member of our staff comes with documentation, references. Familial records." Like the ones Illian forged for me. "No one here would commit such treason, not when it would put their family at risk. I trust my staff with my life."

He's trying to keep the speculation, the focus, off her.

"Is that so?" My father narrows the space between himself and Laurent—an attempt to intimidate, no doubt, though Laurent stands tall. "Are you telling me you have never made an exception? Not even, say, for a friend?"

My knees beg to buckle. I should have seen it coming.

Illian discovered Marian. Is this, in part, revenge against her for denying him? Or is this mere happenstance, because Laurent put her in charge of the cellars to guard the tunnel access?

In which case, if Illian did not know about Marian before, he certainly will now.

Laurent works his jaw. "I will not be subject to baseless accusations, nor will my staff."

"You tread a dangerous ground without proof, General," Anton warns, his eyes flashing, and I glimpse the storm now stirring within, an undercurrent of char and smoke. "I will tolerate your interrogations no longer. The harm was contained to my court, and as such, it falls under my rule."

A valiant effort, but my father won't let this go, and neither will Illian, who now watches me. He nods, the slightest bump of his chin. Silently, I beg him to reconsider, but it's as futile as blowing a breath against the wind.

He raises his hand, ceasing the dialogue. The little food I managed to eat rises in my stomach.

"Miss Moran, is it?" Illian steps toward me, black curls shining like the leather of his boots. "You look ill, my dear. Do you have something you want to tell us?"

Harden your heart, I tell myself. I wish I could rip it from my chest.

He has no room for patience. "Miss Moran?" he urges.

Don't force me to leave you in the dark once more.

I feel the calluses on my skin, the iron around my wrists. I hear the crack of Emilia's bones over dust and stone. I remember how it felt to run after that, what it was like to leave her all alone.

My feet step forward, as if on their own accord.

"Vasalie?" I hear Laurent say.

My eyes burn. The floor feels like sand, sinking beneath me. King Illian presses, "Miss Moran, you have nothing to fear. Please speak whatever is on your mind." Two of his guards move pointedly behind him.

I see it for the warning it is. I try anything, and they will arrest me. Illian will send for Lord Sarden's body, and my life will be over, my hope for justice gone.

Harden.

Stone.

I let my heart drop low, lower, until it falls through the glass floor to sink into the watery depths below.

"I have come to know the Head of Staff," I hear myself say. A hot tear glides down my cheek. I feel it track a line from my jaw to my neck, pooling on my clavicle. "I've come to know how k-kind he is. How generous—" Illian clears his throat. I drag my eyes away from Laurent, unable to watch him when I say my next words. "But the goodness in his heart lends itself to danger. He—" I cough, the words thick in my throat. My cheeks are soaked now. "To help a friend . . ." I omit Marian's name; it wasn't a part of the deal besides . . . "Laurent confessed to me that he once forged documents. There are indeed staff members here without references."

I try not to look at Laurent.

I try, and fail. When my eyes slip his way, I find him watching me with aching betrayal that threatens to steal the last of my strength.

"Staff without references?" King Rurik yells.

"If the Head of Staff allowed unregistered workers into this palace, any one of them could be guilty, including this so-called cellar maiden. In fact, they could both be conspirators!" the general shouts with a zeal I remember. Like when he roared my name, the echo following me through the garden and out the front gates, where I'd taken refuge in a ditch canopied by vines until I could escape under the cover of night, Emilia's ring in my palm.

"Anton, you *must* do something!" King Rurik demands. It almost looks like his glass eye could pop out of his skull. "Is he not a subject of yours? Will you treat our safety so callously?"

"He should be in irons!" says someone else—the Sovereign Ruler of Serai, I think. My head spins. The air grows thin.

"What an embarrassment, Anton," I hear King Estienne mutter. "I expected more of you, truly."

"This is your territory, brother," Illian says. "We defer to your punishment, but do not be so foolish as to do nothing."

Anton steps forward, assessing the room in a cold sweep. Then something like pained resignation weighs in his eyes, and he signals for his guards. "I am sorry, Laurent Achea," he says. "In light of these accusations, you are henceforth stripped of your position and will be escorted from the isle. Until we uncover the truth, you will be held by my guard in the dungeons of Philam. As will this cellar maiden," he says. "She will likewise be held and subject to thorough interrogations, along with anyone else on staff that evening."

I cover my mouth, holding back sobs.

"If any of you are found guilty of these charges," Anton continues, "if you're found to have conspired against my court or anyone at this Gathering, the punishment for such crimes will be your life."

And if I know Illian, he'll make it so. I wouldn't put it past him to force a confession. To somehow frame both of them for conspiring with Razam.

"Meanwhile," Anton says, "we will confirm documentation for every staff member here, starting now."

Don't worry about Annais, Illian had told me. *I have plans for her.*

Plans.

My eyes track Laurent's once more. I expect him to plead for mercy, or at least expose me in return. He could tell the court about Annais. He could tell them what I did, and he *should*.

Instead, he looks tired. Face wan, eyes heavy and sad. Illian was correct when he said that Laurent is too loyal, too kind. So he does nothing, not even as guards shackle his hands.

Not even as they haul him away.

My father is another story. His proud eyes walk a slow perusal across the commotion he's stirred. He performed his part, whether he knows all the acts to this play. He does not care if there's truth to his accusations. All he wants is war and glory, to impress his king, and it doesn't matter who he tramples to get what he wants. He's benefitting from hurting others.

And I am *just like him.*

Emilia, I had asked her once. *If you don't love him, why do you stay?*

It was after a fight. My father had returned from a night with the king, so inebriated he couldn't land one foot in front of the other. It prompted him to pick a fight with us, then, spouting off nonsensical words I couldn't understand. Emilia had grabbed me and my coat, shoved us both into a carriage, and steered us to a late-night tavern. It was there that I found out that she had been in love with someone else, but when my father set his sights on her, he cornered her backstage at one of her shows. They were caught in what looked like a compromising position, effectively ruining their reputation—unless they wed.

I stay, she said that night, *because I love you.*

But what if I turn into him? I'd asked.

She'd cradled my tiny hands in hers. *Darling girl, the choice will always be yours. Refuse to be compliant; refuse to let him mold you into himself. No one dictates who you are but you.*

The choice, she had said, *will always be yours.*

Her words hit me like an axe against wood, and my resolve splinters apart. I chose it. I'm reaping the benefits of hurting Laurent. Whatever my reason—justice, revenge, freedom—it doesn't matter; I will walk free from this Gathering, and he will not.

Emilia would be ashamed. She would tell me to find another way, because the choice will always be mine. Because she never sought revenge for the life she lost, the love she lost, when she was forced into being a bride. She owed me nothing and yet she stayed. And when it mattered, she stood on the line for me instead of protecting herself.

She faced him down.

She defended me.

I wish she hadn't.

An evening storm rages across sky and sea.

I lean over my windowsill, my skirt fluttering in the breeze, my eyes trailing over a dark ripple of clouds. The wind dries my tears, but my heart is soaked.

I'm *drowning*.

The choice will always be yours, Emilia had told me, but she didn't understand. I am the product of lust and greed. I am the result of lies and unchecked power. Darkness choked me until it became my air.

"I didn't have a choice!" I scream. "Because I am alone and no one can save me! You tried; I know that, but you failed, and this—*this* is what I have become!" A squall rips through my voice until it's nothing but the cry of wind. Rain beats down now, slapping my cheeks.

And the lie is sour on my tongue. Because she did save me. And because no matter how I try to convince myself otherwise, I did have a choice.

I *still* have a choice.

I can't live with myself knowing I've failed Emilia again. Because the definition of failure has changed. It means forgetting everything she taught me, everything she sacrificed. The person she wanted me to become. The person she tried to protect me from becoming.

All this time, I've been getting it wrong. I know what Emilia would do because she did it for me.

I shuck off my costume, chuck the jewels from my hair. I pull on my dark leggings, and slip a matching tunic on top. I can't help Laurent or Marian on my own, but there's someone who can. Someone who seems to despise Illian as much as I do, and that I can use to my advantage.

Because he just might listen to me.

Chapter Twenty-Two

I tread soundlessly through the halls.

Pain is a constant, but determination pushes my feet onward. I find the cellar, plunge my hands into the crevice behind that bottle of wine, and yank the lever just as Marian showed me.

Her clock, like Laurent's, is ticking away.

The tunnels blast cool air against my face, and I move as fast as my body allows, ignoring the pain digging deep into my bones. I pass room after room, mosaic after mosaic. *Keep going. Don't stop.*

Different courts hold private after-parties, their carousing echoing through the glass and down the tunnel walls. The palace won't sleep for a long time yet. The havoc from earlier was hardly a disruption.

According to Laurent, only Anton and his most trusted know these passageways. I'm relying on it. And if I'm caught, I suppose I'll find out just how badly Illian needs me, or if I really am no more than a button on his doublet, showy but easily replaced.

Dizziness sways both my vision and my steps by the time I reach the eastern wing. Cold clambers through me, icing my very bones. But it isn't much farther. Anton's chambers are after Illian's, so I just need to follow the outer curve.

Only, as I near Illian's corridor, I can't resist a peek. Is he celebrating his victory? Conspiring?

I let myself approach the glass above his hearth and peer inside.

He's still awake, his quill fluttering across parchment, letters fanning across his desk. He pauses, blows on the ink, then compares it carefully to another letter.

Almost as if he's attempting to write in someone else's hand.

Satisfied, he cracks open a small leather box, retrieving the wax seal inside. I'm too far to make out the details, but not so far that I can't tell the seal he holds is not his own. Because I've watched him sink his fat golden ring into blood-red wax to seal hundreds of letters.

I tuck away the information, about to leave when a voice announces, "Your Majesty, your guests have arrived."

King Illian rises from his seat, stretching leisurely. He scoops the letters into a drawer before arranging himself on a chaise, permitting someone entrance. That ominous, tapered glass chandelier flicks razor-sharp shadows along his face. Behind him, the door is ajar, revealing a luxurious four-poster bed.

Two women enter.

The first is older, severe, her chamomile hair twisted into a tight crown, a modest red garb clinging to her curves. After a reverent bow, she turns, offering both Illian and me a clear view of the second.

My breath hitches in my throat so fast I almost choke. I lend my weight to a jutting stone so that I don't fall. Surely my eyes are deceiving me. Surely, because . . . it couldn't be . . . I pinch my cheeks, but I am horrifically, indisputably awake.

The girl sashays forward, tossing her curls—curls that look so much like my own. Lips, painted like my own. Eyes, winged with kohl, just like mine.

Nausea bubbles up, lurching against my ribs.

Because she's wearing my dress. The very costume I'd sewn myself with Annais's help and worn mere hours ago.

Had Annais retrieved it? Brought it to this woman? Is this girl meant to take my place? But I completed my task; I did what Illian wanted.

No, she couldn't replace me. As much as we resemble each other, her face is rounder, her chin flatter. And she stands a little too upright; someone would notice. Copelan would never allow her to perform in my place.

I don't understand. Or maybe I don't want to.

Illian circles her like a vulture, chin propped on his hand. A curt nod, and he dismisses the older woman along with his guards.

Leave now, I beg myself. I don't want to see this. Yet I can't force myself away.

I need to know.

Illian comes to stand behind her, whispering something I can't hear. She looks up, just as he gathers her curls in one hand, and—

Yanks her head back.

Drags his lips across her throat.

Unhooks the skirt.

Breathes my name.

I jerk away and cover my mouth, swallowing a pool of hot, burning bile. My tongue feels like ash in my mouth.

I wish I hadn't come here.

I wish I hadn't seen.

All of this, I had known, deep down. I had seen the lust in his eyes. But I hadn't known how far he'd taken it.

How many look-alikes has he requested? How many nights has he pretended it was me?

And by the Fates, why not just summon *me*? Why take pains to have someone dress like me when I am at his beck and call? My head whirls, the ground beneath me pulsing. Every inch of me trembles.

I shake myself. I have a purpose, and I'm wasting precious minutes. Hugging the wall, I skirt toward my destination: King Anton's wing. It isn't much farther. If I could find the blue light, that strange room—

A hand snatches my arm.

I shriek, but another covers my mouth. I'm yanked backward and pressed against a solid form, arms pulled tight against me—

"These halls are not soundproof," my captor says into my ear, "so do try not to scream." I attempt to wriggle free, but he tightens his hold. The heavy scent of bergamot fills my nose. "If you promise to be calm, I will release you."

I nod, stifling a whimper, and something clicks onto my wrists. I'm released with a shove. I spin on unsteady feet.

The King of the East stares back at me, jaw working. I almost don't recognize him in the dark. Like me, he's clothed in black, a hood dipping over his forehead, but his sharp green eyes spear through the shadows. "Of anyone I expected to find in my tunnels, my brother's pet is the last."

A mix of fear and fury clogs my breath. "I'm no one's pet," I hiss, writhing to get my arms free, but he's fettered them behind me with irons. Irons, just like in my cell—

"And yet he holds your reins." Anton drags me by my upper arm so fast I can barely keep up, then pushes me into a small alcove, far from any mosaics or windows. Here, it's even darker, and all I see are the whites of his eyes. "What is he paying you? What reward is worth two people's lives?" He practically spits the words.

I press back against the wall. He's blocking me in the crevice; I can't escape.

He could have me killed. He could end it here and now. No one would know.

"Tell me," Anton pushes. "Is his bed worth it? Do you really believe the promises he pants to you in the night?" He tightens his grip on my arm. "I suspected, but I didn't want to believe it. My suspicions were confirmed the moment I saw his face during that *dance* of yours. Really, you and your Master Reveler should know Illian doesn't share his harlots."

His words leech the color from my skin. "I am *not* his harlot!"

Anton's hand snakes forward, covering my mouth again. "What

did I tell you about shouting?" His scent fills my nose, thick like incense. I breathe hot air against the palm of his hand, a half second from sinking my teeth into his flesh, king or not. I came to clear Laurent's name and ask for his help, but here he is, accusing me of *this*.

"Lust is, quite frankly, the most visible quality on a man, Miss Moran. Right next to obsession," he says, and hot tears scald the backs of my eyes. I try to speak, but his palm clamps against my mouth. When he releases it enough for me to talk, he doesn't back away, doesn't even give me room to breathe.

"So you condemn me because of *his* lust?" I manage, an erratic beat pounding through my veins. So typical of a man to think such a thing.

I hate him. I *hate* him.

"It adds to the evidence stacked against you," he returns. "Let's recount, shall we? First, you pull a rather dangerous stunt to nab my attention that first night. I welcome you to my banquet, offer you a night of rest, merriment, and—better—a safe place to talk. My friends welcome you; we treat you like one of our own. And when my closest friend collapses, you happen to be right beside him. Do you expect me to believe it was a coincidence? Then—"

"I know, but I came here to—"

"—*then,* you sidle up to my Head of Staff, learn his secrets, and betray him before the whole of the Gathering. Do you realize who you put at risk? The cellar maiden he helped works for *me*. What a coincidence," he spits, "that she's someone my brother begrudges. I approved the forging of her documents to keep her safe. Did you really think any happenings in this palace get past me?"

He must not know about Annais; Laurent must have kept my secret, even from his king. I open my mouth, but Anton barges on. "While I entrusted the secret of my passageways to Mr. Achea to use at his discretion, I am hard-pressed to believe he had a good reason to allow you inside. Does my brother know?" A breathy laugh. "Of course he knows." I try to squeeze a word in, but still he barrels on. "And to think I liked you. I even second-guessed myself. Tell me, does my brother wait for you in his bed as we speak?"

All rational thought flies from my mind. "If that is what you think," I croak, "go and look. See for yourself what he's doing *right now*."

He brushes me off. "Catching you here is all the proof I need."

I glower at him, the threat of tears glazing my eyes. "Coward."

He scrutinizes me, a second ticking by before making up his mind. Capturing my arm again, he ferries me along with him, and when we reach the mosaic, I turn my head. I can't look.

But I watch Anton as he peers inside.

For a moment, he stares blankly, and I fear Illian and the girl have left. But then his features slacken, his face turning ashen even in the low light. He swallows visibly, and his eyes slide back to mine.

"I have never gone to his bed," I breathe. "Nothing would ever convince me to."

Maybe I would have years ago if he had asked. I might have thanked him for it, might've felt compelled. A part of me had been infatuated with him.

But that part of me is dead.

Anton drags a hand over his mouth, then breathes a sigh. "Is he aware of your whereabouts right now? Tell me the truth."

"I have not told him about the tunnels," I say, "nor do I plan to."

He regards me with such a probing intensity that I feel as if he's making geometry of me, measuring each response. For him, it's nothing new.

Then he picks up my wrist and slides a key into my shackles. As they fall off, he says, "Follow me. And please, don't try to run."

The teacup quivers in my hand.

It's an effervescent floral blend made from a basilica bloom, or so a servant told me, known for its revitalizing properties. Even so, the mere sip I took sends it back up my throat in an embarrassing display, my stomach whirling with nerves while I wait awkwardly on a divan in Anton's antechamber. It's a spacious room awash in color—emerald curtains, ultramarine pillows tasseled in carmine. A plush, vibrant rug. Dichroic, cathedral windows reveal a granulated, prismatic moon. But even the ceiling, with its azure glasswork, is not a reprieve from my addled mind.

He knows I work for Illian.

After fetching himself a drink and muttering something to someone outside the door, he sinks onto the cushion next to me, unabashed at our proximity. Propping an ankle on his knee, he swirls the liquid in his glass with steady hands. He is the Anton I recognize now, all confidence and ease.

He still hasn't said a word about what he saw, though.

"Tell me why you were in my tunnels."

I breathe through my nose and exhale slowly, summoning any ounce of courage I can muster. "I came to plead on Laurent's and Marian's behalf." I hate the tremor in my voice, hate the way it shakes.

"To what end? Did you not stand before every Crown and condemn them? The damage is done, Miss Moran."

"They're innocent," I say, resisting the urge to scoot away from him. "You—you have to know that."

"And what proof do you have?" His eyes track my arms as I hug my own stomach.

He already senses the truth, but he wants me to admit it. I'd known I'd have to give it to him when I'd sought him out, but even so, fear numbs my tongue. My father deserves a knife in the chest, but I won't be the wielder of that blade should I admit to poisoning Gustav. I will never have justice or revenge, much less my freedom.

But that freedom, if I managed it, would be haunted by the ghosts of those I hurt. I cannot shove them in the closet of my mind and forget them. I tried that with Emilia. It didn't work.

"Miss Moran."

I squeeze my eyes shut, forcing an inhale. This—it's the moment I lose everything. He will throw me in his dungeon and forget me, or take what little life I have left.

The truth leaves my lips in a broken, defeated whisper. "I am your poisoner."

Agonizing seconds pass, and Anton says nothing.

I glance up to find him skating a thumb across his bottom lip. "My brother."

My gaze falls, my silence damning enough.

"Would you be willing to testify to clear their names?"

For you, Emilia. It's all I have left to give. "I would."

"You can guess the consequences," Anton says, leaning forward. "Even then? Do I have your word?"

"Yes, but they might not believe me." Illian will expose my time in prison for a murder he will make them believe I committed, and my admission will mean nothing. "I have a past in West Miridran, and he will make it known."

"My brother's hold over you," Anton mumbles, sucking on his teeth. "What has he promised you in return?"

The lump in my throat is like a rock. Still, I push it down, forcing out my rasp of an answer. "My life, Your Majesty. My exoneration."

My gaze dips, catching my reflection in the surface of my tea. Disgusted, I set down the saucer before tucking my hands in my lap. Anton is silent, the seconds stretching between us.

"My brother's plans," he says finally. "What do you know of them?"

"Nothing. He gives me an order and I obey."

I steel myself, waiting for him to call his guards, signal my arrest. I await the clamp of steel on my wrists.

"Vasalie," he says, and I lift my gaze. "I am not going to have you testify before the Crowns. You are right, but whatever your past, it would not matter. My brother would have you slain before you stepped forward."

"If I do nothing," I say, heart careening, "Laurent and Marian won't be absolved. They won't be set free . . ."

A smirk presses on the corner of Anton's lips. He eases back in his seat, sliding an arm across the back of the chaise, looking far too at ease. "A good thing I've taken care of them, then."

"You—what?"

He squints out the window, then holds up his fingers, ticking them off. "In an hour, two at most, a well-paid mercenary will conveniently attack the prison cart in Philam and set them free. They will be directed to a personal escort, who will safeguard them both."

So many words and emotions tangle together in my chest, and all I can manage is a scratchy "Thank you."

It was desperation that brought me here. Desperation—and the small thread of hope that he disliked his brother enough, that he was angry enough about what just happened, at the audacity of the general, that he would be willing to help them. The relief is like a breath of fresh air.

"Laurent is far too valuable, as is Marian. They will continue to work for me back in East Miridran. We will simply have to be more discreet for now. As for you," he says then, and my spine straightens, "you have betrayed my trust and the trust of my friends. Not to mention the whole of the Gathering."

I can't help but drop his gaze.

"But you came to me, willing to take their place. For that, you have also earned my respect."

My head pops up at that. But I dig my hands into my cloak.

I do not deserve respect when I was only attempting to clean up the mess *I* made.

"I don't understand," I whisper. "What will you do with me?"

"Nothing, at the moment."

I blink at him. "You're letting me go? After what I admitted?"

"Ah, you mean your actions at my banquet, where you consumed half the poison yourself? One could say it was an effort to exculpate yourself." He leans in, holding my gaze. "Or one could say you saved his life."

"I still hurt him. And I will hurt others if you don't arrest me. I could do something worse."

"So help me," he says. "When my brother gives you a task, tell me. And when this is over, Miss Moran, I will find a way to help you in return."

Help. He would help me? My heart constricts as hope inches in. Part of me wants to break down and tell him everything. Who I am, where I came from. Everything I've seen so far. The murder Illian would say I committed. But if Anton knew that, and if he didn't believe my claim to innocence . . . I hug my arms around myself.

And then I remember that the word of a Crown means nothing at all. But if Anton *is* letting me go . . .

I could still avenge Emilia and expose my father when it's all over.

I run my nails along the inside of my palm. All that matters is that I did what I came to do. Laurent is safe, and so is Marian.

"Something is happening, Miss Moran. Can't you feel it?" Anton says. "It's like a current under the island, slowly sifting the sand from beneath our feet. Gustav spoke of a prophecy earlier tonight. Do you remember?"

"You stopped him from telling me what it was."

Rightly so, perhaps. He had just realized I was working for Illian.

He procures a piece of parchment from the folds of his cloak, worrying it between the pads of his fingers. "The elder prophets of Mirin sought a meeting with the Syndicate, then went missing rather conveniently," he says. "Fortunately, one of my men attained the message they were trying to relay before my brother abducted them. He was detained as well but managed to escape. And he claims to have seen a tendril of fire above the mouth of the one who spoke it."

He places the parchment in my lap.

Laurent had mentioned the prophets and their capture, but I was so distracted that I had forgotten until Gustav warned of a prophecy—the first in so long. And the fire ...

It means it's confirmed—a true message from the Fates, if I dare believe it. I unfurl the paper in my hands, a peculiar darkness settling in my chest when I read the words.

From Beauty foretold, a trap unfolds,
A return to the living, a plight of souls,
Eyes of shadows, glazed like mist,
Whose touch will kill, and lips will kiss,
Consumed by darkness, His heart a snare,
Those around Him will remain unaware.

I pause, glancing up. Anton's lips are a tight, thin line. He motions for me to keep reading.

Beware, beware, His time is near,
Through one of three sons, He shall appear,
A jewel in His palm, a path divine,
With the Fate of Morta, He will align,
When Crowns divide, and nations collide,
Blood will run, high as tides.

Ice slips up my spine; even my bones grow cold. Beside me, Anton shifts closer. "Back to the top," he says, pointing at the parchment, a sweep of hair falling across his cheek. "Beauty foretold. A return to the living."

He tilts his head at me, expectant.

My voice feels distant as I say, "Eremis."

"Gustav believes it will be Eremis's soul corrupted by the Fate of Morta, sent to carry out her wishes, while others in my council think it will be a new Eremis, a different spirit darkened by Morta's touch." He jerks his chin. "What else?"

My throat bobs. I trace my thumb along the parchment.

"Beware, beware, His time is near," I read aloud. "Through one of three sons, He will appear."

One of three sons.

One of three *brothers*.

Again, I meet Anton's gaze. He sips from his glass, assessing me over the rim. *Who is it, Vasalie?* he seems to ask.

You, I want to say. A return to the living? I know the rumors; they say he, too, cheated death. And there's his oldest brother. I think of Estienne's cruelty, the *drip drip drip* of vengeance.

But I know it isn't Anton or Estienne, because one line stares back at me, stark as a full, unfazed moon.

A jewel in His palm.

The jewel is me. *I* am the Jewel of Illian's court. *I* am held within his palm. He is my prison. Should he close his fingers and squeeze, I would crack in two.

The prophets he captured prove it further. Why else would Illian kidnap them? Why keep the truth from his own brothers? He heard the prophecy, saw the flame, and knew it was about him. Then I remember something else: Morta's statues. There are hundreds of them, maybe thousands. They haunt Illian's palace as if it were a graveyard.

But this assumes I believe the prophecy, or the man who shares it with me. Believing in anything feels like offering something I'm not ready to give.

And yet that line, the jewel it refers to . . .

There are coincidences, Emilia had said when I asked her how she knew where to put her faith. *Then there are revelations that hit you so hard they leave a dent on your soul. Those are truths, my love.*

So I speak my truth. "Illian serves the Fate of Morta."

"If he doesn't yet, I suspect he will soon. And regardless of the prophecy, it's clear his intentions are destructive to Miridran. Help me minimize the damage. Please, Vasalie."

It's then that I realize he's begging me.

Me.

But what could I do? There are times when I can barely stand. Times when walking, let alone dancing, feels like my bones are splintering one by one. I'm so exhausted by the effort required to stay upright. I am hanging by a thread—one single thread that keeps me from lying down and never lifting my head again.

More so, my neck is noosed by Illian's leash, cinching ever tighter. I am caged, wounded. And even if I weren't, how could I ever trust Anton? He paints himself a hero, yes, but Illian was once the hero, too. I can't forget the rumors of his Glory Court, the women that never return—including Copelan's partner, I'm willing to bet. Not to mention his lechery, his constant carousing. The copious expenditure of wealth.

My words are tired, despite the kernel of anger glowing within me. "I suppose I'll end up in your dungeon if I refuse?"

Anton rises, then comes to kneel before me.

"I won't force you," he says quietly. "But I *will* watch you." I think of the tunnels, the mosaics. "If you try to harm anyone else on his behalf, believe me when I say I will make it my personal quest to remove you from Miridran at any cost."

Then he stands, straightens his cloak, as if he didn't just beg for my help and threaten me within the span of a few breaths. "It seems we are finished for the time being." He slides an open palm into my line of sight.

Tentatively, I take it. His hand engulfs mine, and when he pulls me up, he tugs until I stumble toward him, his breath dancing over my cheeks. "You can choose to be his victim, Vasalie. Or, when you walk from these halls, you can deny him the permanence of such a gift."

It's difficult not to stagger back at that.

I want to argue, to make him understand that I could never be anything else. How could I? The constant knot of pain tightens inside me, and I gulp, grasping for the relief of knowing Laurent and Marian are safe. That I am, too.

And yet—I came here tonight at great risk to myself. Maybe it wasn't much, but it did feel like reclaiming a splinter of something Illian took from me.

Anton paces to the pane in the wall leading to the tunnels and slides it open. "Should you find yourself with information that could save another life, you know where to find me."

When I reach its threshold, I pause, finding myself offering him a single nod.

Because if I've learned anything today, it's that I don't want to hurt anyone else. I can't grow numb to it like I thought, not when I think of Emilia. What she did for me.

And whether Anton is a scoundrel or a saint, there's something about him. Something in his voice, the way he speaks, the fire warming the cool of his gaze—that makes me want to fight.

Chapter Twenty-Three

Copelan doesn't come for me the next day. No one does, not even Illian, though I suppose he's content for now. I completed his task.

Annais is also gone. I assume she's with the other seamsters, but I do find it strange that I haven't seen her at all since last night. But she's the last of my worries right now.

My body feels wrecked. My world tilts and sways, and I have so much to sort through: the prophecy, Illian's plans, Anton's intent. When I remember the way Laurent looked at me, another spike of nausea climbs my throat.

So I lie in bed, not bothering with food, not bothering to find Copelan and practice. He no doubt saw what I did. There's no telling what he thinks of me now. If anything, I'm sure it's provoked his ire. Again.

That evening, the sound of soft footfalls draws my attention, especially when they pause at my door. I brace for a harsh knock, for Copelan's voice. It isn't until the lock pops open and the door stretches wide that I realize who it is.

His breath gives him away.

Does he know where I've been? I curl into my pillow and pretend I am asleep.

Will he graze my jaw? Brush his knuckles against my hair? He might not touch me while I'm awake, but what about while I sleep?

Something lowers onto the table next to my bed. The tread of his steps fade after that.

I wait until I'm sure he's gone, then turn to see what it is: a small platter of fruit and nuts, along with his signature card, one he doesn't bother to sign.

Eat, Vasalie.

I ignore it and fall asleep.

The next morning, Annais has yet to return.

I force myself to consume a meager meal and rise from bed. My exertion and anxiety have well and truly drained me, like sand in an hourglass, thieving both my time and my strength. There's so little left these days. My endurance grows thinner with each week, and I wonder if that's forever. If this feeling, this exhaustion, is part of me now, a permanent crack in my being.

A crack that, with each passing day, widens a little more.

I twine my fingers into my hair, gathering it into a quick plait, which I fiddle with nervously as I enter the Dance Hall. My gaze immediately tracks to Copelan as he directs one of the younger troupes through a new routine. When he notices me, a shroud falls over his face, his lips stretching taut. He resumes his focus, perfecting their choreography until their practice ends. The dancers depart in a flurry of whispers, and I'm not oblivious to the shape of my name on their lips or the way they shuffle their gazes between Copelan and me.

I almost forgot he kissed me before the whole souls-damned palace. It feels like a lifetime ago.

I can't get you out of my head. I can't wash you from my skin.

"Vas," Copelan says.

"We need to plan about our next performance," I say, hoping to dodge any talk of the other night.

He blows out a breath. "Right. Yes."

The air is thick and strange like a room full of steam; I don't know how to navigate it. And it stays that way throughout our session. We try to conjure a new dance for the week's end, this time in honor of Serai, but it's far from spectacular and we both know it. Neither of our heads are present. Neither of us wants to get close.

"Maybe it would help if we see the location," he says, swiping a hand across his damp, ivory locks.

"It isn't in the Dome Hall?"

"The Sky Garden, actually."

The Sky Garden is near the northernmost wing. I've heard talk of it, but I've avoided it thus fair, considering that the Brisendali court resides nearby. The last thing I want is to run into my father.

"I don't think it necessary to visit," I start, but Copelan is already moving.

"Unless you have another idea," he says over his shoulder, "we need any inspiration we can get."

I hate that he's right. Serai, a western country across the sea, is a mystery. Not many are invited in, even fewer are allowed to tour. They aren't inhospitable, exactly, but there isn't much to see without mounds of paperwork. Their cities are guarded by twenty-foot walls. It costs a fortune to dock at their ports. They are protective, and I can't blame them for it.

Silence trails Copelan and me through the halls of the northern wing until I catch a glimpse of the Sky Garden in the distance. It hangs over the ocean, a platform of marble. A glass dome shields it from the rough ocean winds, but open pockets still allow for airflow. Gulls flit in and out, clustering on the trees beneath.

When we reach it, a gale sweeps in, disheveling my plait.

The space inside the dome is enormous, crawling with wisteria. Beds of amaryllis, hibiscus, and lotus carpet the ground between walkways, along with other flora unique to Anell. An intoxicating mix of nectar-sweet scents spiral around me, and for the first time, I take a full, satisfying breath.

And though a few courtiers linger, congregating underneath arbors, the magnitude of the place makes it feel as if we're alone. Copelan leads me underneath a flowering willow, its strands swaying in the breeze. I slip through, lavender petals whisking about my feet, and then we come across a large, trickling fountain—

I halt, and Copelan almost rams into my back.

In the center stands the ever-famous Fate of Morta.

Unlike in Illian's palace, she isn't crafted from marble; rather, she's made entirely of obsidian glass, her dress veined like a butterfly's wing. Water escapes from her cupped hands, almost as if she's trying to grasp it but can't.

Copelan plants himself at the bottom of the stairs, so lost in thought that I decide not to disturb him. I wander instead in another direction.

He bounds up and grabs my arm. "Vas."

I turn, a question in my eyes.

He wets his lips, like he isn't sure where to begin. He shoves a hand through his hair, then, with the other still holding my arm, pulls me against his chest. It surprises me so much that I stand there for a minute, arms dangling, until the familiar warmth of his embrace draws an exhale from my lungs.

My eyes begin to sting and the emotions of the past few days catch up to me, siphoning my strength. I press hard against him, clutching his sides.

I thought he was through with me, through with the mess I leave wherever I go. Instead, he breathes against my hair, his thumb rubbing the small of my back.

I know this is wrong, but I need his comfort. "What happened the other night—"

"We'll discuss it later," he whispers, breathing into my hair. "We will figure it out."

How I wish I could tell him everything; I wish it so much my mind aches holding it in. The other night, I'd wished Anton had seen it, too. For a moment, I swear he did. The enormity of my past, the way I'm suffocating beneath it, the way my chains grow denser, heavier, each day.

And I'm so afraid. Not just of Illian, but of myself. My ability to disappoint Emilia, to not rectify the past.

Most of all, I fear my own body—a body I no longer understand.

I fear the time might come when the pain is too great, my fatigue too deep, that I can no longer move, let alone dance. I sometimes think the only thing holding me upright is grit. Dogged determination. Because if I can't dance, I am not useful to Illian.

Copelan tilts my chin, watching me now. I wonder what he would do if I indeed gave him my truths. He already knows about my father. What would he do if he knew the rest?

But no, I couldn't. I recall Anton's warnings, Illian's threats. *I am watching you, always.*

The truth of it seals my lips yet again.

Still, I can't seem to break away, so we stay in this embrace until voices cleave through our reverie, splitting us apart.

"Copelan, my, what a timely surprise." Princess Aesir parts the willow branches like a curtain, her lips tipped up in a lupine grin.

"Princess," Copelan replies, his tone surprisingly flat. We give a short bow, in sync.

She sweeps her braid over her shoulder, looking more Brisendali than ever with an ultramarine tunic and leggings plated in silver-embellished leather.

The princess of a kingdom preparing for war. Why she feels the need to show it here is unclear. Unless she plans to fork some fish from the sea, the ensemble is entirely ridiculous.

"It so happens that we were coming to find you," she's telling Copelan. "I was told you might be here."

Copelan scratches his head. "We?"

Another wind blows through, and I rub my arms against the chill.

"Yes, we," she says, blinking innocently. She glances about, seemingly looking for someone who should be there.

Then a woman with raven hair and moon-white skin slips into view.

I recognize her instantly.

Esmée Fontaine looks just as she did all those years ago: simple yet beautiful, slender and elegant with her bowed lips and big eyes, cheekbones carved to perfection. I search her willowy frame for evidence of her injury, when she snapped her wrist before Illian, but find none.

Illian's former favored dancer, one of the most revered women in all of Miridran, is here.

She does not notice me. Instead, she offers Copelan a wistful smile. I follow her gaze, an odd feeling in my belly, only to find him as still as the statue over my shoulder.

And it hits me then, who she is to him.

I had a partner my first year here, he had told me. *It didn't end well for her.*

The Gathering, nine years ago.

She involved herself with a Crown.

Esmée was Copelan's partner. Then, nine years ago, at the Gathering, she captured Illian's eye. Illian, not Anton, like I had assumed. And Illian took her away, took her for himself, and Copelan never saw her again.

Until now.

But no one could enter the isle once the Gathering had begun unless all the crowns agreed. How had they managed?

"Esmée," Copelan breathes. He says her name like it's the answer to a long, unanswered prayer. "How, why—"

"I heard what a show you've been putting on," Esmée says, her dimples deepening.

"I admit I had hoped to make a reunion of this," says Princess Aesir. "I was younger, then, barely seventeen, but I so adored the way you two performed together." She lets out a breathy sigh, throwing her hands against her heart. "Like fated doves. And it seems I was not the only one to feel this way, because when I proposed the idea to the other courts, they agreed she would be an honored guest."

Then she pivots a glance my way, mouth curling. Copelan follows it, then scrubs a hand over his face. He mutters a quick introduction: her name, my name. Esmée doesn't recognize me. She wouldn't; we only danced together at the Melune for a few weeks, and even then, I had been in the background.

I wonder where she's been in the years since. She tips her head in greeting, and though her gaze isn't unkind, I feel small enough to sink through the cracks in the walkway.

They talk. She tells him about the job she took in Brisendale in a boutique theater near Kurst, the capital, and all the while I stand there, awkwardly, trying not to read their expressions. But I can't help it. They look at each other like they were lovers. Like they were ripped apart, and now, all their feelings have slipped back through time.

I sense the princess's gaze once more. Then she claps once, loudly, grabbing everyone's attention. "Oh, I have the most fabulous idea. Why don't you two perform together for us? My, what a treat that would be after all this time!"

Esmée bites back a smile, but Copelan does not. His cheeks spread, but then he shakes his head and scrubs his hair. Meanwhile the princess ticks off her ideas.

I stop listening, watching Princess Aesir.

I tell myself she couldn't have planned this for me, but then I remember the time I'd seen her sitting with Illian that night, talking for hours. I've found them together several times since, both watching me whenever I stepped in the room. Then, after the Razami dance where Copelan kissed me, she'd pulled him away. *So then, if you're not lovers,* she'd said, *that means you're free for the taking, no?*

It's as if she tried to lure him from my side. And when she failed to keep his attention, she found the one person who could. She then convinced all the other courts to break the rules and let that person in.

It would almost be extraordinary if it did not send shivers up my spine.

You can keep your pup for now, if you manage to hang on to him.

Somehow, Illian knew where to find Esmée and must have had the princess collect her.

If only she had been his Jewel instead.

After dinner, where I barely managed to keep down a slice of cheese and a sliver of bread, I take a walk. My mind is spinning out of control like a runaway wheel. Nothing adds up. What does Illian want? Why does he waste his time with trivial matters such as Esmée? All he has to do is order me to avoid Copelan and I would have to listen. So why go to the trouble?

Why care so much about what *I* do, when I have no choice but to obey him?

Then I recall the girl he had dressed like me, what he did to her in the night.

His tongue, tasting her flesh.

My name, a prayer on his lips.

The image is imprinted onto my memory with the permanence of a stain.

I shake my head and press on. I still need inspiration. I could still be kicked from the Gathering if I don't play my part, as meaningless as performing seems right now.

I enter the Dome Hall and slip onto the veranda. I sit, squeezing my legs between the balusters, allowing my feet to dangle in the air. Rainfall drapes over the ocean in the distance, a few flashes of light contouring the clouds. I watch it, letting the wind pull curls from my braid. Below, commotion bustles about a pavilion, but I'm so high above it, I can't hear.

So I focus my thoughts, leafing through what I know of Serai:

mellow mountains; dry, cracked earth. Big walls. Ahead of me, the sun inches through the clouds and mist, and threads of color light the sky in a brilliant arc. I breathe out.

Color. Why hadn't I thought of it before? Emilia once told me that it was Serain artists who first designated the significance of color and its meanings, and even now, creators from around the world strive to mimic the vibrancy and elegance of their palates.

An idea knits itself together in my mind as I study the rainbow before me, memorizing which color laps over the next. I think of what I can sew, the dyes I can use. I think of their fashion, the way they bespeak rank and emotion. While the Sovereign Lord's robes were dark, void of color, his court is swathed in vibrant hues—rouge draped in orange and gold for energy and stimulation, blue scalloped with violet and emerald for peace and harmony. Carefully selected analogous hues, paired together with purpose and a discerning eye.

I leap up. I have to find Copelan. It's a stretch, but if we start right away, we might manage. It's the perfect idea to follow last week. Not too risky, nothing risqué. It'll be eloquent, soft. I hasten back inside.

Copelan idles near the stage inside the Dome Hall, almost as if I'd summoned him. He's surrounded by performers. Even so, I race to him, barely containing my excitement.

When he notices me, he excuses himself and pulls me into a private alcove that opens into a small, covered veranda. Bougainvillea crawls along the walls, festooning the balustrade and columns, one of which I lean against as I compose myself.

A salt-kissed breeze sweeps in to ruffle our clothes. Courtiers flit by on a passing walkway, fragments of alarmed conversation drifting past us.

"I was about to look for you," he begins.

"I have an idea," I cut in. It feels like a victory to say those words again. Despite everything, the creativity is like a rush. A breath of air when my lungs felt starved for it.

I lay out my ideas in a string of breaths.

He watches me, his expression inscrutable. It is my first inclination that something is wrong. And finally, when I finish, he scrubs his hair. "I appreciate that, Vasalie. I really do."

I blink at him. "But?"

"But I've decided to give you that night off. You won't have to perform the signature dance. You may enjoy the evening as a member of the audience."

My brows knit. "I don't understand. Just this afternoon—"

"I know," he says. "But you can relax now. I'm sure you need it."

Perhaps, but I don't care for someone else dictating what I can or cannot do. That, and it feels like a deflection. "Will you perform alone, then?"

Copelan's gaze slips from mine, and I realize, then, what he intends. It's like a blow to the chest. "Esmée," I say.

"Try not to take it personally. You and I will still perform the next signature dance in just over a week." And then, noting my expression, he says, "It wasn't my choice, Vas. It was a request from Princess Aesir."

You can keep your pup for now, if you manage to hang on to him.

I swallow, my fingers curling into fists. "And you agreed?" I shouldn't be angry; it isn't his fault. But I can't help it. For once, I want someone to deny Illian something he wants.

"Of course I did, Vas. She's a *Crown*."

"One of many. And you're the Master of Revels. You don't answer to her alone. You could have told her others requested that it be *us*. You and me." I know it's irrational. It's jealousy, and I have no right. I denied him. I turned him away. But when he held me earlier, I hadn't realized just how much I needed that comfort.

I need it still. I need those arms, need to be held. I need to dance with him, because it's the only thing holding me together.

My heart is pounding, throbbing.

I am losing him.

"My hands are tied, Vasalie," Copelan says. "I'm sorry."

I shake my head, my composure disintegrating, especially as I remember the way he beheld her. He doesn't look at me like that. Not with that particular type of yearning, something that runs deeper than infatuation, deeper than lust. "You want this," I say. "I can see it."

"So what if I do?" he throws at me, irritation surfacing. "Esmée is a friend."

Or more.

"At least answer me this," I say. "King Illian. He was the one who took her away, wasn't he?"

"I can hardly fault him for seeing her talent," he says, though I don't miss the grimace he tries to hide.

"Do you really think Esmée's arrival is mere coincidence?" The words—they're spilling between my teeth before I can catch them. "And what about that cosseted, self-imposing princess? Haven't you ever stopped to wonder what her intentions might be?"

"Vasalie," Copelan warns. "You forget yourself."

"Answer the question!"

"I don't form opinions on the Crowns," he snaps. "It isn't my place, nor is it yours. Now, can I rely on you for the rest of the Gathering? If not, tell me now, so I can send you far, *far* away."

"I'd really prefer that you didn't," says a voice, deep and cool. Authoritative.

Copelan tenses.

Anton, surrounded by courtiers, pauses in the walkway next to us. "Is there a problem here, Master Reveler?" he asks. I wonder how much he heard.

"No, Your Majesty," Copelan responds, barely keeping the strain from his voice. "We were working out arrangements for the next few days."

"Master Reveler," Anton says, slanting a glance toward him, "if you please, I would like a moment alone with Miss Moran. And I urge you to withhold your accusations," he adds. "She has done nothing wrong; I merely seek to ask a favor, which she can relay to you as she wishes. It is nothing you need to concern yourself with otherwise."

It takes Copelan a moment to register that he's been dismissed. He nods tightly, utters a quick, "Yes, Your Majesty," then trudges down the hall.

I watch him disappear, wondering if he'll scold me for this later. The thought alone sends a spike of panic through my heart.

Anton puts his hand on the small of my back, nudging me toward the balustrade, until we're looking out over the ocean, a jut of rocks piling along the side of the palace beneath us. "Breathe, Vasalie," he says.

I wet my lips. "A favor, Sire?"

He folds his arms together, sunlight catching on his golden cuffs and the sun-warmed tones of his skin. "I merely thought to break up whatever *that* was."

That—referring to Copelan and me.

I run my finger along the strand of bougainvillea lassoing the baluster, then press my palms flat, a swirl of dizziness spiraling my thoughts. "It was nothing, truly."

"Oh, certainly." He leans against the rail, elbows propped, his dark hair tousled by the wind. "That couldn't have been a *bout* I witnessed. Your brand of foreplay, then?"

"I—" Anger blazes across my cheeks. "You are foul to imply such a thing!"

"I am wonderful. A joy. A gift to mankind." He slides me a devilish grin. "But I find myself unable to resist getting a rise out of you."

"Let me get this straight," I say, folding my arms. "You play a hero, swoop in to save me from the terrible, awful Copelan, and then proceed to badger me yourself?"

"Yes, but you enjoy my badgering. I am heaps more pleasant."

"What is *that* supposed to mean?"

"Just that your Master of Revels is broodier than a souls-damned thundercloud. And Illian is an absolute brute. Try spending time with someone who makes you feel good for a change."

"And you're suggesting that's you?"

He pushes off the railing, straightens a button on his lapel. "I have many talents and appeals, Vasalie, should you care to find out."

Words desert me at that. And before I can find them, he affords me a last smile, bowing his head. "A pleasure, as always."

Then he's gone.

Chapter Twenty-Four

Copelan waits for me in the Dome Hall, his face flushed.

He stalks to me, no doubt intent on demanding that I explain what just happened. But before he can speak, a frenzy of figures barge into the Dome Hall, shouts erupting.

Copelan and I whirl in tandem.

I barely have time to react before King Estienne of Central Miridran strides through, along with a multitude of guards, a variety of courtiers—

And a screaming, thrashing Annais.

"Show him to me!" she shouts, kicking and clawing at the single guard gripping her arm, her cheeks so florid I almost don't recognize her.

Annais. Quiet and subtle Annais, whom I snuck into the palace.

"Let me see him," she wails, so loud it echoes about the walls. "Let me go!" More guards spill into the room, rushing past me so fast I stumble. Copelan steadies me, then inches me out of the way as they surround her in a barricade. "My son," she screams. "My son!"

My son.

"Estienne," she cries. "*Estienne!*" But his guards press him back toward the entrance, away from the hysteria. An ashen pallor drains his already pale skin, though a patch of red laces up his neck.

I turn to granite.

She can't possibly be his mother. It's a farce, surely. But then I see them together. The tilt of their nose, the scatter of freckles patterned just the same . . .

I'd thought King Estienne looked familiar that first time I'd seen him. Now it's unmistakable.

"Vasalie, we should leave," Copelan is saying, guiding me toward the back doors.

They fling open before we can reach them.

Illian stalks into the room with Anton at his side. Close behind is King Rurik, followed by his steel-clad guards. Yet another assembly spills inside after him, a mix of courtiers from every court, all curious and pressing closer, eager to witness the drama.

"What is the meaning of this?" Illian demands. His golden circlet catches the light from the dying sun; it almost looks like a halo, as if he knew just where to stand to make himself a god.

"I've never seen this woman before in my life," King Estienne says, glowering at the guards who still wrestle with Annais, snapping shackles over her wrists.

It's as if the iron bindings snap any last shred of her composure. Thrashing even more violently, she shrieks, "I can prove it! Let me go!" She plunges forward, only to be slammed down, her bones smacking audibly against the floor.

Acid floods my throat, and I only just stop myself from lurching toward her. That treatment, the cruelty from the guards—I know it. And all the while, no one bats an eye.

Shame drains my face of color.

This—it's my fault. I am the reason she is here. I could have told Anton, but I had held my tongue . . .

"Prove what?" King Rurik is asking. "By the Fates, let the woman speak!"

A guard tries to lift her, but she throws her weight forward, clawing uselessly at the floor. Her curls are drenched in sweat, plastered to her cheeks. "My *son*," she cries. "Let me go to my son!"

"Who is it you speak of, woman?" Illian says, a façade of concern.

"Estienne was born from my womb," she says, a palm to her stomach. "He is my *son*." Tears run in rivulets, a glistening path that glides down her chin. My lungs constrict beneath my too-tight tunic.

She is telling the truth.

And Illian knows it.

"I advise you to consider your words carefully," says King Rurik, his tone fringed with frost. "You are speaking about a Miridranian king. This accusation challenges his legitimacy, and should we find your words to be false, we would have your head."

Legitimacy.

Miridran could lose a king right before my eyes.

"I do not lie," Annais rasps. "He is my *son*." She whips her head to King Estienne again, eyes pleading. "They kept me from you. All your life, they kept me away, and they turned you into *this*. But you are better than this. *Please!*"

They kept her away. And then Illian used me to sneak her inside.

What had he promised her? What does she think will happen? Does she know the cold of his ice-laden heart? More people pour into the room, drawn by the commotion. My father is among them, his hard eyes cutting over the crowd as he takes his place next to Rurik.

I shake my head, mouth drying. Anton, hovering behind Illian like a shadow, finds my gaze. He no doubt wonders if this was me.

It was.

"The absurdity!" King Estienne yells. "This is but a treasonous plot. You will receive nothing, woman, beyond a blade to your *neck*."

Annais shoves forward, pushing to her feet. Her linen smock is torn, fraying along her busted knees. "I have risked everything to come here. *Everything*, so that I might take you home to where you belong. This," she says, "is not who you were meant to be."

"Arrest her at once!" King Estienne demands, looking as if he's only just managing to hold back from attacking her himself.

"Wait," implores a voice. The Lord Sovereign of Serai. He cuts through his courtiers, his dark purple robe slung open to reveal the expanse of his smooth, deep brown chest, draped with colorful beads. "She claims she has proof. We deserve to hear it."

"Let's have it and be done with it, then," Illian says dismissively. Like he's grown bored. "I, for one, would like to retire for a glass of wine."

Donning an overtly bored visage, Anton asks coolly, "Why's that, brother? Something to celebrate?"

An accusation. But Illian merely flexes his jaw.

Annais swipes the guard's grip from her arm, taking a step forward.

She directs the full force of her attention toward King Estienne. "I worked in your father's palace before the Miridranian territories were split into three. I attended him directly, and after some time, he began to request me each night. His Majesty had just married his queen a year's previous, but they struggled to get with child. With the mounting pressure from the court to produce an heir, he took me to bed." Her words feel brittle, as if she's worn from a fight, but she maintains her conviction all the same. "Once you were born, they wrenched you from my arms. Claimed the queen birthed you. And they turned you into one of them—a Crown raised by gold-coated lies!"

"Ludicrous!" King Estienne hisses through bared teeth. He swivels his head toward the other Crowns. "Have you not heard? She insults us all—"

"Let her finish," someone says—another Crown, I think—but King Estienne can't contain his fury.

"I will have her head!"

"Contain yourself, brother," Illian says. "We must allow her to finish. If she digs herself a deeper grave, so be it."

Such false camaraderie.

Annais knuckles a curl from her face and takes a shaky breath. "When I became with child, they kept me secluded, cut off from the world—even from my own husband. And the moment I gave birth, I was never allowed to see you again. But I came here to find you and take you home. You are the heir to our clan, Estienne. I can prove my words as truth."

Her clan.

Clans still exist in the mountains, I remember. After the War of Rites, Mercy, the first Miridranian Queen—who some believe later became the Fate of Morta—granted many of them their lands and allowed them to live in peace.

Annais yanks her tunic back, then turns to reveal the back of her neck, where a large patch of red in the shape of a star marks the base of her spine. "This is a birthmark that's been passed down through our family for generations. You will have it, too."

"You have nothing to hide, brother," Illian says, straightening his lapels. I can almost feel his inward smile, like sludge against my skin. "Remove your jacket and prove this woman false once and for all."

He knows good and well what we're about to find; he wouldn't have brought Annais here if her claim was false. If he didn't know for certain the birthmark Estienne inherited.

He is about to dethrone his brother.

"Show them, Estienne," urges King Rurik. "This accusation—it's a stain on your father's legacy. How dare you allow his name to be tarnished so?" There's real fury in his one good eye, and I recall how he'd been mentored by Illian's father before he took his crown.

The panic in King Estienne's features is almost enough to condemn him. He throws up a few more feeble arguments, but the Crowns have spoken. They want their proof.

Reluctantly, he turns around. Drags his jacket and collar down.

A collective intake of breath whisks across the room.

The mark is clear and red as a drop of blood.

"I wrote you," Annais weeps. "I sent a letter when you were sixteen. I sent it through your maid—which put us both at risk. I told you everything I've said today. I asked you to come find us when you were of age, but you never came."

Illian wraps a palm over his mouth, and so ardent he is in his performance that I even see the sheen of tears. "How," he says, "could you not tell us?"

Then he strides over and yanks the crown right off his brother's head.

Estienne's guards shove forward, leaving a sobbing Annais on the floor, but Illian's men block them, hands shifting to their hilts.

"You ignored your own mother. You and Father hid this for years," Illian says. "It's disgusting! Yet you stood at your coronation, knowing Miridranian law?"

Miridranian law, which dictates a Crown must be of full royal blood. Bastards cannot rule. It means that Illian's father put Estienne on the throne illegally.

"Explain yourself, Estienne," King Rurik demands. A hum of agreement follows him.

"He's a hedge-born!" yells a courtier.

"Lowly scum!"

The Queen of Razam nudges past me, her long amber cloak flowing like wind. Her regalia underneath is black silk, like her hair, which is woven up into a glittering circlet.

I hadn't even seen her enter.

"Since when did bloodline dictate a higher calling to rule?" she asks. "Perhaps it is time to reexamine your own traditions."

Interesting, that she speaks directly to Illian, whose eyes flash in answer. But I don't understand why she would challenge him. She has no allegiance to Estienne.

I wonder, though, if she thinks Illian is worse.

"The issue is not just tradition and law but deception." King Rurik approaches Estienne. "This pains me more than I can say, but the least you can do is make it right—"

The room erupts into a maelstrom of voices. More guards enter.

More swords are raised. I slink back until I bump against Copelan. "You should leave," he begins, hands on my shoulders, but Illian's voice rises over the chaos.

"Step down now, Estienne," Illian declares holding up the crown, "and it will be with honor. If you do not, your land will be taken from you before the whole of the north."

"And I suppose you'll keep it for yourself?" Queen Sadira sidles up to him—even managing to look down on him. "Will you take his territory for yourself, Illian Orvere?"

His jaw ticks. "You forget, Sadira, that I have *two* brothers. Do you dismiss Anton so easily? Estienne's territory will be governed by us both."

"Then will you make that promise before us, right here, right now?" Her gaze reminds me of a cat readying to pounce. I want to tell her that Illian's promises mean nothing, but then I recall something Gustav mentioned the night of Anton's banquet. In Razam, oaths hold great meaning. They don't sign contracts because they aren't necessary. Foreign letters are often denied; they prefer face-to-face. An audience. Tone and intent aren't easily derived from ink and quills, and the people of Razam are known to be sharp judges of character.

She hopes to bind him with his words.

But Illian is not so easily led. "Miridran will not answer to Razam, Queen Sadira. I take offense at your insinuation."

I don't believe him for a second.

Then say something, a voice inside me urges. *Step forward and tell them about Illian, about everything that has happened thus far.* But it wouldn't help, not when Annais is speaking the truth.

And not when King Illian could nail murder to my name.

I divert my gaze back to Anton, who remains eerily silent. He looks untroubled in his deep viridian waistcoat over a crisp white shirt, his hands tucked in his pockets. By the lack of expression on his face, it's almost as if he isn't actually here. Like he's witnessing a puppet show, not a coup.

Then, as if he feels my stare, his eyes flick to mine.

Do you see, now? he seems to say. *Do you understand his play?*

Part of me is glad for Estienne's disgrace. I remember what he did. I remember that wall. He deserves to lose everything.

But my jealous king will not stop with Estienne. I know him too well for that, and his apparent distaste for Estienne pales in comparison to his hatred for his younger brother.

I see it now, clear and sharp, like the edge of glass.

He will go after Anton next.

Chapter Twenty-Five

The revelry does not stop after Estienne's banishment. It doesn't even pause.

The two days before the next signature dance inch by, during which I avoid the training halls and keep to myself. I perform once for the Kasimi court—a small affair, where I pick up only fragments of gossip about Estienne's dethroning.

It seems Estienne will be allowed to return to Central Miridran, where he will reside until the Gathering ends. Afterward, he will be afforded an estate in the countryside near his mother's clan, where he may live out the rest of his life.

That must be how Illian convinced Annais. He promised he wouldn't harm Estienne, that he would allow him to return with her. I wonder if he will stay true to his word.

But Estienne's rulership is revoked. The Miridranian court, I hear, will spend the next few days deciding how Anton and Illian will divide his territory. I haven't seen either of them since.

When the day arrives for the third signature dance, the one meant to honor Serai, I consider not going at all. My presence isn't required. I try to stay away, but curiosity hooks its claws in me and draws me out.

It's hard to tell where the garden ends and the sky begins.

Thin clouds smear the sunset in swathes of pastel that seem to wrap the glass dome in a cocoon. Reds and golds bleed onto the leaves above, and underneath the trees, the garden is latticed in shadow and color.

Tables are spaced around the center of the garden, draped in linen that sways in the wind. Lanterns hold the tablecloths in place, glowing embers against a receding sun. The slow hum of a violin underscores the chatter of guests.

I stay hidden from view, weaving between the outer trees as the Sky Garden fills with Crowns. They filter in slowly, jovially, and once again, their revelry turns my stomach to stone. Tonight is just another night, as if a king wasn't dethroned before the entirety of the north.

Ever since, I've leafed through my mind, sorting through what I know, what I've seen, however inconsequential the clues might seem. The poison that wasn't fatal. The letters I saw Illian scribe and seal with a ring that wasn't his own. Laurent's suspicions.

Then there's the prophecy, and the blood it foretells. The signs point to a war of some sort. Yet there's something personal about Illian's moves.

Maybe the prophecy is real. Maybe Illian is aligned with the Fate of Morta somehow. For all I know, he's sold her his soul—if such a thing is possible. Either way, I understand him well enough to know which name he hopes to scratch out next. Which brother he wants to wipe from the board. And I might not trust Anton any more than I trust the temperament of a cat, but he's the only one who can take power from Illian.

And I am going to help him do it.

I pause behind the same lavender willow I'd stood under when Copelan wrapped his arms around me and breathed into my hair.

Until Esmée, that is.

I should not be here. But I want to see how perfect she is, how well they fit together.

I prop myself against the trunk, taking a moment to breathe. To let the willow's crisp perfume infuse my lungs and soothe my weary soul. To my right, the Fate of Morta fountain trickles faintly, music swelling beyond from the makeshift stage in the center of the garden.

A breeze sweeps about, swaying the branches, and through them, I can see Copelan. He positions himself in the center, and around him, a hundred strands of color unspool from the tree above.

Ribbons.

And with them, a figure descends, lowering little by little.

Esmée.

Her dress is made of the same silk she hangs from, a radiant spectrum of hues. She's tangled inside a rainbow, using her strength to weave through it.

So they used my idea, then. Down to the attire.

The melody is soft, delicate, befitting the way she moves. She twists, banding silk around her legs, before allowing herself to fall upside-down to the stage in one, graceful swoop.

Copelan takes her wrists.

She pulls him up, up, up into the air.

Locking onto her, he swings himself upward, then flips to wrap his legs around her waist. Chest to chest, they spin together, upside-down in a swirl of emeralds and pinks, golds and blues. Awed murmurs fan out across the audience, sprinkled with applause.

Esmée adjusts the ribbons and they slide to the floor.

Upon landing, they loop separate ribbons around their wrists, then circle each other until they're going fast, faster—

One leap and they're off the ground, flying around each other like birds seeking their mates. This is where they deviate from what I had planned, and I can't help but recall Copelan telling me they didn't have the setup for aerialists. Not that it matters. I'm not strong enough for it. Still, the reminder sits like soot in my belly as I watch them swirl and glide with incredible poise until the ribbons twine them together into a single, corded rope.

Esmée coils her legs around his torso. Copelan releases his ribbons. Just when I think he might fall, Esmée clenches her thighs tight, catching him so that he's suspended between them.

Even from here, I can see the breadth of his smile. They take turns, using muscles I forgot existed to form shapes in the air—shapes made together, balanced between each other's arms.

And I'm so blindingly jealous. Tears sting my eyes and I swallow and swallow, willing them to disappear. I don't want to be jealous. But the bitterness—it surprises me, because it isn't her proximity to Copelan that I envy. I thought that would bother me, but somehow, it doesn't.

It's *her*.

Esmée. She's everything I admire; everything I had longed to be. I imagine that, if given the chance, we would even be friends.

But what hurts the most is how *whole* she is. How strong. All the things I wish my body could do, she does with ease. She can dance without limit—spin and leap and curl into the air with an effortless sort of grace. Oh, how I had taken my abled body for granted. I hadn't realized what a privilege it was, how thankful I should have been.

She can do things with Copelan that I never can.

More so, she is the embodiment of confidence and poise. The type of woman who could look down her nose at my father. The woman I failed to become.

With the back of my hand, I swipe away a tear. I shouldn't have come. I shouldn't have watched this. As for Copelan, I can't have him. I see that now. She's a star and he's her moon. They belong together, in the air, surrounded by the glimmer of a thousand lights.

I press a hand to my heart, willing it to freeze.

I made myself a promise. And though things have not gone as planned, there's still an inch of hope. Hope that Anton was truthful about his intentions. That he will indeed help me. That we will thwart Illian, and that I will keep my promise to Emilia. *Somehow.*

I must cling to that hope. Because without it, I will sink into the earth like rainwater, then cease to exist at all.

Copelan drifts down once more, and during his descent, Esmée peels off his shirt. On his chest are painted stripes of color, as if the ribbons bled onto his skin. Once again, the audience crackles with applause as he lands on his feet. He stands there, collecting his praise, with Esmée suspended above him like a swan eclipsing the now-emerging moon. My breathing turns ragged, and no matter how much air I drag in, I don't feel replenished. So labored are my breaths that I don't hear the footfalls when they approach.

"Impressive," a voice drawls. "I suppose I see the appeal."

I afford Anton a sideways glance before turning back to the stage, so consumed that I forget to bow. Esmée descends in a waterfall of spins. Copelan catches her in his arms, then swings her around in a triumphant twirl before placing her on her feet. It's her turn for applause now. What a vision they are as they clasp hands, raise them, grins aimed at each other.

I turn away, breathing out the last bit of pain residing in my chest.

Anton tsks. "Trouble in love?"

Of course. He saw our kiss, as did everyone else. All of whom see them together now.

I wrap my arms around myself, trying not to fall apart.

"A shame," Anton continues, stepping beside me. His eyes are dark, lined in glitter, and a sleeveless emerald jerkin rimmed in gold reveals his sculpted arms. When his shoulder brushes mine, I'm not naïve enough to think it wasn't on purpose. "He's attractive, you're attractive," he muses. "What fine and talented offspring you might have made."

Offspring? I wheel around, all rational thought flying from my head. Sparks fill my vision and I shove him backward. "How dare you insinuate—"

He slams against the tree and my eyes go wide, a mirror to his shock, and it hits me what I've done. I just assaulted a Crown. I rush to him. "Your Majesty, I'm sorry—"

He snags my wrists and yanks me toward him. His breath is hot, full of fresh peaches and wine. And he's grinning.

Grinning.

"There you are," he says. "I so enjoyed your snark from before; I'd hoped you'd find it again."

My cheeks flame. But then his fingers tighten on my wrists, and all I can feel are shackles—binding me, locking me in place. "Release me," I say. "At *once.*"

His eyes lose all humor. "I apologize," he breathes, dropping his hands, and I blink at him. He just apologized. To *me.* "But surely you must know everyone at this Gathering can't keep their eyes off you—including me, if it wasn't perfectly obvious. You do not need the one man who gazes elsewhere."

"Says the man with the Glory Court at his disposal. You have eyes for a hundred women, do you not?" I say it because I have no idea what to make of his statement or the annoying little sparks filling my belly like a swarm of fireflies.

He's merely trying to get under my skin—because he enjoys that, apparently.

"Still on that, are we?" Anton asks, rubbing his neck. Then he straightens, picking something invisible off his jerkin. "Despite what you might think, I find no sport in trampling on hearts, Vasalie. Hearts are fragile things, like glass. They break far too easily in the wrong hands. Offer them only to someone who can care for them, who might polish them until they glow." He laughs a little. "Now *that* should be made into a serenade, no?"

He mimes a chef's kiss.

I resist a scoff, wrapping my arms around myself instead as his words sink into me in ways I wish they wouldn't.

I wish my heart was more like Anton's sea glass. Harder, stronger, less breakable. But as I see Copelan pulling Esmée into his embrace before the still-cheering audience, I still feel a pang of loss, even knowing the root of those feelings.

Because I *did* let Copelan borrow it. Not for long, but long enough that he left a bruise. I told him the truth of who I am. My childhood, things I hadn't let myself think about in far too long. And he'd listened.

Maybe it isn't losing Copelan that bothers me so much as losing his comfort or the ability to feel powerful in his grasp.

Perhaps we were just using each other.

I was a replacement for Esmée. He was a rock when I needed to stand. Arms, when I felt lonely, when I so desperately needed to be touched. But it doesn't make it easier, because he saw me for all my weaknesses and still he chose someone else. Someone better than I am.

"It's just that I felt something I hadn't felt in . . . forever maybe." Not love, but certainly something better than pain. "It was small and insignificant, but there, and now I feel . . ." I tighten my fists. "Ashamed."

I'm a fool to have allowed it. I knew the reason I was here, yet even after I rejected him, I clung to him. And now, I'm a fool to be standing here, spilling something so private, so embarrassing, to a *king*, no less.

I'm a fool to let my ruined soul feel at all.

I slouch against the trunk of the tree, hands curling into the bark. Copelan and Esmée parade around, smiling, greeting guests.

Anton paces in front of me, blocking my view. My lips part, but he plants an arm over my head, leaning so close we share breath. "If you think he's the only one who can make you feel," he murmurs, his lips against the shell of my ear, "you are so very wrong."

His words steal the air from my lungs.

I expect him to move away. Instead, he takes an errant curl, spiraling it with his fingers before tucking it behind my ear. Heat whisks over me, leaving me feeling intoxicated, dizzy—and more so by the way those deep, sea-green eyes hold mine in a terrifying, exhilarating grip. I glimpse it again, that otherworldliness. It's in the way his gaze seems to shine, even in the shadows, like the sheen of a pearl.

I press a hand to his chest. And whether it's to shove him away or pull him closer, I don't find out, because Copelan shoulders through the willow's branches.

He halts at the sight of us.

Anton doesn't bother to acknowledge him, instead lowering his voice so only I can hear. "I came to find you because we have much to discuss regarding my so-called brother. Come to me later. Use the tunnels."

"Vas?" Copelan says. His voice is strangely thick.

Anton backs off—slowly. When he turns to Copelan, his lips peel back in an insufferable, knowing smirk. "Spectacular performance, Master Reveler. Vasalie and I admired it *oh so* much."

A torrent of heat floods my cheeks and, no surprise, I want to shove Anton yet again, Crown or not. He knows very well what he's doing.

Copelan's eyes slide to mine, and I want to be anywhere but here.

"Well." Anton straightens his lapels, as if his work here is done. "You two enjoy the rest of your evening. Vasalie, it has been a pleasure, as always." He strolls off casually, *whistling*, like he hadn't just erupted something inside me.

"Souls below, Vasalie. What was *that*?"

The branches still quaver from Anton's departure. I stare at them, unable to form words. Not when his scent lingers in the air, trapped between the leaves; not when the taste of his breath still hovers atop my lips.

"It was nothing," I finally hear myself respond.

"Nothing?" he asks. "That didn't look like nothing."

"We watched your performance together. That's all."

"You shouldn't involve yourself with a Crown, Vas. Haven't you figured that out by now?"

Aggravation swarms under my skin at that. I know what he's

doing, yet he has the gall to compare me to Esmée—especially after what I just saw. "What are you accusing me of, exactly?"

"I . . ." He lets out a weary sigh. "Seeing you two, it was unexpected. And it just looked like—souls, I don't know. He looked like he wanted to carry you off. Or devour you."

Like you look at Esmée, I want to say. But once again, I suppress the anger building inside me. "He is a Crown. He may look at me however he wants." Another truth. "I'd have thought you'd be relieved."

It's my turn to deprive him of words, it seems. He threads a hand through his mussed locks—that all-too-familiar gesture. Paint slathers across his bare chest, though it's beginning to crack. Just like me.

Our stalemate lasts for several seconds until, finally, he curses. "I didn't expect any of this, all right? I was an overseer. A soloist. But then you came and changed everything. And when you're around . . . I don't know. I become someone else when I'm with you. But trouble seems to follow you wherever you go. You're like a cyclone. Reckless, dangerous. Dragging me in. And Esmée—" He grimaces, cutting himself off.

"She's safe, and whole," I finish for him. I press my hands to my stomach, feeling my nausea swell. It's everything I can do to keep from vomiting on my feet.

"That's . . . not true, exactly," Copelan says, grappling with himself. "I didn't expect to see her again, and then she came back, and I can't just . . . I can't turn off the way I feel. For you, for her . . ."

If you think he's the only one who can make you feel, you are so very wrong.

All of this . . . it's so irrevocably foolish. I don't have to stand here. I don't have to hear this. And in the grand scheme of things, it matters so, so little.

My conflict isn't with Copelan. It's with Illian, and my father. I had forgotten that tonight, in the rush of emotions. They are the ones who took everything from me. My title, my passion. Years of my life I'll never get back. Years that punished my body in ways I can't undo. My friends. Laurent, Copelan, and whoever I look at next, they will be taken, too.

And Anton . . . I flex my fingers.

I will never have anything for myself, not until I am cut free from Illian's noose. And after what I witnessed in his room—the girl, the way he had her dressed like me—I am coming to realize something else, too.

Illian will not keep his promise to me. He is not going to let me go.

Not unless I do something about it.

Copelan stares at me, awaiting a response.

I slip around him and push through the trees, disappearing into the night beyond.

Chapter Twenty-Six

The tunnels feel different.
Or maybe it's me. I find my way through the darkness, determination threading through my veins. Illian will not grant me my freedom; of this, I am certain. But I now know who might help me cut his strings.

My memory serves me well, and I find the mosaic leading to Anton's antechamber. I rap against the pane and he opens it on the third knock, shoving a heap of fabric into my hands.

"Put this on," he mutters. "Quickly."

I examine the fabric, rolling it out. It's a long black cloak, finer than the one I wear now. "Your Majesty—"

"You dropped this," Anton says, bending to hand me a length of red velvet. I take it, frowning as I examine it. It seems to be a dress—but barely. My head snaps up. "Is this a joke?"

"Not at all," he says. "Be quick about it."

"You want me to wear this? *Where?*"

"Did you notice your king was nowhere to be seen tonight?" he asks, and I remember he's right. "My men tracked him to Philam; I just received reports of his whereabouts."

I push the fabric back into his hands, flushing. I came to help somehow, but *this* . . . "I'm not your doll."

"Miss Moran, I'm very good at reading people; let's call it one of my many special talents. You know as well as I do that he will not stop with the girl he festooned in your clothes and bedded like something from a nightmare. So either you do nothing—let him keep you as his souls-damned marionette and be complicit to whatever vile plans he unfolds—or you can help me thwart him and be free of him once and for all."

Free, once and for all.

Once again, my anger rises to the surface, a beast ready to attack—but not him, because he is right. And hadn't I already made my decision?

And yet . . . "I am but a lowly dancer. I have no power against him."

"You are the object of my brother's obsession," he says. "I have a feeling everything he does revolves around you. And that, Minnow, is a very special kind of power."

Bile burns deep in my belly and I pick at the fabric in my hands. "Why trust me? For all you know, I could betray you. You already know I was working for him." If I have any hope of escaping Illian, I have to tell Anton the truth before he finds it for himself. "And there's more—"

"Ah, yes. Like how you spent two years in prison for supposedly murdering one of Illian's advisers whose death hasn't even been publicized? You can tell me all about it on the way."

"I— How did you . . ."

"Really, Minnow," Anton drawls. "I wouldn't be much of a king if I didn't have my sources . . ."

But no one even knows Lord Sarden is dead, save for Illian and a few of his guards.

And . . . Brigitte.

". . . I also know Lord Sarden would not have come to your

rooms on his own, that he was devoted to his pregnant wife. He made a mockery of Illian in the weeks before, I am told, insulting him before his court after dearest Sadira refused a meeting yet again. Now can you *please* get changed?"

When I emerge from a guest room, my outfit changed, I pull the cloak tighter around myself, securing it with a tie at my waist.

I find Anton waiting restlessly by the hearth, his foot tapping a rhythm against the parquet floor. And I notice, then, what I hadn't earlier. His clothing is simple: a plain leather jerkin and dark breeches, free of his usual embellishments and jewels. No rings adorn his fingers and ears; no kohl sweeps under his jade eyes, though they're still dark, accented with long, defined lashes. And his hair is gathered at the neck, the smallest knot already slipping out.

When he notices me, he ushers me through the pane in the wall and into the tunnels. It takes all my effort and more to keep up with him, but I press on, ignoring the ache in my knees, the exhaustion in my bones. When we reach the beach outside, he guides us away from the dock along the dunes, hugging the palace until we reach an inlet hidden by rocks. There, a small rowboat drifts in the shallow water, secured to a post by a corded rope. Across the channel, Philam's lights sparkle against the waves.

Anton wades into the water. I slide my slippers off and lift my cloak, shivering as the water laps around my thighs.

"Your brother, King Estienne," I begin. I had been meaning to ask him, but my thoughts were foolishly occupied by Copelan, the dance. "I am the one who brought Annais inside the palace. Only I didn't know who she was—"

"I had guessed that much. Laurent said something about a new seamstress after the tunnel debacle. I suppose it's my fault for not digging into that further."

"Did you know?" I ask. "That he was . . . illegitimate?"

"Illian and I both suspected," he says, "but Illian had no real proof until he managed to find Annais." He reaches the boat and unloops the rope. "There's a long history there, one I don't care to repeat at the present. But suffice it to say: It was only a matter of time. In fact, I suspect that's the only reason he hasn't made any of his moves until now."

"And now," I say, "you are the only thing standing in Illian's way."

"I intend to keep it that way, futile as it may be. What with the prophecy and all."

"Can a confirmed prophecy be subverted? Avoided?"

"Not according to the prophets of old. Once confirmed, it is permanently etched into the stone of time. Their words, not mine."

A chill raises the hairs on my neck. At least we are in Anton's territory. Surely he is safe here. Protected. Except . . . "Your guards," I ask. "They allow you to leave without them?"

Anton collects my shoes and lifts me into the craft with ease. "They are, ah . . . rather accustomed to my tendency to vanish. I am a pain to guard; I'm fairly certain the captain of my personal guard is dead inside."

"But why not send them to Philam instead? You could have them report back, rather than put yourself at risk . . ."

"Because a king's word carries more clout," he says simply, jumping in beside me. He grabs the oars, which I'm grateful for; though I've rowed before, it isn't an easy task. Then he adds, "And there are some things I need to see for myself."

That, I can understand. I need to see it, too. Need to see what Illian is planning—especially if the prophecy manifests. Still, I ask, "What do you think we will find?"

"I think," Anton says, "we are about to discover out who, exactly, is under Illian's employ."

Who else aside from me, he means. Because he knows everything about my life in Miridran, apparently. The shock of it still hasn't worn off, but at least he doesn't seem deterred.

The ocean is smooth, and I can't help but watch Anton as he rows, a notch forming between his brows. It isn't from the effort;

the craft glides easily under his strokes—an impressive feat. No, he looks like he wants to say something.

It isn't until we're halfway to Philam that he breaks. "Tell me one thing." His tone is sour, almost harsh. "My brother. He chained you up for two years, kept you malnourished, weak, and yet he expects you to do all this—" He gestures around him, like the sea holds the answer. "Dance for him, perform for the Gathering every souls-damned night while you're clearly in pain, *and* do his dirty work?"

My throat constricts, and I take a moment to swallow.

He's right, mostly. What he said feels both too big and too small to describe what happened. The chains, the darkness—I am still there when I close my eyes. It damaged me in ways I'll never recover from. I have accepted that.

Except I wasn't malnourished—or at least, not compared to the other prisoners. I was allowed food, and it wasn't moldy nor was it old. I was provided a pail of fresh water daily from which I could drink. I was not crammed onto a floor with other prisoners and their illnesses, many of which were contagious. My cell had a hole for waste, and as small as the space was, it was larger than the other cells, all of which were packed with people. I had seen that when I was taken in.

I had assumed it was the one kindness Illian had left. Or a kind of torture, to keep me alive so that I might suffer longer, when he knows I must have wanted to die. And I had tried. I refused his food until I couldn't, when the pain of hunger forced me to eat.

I don't know how to answer Anton, what words could possibly convey the truth of what happened to me. I end up deflecting instead. "I am sorry, Your Majesty, if my performance has not been adequate—"

"Souls, Vasalie," he says. "That isn't what I meant. It took me a while to notice, in fact, as you hide your pain well. I see it only in the press of your lips, the wince when you turn away. The occasional stumble you cover impressively well."

I knew he had been studying me, but I suppose I hadn't realized just how closely.

"I am sorry for what I accused you of," he continues, "and for what you have gone through, when souls know I am not nearly as strong as you."

Strong?

No, I am not strong. Not my bones, not my spirit. Not when I can't move or dance like I used to. Not when I shoved Emilia and my father and all my pain into a box and locked it away like the coward I was, all before Illian ever wronged me. Not after everything else I've done under Illian's command. My hands find my stomach, and I press against the nausea threatening to erupt inside of me.

For once, Anton doesn't notice, occupied as he is steering us into Philam's bustling docks. Even at night, the city teems, thanks to the marketplace scattered along the water's edge.

Two dockhands assist us as we scramble from the craft. Anton tosses them each a sack of quatra, then shakes their hands. They must know who he is because they dip in reverence when they accept the payment. A minute later, we're on our way.

Melodies spill from taverns, the amalgam of jaunty rhythms clashing together in a lively yet dissonant ensemble. Sellers hawk their wares, even this late in the night, while others haggle over prices. Horses trot over salt-smeared cobblestones. Women lean over balconies, cat-calling sailors and passersby. The smell of sweat, sea spray, and manure hangs thick in the air. I almost have to run to keep pace with Anton, who strides ahead of me, shouldering through the crowd.

Only when he turns down an alley does he slow. "Stay close," he says, placing a hand on my lower back. I pretend I don't shiver from the contact.

I pretend, too, I didn't hear the marvel in his voice, the respect, when he called me strong.

An array of saturated colors illuminates the walkway ahead. When we reach it, Anton turns, a smile curling the corner of his lips. "Welcome, Minnow, to the Heart of Philam."

Canopies enshroud the moonlit sky, but light glows from every direction. Craftsmen rotate metal pipes, shaping what looks like molten fire. Behind them, large, concave furnaces spit sparks into the air. Then there are the tents stacked with artifacts and trinkets, not to mention walkways that ramp upward toward more shops on different levels—

"The Glass Market," I surmise. I'd heard of them, but this one is large, like a city in itself.

"One of many throughout my territory," Anton says. "See those men? They're glassblowers and gaffers. Each works for one of the many merchants. While there are ready-made items available, a patron may commission something, too, whether it be decorative or useful—the possibilities are endless—and they can make it on the spot. And this particular market uses recycled glass," he says, redirecting my attention toward the furnaces. "It's heated in a tempering oven and then quickly cooled, which makes for stronger and more durable glass."

I slow, unable to keep my gaze from roaming about as we weave through the market. Anton points out some of the commissions: vases; windowpanes and doors with family crests or other unique stains; tabletops; chandeliers that look like hanging gardens.

"The colors," I ask, speeding again to match Anton's stride. "How do they do it?"

"Minerals and salt," he answers. "Copper turns it red, and adding iron or chromium stains it green, for example. Cobalt for blue, silver for red to yellow, depending. I promise to bring you back one day, but for now, we shouldn't linger."

I keep moving, not allowing those words to take root inside in my heart. *I promise to bring you back one day.*

We pass a small bunker at the back of the marketplace hidden by a copse of flowering jacarandas. Racks of weapons with metal hilts and glass blades glint in the torchlight, and I recall the halberds from Anton's guard. They must be crafted here.

He must sense the gaze I press between his shoulders because he glances back, a half grin on his lips. He nudges me along.

"I've been meaning to ask you something," I say as we stride down yet another alley, this one a flower market packed with rows of stalls.

"Mm?"

"Queen Sadira. What did you say to her to stop the war with Razam?"

"Nothing," he says.

"So the story isn't true, then?"

"What I mean is . . . I said nothing. Not one thing. I merely . . . listened," he says, guiding me around a pothole. "That's the problem with so many of us who hold privilege and power. We talk too much. We talk above others."

The answer surprises me, coming from him. And I think that he's . . . right.

"If only others saw it that way," I say.

"It's something I'm still working on, admittedly. For so long, we've expected Razam to conform to our views, and the views largely held by the Syndicate. But Queen Sadira has her own traditions, her own values—for trade, security, and so on. Not to mention, her borders are constantly under threat by the southern lands. She came to us, asked us for help, and Illian—among others—used her pleas to try to pressure her into reducing trade taxes, allowing Miridran a military stronghold on her land, and so much more. We would suffocate her in exchange for our assistance. At first, I didn't see it that way, however; I couldn't understand why she wouldn't compromise on some level. But as tensions increased, she threatened to sever ties with Miridran and even break from the Crowns' Syndicate altogether in response to that pressure—to which Illian responded with the threat of war. It was during that escalation that I began to wonder if her stance wasn't out of selfishness but for reasons we never bothered to understand. So I went there to simply . . . listen. And once I understood her, I was able to advocate for her and leverage resources from the rest of the Syndicate."

I wonder if he knows just how much this shifts my opinion of him.

The streets are less congested the farther inland we go. We turn again, down an even thinner alleyway, this one empty and quiet, the back entrances of buildings crammed together in the dark. Anton tugs his cloak to cover his face before adjusting mine, his fingers brushing my cheeks as he does so.

Then he hesitates, his green eyes flitting to mine. Just when I think he might say something, he pulls me along instead, up a set of stairs. He raps twice on a nondescript door, then pauses. He repeats the action, this time with four knocks. The door cracks open at that, and a woman ushers us inside.

"Quickly," she says.

The door squeaks shut behind us, and the inside is so dark I have to squint. The woman, whom Anton introduces as Mistress Sezar, shows us down a long hall, then up another set of stairs. She unlocks one of several doors along the narrow top floor. "They're in the next room, right wall," she whispers. "Be careful. Ring if you need anything." She's referring to a bell hung next to the door, and only then do I realize where we are.

"A *brothel*?" I ask incredulously as Anton closes us inside.

"Many don't trust my little seaside palace, so they come to Philam under the illusion of privacy. My brother believes he's paid off Miss Sezar so that he might use her establishment discreetly—right under my nose," Anton says, then slips on a smile. "He is, of course, mistaken."

He moves to run his hands along the wooden boards that make up the right wall. I take the moment to orient myself, to measure my surroundings. Plush, amaranthine drapes shroud the window, and the bed is strung with a matching gossamer canopy. Underneath, a red velvet duvet is neatly peeled back over matching sheets, a whisk of petals delicately strewn about. Two full flutes of wine occupy the night table, along with a decanter. And the walls—

My blush deepens further. Risqué paintings line the left wall, each displaying a nude figure balanced in various poses, ribbons obscuring their eyes. Dizzy, I perch on the bed, trying to discern what Anton is looking for as his hands skim the wall near the floor.

He peeks over his shoulder. "I wouldn't sit on that if I were you. You never know who was there last, or if they had time to clean up."

I leap up as if I'd been burned, only to realize that it was a joke. He chuckles and nods me over. "When I lift this," he says, tapping a minuscule, nearly invisible knob in the wood, "it will open a spy hole in the wall. There's one built into every room for such an occasion; the trouble is finding it."

"By the souls, do you have your entire territory rigged?"

"Only about half."

"You can't be serious." Except . . . I think he is.

"Can you blame me for using every tool in my arsenal when someone enters my home and tries to murder my kin?"

"I cannot," I agree. "I can't imagine what your actual palace must be like, though." I bet there isn't a safe corner there.

"My palace is absolutely lovely," he says as I settle beside him on the floor, "and you would enjoy yourself very much."

But I only vaguely hear him, dread pooling in my chest at what I'm about to see.

"Vasalie," Anton says, grinning. He's always grinning, even at a time like this. "You can breathe, for Fate's sake. Just keep silent."

He tugs the nob, and a splinter-thin crack of wood slides open. Anton pulls me in by the waist so I can look through with him. I ignore the shiver that sweeps up my spine and turn my attention to the scene in the other room.

At first, I don't understand what I am seeing. I must be mistaken in fact; surely this is a nightmare sent from the Fate of Morta to torment me, because this is too horrific to be real.

But then I hear my father's gravelly voice, and I know I'm not asleep.

Chapter Twenty-Seven

The blood drains from my face.

My frame of view is narrow but clear. The adjoining room is small yet long—a repurposed bedroom, it seems. Two wing chairs point toward a makeshift stage, where a trio of women dip and twirl about on swathes of cloth suspended from the ceiling like swings. A mellow beat carries idly, thumping against my breastbone, and upon closer inspection, I recognize one of the women. She looks different this time, not as much like me without the intrinsic tailoring.

But she is not the reason bile claws at the back of my throat.

Illian lounges on the chair to my left, a glass of bourbon in hand. And though he's angled away, I would know those ruby-red rings anywhere. Just like I know the profile, the boots, and the weathered hands of the man next to him, uniform or not.

My *father*.

Pain and panic lace between my ribs, knotting my insides, and I can't seem to pull in a breath. The monster who murdered Emilia is conversing with the man who holds my noose.

I had assumed Illian was working with King Rurik, not with my father. Not directly.

Anton slides the wooden slat closed, and distantly, I hear him whisper my name. But my head is spinning, the room twisting, turning, like I'm on the bow of a ship being knocked about by vicious winds—

He cups my face, brings it toward his own. "Vasalie?"

I snap my gaze toward his but his expression isn't one of concern. It's urgency. "I need you to tell me what's going on—and fast."

I force a breath, hanging on to his green-gold gaze like an anchor. "That . . ." I rasp, "is General Stova."

"And?"

I shut my eyes, squeezing them tight, but Anton runs his thumbs over my cheeks. "Look at me," he commands.

With an exhale, I obey, forcing out my next admission. "Vastianna Stova," I say. "It is the name I was given at birth."

"You are his daughter?"

"Yes." I breathe, rubbing my arms against a sudden chill. "I ran away. My stepmother was supposed to come with me, but he"—I swallow—"he found out."

At that, Anton goes very still.

"Vasalie," he says softly, "why were you running away?"

I turn my gaze toward the wall, as if I could see through it to the demon beyond. "Because he promised my hand in marriage to a suitor across the sea, effective immediately." I look at Anton then, my fingers balling into fists. "I was thirteen."

He lets out a curse, his hands falling away.

And the story breaks from me, a gush of water against a collapsing dam. "My stepmother, she begged him. *Begged* him not to go through with it." Because while I hadn't known my suitor, Emilia seemed to. I remember her shouting at my father, saying he was dangerous. Vile. Not to mention how young I was—"My father had become increasingly violent over the years. And when he found our bags . . ."

I trail off at that, unable to say more, but it doesn't matter. Anton must see it on my bloodless face.

He squeezes my arm. "I have to open the slat again; I need to know what they are saying. Do you need me to take you downstairs first? I can, but we may not have much time . . ."

"No," I say, frantic, even as my stomach tightens. "I—can do this. I can stay."

I *want* to stay. I have to know why they're together.

A nod. "Squeeze my arm if you need anything."

With that, he reopens the spy hole. When he leans in, I do, too, straining to hear over the music.

". . . and you're certain that she'll go through with it?" Illian clanks down his glass on a side table.

My father shifts in his seat. "The little princess wants her power, prepped and presented like a cake in time for her next name day. I am the only one who can give it to her. She knows this."

"Bold of you to think she won't dispose of you and keep the crown for herself once Rurik is dead."

King Rurik.

Dead?

"Laughable," my father says, flexing a broad-knuckled hand. "The army answers to *me*. If I perish by her hand, not even a Fate could maintain command over my men. Of this, she is aware." His voice turns feral, then, bitter as gall. "I earned their loyalty, plain as that. I raised them. Bred them. Proffered their earnings. I knocked them down and built them up again; their loyalty is to *me*. Aesir is no different. I've groomed her, primed her, ever since she was little."

So that was how he did it. The times he was gone, neglecting Emilia and me, he was there, making sons out of comrades, followers out of allies.

And Aesir . . .

"Furthermore, she knows the position Brisendale will be in once the Gathering concludes; we will need to create a strong front in case Razam retaliates—"

A shuffling sound next to me breaks my attention, and when I cant my gaze, I find Anton digging deep in his cloak.

". . . logical, but women never are." Illian stands and stretches, emptying the dregs of his glass. "I trust you will keep her in line." His gaze skims over the girls before he bats a hand in dismissal. They slide robes over their scantily clad bodies and exit the room.

A clank draws my attention back to Anton, who fiddles with what looks like a golden tube or a miniature spyglass about as wide as my thumb and maybe twice as long. He positions it near the widest part of the spy hole, then twists it, back and forth—

"Let Rurik play his role," my father says. "Everything will proceed as planned. Morta's hell, his demise will be a relief."

Demise.

Because my father is planning treason against his own king.

"Do enjoy your new bride," Illian drawls, clapping him on the back. "I can't wait to see *that* play out, old man."

Their exchange knits together in my mind, and I understand with sudden, horrible clarity.

Princess Aesir is going to marry him. My father.

She is going to make him a king.

When Crowns divide, and nations collide,
Blood will run high as tides.

Nations collide.

The prophecy, Illian's plans. There's so much more to it than I'd imagined. I dart a frenzied gaze toward Anton, but he's . . . occupied. Toying with a new trinket, one that looks like a miniature chest—wooden, rimmed in gold, brass hinges on one end. I want to shake him. Is he not paying attention?

My father's voice carries through once more, and I watch as he secures the brass buttons on a dark, wool coat—the one Emilia made for him. "Greedy she might be, but I can satiate her well enough. I've had years to perfect my craft on girls her age. You understand what happens in encampments, yes? Free for the taking." A snake's smile inches across his lips as he holds out a hand.

The meager contents of my stomach threaten to spill even as a fire lights behind my eyes. Anton nudges me aside, having hooked the miniature spyglass to that strange, wooden box. He nudges it against the spy hole, then draws a key from one of the necklaces on his chest.

He places it in a small groove and twists.

Click.

Both my father and Illian turn.

In a dizzying rush, Anton pulls me away from the wall—

They heard it, the click. Had they seen us, too? Anton drops the slat back in place, but if he does it in time, I can't tell. I open my mouth, but he presses a finger to his lips.

We listen.

The muffled sounds of voices slip through, though I can't make out their words. Anton presses an ear to the wall. His eyes widen.

In one swift motion, he sweeps toward me. Grabs my cloak—throws it aside. I gasp. Underneath, I'm left only in a short scrap of velvet that hugs my bust and flares high around my thighs—

A garment appropriate for a place like this.

A knock pummels the door.

Anton yanks off his cloak, his shirt, then his pants, until only a pair of drawers remain. Snatching a wineglass, he slings the liquid across the ivory rug at the foot of the bed. The knock pounds harder, insistent. Then Illian's voice, calling for Mistress Sezar . . .

Anton musses his hair. I realize, then, what he's doing, and when his gaze finds mine, there's a question there. Somehow, I understand. I nod my permission.

Keys jingle from outside the door.

Anton scoops me into his arms—and lowers me onto the bed. He wrenches the sheer canopy shut for the modicum of obscurity it offers. Drawing back the covers, he presses me deep into the sheets, slides my slip high enough to reveal my bare legs—

A click, and the door swings wide.

He covers my lips with his own.

One beat, two. His mouth moves against mine, urgent. *Sell it,* he seems to plead, coaxing my lips apart, one hand threading up the base of my neck and into my hair.

And so I do.

I curl my hands around his shoulders. Press up into him. Hook my legs around his waist. He deepens the kiss, his chest heaving; I pull him closer. My heart slams against my eardrums. Surely he can feel it, but he only leans harder against me, using his body to shield my own.

He is a client and I am his muse.

We are supposed to be here.

At least the light is dim, almost nonexistent, and the canopy veils us somewhat, but none of that slows my roaring pulse . . .

"It's nothing," comes the general's voice, the door slowly screeching shut. "Let's go."

"You're certain?" Illian says.

I rake my nails down Anton's back, relishing the moan he releases onto my lips. And when he glides a warm palm along the back of my thigh, one escapes my own. Then he drags it up, up, until he captures my arms—

He raises them above my head.

Instinctively, my hands clench, but he opens them, parting my fingers with his, and the intimacy of it, that slow, languid glide . . .

Reality slips from my grasp, and I forget.

I forget who I am, who he is. I forget my chains or the man who holds them, standing feet away. I forget how little I trust Anton; how all of this means nothing—especially to a king like him with a Glory Court at his fingertips. His lips aren't soft and neither are his kisses, but I don't want soft. I don't want to feel fragile; no, I want *this*. I want passion, hunger, the beat of a rapid pulse. After he left me under that tree, after what he'd said, I hadn't dared imagine what it might be like with him. But *this*—

"One of our newer girls," says Mistress Sezar. "But the merchant paid well, drunk as he is, and I'd rather not lose a client. I won't risk disturbing them any longer."

Anton's lips break from mine, sliding to my shoulder. He pants along the curve of my neck, damp and soft. His scent, his warmth—

it clouds my head until there's nothing else, not even the faint receding of footsteps.

I come to only when he cups my face, thumbs brushing the hair from my cheeks. I glance up at him, dizzy, and he presses a last, chaste kiss to my lips before whispering, "They're gone."

I can't seem to move. It takes me a moment to remember myself and why we're here. Anton slowly pushes off me, then holds out a hand. "My most sincere apologies, Miss Stova."

Stova.

It's the wakeup call I need, like a smack to the cheek. I run my hands over my face, then straighten my slip of a dress. Anton snatches my cloak from the floor and wraps it around my shoulders, but it does little good. I'm trembling, and not from the cold. What we just did . . .

Another wave of heat spirals beneath my skin.

Nothing has ever felt like that.

But I can't focus on it. Can't dwell on why that was even more invigorating than the most intimate dance.

That, of all things.

Him.

He kissed me like it was inevitable. I suppose we had been dancing around each other all this time, and yet we moved like it was a *challenge.*

I shake my head, trying to regain a bit of sense. I tell myself it was just the unexpected rush of it all. That's what got to me.

Not the way it felt.

Because it wasn't real.

It was *not* real.

He gets dressed, but not before I catch a glimpse of his physique—lean, muscled. Not that I needed to see it after I felt it on top of me. "We need to get going. In case brother dearest decides to come back," he says.

I nod, using my still-shaking fingers to arrange my hair into a braid.

Anton, finally seeing me, smirks. Just a little, his lips tipped up at the edges. "I suppose we got what we came for, however unseemly," he says. His hair is still mussed, tangled.

Unseemly. I don't know what to make of that.

Words gather inside my mouth, but I don't know which to spill first. I want to ask about what we just saw, what it means. What he plans to do about it.

I want to know how Illian and my father met.

I want to know if the grins, the smirks, are just Anton's way to get me to do what he wants. If I'm being used by yet another Crown as a play for power. But if it brings me answers, or my own bit of power . . .

Mistress Sezar's voice breaks our trance. "They've left," she says, cracking open the door. "If you hurry, you can sneak out the back and reach the docks before they do."

"I need to get back," I say, "before he finds me missing."

Anton frowns but grabs my hand, pulling me out the door.

Water laps over the edges of the boat as we row back to the island. Cool water pools around my ankles, but I hardly notice. I'm consumed by my thoughts. My anger. Now that I've had time to compose myself and process what happened, I'm steam in a kettle, ready to scream.

A king. Illian plans to help my father become a *king.*

No. I won't watch it happen.

"I'd hope," Anton says, breaking the silence, "that we are, at the very least, allies after that. Common enemies, and all."

Allies? Is that what we are? I feel like I'm swimming in sand.

Allies. But it doesn't matter what he calls it, because even if he's using me, I will help him. Whatever it takes to knock my father to his knees.

"They deserve to burn," I breathe, fingernails digging into my thighs. I picture my father and what he did. I see Emilia's face, already lifeless, right before he swung her over our balcony, let her tumble down the mountain below. And Illian, what his guards did to me, the way he watched them break me, silently—and the way he's watched me ever since he plucked me from his souls-forsaken prison. The way his breath felt along the back of my neck when he spoke my last task . . .

"They deserve to burn," I say again. "And I want to strike the match."

"Good," Anton says. "Then it's time we talked. *Really* talked." He heaves the oars, pushing us over a larger wave. Clouds thick as quilts drift over the moon, bathing us in shadow, the calm seascape now stirred by a current of wind. "My brother is a powerful man, and he's been playing this game for a very long time—perhaps longer than you realize. Until now, he has failed in his endeavors—because every time, he made *me* his first target of disposal."

I don't understand. "He . . . tried to dispose of you?"

Again, that devious tilt slants his lips. "Oh, you've heard the story. Everyone knows about my supposed death."

Philam's night bells chime as if in emphasis, ominous in the gloom. Mist sprays my tongue and coats my skin.

"Mount Carapet," I say. "You—you fell."

"Shoved," he clarifies. "By my doting older brother, at the ripe age of sixteen."

The story is true, then. Only, Illian was the cause.

Even so, whether Anton fell, or Illian pushed him, he is here. Alive. "How—"

"Did I survive? I woke on a jut of rocks along the mountainside. His men were searching for me, so I smeared my own blood along the rocks at the bottom near a waterfall, so they would assume he succeeded. A week later, I gave him a pleasant little scare at my own burial procession." He sighs. "But he had crafted such a convincing show, mourning in public for days after my so-called demise. I realized that, should I try to expose him, I would have no proof to back my claim, and so I remained silent. Learned to watch my back.

"A year after, he sent a troupe of assassins to greet me when I returned from Razam. He wanted that war, and he was rather displeased that I had managed to prevent it." He leans back, resting his elbows against the oars. "Unfortunately for him and his little miscreants, I had an escort: the queen's own sons. Since, he's tried and failed to kill me multiple times. Deathnettle vipers in my bed, suspicious rockslides, and the like. Alas," he says, "this time is different. He hasn't just changed his game. He's brought in new players."

Players, like my father.

Or perhaps the Fate of Morta herself.

"Because of my reputation, I have to tread very carefully around the Crowns. Already, they struggle to take me seriously. And I can't make a move against him publicly without cause."

"But you could warn King Rurik," I point out.

"After our little poisoning incident?" He shakes his head. "If I were to tell Rurik that his beloved general plans to betray him, he's likely to laugh in my face."

"But the prophecy. Surely you could—"

"Even if I share the prophecy with them, they would have no reason to believe it. Not without proof, which is why I've sent a crew to retrieve the prophets my brother captured. Their testimony—well, it would be a start."

"And if they're dead?"

"A possibility," he admits. "Which is the reason I'm here in search of tangible proof. I need to expose the general and my brother not for what a supposed prophecy says but for what they plan to do. I need concrete evidence."

But that isn't good enough. Time is slipping away. "What happens when you can't find enough?" My palms grow damp. "I won't watch this happen—*won't*." I'd rather sneak into the tunnels and slit their throats myself than risk them rising to unthinkable power.

"I know where those thoughts are taking you, but you must resist," he warns. "There is no victory in that." Then he leans forward, his jaw set. "I have no intention of bowing before my brother or your Fates-damned father, Minnow. I asked you once before, and I am asking you again. Work with me. Help me stop them."

My fingers tighten, curling into themselves. "What do you need me to do?"

He considers me. "Is my brother aware that you are the general's daughter?"

"He isn't," I say. "He would use it against me if he found out." Maybe even against my father, too. I have no doubt that should either of them have leverage over the other, they wouldn't hesitate to wrangle that control.

Anton nods. "What else can you tell me about your history with Illian?"

"Other than his framing me for murder as an excuse for tossing me in prison until I begged for death?" I blow out a breath.

"Before that," he clarifies.

A wave rocks the craft, and I grip the rough wood edges. The glass palace floats into view, dimly lit, studded with torchlight from within the arches like a multitude of stars.

I tell Anton what happened. I tell him about the day Illian found me, what he offered, how I worked for him and earned my place and title. The King's Jewel.

"And he never took you? In . . . that way?"

"Not once. He has never touched me, not even a pat on the back. It's why I trusted him. He never took advantage of me, and he shielded me from the lustful eyes of the court. He took care of me. He . . ." I take a breath, waiting for the lump in my throat to dissolve. "He promised to always protect me. He lied."

And that's the reason I can't hand my trust to the king before me, even if I help him. Words mean little, and promises even less.

We reach the post and he secures the boat with the rope, then he leans in, catching my gaze. "Helping me is dangerous, and foolish, probably. But I don't make offers I can't keep, so listen carefully." He hops out of the craft and into the water, then holds out his hand. "I cannot protect you, Vastianna Stova. But I *can* arm you."

PART THREE

Queen of Souls

Chapter Twenty-Eight

By the time we make it back into the tunnels, I'm so weary I can hardly stand.

I follow Anton until my legs crumple beneath me. Then I feel myself being scooped up and carried, but only for a moment until my vision blots and I see no more.

Only when he slides open a pane in the tunnel wall, a lambent glow falling over me, do I come to. I glance about as he sets me gently on my feet, somehow knowing to wait before releasing me so that I do not fall.

"Your wing," I breathe. "No—I must return to my room. If he finds that I'm missing . . ."

"It would be far more dangerous if he hears of you sneaking back to your room the very hour he himself returns from the brothel."

I blow out a breath. He's right.

He tugs me along, guiding me to a guest room off a branching hallway. "You can sleep here."

So matter of fact. "Someone will see me in the morning, surely."

"In the morning," he says, "I can create enough of a distraction that you can slip back out undetected. I'm rather good at that."

Exhaustion rakes over me again, so I merely nod and slump on the bed. The room is small and windowless, alabaster stone wrapping the walls aside from a painting or two. At least the bed is soft and pillowy. Anton tells me he will have someone send me breakfast in the morning and that we will figure the rest out after that. I barely hear him, already half asleep.

This time, I dream of a throne.

It is familiar. A pillar of carved stone filigreed with iron, set high on a dais before which I stand. But try as I might, I cannot see who sits upon it. So I turn.

And forget that I am dreaming.

Gore paints the room in shreds of red and black, blood thick as tar smeared across the floor. I trip over my heels as I stumble back, only to hit a wall of glass. I try another route, but the same glass blocks me on all sides, caging me in—

I throw myself against it, but it doesn't budge. I kick and claw, but it only shrinks until I can't move at all.

A prison.

No.

I splay my hands, glancing about for any sign of help. Beyond the horror, doors open to flitting figures. A battle. A *war*. Spears are thrown. Axes swing past. Heads are severed, and I cannot, cannot get free, the blood about my cage rising like a flood—

I don't know where I am.

I wrench forward, only to slip, my legs splayed beneath me. And I am bound, cocooned in fabric that sticks to my sweat-slicked skin like glue. The air is stale. Hot. Unmoving. My heart riots. I follow the line of the wall, but that too is stone—

A prison.

A cell.

Darkness, shrinking.

I cannot breathe.

I cannot *breathe*.

Panic swings me into full hysteria. I claw forward, wrestling against whatever it is that clings to me, until I find a faint sliver of light like a crack in the wall. I scamper toward it, shove my fingers into the gap, pull—

A door. It's a door. I manage to pry it open, then I'm spilling outward, into some unknown hall, my equilibrium tilting like a wave-thrown ship. I knock into a plinth, the vase atop shattering across the floor, but I need air. I stumble on, the tile cold against my feet. Dimly, I hear someone calling my name.

The voices. Always the voices.

I collide with something hard.

"Minnow?"

I try to look up, but the rhythm of my panting sends a swirl of stars across my sight.

"Vasalie," says a voice, soothing, soft. A voice I know. "I need you to do something for me. It will sound strange, but it will help. I need you to breathe in and tell me what you smell. Give me three words for it."

I shake my head, because he doesn't understand—

"Trust me," he says.

With no short amount of frustration, I turn my focus to the scent corralling me.

"Warmth," I rasp. Musk. Something else I can't name. "Clove." But my chest grows tight, as if it's about to cave.

My weight rocks sideways, but strong arms catch me. I feel myself being hauled up, carried—

Quivering curtains slink back, then a vortex of sea-kissed air whisks about, tossing my hair. I'm settled onto a wide balustrade, one hand cupping my waist. The other settles against my cheek, and only then do I feel the line of tears tracking down my face.

"Let's try it here. Something else, now. Tell me five things you can touch. Describe them."

Dimly, I understand what he's doing.

Use all your senses when the pain is at its worst, Brigitte had told me. Maybe—maybe it will work with this, too.

"The stone beneath me," I say, shaking my head. "The wind."

"And?"

And I can't concentrate anymore, can't—

He takes my hands in his. Puts them to his chest. "What do you feel, Vasalie?"

The silk of his nightshirt. The zigzag of its golden hem, rough beneath my fingertips. The sturdy planes beneath. I press harder in my desperation, then flatten my palms.

"Your heartbeat," I breathe.

"Tell me more. Four words for it."

"It's . . . slow. Steady," I force out. I squeeze my eyes shut, narrowing my focus to my hands, to what I feel. He's so . . . "Solid, and firm."

Heat builds beneath my cheeks, my heart easing its pace.

"Tell me three things you see."

I open my eyes.

"*You.*"

He quirks a soft smile. "What else?"

But I can't look away. His gaze transports me somewhere . . . *else*. Somewhere mythical, a place that only exists in my dreams—or perhaps far beyond even those. Because there is something so very *unreal* about him. As if he might vanish beneath my touch.

It's then that I realize my fingers are digging into his shirt.

But I can't seem to let go, afraid that if I do, I will fall into the world below. The Lair of Morta, perhaps. But maybe I am headed there anyway.

Dark hair whisks about Anton's face, the pale kiss of moonlight silvering his cheeks. A shiver glides across my arms.

"I am broken," I say. An admission, or explanation. The only words I can string together.

"You are art," he says in response.

Once more, I latch on to his gaze, trying to make sense of that. But my mind—I feel it slipping, feel the weariness settling over me like an unwelcome embrace.

But I am no longer starved for air. Especially now, with a heavy wind whipping past, plunging air into my lungs with ease. My vision clears, the fog of panic dissipating.

"I . . . broke your vase," I say, tipping my gaze away.

"I hated the thing anyway."

"You didn't even see which one."

"I'm really not fond of vases."

I let out a huff, allowing my hands to fall. "I can't go back there." I don't care that I'm in the thin, velvet nightdress I had worn into Philam, a mere slip of fabric that now rides all the way up my thighs. But he isn't looking at that.

He's looking at me, his verdant eyes limned in starlight.

"I know what it's like to feel lonely and stifled by the dark. I should have taken more consideration with the room I gave you." He swipes away the tendril of hair plastered to my cheek. "As it happens, it was the only one with fresh linens, and I can't risk sending you back to your room just yet. We have another three hours until dawn."

Even sitting as I am, I begin to sway. Not from panic now, but exhaustion so deep even my bones ache. "Here. I will stay here."

"On my balcony? I think not." He takes my hand and helps me up, guiding me back through sheets of rustling curtains and into the room beyond.

It's a large, circular expanse plush with rugs, flooded with wavering firelight from a hearth to my right. To my left is a wide, four-poster bed. A duvet sits askew, sheets and pillows strewn about, the ceiling domed and painted like an aurora borealis above.

I turn back to Anton, taking stock of his attire. The silk pants in particular, the way his hair is disheveled, tossed about by the breeze. "I can't stay here," I say.

Because this is his *bedroom*.

"I rather think you should. It's open, spacious, and the fire lends just enough warmth against the cool nighttime breeze," he says, moving to kindle the hearth.

I back up, my shoulder blades hitting an armoire, and blurt the first excuse I can think of. "I might be sick. I would ruin your coverlet . . ."

"All the more reason to let me keep an eye on you."

"You expect me to sleep in your bed."

"I will not lay a hand on you, Minnow. I swear it on my life."

I believe him. I do.

But then, why does my throat constrict at the thought? At the prospect of trusting him, of burrowing beneath his sheets, even after what we did in that brothel . . .

I am not afraid of him. So why the fear?

Then my mind snags on the night I found Illian next to my bed, watching me. The way he wanted something I didn't understand. And Anton—

Anton is his *brother*.

He watches me now, frowning at the distance I've put between us. Then he grabs a bottle in a drawer beneath the night table. "This is brazenflower oil." He dabs several beads on his wrist, and immediately his skin reddens and swells. "Not a soul knows about this, but I am allergic to it. Of course I'm trying to change that little by little, but I have not yet succeeded."

He strides toward the bed, then lugs something from underneath it. A sword glints, his hand coiled about its hilt. My breath catches, but then he lacquers oil over it in a generous sweep and places it on the center of the bed, dividing it in two. "Should I so much as lean your way, one nick with this blade and I am unlikely to survive it."

I . . . "Why would you do this?"

"Because I am exhausted, and so are you." He grabs a rag and soap from a washbasin and scrubs his arm, then dims the fire to a subtle glow. "And because you are not the only one with nightmares. Another presence in my room might benefit me, too."

"Because this is the one night you are deprived of your usual company?" I hedge, making my way toward the bed, opting for the unruffled side. Tentatively, I peel back the covers.

I am decidedly unprepared when he shucks off his nightshirt, the hard cut of his chest glazed under a spill of moonlight. But the distance in his gaze brings me up short.

Guilt corrals me at that. Earlier this night, as long ago as it feels now, he had told me his brother made not one but several attempts on his life.

I know what it's like to feel lonely and stifled by the dark.

But the shadow disappears a moment later, the light in his eyes returning. "We all have our comforts, Minnow. I wonder if you might be mine."

I awaken a few hours later as the sun first teases the horizon, a barely visible flush cast upon the sea and sky. And this time, I am at peace.

The soft sound of breathing stirs the air.

Slowly, gingerly, I turn over, still toasty under the warm duvet. Anton's hair is splayed about the pillow, his lids sealed shut. I withhold a smile when I see the puddle of drool on his pillow, and even more so when a snore pipes through his lips.

We all have our comforts, Minnow. I wonder if you might be mine.

For long moments, I just watch him.

The King of the East is an enigma, my opinion of him shifting every passing day. He is both beloved and despised, admired and envied. Rumors sully him on all sides—rumors that, if they are to be believed, say he is no better than his brothers.

And yet he laid that sword between us.

I wonder if anyone truly knows him at all.

I wonder, too, if his kindness, real or not, might be what breaks me in the end.

Tentatively, I ease up. Take its hilt in my palm.

I lift it from between us and place it on the floor, out of reach, before sliding back into bed. His gesture by placing it there in the first place proved to me I do not need it.

Chapter Twenty-Nine

A breath along the dip of my neck pulls me from sleep once more.

This time, the sun pours generously over the room. I squeeze my eyes shut against the onslaught of light and nuzzle back into a cocoon of warmth.

Only that cocoon is vibrating.

I angle my head and find Anton shaking, a sheen of sweat coating his brow. His muscles are locked, as if tensed for danger. The smooth, bare skin of his chest is damp, too, and his arms come around me, fingers splaying about my abdomen.

A burst of panic jolts me, but I can't seem to pull away. Not when he looks like he's in . . . *pain*.

A nightmare.

Before I can stop myself, I roll over and reach out. Cup my palms over his cheeks. "Anton?"

He does not wake. His hand comes up to grip my wrist, his breathing shallow—

I throw my arms around him, pull him against my chest as if I could protect him, shield him. My lips find a spot just over his brows.

Green eyes, vivid in the morning light, fly open.

I withdraw, my own chest heaving now. "You—you were having a nightmare. I couldn't wake you."

He takes a long moment to process my words. Our proximity.

"The sword," he murmurs.

I bite my lip, unable to voice that, yes, I moved it.

I moved it, perhaps in a state of delirium, because what could I have been thinking? He is a king. Not to mention a charmer, a seducer. And here I am, in his bed, wearing almost nothing. But before I can put distance between the heat of his body and the stuttering pulse of my heart, he slowly props himself up on his elbows and pulls the sheets over my shoulders, saying, "Fates, does it pain me to do that."

I breathe out, grateful, even as an embarrassed heat rises within me. Until he adds, "You do look like you belong here, however. Truly, you are welcome to stay any time. Or *all* the time."

Again, that mouth. I glare at him. "And what expectations might that impose on me, exactly?"

"Only that you grace me with your adorable little pouts more often," he says, tapping a finger to my nose. "I admit they are a weakness. You scowl so beautifully."

I sit up, bringing the sheets with me. "What a charming tongue you have, Majesty. I wonder: Do you recycle your lines often?"

"My tongue is dedicated solely to you, for as long as you want it."

"Sometimes I hate you," I say, resisting the itch to whack him with a pillow.

"Ah, but hate and love are two sides of the same blade. They share the same passion, besides."

My fingers do reach for the pillow at that, but he places a hand on mine before I can grab it, his expression shifting into something softer, more somber. "Vasalie, I want to apologize. For what I did at the brothel to try to hide you . . ." He trails off, a soft, creeping pink painting the apples of his cheeks.

I can't help my amusement.

Anton Orvere, the famed King of the East, is nervous?

He clears his throat at my silence. "While I realize we had little choice, I may have lost control, and I didn't mean to take advantage of you, which, of course, I did. Inadvertently."

The man with the Glory Court is apologizing for a mere *kiss*?

Yet it wasn't a mere kiss, was it? The way his mouth played with mine, the way he wove his fingers through my own—

He says he lost control. He is not the only one.

Then that last kiss, the one he gave me even after the door had clicked shut . . .

"Please accept my apology."

The look on his face is so endearing that I begin to laugh.

He arches a thick, manicured brow. "You are laughing at me. I cannot believe you are laughing at me." A grin peeks from his lips then. "I rescind my apology, considering you quite enjoyed it yourself."

"Shaping the tale to your liking, I see."

"Your little moans spoke volumes as to your level of enjoyment, Minnow."

A flush blazes up the back of my neck. "You could use a dose of humility, Sire."

"Why would I dose myself with *that*? Sounds terrible."

I can't help the laugh that spills out next. But then he takes my chin with his fingers. "Your laugh," he breathes. "I could drink an ocean's worth."

That draws me up short.

He watches me through the fringe of his lashes, his thumb tracing my bottom lip—softly, like he wants to capture my smile. Pocket it. Like it's fragile and rare, and he can't believe it belongs to him. And in this moment, the horrors of this place fade away, and so does the pain, and I can breathe. Fully and completely.

I feel like a thousand tiny stars, bursting and shimmering all over.

But I have felt this way before.

I soaked in Illian's adoration, his praise. He made me feel more valuable than the crown gracing his head. He kept me on a string, dangled his promises on a hook.

Anton mistakes the change in my demeanor for worry. "Just a little more time, and this will all end. I promise."

Just a little more.

I will give you more.

I promise, I promise.

I don't want to compare Anton with Illian, but how could I ever be sure of his intentions? While I trust that he won't hurt me, or touch me unless I wish it, I am here because he needs me, in the end.

He plays a wonderfully convincing hero—an act I am starting to believe, admittedly. But how can I trust that he's a better man when, upon his coronation, he established that Fates-forsaken court?

He notices the change in my demeanor, his smile fading.

"Your Glory Court," I whisper.

His brows furrow. "Oh, Vasalie, it isn't what you—"

A knock interrupts him, two raps in quick succession. Anton slides from the bed and, before I can so much as hide under the covers, says, "Yes, Basile?"

I squeak and bury myself under the duvet, but all that comes is a deep, "Your Majesty, the breakfast bell has rung. I've brought the clothes you requested."

"Thank you, Basile. We will leave right away. Vasalie, my dear, you can come up for air. Basile is the captain of my personal guard. He is not only sworn to secrecy but is fully aware of who you are and why you are here. I informed him last night."

Humiliation colors my cheeks as I peek above the covers. Anton tosses me a cloak. "Wear this. You can't be seen in the same dress you wore in the Sky Garden in the unlikely case someone notices you this morning."

Hesitantly, I take it, arranging it around my shoulders before sliding from bed. To my further embarrassment, Basile—a broad man with rich brown skin and a mane of thick curls sectioned into several braids—stands in the doorway, blank-faced, unmoving. He's plated in sea-glass armor and pads of leather, looking as bedecked as his king usually does. At least he isn't looking at me. "Sire, I recommend that you put on actual pants."

"Thank you, I was getting to that," Anton says, snatching a nearby set of trousers. He's wearing a set of loose drawers that indeed cut well above his knees.

"It's only that I have to remind you often, Sire."

"I am sorry that my thighs offend you, Basile."

"Sire, after eight years in your employ, nothing offends me."

Anton sends me a coy grin. "See? Dead inside."

"That would be your fault, Majesty," Basile retorts.

"Indeed. However, my astounding supply of charisma resurrects you on the daily. Does it not?"

"If by charisma you mean chaos, then yes, I am revived daily."

"Stop stealing all the good lines," Anton mutters, buttoning his tunic.

Despite myself, I can't help a small smile. Anton adores Basile, and it shows. And the affection seems to be mutual.

After donning a vest, Anton ushers me from the room, instructing me on which path to take while he arranges a disaster involving the delivery of my millen and a small-scale fire, which will inevitably draw most of the staff out into the halls while I slip from the cellar.

But as I reach the pane of glass leading into the tunnels, Anton calls my name. I swivel as he advances, and he takes my hands in his. "Promise me you will not act on what you saw last night. Do not move against your father or Illian yet."

It is a wise move, making me promise. The temptation to end this now is all too great. Yes, Maksim Stova deserves torture, shackles, the dark, endless grip of a cell, but he also deserves death, and I want to give it to him.

I clench the folds of the cloak.

"Promise me," he urges. "We will bring him a fate worse than

Morta's revenge. Your life is not worth risking only to bring your father a few seconds of pain he'll scarcely feel."

For that, I finally agree. And I cling to that promise even as I leave his rooms and traverse the tunnels. Yet even as I do, I find myself replaying the night's events. The morning's, too, in an endless loop. I practice my breathing as I take it all in, and then I realize something else.

Anton promised me he would unearth my secrets.

Now he has them—every last one.

It's unsettling. Frightening.

But in a way, it's also freeing.

Chapter Thirty

Illian's next task is waiting for me when I arrive back at my room. The letter is tucked into a stack of neatly folded linens, and when I lift it, it's stained with lye.

I was correct, then, about the maid working for him. She must have just delivered it only moments ago, thinking I was in the dining hall.

I scan the letter. The task isn't what I expected. I assumed each one would be worse than the last, but this one is simple, seemingly harmless. For the next few nights, I am to entertain two smaller courts, both of which he will attend. He merely asks that I divert attention while he secures a few deals, which I will, admittedly, try to overhear.

Sweat beads on my skin despite a mid-morning chill. Last night hardly seems real, and now, I can't help but clench my quilt, my father's voice encircling my thoughts like a fist around my throat.

He wants to make himself a king.

And if he does, Emilia will have died for nothing.

I think of her more than ever now, especially the way she'd looked that day, her gold locks swept into a coronet, her pink wool dress perfect for traveling through the harsh mid-winter cold. The too-big coat she made me wear, and how it itched against my skin, how I'd used it to cover my sobs when I realized she was gone.

Another sob breaks loose at that. But I quickly compose myself, repeating Anton's promise in my mind.

We will bring him a fate worse than Morta's revenge.

I coif my hair and wander to the Dance Hall, dreading each step that brings me closer to Copelan. After last night, our quarrel feels insignificant in the scheme of things, but we have one last dance to plan. Unless he's decided to use Esmée for that, too.

But the Dance Hall is devoid of its usual bustle, the single curtain drawn.

"You're late," comes Copelan's voice. My eyes drift to where he's slumped on the floor, propped against the mirrored wall. He's as pale as a wraith, almost ghostlike in the dark. And his eyes are shadowed, his brows a dark slash as he regards me angrily.

I approach warily. "Late? For what?"

"We gave instructions after the performance last night," he mutters. "I couldn't find you, so I searched for you. Odd that you weren't in your room, even in the dead of night."

"I couldn't sleep, so I went for a walk," I lie, only to have Copelan toss a lump of fabric at my feet.

I bend, gathering the outfit I had worn to the Sky Garden last night. I had left it in Anton's wing after he asked me to change.

"A maid found it this morning," he says. "She thought you left it. Any guess where she retrieved it from?"

When I don't reply, he shoves up from the floor and stalks toward me. "You know the rules, Vasalie; you know them damned well—"

"Yes, and if you send me away, what do you think he will do? Do you really want to be responsible for angering a Crown like him?"

"That's exactly it, Vasalie. A Crown like *him*. You know his reputation, what he's known for."

But do we really?

"Fates, you two. I'm not so terrible as that."

Copelan swivels, and so do I.

Anton leans against the doorframe, arms crossed, his velvet waistcoat bunched against his broad shoulders.

He sinks his teeth into an apple.

Copelan stares for one second, then two, before he remembers himself and bows. When he straightens, he juts his chin just a little too high. "Your Majesty, what can we do for you?"

I don't miss the edge in his voice.

"The final performance is approaching rapidly and, due to recent events that rather disrupted my country's rulership, I would prefer to oversee this one. Apple?" He displays it between his fingers after another loud crunch.

And I want to disappear into the floorboards. I may have agreed to work with him, but he said nothing about interfering with our performance.

"Your Majesty," Copelan tries. "We wouldn't wish to inconvenience you—"

"Nonsense," Anton drawls. Swiping a piece of apple from his waistcoat, he slaps Copelan on the shoulder like one would a friend. "Let's walk through the ideas you have and go from there."

Copelan, looking as if he's on the brink of exploding, glares my way as if to say, *This is all your fault.* "We're styling it around the Carasia Gardens."

The Carasia Gardens aren't gardens in the traditional sense. It refers to long swathes of ivory wildflowers that bloom in the summer and fall and grow like weeds all through winter, only to die upon the arrival of spring when rain sluices the land. They carpet the southern border of Miridran's three territories and stretch all the way up into the mountains. Most people, farmers especially, consider them a nuisance.

Anton must agree. "Weeds? You're telling me you intend to represent Miridran through the weeds that fester through our lands like a plague?" His teeth, once more, crunch into that apple.

Copelan's face reddens. "I assure you, the choreography and music will be quite spectacular—"

"I'm sorry, Master Reveler Copelan, but the answer is no."

"The planning is well under way," Copelan pushes back. Bold, especially for him. "The outfits are already in production, as are the props, the music. Shifting now would be impossible—"

"Eremis and the Fate of Morta," I blurt.

Copelan's eyes slide to mine, narrowing, but I ignore him. "Eremis was Miridranian, and his story is our most legendary tale. Even you, Sire, pay homage to the Fate of Morta throughout this palace. If we must shift our plan, we could repurpose what we've acquired so far."

"Do go on," Anton says, a grin playing on his lips.

By the look of it, Copelan thinks we planned this, Anton and I. Especially after finding my clothes. I try not to grimace as I ask, "The white silk costumes that have been finished are supposed to mimic the flowers, no?" It's the first performance that would unite all the dancers—another of my ideas.

His lips flatten, but he nods.

"We can keep them, use them to depict the Souls in the tale. And Eremis can wear anything depending on what version we decide on."

"And the Fate of Morta?" Copelan asks dryly, pretense be damned, as if he's lost all sense of self-preservation.

"Leave the gown to me," Anton says, eyes sparkling.

"And props will be simple," I say. "I can walk through staging with our performers today."

"Whatever else you need, draw up a list and I will see it done." He tosses the apple core to Copelan as he strides off, only to pause on the threshold. "Vasalie, a word?"

I don't dare look at Copelan's face.

I step out, joining Anton in a nearby alcove with a small window open to the glistening sea. When I look up, his usual arrogance fades into something softer.

"I came to answer the question Basile so brusquely interrupted."

"You . . . came to explain your Glory Court?" I ask, unbelieving.

He glides his hands into his pockets. "It's a healing house. A refuge for those who need shelter and protection. It's simple, really. We orchestrate a seemingly forceable seizure—enough to be credible by whoever is a danger to them."

But if that's the case . . . "The ones who go missing. What about them?"

"Not so much missing as relocated, new identity intact. A strategy we use when they cannot return to their homes. You may confirm this with Laurent. His sister spent time there herself as a glassblowing instructor."

"You're telling me the rumors are for show?"

"Indeed, and it must stay that way."

"So those who you purchased in Estienne's *auction* . . ."

"They were offered the very best of accommodations until they can reintegrate into society, which I will help them do. They are free," he says. "And I wish that for you, too."

My throat tightens. I can't fathom how all of this could end well, but another glimmer of hope invades my heart.

I almost reach out and grab his hand, but I stop myself when he adds, almost reluctantly, "You should know that the other rumors surrounding me are mostly true, however. I spend my nights trying to forget the days. I rely on drinking and sleeping with women I forget all too easily come dawn, if only to stave off the loneliness—which never works. I am greedy, wasteful, and far too proud."

"I am fearful, damaged, and angry," I offer—as if it might smear away the shame I am not certain he should feel.

He bites his lip. "I have never really loved anything or anyone. I wonder at times if I am capable of it."

My heart constricts.

Even so, I feel myself retreating, my walls inching up. Because while I am beginning to trust him, trust is where it must end. There is nothing for us beyond this Gathering, nor can there ever be. However charming and flirtatious he might be, it's time I remember that.

I lift my shoulders. "Love is often linked to pain, so perhaps that's a blessing, Sire." His brows squeeze together, but I quickly change the topic, lowering my voice. "I'm to attend a handful of soirées over the next few nights. That's all I know."

A nod. "I will begin on the Fate of Morta gown, among other things. Now, let's get you back to killjoy in there before he bursts a vein."

When Anton returns me to the Dance Hall, he pauses in the doorway. "I will have the gown ready by tomorrow night."

Copelan and I bow as he exits the room, and under his breath, I hear Copelan murmur something a lot like, "I'm sure you'll deliver it *right* to her room."

I rub my temples.

Silence lingers, until finally Copelan sighs. "Esmée and I are a thing of the past, Vasalie."

Is that supposed to mean something? "I don't know what you want me to say."

He slicks back his hair. "I didn't merely come last night to tell you about the plans you missed. I wanted to apologize. And to tell you that this," he says, motioning between us, "is something I don't want to lose. You make me feel alive, Vas. When I'm around you, I feel . . . I don't know. *Passion*. And it's something I haven't felt in a long time."

But it isn't my job to make him feel alive, or better about himself. And I'm tired of him looking at me with either lust or scorn.

Because it *was* lust, I realize. A different kind. Not like Illian's, but lust in that he wanted me for the way I made him feel about himself. And I allowed it because I wanted the illusion of his protection—and because I was trapped. Lonely. Desperate to feel something other than pain and regret.

But what I should have wanted was empowerment.

"Then this morning," Copelan continues, "after the maid returned your clothes . . ." He shakes his head. "Tell me it isn't what it looks like, Vas."

"Why?" The bite in my voice comes as a surprise, but I square my shoulders. "So you can sleep better at night?"

He lets out a breath. "I know you felt what was between us. I know the way your body works. It responds to me with ease. We dance, and you come alive the way I do. Can you say the same when you're with him?"

He really doesn't want me to answer that. Not after last night.

I can't deny that Copelan and I had chemistry. Perhaps we still do. But chemistry is not finite. It's a shifting thing, malleable as it is predictable. With Copelan, I needed to be touched, held, comforted in all the ways I was deprived of. And with Anton . . .

It was unexpected, like a strike of lightning far outside a storm, one that left me warm and shimmering all over. He unearthed something buried within me—an intrinsic desire I still can't name. Even now, I don't fully understand it.

But it doesn't matter, because I am afraid I'll never feel it again.

"At least consider the rules, for Fates' sake, Vasalie," he says at my silence.

"The rules say nothing about Crowns, only guests, and King Anton is not a guest in his own palace." I traipse to the center of the room and stretch. "Think what you want. You always have."

Chapter Thirty-One

That night, I am sent to perform before the Serain dignitaries aboard a docked pleasure barge.

The barge itself is an impressive vessel—a congruence of carved, ornate wood. Flat, multicolored sails ripple like the gills of a fish, and a garland of silk lanterns bedecks the masts, fluttering in a gentle, evening breeze. Lounges entice guests at both the front and the rear, and a golden structure crowns its heart, hosting an inside bar.

It's a larger event than I had anticipated. Several courts meander on and off the ship throughout the evening. A multitude of performers grace makeshift stages throughout, a constant stream of entertainment. I'm thankful for the paint on my face, applied like a golden mask around my eyes—similar to what I used to do in Illian's court.

Illian, for his part, idles nearby, speaking with two Serain lords, no doubt trying to sow the seeds of doubt against his brother and Razam both. Only they seem distracted by the festivities.

And me, as I dance.

Seeming to give up, he slinks away soon after.

I finish my performance—a slow, artful dance to a harpist's

strum, subtle slips of millen glittering about my hips as I release them.

Despite the steady pace, sweat still clings to my brow. The slower songs prove the most difficult, each movement requiring a precision I barely achieve. Afterward, I perch on a bench and rub the numbness from my calves, then check the pins holding my chignon. The ocean lies unusually tranquil, a pane of glass mirroring the starlit night.

An emissary from Kasim approaches. Her blue-black hair is longer than mine but swept into a high arrangement, her floor-length organza vest cinched at the waist. She lifts the backs of my fingers to her lips, then removes them—the Kasimi sign of appreciation. "Pardon, but my friend and I have been longing to know the inspiration behind your dance. The powder, specifically."

"Oh," I say, forcing myself to stand, straightening the copper hem of my lapis silk dress, fringed just above my knees. I scramble for an answer that might appease her.

Then I wonder why I have to hide it at all. Perhaps it's an act of defiance, a small glimmer of my rage, but I find myself telling her the truth. "I have a condition that makes movement rather difficult," I explain. "I can't dance the way I used to, so I needed an element of creativity to allow me to perform."

As I say it aloud, a glow of pride falls over me.

I did that.

And it makes me feel as though . . . as though I not only accept myself as I am now, but I'm proud of it. I'm proud of surviving, of persisting, despite my pain.

"And this is . . . ?" She takes my hand, dabbing a finger on my palm, where a smattering of millen still lingers. It isn't meant to be rude; in Kasim, a casual touch is as natural as breathing, their culture one of respect.

"Millen, actually. A flour created here in East Miridran."

"Ah!" says another Serain courtier, joining in excitedly, her tight black curls strung with tourmaline stones. "That's Lord Bayard's doing! He told the story just the other night; he discovered the girl who came up with the process for grinding its stalk."

Gustav.

He was the one who found Marian.

"How very clever of you to think to use it in such a way," the Kasimi emissary says.

A new song picks up, jaunty in its rhythm. Excitement sweeps over the deck as couples pair up, readying to dance, including the two emissaries I just met, giggling as one embraces the other and leads her away.

Surprise bubbles through me when I feel an arm around my waist.

Then Anton is luring me into the throng.

"Sire, what are you doing?" I rasp, scanning the crowd, but Illian is nowhere to be seen.

Anton leans in, his gaze radiant beneath the dancing of light. "Playing into my façade, Minnow. This is nothing if not believable for me."

He guides my arm over my head.

We're but two bodies engulfed in a multitude of them, I assure myself.

We circle each other. He's practically glowing, a canvas of ivory from his tunic to his pants, like a pearl against the night. Gold hangs from his neck and ears. My knees go weak—even more with the skill at which he moves me through the dance. It unfolds like a spirited waltz, only more vigorous. I twirl away, then spin back into the crook of his arms.

He's grinning his customary grin, his cheeks charmingly dimpled.

I swallow the desire burgeoning within me, the joy—pretend it away.

On cue, he lowers me into a dip.

"By the way," he says, his breath ghosting my clavicle, "did I ever tell you I took dancing lessons? One of my many favorite pastimes growing up."

With that, he lifts me upright, whirls me away—

And releases me in a blink as he switches partners.

I am left breathless, my stomach aflutter. A lick of heat slides up my neck.

I lose sight of him soon after, couples whirling by. I decline the next courtier vying for a dance, charting a course for the bar. Filling a glass of water, I gulp it greedily, waiting for the twinkling in my vision to recede. When it does, I break for the exit.

My breath hitches when I find Illian blocking my path, his long fingers curled about a chalice.

A menacing calm cloaks his countenance, though he merely moves aside with a simple, "Evening, Miss Moran."

I want to be relieved as he lets me pass.

Yet a frightening suspicion makes me wonder if tonight was less about his order and more about watching me.

The next three days before the final signature performance tick by, uneventful.

I spend each morning practicing, ignoring my exhaustion. I act as though I am not haunted by Emilia's cries or the nightmare in which my father finally recognizes me.

I pretend away the pain in my body, or try, but despite that I feel it in every step, and I swear it's growing worse.

Worse still is the tension between Copelan and me, as dense as a heavy fog.

In the evenings, I swathe myself in costumes and paints and perform where I'm assigned. First, for a Kasimi councilor and her wife, who dismiss me the moment I finish; second, for Raiden, the Prince of Zar, who falls asleep halfway through my dance. Finally, I perform for Queen Sadira and her sons. That evening, Prince Sundar coaxes me into a game of chess, which he loses promptly, in such a way that tells me he let me win on purpose. More and more, he reminds me of Anton. It's his charm, the smiles he can't seem to hide, and his penchant for exquisite fashion.

It makes me remember that I haven't seen Anton since the barge, or heard anything more about the proof he vowed to collect.

And the Gathering concludes in just over a week. Whatever move Illian plans to make, he will do it before then.

I can't sit idly by when the stakes are so high. So I whisk on my cloak and make my way to the kitchen.

And slow at the sound of voices. I hadn't expected so many at this time of night, and so I slip between familiar crates and pad toward the cellar door, only to halt at a flash of white-blond hair.

Copelan.

He's leaning against a pillar, a confection in hand, talking with Laurent's replacement—a stiff, older woman I have made a point to avoid. When Copelan angles away, I flit around the corner and out of sight, parting the cellar door as swiftly and silently as possible. In the tunnels, I pause only once, when I pass Illian's quarters, but they are unlit. Dark.

I tread onward until I reach Anton's room. I slide the pane aside, a demand on my tongue, only to freeze at the visitor standing wide-eyed at my arrival.

"Laurent," I gasp.

I long to run to him, to fall at his feet and beg for his forgiveness, but I hold myself back. How he must hate me. How he must loathe my presence after what I've done—and rightly so.

Except he breaks into a wide, familiar grin. "Vasalie, my sweet!"

"Words can't convey," I rasp, "how sorry I am—"

"Sorry?" Laurent says. "I should be thanking you! His Majesty was guilted into not doubling but tripling my salary. *And* I was given a suite in his palace. I requested a pet tiger—though even a lynx would do—but that's still a work in progress."

Tears burn behind my eyes as I dash over and fling my arms

around his neck. He smells like cinnamon and fresh rain. "I was so worried about you," I breathe.

"I'm worried about *you*," he returns, gathering me into a gentle hug.

"I— How are you here? You should be far away . . ."

"His Majesty brought me back—with great precaution, I should add. He needed help constructing a gown." He grins.

The Fate of Morta gown. My heart flutters. "If anyone saw you . . ."

"No one knows, nor will they find out. Unless you tell them, of course."

Horror pales my face. "I would never—"

He holds up his hands, chuckling. "I know; too soon. But while I have you, would you like to see our little project?"

He pivots, but I grasp his wrist. "Laurent, I mean it. No sword, no fist—nothing could make me betray you again."

At that, his smile falters. "I won't deny how it felt, Vasalie, but Anton also told me that you came to make it right. For that, I am grateful. There is no quarrel between us."

"Even so," I tell him as he ushers me down the hall, "I will never forgive myself for it."

"Guilt eats up entirely too much energy. I'd rather you spend it on justice," he says, cerulean light seeping onto the copper floor from underneath a nearby door as we pass.

Blue light, like from the strange room I had witnessed in the tunnels that first time. The one with the portrait of Anton. I had almost forgotten it. Laurent nudges open a door on his left, revealing a small but breathtaking study. A Palladian window arcs along the far wall, moonlight limning stacks of tomes to my right. An embellished mahogany desk stretches the length of the room on my left.

But my attention latches on the sea-glass bust in the center of the room—and the gown upon it.

If it could even be called that.

It's as if he crafted a mural. It's half beadwork, the fabric barely visible on one side. The bodice is made from flat, reflective shards, and the pattern wings upward like a hellebore in bloom, each petal veined by copper threadwork. Then, like a reflection in a lake, it fans out into the skirt, the bottom elongated with a train.

"You made this?" I breathe.

A shuffling comes from behind the statue, then Gustav's head peeks out. "Vasalie? Vasalie!" Clanking down a set of tools, he runs over, his usual grin intact. "What do you think? I've been helping Laurent on the steel-boned corset and bustle. We are almost finished."

"I think I am in a very strange, very surreal dream," I say, giving the gown another perusal. The glass beads fragment light the way the sun sparks across scales.

Gustav chuckles. "This was from a concept His Majesty began a few years back. It was meant to be a wedding gown one day, but he never completed it."

"He . . . was planning to marry?" It's the first I've heard of it. An uncomfortable feeling crouches in my belly.

"A proposed arrangement since he was a boy that never came to fruition, with the Lord Sovereign's niece, Princess Ademi," Gustav says. "They wrote letters. She visited often. But the summer they were to make it official, right after his coronation, she called it off, and he's refused to speak of it since. I think it hurt him more than he wants to admit."

"Is she . . . here? At the Gathering," I ask.

"She's never attended. Not sure why," Gustav says, making another adjustment to the back of the gown. "Look at that. Bustle's done. It will help lift the weight when you wear it."

I dare a touch, dragging a finger along its uneven surface, down to where the pattern flares into the skirt.

"Those are made from aranian glass," Gustav tells me. "It's rarer than diamonds, made only when Mount Aran erupts every twenty years or so. Not particularly durable, so we can't use it for much else, but stunning for a gown such as this."

Mount Aran, a small volcanic mountain on an island north of Razam.

"I don't know what to say," I tell them. "It's exquisite, but it hardly seems worth the trouble . . ."

"Indeed," Laurent says. "It's almost as if His Majesty wants to make a statement." At my questioning glance, he shrugs. "King Illian has made not one but several attempts on his life, ever since he was barely out of adolescence. Their feud has been long and arduous, yet still, Anton lives. Thus, by putting you—his brother's so-called pet—in a gown of glass, he is telling Illian that he hasn't only cheated death, he's cheated *him*."

"Almost as if he turned his own Jewel against him," Gustav says.

I wrap my arms around my ribs. Despite Anton's flirtation, I haven't let myself believe he wants me for anything beyond thwarting his brother. Hearing Laurent's speculation is only further confirmation.

But I am not a thing to be taken or turned against anyone. I am my own, and I deserve justice as much as he.

Then Gustav's and Laurent's words hit me. *His brother's so-called pet. His own Jewel.* "You two know everything then?"

Laurent smiles sadly. He grabs my hands, squeezing them with his own. "I only wish I could help."

I turn to Gustav. "I owe you an apology, too—"

But he waves me off. "I understand the stakes for you, had you not followed through on your king's orders." His smile is so kind it hurts. "Take comfort, my lady Vasalie, in knowing you are on the right side. King Anton is a good man."

"I believe you," I say, rubbing my arms. And I do—especially after last week. "It's just that I thought the same of his brother, who had me fooled for years. It's hard to forget that."

"Illian had many of us fooled for a time," Gustav says, drawing my eye. At my quizzical glance, he explains. "I grew up in the palace. My mother and his are cousins, if you can believe it . . ."

"You were raised alongside them," I say. Illian never spoke of his mother, let alone his past beyond his strenuous relationship with his brothers. And even then, it was cryptic. Small remarks, nothing more.

"Indeed. He was Queen Saskia's favorite. For a long time, I couldn't understand why she never favored her eldest."

At least now we know why; Illian was her eldest by blood.

"But though she doted on Illian, souls, she smothered him, too. She forced him into lesson upon lesson while his brothers galivanted through Miridran in whichever way they so pleased. She practically ignored Anton's existence altogether. And Illian . . . I don't think I ever saw him without a book in hand, and by the Fates, even as a boy, he never learned to smile. His whole life was centered around a single purpose: preparing for the throne.

"I remember Anton and I overheard him and Queen Saskia once after he was caught skipping a lesson. It was"—Gustav counts his fingers—"two years before she passed. She berated him relentlessly. It didn't matter that Estienne had always intended to step down as crown prince, that everything would go to Illian automatically. That was not enough for her. Illian had to earn it. Prepare. And so he did."

"But then King Junien split the kingdom," I say. After all Illian's hard work.

"Yes, after spending time in Razam with Her Grace. The two grew close—closer than Queen Saskia was comfortable with. She didn't like it—misunderstood it, even, because it was never romantic. But even she couldn't convince her husband to abandon his plans before the Gathering took place. She died that year.

"Once the announcement was made, Illian . . . grew bitter."

In some ways, I understand. Illian thought he was owed Miridran in its entirety. He had prepared for it all his life, to the exclusion of all else. It had been *promised* to him.

I, too, know what it is like to be raised solely for a purpose—a commodity more than a child. It's almost enough for me to feel sorry for the boy Illian was.

But not quite.

I think of the attempts Illian made on Anton's life. I had accused Anton of carousing, and while that is true, his adolescence was also spent simply trying to stay alive. I do not know the nightmares that follow him to sleep, but I suspect they are many. I wonder if they might be as vicious, as numerous, as mine.

I know what it's like to feel lonely and stifled by the dark.

He's surrounded himself with good people—Gustav, Laurent, Basile. The company one keeps is an indication of character. Yet I sense that they might not fully comprehend the depth of his pain, and he, in turn, chooses to shield them from it. His brothers, his mother, and even his future wife rejected him, all in their own ways. And with the pressure of a kingdom on his back . . .

"Please, I need to see him," I say.

"He's on the balcony off his room last I checked," Gustav says, a coy smile brimming. "I believe you know where that is."

The balcony, where he perched me on the balustrade and broke my spiral of anxiety and fear.

Where he said: *You are art.*

Somehow, I don't even mind that Gustav knows. I follow the hall, past the empty plinth where the vase I broke once stood, and beyond, into his bedroom. It's dark aside from the orange light of the hearth, the doors leading to the balcony spread open. A current of sea air rushes past, carrying the song of softly rolling waves.

I find Anton on a lounge, the breeze toying with his loose hair. He's propped up, nose buried in a book, a small lantern flickering a soft glow onto the page. A pair of endearing spectacles are perched on the bridge of his nose. Beside him, Ishu is curled on her side, snoring softly.

He's so engrossed that he doesn't even notice me.

My heart whirls like a carousel in my chest, a gyre of feelings that make it seem like the balcony is tottering beneath me. Like the palace might topple, crumble, and me with it.

I haven't known him for long, but something about the sight of him dispels the last of my reservations. Here, and perhaps always, he is just a boy. A curious boy who loves to learn, to laugh, to *save*.

A boy chased by nightmares, even when he's awake.

A sly little curve turns his lips without him glancing up. "Enjoying the view, Minnow?"

Embarrassment suffuses me. I wring my hands, idling awkwardly by the door. "It's been days, Sire. You said you were gathering proof, and I was worried—"

"I have been," he says, grin softening. "I am. I need another day or two at most, and we have just over a week before the Gathering ends."

I nod, but it does little to ease my anxiety.

Placing his book down, he rises and strides toward me. My stomach swoops, and I find myself blurting, "I—I am not a thing to be used."

Tenderly, he cradles my jaw with his hands and leans his forehead against mine.

"You are not," he whispers.

His thumbs are smooth as they graze my cheeks—as if he can sense the war inside me.

And when his nose brushes mine, I can do little more than inhale him for long moments. I want to close out the world. Forget who he is, yet again. And here, sharing breath, I almost can. His scent fills my lungs—a welcome. A warning.

My hands move without my consent, wrapping around his waist.

I lean my head against his heart, feeling the way it beats. Races.

For me.

He cups my head, bringing my gaze back to his, and something about the gesture is irrevocably tender. A need shivers through me—one I don't even fully understand.

"May I kiss you for real this time, Minnow?" he whispers, tucking a spiral of hair behind my ear with his free hand.

We shouldn't, I think.

Please, I think.

I twist my hands into his tunic and nod, only when I glance up, he doesn't move.

"Well?" I prompt, at last.

"I'm not going to do it when you're *expecting* it."

"Menace," I say. I yank him toward me—

He presses his lips onto mine.

If there was a game between us, it vanishes. I tug him closer, as if I could burrow inside him, and then he's challenging my force with his own, his other hand pressing against the small of my back. And all I can think of is desire. Desire, to be closer, to—

His arms come underneath me, and then he's sweeping inside, situating me on the dresser beside the door. His hands grip it on either side of my legs.

I feel so small, so engulfed. Liquid, from my head to my toes.

My eyes fall shut, and though he isn't touching me right now, I feel him everywhere. In my lungs, in my bones. In my *pulse*.

He removes my cloak. Lets it fall around my hips. Underneath, I am wearing only a simple black dress with a neckline that scoops down far too low.

His knuckles glide along the arc of my neck.

I release a breath.

He swallows it, his mouth on mine once more. He smells like the zest of an orange, the salt of the isle, a scent that lingers even on his lips. I bring my hands to his chest, splay my fingers across it.

He releases a long-suffering groan. "Vasalie, please, spare me and pull away before I lose myself and carry you to bed."

I should do just that. But this is a moment we might never have again, and try as I might, I can't back away. So what if I am selfish, just this once?

I can't put words to what I want from him right now. I just know I want . . . *more*.

I shake my head, my fingers twining around his neck. His breath shudders, and in return, a hand flirts with the hem of my dress. He watches me for any hint of discomfort, then his palm travels up and over my thigh, and farther still, to curve around my hip.

Once more, I am intoxicated. And more so, when he slides my sleeve down with his other hand, his lips kissing a path along my neck. I tangle my fingers into his hair.

The air changes, like an updraft in the summer, simmering with heat.

The lacing on the back of my dress is simple.

He looses the ribbons with ease.

Cool air grazes my shoulders, my back, and then I am in his arms.

He brings me to the bed, just like he said he would.

There, he eases us down until he's sitting, his back against the headboard. His mouth never leaves mine as he gathers me up toward his chest, his arm underneath my knees. My skin is glossed with a light sheen of sweat. I could melt, here. I think I already am, and I am okay with that.

He pauses once more. Looks between my eyes, his breathing as ragged as my own.

I am frightened—but only of the way I feel.

With an arm keeping me tucked, he turns us, rolls us around until he settles me beneath him, his weight a pleasant thing. My eyes fall shut. I am nothing but sensation and coiled, frenzied nerves as he sets a palm underneath my knee, drags it up—

"Your Majesty," comes a voice just outside.

We freeze, but neither of us speaks. My heart feels as if it might fly from my chest.

Whoever is outside the door knocks twice, then again . . .

Anton squeezes his eyes shut for a moment before dragging a

quilt over, wrapping it around me so I am covered in full. "What is it, Basile?"

The door cracks open. "Your presence is requested in the studio, Sire."

"I will be there shortly," Anton says.

"I recommend now, Sire."

"You have the absolute worst timing, Basile."

"It is a new development, Sire, which you demanded I inform you of should it come to"—Basile glances at me, unreadable—"fruition."

Development?

A slight groan slips from Anton's lips. Once more, he cups my face. "Vasalie, I—"

A very prominent clearing of the throat jolts us both, and Anton finally pulls away. "Basile, in this moment, I do not like you very much."

"I know, Sire."

Anton groans as Basile lopes off, leaving us alone.

"We will talk soon," Anton says apologetically, after giving himself a moment. "I'll send someone to deliver your gown within the hour."

Dazed as I am, he leads me back to the workshop where Gustav and Laurent are. Gustav follows him away, the two of them shoving each other playfully before disappearing around the bend. Laurent, grinning knowingly, offers to escort me out.

But he pauses, sensing the tumult within me.

I almost lost myself, just now, with Anton. And it leaves me both exhilarated and terrified—of what the future looks like when I have to forget him, when I must move on from all that's happened these past several weeks.

That assumes we make it out of this mess, what with my father, and Illian . . .

"It's going to be all right, sweet," Laurent says.

"I hope you're right."

Laurent snuffs the lantern. I pivot to follow but pause at the sheaf of moonlight falling across the desk. Or rather, the ring glinting at me like a winking eye.

His signet ring.

"Anton isn't wearing his ring," I note, unable to look away.

Crowns always wear them. Illian never let his leave his hand.

"He prefers not to wear it when he's in his studio."

But I can't focus on Laurent's words, because my mind is elsewhere, hung on the edge of a memory.

The banquet.

I replay the night in my head. I had always felt like I'd forgotten something. Missed something. So I allow the memories to resurface, one by one.

Gustav's legs buckling beneath him.

Anton rushing over. Shouting for water. A physician.

A servant ambling forward, a glass in hand.

Except he spills it. And so he bends, wiping his rag . . .

The rag. What am I forgetting? I shake my head, trying to clear the murk from my mind. The poison had begun working by that time. But if I could just—

Eyes, sliding intently toward mine.

A smirk on knowing lips.

The servant. I had recognized him from Illian's court. And Anton—he had been wearing his ring that night. I remember seeing it, remember the cold of it against my hand.

The servant had a small box. Not a ring box, but . . .

I approach the desk, considering the ring, and that's when I see it. A small block of red, unmelted wax.

It wasn't a box in the servant's hands. It was *wax*.

"The banquet," I breathe. "The poison, it wasn't just to harm Gustav. I think—I think it was a distraction while someone duplicated Anton's seal."

Laurent relights the lantern and paces over.

"Illian," I say, the pieces snapping together. "He was composing letters using a seal that wasn't his." I remember it clearly, the first time I found the tunnels. I hadn't thought much of it, but now . . . "I think he is writing in Anton's hand."

Apprehension accompanies me on my journey back through the tunnels. Once more, I try to align the pieces of Illian's crooked puzzle, fit the discordant notes into some kind of rhythm I can follow, but I can't make sense of who he would be writing to in Anton's hand or what good it would do here when any misconstruction could easily be exposed by Anton himself?

Laurent promised to warn Anton, but even so, I feel as if each passing second is a stride toward King Rurik's death and a dangerous, inevitable war. I can't understand why Anton is waiting, why he needs so much time. I should have asked him when I had the chance.

But instead, I had kissed him.

I groan and bat a flurry of dust from my face, then yank open the cellar door, registering too late the light bleeding from the other side. The moment I step through, a rough grip seizes my arm.

Then I'm dragged directly into a column of light.

Chapter Thirty-Two

The lantern cuts a harsh shadow against Copelan's pale face, carving his cheekbones into razor sharp lines.

"Where have you been?" His grip is punishing as he swings around me, peering into the tunnels for himself. "Souls below, you were sneaking about the palace. I saw you disappear, but what in the Fates is this? How did you know of it?"

My mouth parts, but I'm so stunned I can't even conjure a poor excuse, let alone a believable one.

He laughs, and it's a pitiless, merciless sound. "One deception after another. Really, I'm dying to know what lie you have for me this time."

"It was . . . an errand. At King Anton's request." I hate myself for lying, but I see no other escape.

His eyes dip down in a mocking perusal. "And what type of errand would that be, Vasalie?"

I've never seen him so cold, so finite. It's as if he's slammed a wall between us. "Please, Copelan. You can ask His Majesty. He will verify—"

"It's too late for that."

My face drains of color. "Too late for what?"

"I've already reported you. I wash my hands of this. Let the Crowns judge you." One stride brings him to the kitchen door, where he knocks twice.

Horror leeches my breath. "Copelan, no—"

Guards pour into the room like smoke. I'm torn from Copelan's grip and thrown to the ground, breath fleeing my lungs in a whoosh. I gasp, panic speeding through my veins like cold fire.

He turned me in.

He reported me.

Boots step around me. A hand grips my hair and wrenches my neck back.

A figure strides into view, a shadow against the blinding light, but I know that shape.

It's happening—*again.*

"After all I've done for you," comes that familiar drawl, followed by the cluck of his tongue. "This is how you repay me."

My stomach churns at the low, smooth tenor of his voice. He tugs his hood down, his curls spilling out. One flick of his wrist, and a guard jerks me to my feet, fingers digging into the soft flesh underneath my arms. Even so, I struggle to find purchase, scrambling to stand on my own.

And the tunnels are wide open, yawning behind me.

If I could make enough noise, perhaps it would warn my friends—

"Release me!" I shout. "You have no reason—"

A gag is shoved into my mouth, then banded tight. "What a little snake you've turned out to be, coiled around another's arm."

I thrash, screaming against my gag. Meaty fingers squeeze my throat until stars splatter across my vision.

"Don't hurt her," comes Copelan's voice. He steps forward but is promptly blocked. "Your Majesty, she was to be brought before the Crowns. This is unjust—"

"I'd advise you to hold your tongue, Master Reveler."

"With respect, Sire, I am obligated to remind you that we are in East Miridran, and punishment must be carried out in accordance to its laws and to the laws of the Gathering."

I notice, then, how ashen he is, even amid my panic.

"Her registration puts her from Greenwood, a village south of Irivan," Illian drawls. "Seeing as Central Miridran is now split between my brother and me, she falls under my judgment. I may carry out punishment as I see fit." He pauses. "I'd hate for my wrath to extend to dear Esmée, who is here in hopes that I might offer her another position once more."

Esmée.

She's still here.

Copelan's features slacken.

"Come now, Master Reveler. Your pity is misplaced." Illian cocks his head to the side. "Did you know that our Vasalie here is a suspected criminal? Rather damning letters of hers were found just recently alongside a murdered courtier from my territory. Perhaps you will be less hasty to defend her now."

I suck in a breath. He signaled for the body to be found—he finally invoked his true hold over me. Or is it merely a bluff, a way to shut him up?

Copelan's eyes find mine.

I shake my throbbing head. *Please, see the truth in my eyes.*

Illian continues, "What a favor you've done, reporting her. During our investigation, I will allow her to finish her role here, albeit under watch. And, seeing as I am repaying the kindness for your Esmée, may I count on your discretion?"

Again, Copelan locks eyes with mine. A tear tracks down my cheek.

Please, I beg him silently. *Do something.*

But I know he won't. And so I am not surprised when he tightens his lips and nods like the coward he is.

"Excellent. Before you go," Illian says, "what do you know of these tunnels? Where do they lead?"

"I was never made aware of them, Sire."

I can't tell if Copelan is telling the truth, but it does not matter. "Search them," Illian orders his guards, and my stomach drops. "Find everything there is to find, but be discreet."

Guards rush past, torches blazing as they plunge into the tunnel. And like batting a fly in the air, King Illian waves Copelan away.

Don't abandon me, I silently plead.

His brows notch together, a flash of pity within, then his shoulders stoop and he walks away.

Once again, I am alone with Illian and his guards. I wonder if he will finally have me killed or if he has something worse planned.

Fear runs cold through the marrow of my bones.

"Tell me where you were going," he says, narrowing the distance between us, his voice softening into silk. "Tell me before they find out, and I might find it in my heart to extend you mercy once more."

The guard holding my arm yanks away my gag.

I bark my answer. "Was it your mercy I just witnessed?" I run my tongue along my lips, tasting blood. They must have split when I hit the floor.

Illian follows the movement, gaze dropping to my mouth. The echo of footfalls reaches my ears as the guards swarm the tunnels, splitting off in different directions. I pray my friends will hear their approach.

My eyes burn like hot pokers as I stare at Illian. I want to claw at him. I want to curse his name. I open my mouth but stop myself. Should I try for mercy or invoke his wrath? *Survive*, a voice inside me says; it sounds like Emilia. *Live to fight.*

Illian studies me for a long moment, two fingers rubbing his chin. "It pains me, you know. All of this. Contrary to what you may believe, Vasalie, I do not enjoy seeing you suffer."

I lose all sense and spit in his direction. Blood lands on his brown tunic. His eyes dip down, assessing the damage, before returning to mine. I can tell he itches to reach for me, to jab his fingers into the soft flesh of my neck until the air is squeezed from my lungs.

But then I study him closer, and my breath recoils.

There is an ache in that gaze. A want. And all over again, I recall the girl. My dress. What he did to her while pretending she was me.

His fingers twitch at his sides.

Then he lets out a long sigh. "I thought we had an agreement. I thought we had made peace, after everything." He pulls a kerchief from his pocket and dabs the blood on my lips with a tenderness that makes my skin crawl. "But know this," he tells me. "Whoever you are helping, whoever you have manipulated onto your side—whether my brother or his minions on this souls-forsaken isle—I will find them. And if you do not play your role, their every plea for mercy will reach your beautiful ears until you beg me to cut them from navel to neck."

With that, he breezes away, and the guards heave me toward the door.

"And remember," Illian shouts over his shoulder, "not a word, my Jewel."

I launch my weight toward him, my vision sparking like the end of a torch. I want to rip him apart. Dig my nails into his face and shred it until there's nothing left but blood and bone.

But my strength is no match for Illian's guards. One grabs a handful of my hair and jerks. "Stand straight," a feminine voice hisses into my ear. "Walk on your own legs or I'll drag you down the hall by your braid."

My pulse pounds against my skull. The guards press tight on either side of me; I have no choice but to walk on.

When we reach my room, one barrels in ahead of me. "What in Morta's Lair is this?"

The other guard lugs me inside, and I hold in my gasp. In the center of my room is the bust with the Fate of Morta gown, gleaming like moonlight against black, jagged waves, a hooded cloak draping over the ensemble.

They managed to deliver it.

I take a shaky breath, steadying myself as my guards circle it like vultures.

"Don't you dare touch it," I hiss. "It's a costume, designed specifically for the upcoming dance. If you so much as pull the wrong thread, it could fall apart." A lie, or maybe it isn't, but I don't want their filthy hands on my dress.

But then I notice something different about it. I wait until the guards are distracted, leafing through my room as if to find damning evidence or some nonexistent passageway, one knocking against every last stone in the souls-forsaken wall.

I tug down the hood.

Underneath is a silver circlet ornamented with twining glass, and on the front, two opposing obsidian shards jut up proudly.

No, not shards. Daggers, the apex of their blades forming a point.

I cannot protect you. But I can arm you.

I press my finger to one of the blades.

It moves within the frame.

I'm herded to our final practice the next day like a muzzled ox, my guards crowding me with every step, and only when I reach the Dance Hall do they allow me room to breathe.

"One word, one wrong move," one whispers in my ear, "and you'll be dragged from this hall in chains."

Our performance uses a multitude of performers, who Copelan directs in turn.

He makes a point to avoid me.

Whether it's fear of retaliation from Illian or simply shame, I don't know. Perhaps the knowledge of my past, the lies Illian told, disgusts him. Still, I sear him with my gaze, knowing he can feel it, and bide my time, praying my friends weren't caught in those tunnels.

My friends, who I do not deserve, but who have lent me their kindness all the same. As I tossed and turned last night, sick with worry, I decided that—for them—I would fight back. I would destroy myself to protect them. Because Emilia had fought for me, and Copelan had not.

I will not turn my back like he did.

Then there's Anton.

A good man, Laurent said. I'm beginning to think he's right. Despite Anton's arrogance, despite his beautiful, insufferable smirks. Despite his silver-tongued glibness. What he did for Laurent, for Marian, for the members of the Glory Court . . .

There is good in him.

Then there's the way he makes me feel—like I have a bit of fight left in me. Like joy, laughter, and pleasure are not so far out of reach. Warmth rushes through me like a summer wind, until I remember that he is a Crown and I am a broken dancer with little to her name. I have nothing to offer him beyond the little help I can give. And when everything is said and done, I will disappear into the cliffs of Brisendale and never see him again.

But I will make peace with that when the time comes. First, we have to survive this mess.

Just a little more time, Anton had said, but I can't do nothing. So the one time, that one *single* beat in our dance where Copelan cannot avoid my gaze—when he is forced to fall into my embrace—I breathe a single whisper into his ear.

And pray it hits its mark.

"What, did he threaten to cut your tongue to ribbons if you speak?" I ask Sana, the guard leaning against the back of my door on the evening of the final performance.

As always, I am ignored.

For now, she is my only companion until the other guard, who I now know as Aemon, returns with our food. As per Illian's command, I have not had a moment's reprieve. They even take turns sleeping in my room each night to ensure I am watched at all times. That I couldn't somehow escape.

If I could, I would have.

If I can just find Anton tonight at the final performance, I can warn him—during the dance, somehow, if I must. Even if not, he never fails to read me. He will know something is wrong.

Soon.

I sit before my vanity, artlessly brushing a pearlescent powder over my cheekbones, eyelids, and nose, before stroking kohl above my lashes.

"Can you arrange a coronet?" I ask Sana. "You might as well make yourself useful."

I am met with silence. But if my talking annoys her, I will keep at it. "You know, Illian prefers a bit of spice. If you are hoping to impress him, which clearly you are, being that you enabled the abuse of a defenseless woman, you may want to liven up." I feel her gaze on the back of my neck, so I press on. "Or you can choose to work for someone who doesn't prey on women. There's always that."

In the mirror, I note the ever so slight tightening of her jaw. But she swings her gaze at the sound of a knock, then slants me a warning look. "You are not to reveal anything in regards to your king."

Like I would listen to her. But when she opens the door, the last person I expect flits through.

Esmée Fontaine.

In her hands are a bundle of pins, a comb, and a jar of scented oil. "I was sent by His Majesty, King Illian, to assist you in your preparation," she says, her gaze darting about the room. "Might you allow me to fashion your hair?"

Her voice is feather-light, serene, as if this is all perfectly normal. But she might be my only hope, and so I nod and settle back into my chair as she twines my hair in sections, securing them with pins before pulling pieces loose. Those, she coils with her fingers. Aemon returns with a platter of food, relieving Sana of her post, but I'm far too queasy to eat.

Once I am finished, Esmée turns her gaze on Aemon. "I will need to help her dress."

His cue to leave.

My heart jumps, and a fool's hope slides in—that my last, desperate appeal to Copelan got through. That he sent her here to help. But that can't be. This is Illian's work.

She must know who I am.

As expected, Aemon shakes his head. "I can't let her out of my sight."

He doesn't even offer to turn.

"The room is too small, what with the size of this dress," Esmée says. "The window is a steep drop, and you will be right outside." She glides over, placing a careful hand on his arm. "Please. It would mean a great deal to me—a favor I shall try to repay."

To my surprise, he gives her a sweeping appraisal before assenting. "Three minutes."

"Five," she says, gesturing at the costume. "It's a complicated piece."

"Five, then, but not a second more," he murmurs.

The moment the door shuts, she spins to face me. "I just bought you a few minutes of privacy. In exchange, I want to know what has happened between you and Illian."

"Why?" I ask as she reaches for my gown. "Because he abandoned you, and now you want him back?"

"What makes you think—"

"I was there when you broke your wrist."

She pulls her lip between her teeth as she unlaces the ties on the back of the costume, the ones holding it to the bust. At the way her fingers tremble, my heart clenches with a sudden pang. I halt her with a hand on her arm. "You aren't the only one he wronged."

But she blinks at me, almost doe-eyed. "Wronged? His Majesty . . . did not *wrong* me."

"Didn't he, though? He took your position from you."

Again, her gaze flits across mine. She releases a long-suffering sigh. "It's my fault, really. I . . . we shared a night together. Just one, but things changed after that. It was perhaps my greatest mistake."

My vision tunnels, the room closing in.

He slept with her?

Touched her?

The knowledge bears down on me like a portcullis ready to sink its teeth into my shoulders. Illian never laid a hand on me. And while I'm thankful, I can't understand it. Can't fathom *why*.

"You say it was mistake," I hear myself say. "Is that because you both regretted it?"

Esmée shakes her head, fingers fumbling with the gown again. "I should have known he would tire of me thereafter."

"But he came to see you—at the Melune," I say.

"It was . . . an attempt to remind him of what he was missing." She swallows, unbuttoning my shift. "I heard he found you afterward. His Jewel. It is a shame you ruined your chance to win him back, but do not begrudge me the same opportunity."

"You're only here to try to reclaim your position, then?" I was beginning to think Illian sent for her, somehow. But if she came on her own . . .

Esmée takes Morta's crown, fashioned by Anton himself, and places it gently on my head. Arranging my hair around the circlet, she says, "The princess offered me a full month's salary if I came as a stand-in. It was an opportunity—both to see His Majesty again, and to . . . resolve some unfinished business. With a friend."

Unfinished business.

With Copelan.

Copelan, who nearly got me killed. Who abandoned me. Revulsion swims in my belly. Convincing her to help would be fruitless because she doesn't hate Illian. She *wanted* him. She craved his affection like I had, only I had gotten so much more than I'd bargained for.

She steps back, admiring her work, and I decide that I can't waste this chance, even if she might not believe me. If anything, I'd say she's as trapped as I am, only by her own delusions. "Things aren't what they seem," I say. "There's so much you don't know. We're all in danger. Please, if you could send word to—"

The door flies open, and Aemon's voice cuts through my plea. "Time's up."

Still, I angle away, praying she reads my lips. "Find King Anton. Tell him—"

Aemon wrenches Esmée away, and Sana appears, ushering her out. Esmée shakes her head in a pitiful gesture, not understanding, and my hope tumbles from my grasp into a heap on the floor.

Sana secures a set of manacles on my wrists after allowing me to gather my cloak and adjust my costume.

When the time comes for them to escort me to the boat that will carry us to the small, adjacent island for our final performance, I walk as a Crown would despite the deep-seated ache in my bones, the pain in my ribs, the fear compressing my lungs. Head high, shoulders back, I summon the confidence the real Fate of Morta would have.

Chapter Thirty-Three

Bonfires heave smoke into the air as our boat approaches the small island off the northern end of Anell. It smells of a pyre lit with incense—sage, black currant, myrrh—like an offering to the Fate of Morta herself, while clouds of gray catch the smoke and blend it into the evening sky.

One long dock curves around the southern half like a crescent moon, and from it, a single bridge reaches onto the island itself. The Crowns and courtiers are escorted off small, elaborate crafts and directed toward the entrance—a stone tunnel that proudly displays flags from each country.

Our boat, however, drifts toward the eastern side of the island. My guards and I dock near a set of rocks and unload, then join the performers around the back of the stage. My cape billows in the wind over my costume, which is surprisingly light thanks to the corset and clever bustle sewn into the design.

I peer around the stage divider, the air heavy in my lungs.

It looks as if a giant scooped a handful of the island and tossed it out across the rocks. A dip in the center creates the perfect curvature for carved stone benches, like that of an arena, and on the lowest level is the stage. Around it, juts of stone form barriers, blending in with the curved stone wall and archway like a cave with its roof blown off.

I skim the crowd for Anton. If I could just catch his eye, I can signal him back here while the audience settles. I need to warn him about Illian and the tunnels. Ask him if he's found anything. Time is running thin, and King Rurik is in danger.

But I can't find Anton anywhere. Not as the musicians slide into place throughout the stage, not as massive pots blow steam across the makeshift stage's wooden planks. Not even as the dancers and bards take their positions, their costumes drifting about in the wind.

I do, however, spot my father. He reclines beside King Rurik in his crisp blue uniform, sharp as the harsh lines scoring his forehead and lips. His eyes, severe and emotionless, cut across the stage like a carefully wielded blade.

The Lair of Morta. That's what we have created here. I hope he knows he'll face her soon. I'd gladly trade my soul if it meant his would be lost.

A harmony stirs the air, soft as breath.

Four dancers dressed like souls flutter a long, tapered stretch of fabric in the center of the stage. With the sweep of their hands, it bounces, flows, and with one last exaggerated swing, they release it.

Underneath, Copelan is revealed.

He lies on the stage floor, knees bent at odd angles, a plunging red stain evident on his doublet.

Eremis, slain on the battlefield of his first war.

The last time I saw him, I had whispered in his ear, *Your complicity reveals your cowardice.*

A violinist's string pierces the fog, sharp as a pin prick. Copelan jolts, awakening in Morta's Lair.

Souls circle him in their wraithlike attire, taunting, beckoning, grabbing fistfuls of his clothes. He tries to run, to flee, but they tear off strips of his jacket, ripping at his buttons—

Through a plume of fog, I enter, a whisper of darkness and shadow.

The commotion comes to a halt. Copelan, as Eremis, is unaware of who stands behind him, ready to pull him into the void. Anticipation builds until he senses my nearness, and finally, he turns.

He had stood idle while I suffered, idle while guards threw me down.

We watch each other—me, a veiled figure, and him, with his slicked-back hair and kohl-lined eyes, as defined as Anton's in the low light. I chance a glimpse at the stands, but Anton isn't there. Unease sits in my stomach like spoiled meat and it takes everything in me not to double over with worry. Something isn't right. He would not miss this.

The vocalists spin the lines cueing my next step. *Take my hand, Eremis of Lach, for I promise not a scratch.*

I have no choice but to focus, so I tug down my hood and reach out my hand.

True to the myth, infatuation cajoles Eremis toward me, as I am beauty personified. Copelan unfurls his fist, stretching his hand toward mine. But at the last moment, he jerks it back as the song continues.

You will not trap me, Morta. Your beauty, while lovely to be sure, is that of an agate, clouded and veined. I am an ammolite, iridescent and rare; next to me, you cannot compare.

He plucks the tapered cloth from the ground, whirling it about. In a blink, he disappears, the trapdoor perfectly timed.

But while he has escaped my Lair, he has not escaped me. That sepulchral, blue-gray light dwindles, the sea glass on the torches replaced. Pale amber and sage envelops us now, shifting us into the land of the living. The souls spin out of their robes, earth-toned linens beneath, the costumes that of street-goers, traders, bakers, and merchants. Dancing around, they sing their wares amid carts wheeled out, our surroundings that of a bustling street.

I, too, sweep off my cloak, revealing a softer one the shade of dusk—a maiden in the crowd.

From beneath the archway, Copelan enters the stage once more, an arrogant smile in place. He escaped death, after all, and now he joins the living, unaware of the specter who stalks him; in our version, it isn't the prophets who follow, but Morta herself.

A bard sings my thoughts aloud as I follow him, as I vow to find his weakness. I move around him, dodge him before he can notice me, weaving among the bustling crowd. He turns back, sensing my presence, and I dip away. He dances from vendor to vendor; I spin and whirl about, unseen.

Until finally he pauses at a fruit cart, shucking a few coins in exchange for a pomegranate. I use the distraction to draw near, snatching a metal pitcher to hide my face.

He turns, pausing at the sight of me.

Only, he isn't looking at me, entranced as he is by his reflection in the pitcher. He angles this way and that, flattening an errant hair before giving himself a wink.

And I've learned his secret.

His weakness I have unmasked.
His beauty shall trap him at last.

Beauty. The lyric snaps me out of my performance. Illian, the prophecy . . .

I flick my gaze to where he sits, and seeing him is like a blow. My skin still stings at the memory of last night.

He smiles when he catches me looking, smiles at the way I fumble a step. Then, deliberately so that I don't miss it, he slants his head toward Anton's empty seat.

No.

My heart slams my pulse into a frenzy. Anton, my one chance at justice. Freedom. Miridran's only hope for a decent king—Illian has captured him, somehow. He shows it to me in that smug, satisfied smirk.

I don't see Gustav, either. Or Basile.

I can't catch my breath. Copelan notices. He spins away, drawing the audience's attention with him. The dancers play along, and I'm grateful, even if it isn't for me; a poor performance would reflect on us all. Attackers ready themselves in the bushes to ambush Copelan when the music swells. I have precious minutes to compose myself and finish my act and then . . . then I will make a plan. I will find Anton. Somehow.

Breathe.

But Laurent and Gustav. Are they safe?

I can't . . . *can't* let Illian win. I won't let my father win. I will *not* let him claim the Brisendali throne for himself. Anton and I are the only ones who overheard their plot, and that means no one else can stop it. And if something happened to Anton, it's up to me.

I must warn King Rurik.

A loud clash, and Eremis falters, slain once more. His attackers were swift, precise, and once more, the stage transforms back into Morta's Lair. I drop the dusky cloak to reveal Anton's creation: the gown of stained, molten glass—with a crown to match.

I feel the intake of breath like a drop in pressure.

For the second time, Eremis awakes in a bath of fog, souls chanting around him. Azure light focuses in on me. Copelan pulls himself up, only to freeze.

This time, he does not see me. Because there, in my dress, my crown, the mirrored sea-glass mask I slid into place, he finds his reflection gazing back at him. Just like the statue from the fountain.

For the second time, I stretch out my hand.

Eremis, whose face do you see?

Let's see how easily you are deceived.

Our hands link, his heady pulse thrumming against mine. Souls bound around us, exuberant in triumph. We have bested an arrogant man, and we intend to feast. I drag Copelan deeper, deeper, spinning us lower and lower in the center of the stage until the mist swallows us whole.

The music settles, and applause breaks out, only to be overpowered by one slow, thunderous clap.

Illian is impossible to miss, his slim, crimson doublet trimmed with diamonds, his smile like that of a cat. He continues that clap, loud as the clank of a blade against steel, as he joins us onstage.

"Extravagant, as always," he says. "Alas, I have an announcement that cannot wait." His tone fails to hide his eagerness as he strides toward me, his gaze roaming where his hands itch to, until it clings to the glasswork details of my dress.

His smile falters when he realizes who made it.

Good.

"First and foremost," he calls out, his expression one of concern as he turns to his waiting crowd. "I wish to convey the depths of my gratitude that you have all chosen to attend the Crowns' Gathering. It is a show of dedication to the greater good of our world; we better serve our people by setting aside our differences to strengthen our relations and forge new ones. Miridran has always been proud to host such an occasion. And to honor that spirit, I vow to deliver the truth, no matter what imprecations it may bring against me."

My stomach swims with dread. Anton is still missing. King Rurik, on the other hand, sits next to my expressionless, deceiving father.

"My father once said that Miridran is like an evergreen tree. We remain strong season to season, but to do so, we must shed our weakest branches—those brittle with mold and corruption. We witnessed such an occasion last week with the heartbreaking news of Estienne's deception and illegitimate claim, yet I am afraid I have even more disturbing news. Our host, and my younger brother, Anton Orvere, Crown of East Miridran, is not so benevolent as I believed."

Murmurs spread, yet Illian barrels on, "As much as I wish to deny it, I have learned that he has used the Gathering as a way to plot against us all." A guard approaches, handing him a bundle of letters. Illian holds them up, each one sealed with a pool of emerald-green wax.

And the imprint of Anton's seal.

"We intercepted a series of correspondences from Anton himself to Queen Sadira. Razam intends to cease all weapons trades with Brisendale," he says, "and Anton intends to replace them with newly forged weapons from sea glass—weapons he has thus far restricted to his own use. Not only has he undermined a ten-year trade agreement we signed into operation during the last Gathering, but he has since transported illegal weaponry. Such astonishing findings have left me no choice but to expose his schemes."

I expel a breath as if I've been pierced by a lance. Two Crowns—no, three—spring from their seats, accompanied by guards. The rest of the audience follows, murmurs and shouts erupting like a hot spring. "Let us see the letters," I hear someone shout. "Hand them over!"

The Queen of Razam sweeps upward, a devastating fury darkening her gaze, but two of her sons clasp her arms, restraining her.

Illian disperses the letters among the crowd. "All their plans, laid out before you," he says. "Anton has been arming Razam behind our backs; see for yourself."

"No," I say under my breath. My palms are hot, shaking. *Speak out*, something inside me begs, but my word will mean nothing here. I am as insignificant as dust. I look to Copelan, but he's occupied, shuffling the other performers onto boats. As if at any minute this island could sink.

The letters seem to multiply. How many had he forged? The King of Brisendale bounds into sight, grabbing one and unfolding it. I'm sure it is every bit as incriminating as Illian suggested.

Because Illian wrote it.

"The entire Gathering has been a farce," Illian calls over the noise. "By bringing you here, Anton was learning your secrets. His entire palace is riddled with hidden tunnels; my guards came across them just today." The liar. "We've been scouring them for the last hour. I plan to open them up to you all so that you might witness them for yourself."

It's like a string of tension has snapped. A cacophony of voices fights for attention—some shouting for Anton's head, others for his presence. The Gathering is in pandemonium. Guards form blockades, eager to protect their Crowns. I spot Aemon and Sana at the edge of the stage, tracking my movements.

When Crowns divide, and nations collide,
Blood will run, high as tides.

"Let Anton speak for himself!" says Prince Raiden. "He owes us an explanation. We deserve to hear it from his own lips—"

"He absconded upon learning that he was discovered, I'm afraid. However, we have taken the whole of his court into custody until he's found to answer for his schemes."

I stop seeing, breathing. I don't believe Illian. He found Anton—found him through the tunnels.

"This should come as no surprise," General Stova says. "Has he not been under Her Majesty's skirts ever since the almost-war?"

"A war is what he wants!" says someone else.

"Let the queen answer for this accusation!"

Queen Sadira's seven sons surround her, tulwars drawn. But she pushes through them now. "You are all fools if you believe this nonsense."

I have to do something. Another glance at my guards tells me they're momentarily distracted by the mayhem surrounding the queen, so I snatch the train of my gown, wishing I wish I had time to discard the costume altogether.

Skirting the edge of the island is my best chance at going unseen. I trail around the rocks, blending into the back of the crowd. If I can reach the archway, I could grab a craft and row back to the palace.

I must find Anton.

I'm a few feet from the archway when King Rurik's voice booms through the dissipating mist from our performance like the growl of thunder. "We have been deceived for the last time," he says, silencing the Gathering. He has that much power, I realize. Few would risk angering him. Fewer would risk tampering with their trade agreements, provoking his army.

And yet he's a dead man walking.

I pause at the mouth of the open cave.

"We have had enough of Miridranian turmoil," he declares. "Let us settle this once and for all. I may have admired the late king's intent in following the ways of Razam, but his experiment has been a failure. Miridran needs one king, not three, and King Illian has proven himself the only honorable candidate."

No. He can't side with them. Rage courses through me as I gaze around, waiting for someone, anyone, who might see through it, but even Prince Raiden, who looks skeptical, holds his tongue.

"The claims against Anton are irrefutable. Illian Orvere, should you choose to ascend to High King, you have Brisendale's support in full." He levels a gaze toward the other Crowns; none dare to oppose him. "And that of our army."

Beside him, my father stands tall, smug, like he's already made himself a king. Even his silver hair is missing its usual peaked cap, as if awaiting a crown.

His cap. He must have removed it, perhaps during the show.

An idea strikes me. My words would mean nothing to them, but words aren't the only way to speak.

There might be a way I can warn King Rurik that his general is conspiring with Illian.

In the shadow of the cave walls, I go unseen, skimming the edge of the rocks until I'm behind where they had sat during the performance.

And there, in his seat, is my father's cap. I use the distraction, careful to stay low, and lunge.

I snatch the rough, weather-resistant cap.

"I am honored," Illian says as others voice their support. "In the wake of everything, truly, I am more than humbled to serve Miridran this way, but only with the support of the Crowns' Syndicate."

Slowly, I release the daggers from my crown. It takes me a moment to pry them loose, but they slide free, small and perfectly shaped for my hands.

"We should put it to a vote," Illian says.

A vote will be pointless, when everyone will back him now that Brisendale does.

"But the queen—"

"Will be served her justice. She will be held and put to trial before the Gathering ends."

"Lay a hand on her and you will lose it," Prince Sundar growls, his brothers and guards forming a blockade against the riotous assemblage.

Riveted by the turn of events, no one watches the entrance to the tunnel or the wall of flags, each one strung top-down like a banner. Over my shoulder, I catch sight of Aemon and Sana scouring the stage, wondering where I've gone.

The Miridranian and Brisendali flags are next to each other, there in the center, and impossible to miss.

Tucking one dagger into my belt I plunge the other into the Brisendali flag and drag it down, threads ripping apart like a knife tearing through flesh and muscle. I don't stop until I split it in two, both ends fluttering in the salty breeze, tapered and torn. Behind me, King Rurik asks if any oppose the motion.

When no one comes forward, he says, "It is settled, Illian. By vote, by heritage, and by right, the Miridranian throne is yours."

His role.

His role, that Illian said he'd play. Unknowingly, after my father no doubt whispered into his ear.

I take the same dagger and jam it through my father's cap.

And with the blade still stuck in its thick wool fabric, I pin it through West Miridran's flag, directly into Illian's golden-threaded chalice.

Chapter Thirty-Four

I don't wait for them to see what I've done. I run.

Hard-packed sand and shells jab into my soles as I flee for the boats. Voices echo behind me, but I press on, praying King Rurik will understand the message I left for him and the rest of the Gathering.

That his general plots his destruction, alongside Illian.

My guards know I'm missing, so Illian will know it was me—especially when he examines the dagger I left stabbed into my father's hat. The other, I still carry with me.

I clamber inside a small craft and grab the oars, pushing off into the waves. At least the current drifts south, the wind helping me along. Even still, rowing is no easy task, and the effort burns hot in my muscles, my arms shaking. Mist sprays my skin, cold as ice. A storm is rolling in.

My chest grows tighter with every near-impossible breath.

I must find Anton. Despite what Illian claimed, Anton would not have run.

Steering toward an inlet, I see Copelan and the other performers already there, emptying onto the docks. I watch him, his blond hair tousled by the breeze, the lines of his jaw hard with tension. For a moment, I remember the feel of his arms and the warmth of his skin, and I consider dropping everything and begging for his help. He listened to me once.

But when it mattered most, he did nothing. He didn't bother to learn if Illian's accusations were true. He abandoned me for a girl who couldn't see past Illian's lies. It hardens something in me.

Copelan disappears behind the palace doors as I tumble from the boat and wade through the water; it's much higher this time of day, reaching my chest.

My dress catches on the oar.

The tide is strong, and with the weight of the fabric, I can't get free. I tug. Groan. *Pull*, even as exhaustion overtakes me.

I can't do it.

Frigid waves topple over me and I gulp for air, choking on my own breath. My muscles feel like porcelain, ready to shatter. I lean against the side of the boat, clinging to it with the last of my draining strength. Each brush of the waves yanks it from my grip.

My hands loosen, and my fingers slip.

The water pulls me under.

My world grows dark, the oar dragging me on its path to the bottom like a cluster of seaweed, and I'm so tired, so weak. Sink— I should let myself sink. Why bother? Hope is frail, all but lost. There's little left worth fighting for.

Then eyes, green as rolling hills, fill my mind like a phantom. I hear his voice. It's far away at first, but it echoes, reverberates like a ripple of water—

I cannot protect you, Vastianna Stova. But I can arm you.

My hand falls to my side, my fingers brushing against something sharp and cold.

The second dagger. It's tucked into my belt. I fumble to unhook it, then cut and slash at my gown until the layers of heavy fabric release their grip. Left in nothing but a slip, I rise to the surface, inhaling deeply before swimming to shore, battling fiercely against tendrils of coiled seaweed and the growing current. My lungs are tight, my heartbeat so rapid I fear it might give out. Still, I clutch the dagger so tightly the embellishments imprint onto my skin, afraid the sea will rip it from my hands.

Once ashore, I find the tunnels, begging the Fates for the strength to keep moving. I've built up more stamina over the past month, but I'm worn and weary, always, and I don't think the fatigue will ever go away. So I make myself another promise: I will find a way to live with it. Because I am grateful that my heart still beats, grateful that this body, however pained, has not crumbled beneath the weight of all that has been done to me.

Inside the tunnels, I expect to find a guard at every turn. Instead, I find only an unsettling emptiness. I curl my fingers around the dagger's hilt, and just when I feel like I might collapse, I reach Illian's chambers. Through a mosaic, I note four guards outside his suite, and even more stand sentinel just outside the doors to his antechamber.

But why not monitor the tunnel's entrance? Surely they know about this one, where it leads. I move to the one above the hearth, and my breath stops short.

Because secured to a chain hanging from that ominous, glasswork chandelier is Anton, his hands bound above his head, a strip of cloth gagging his mouth. The tips of his toes graze the floor, probably the only thing keeping him from a substantial amount of pain. Several cuts nick his face and neck, but he has the gall to look entirely bored with the guard who is circling him insouciantly on the carpet beneath that array of glass, quite clearly taunting him. A guard who, if I had to guess, is supposed to be guarding the pane in the wall I'm looking through.

Anton mutters something through the gag, a grin creasing his eyes. It earns him a fist to the face, his head snapping to the side. My hand flies to my mouth; it takes everything in me not to barge into the room.

But he is alive. That's what matters.

I have to think—and fast. Only two guards are inside the room with Anton. I don't have to fight them; I need only to outsmart them. My whole body trembles, but a new wave of adrenaline keeps me on my feet, so I swallow the nerves bundled in my throat and move.

Snatching a pebble from the tunnel floor, I tap lightly on the glass. Enough that it could be nothing, but they will have to investigate. When they drift over, I slink around the bend until I'm out of view.

The glass pane screeches open. "Stay here," one says. "Probably nothing, what with everyone on the island still, but I'll take a look."

The mural is like a window, and he has to climb on top of the mantle before he can crawl in. He does so with ease; first, his boots pop through, then his hands, until finally, he slides down into darkness.

I toss the pebble down the corridor. It clatters, echoing like the clank of a faraway sword.

He jolts, then stalks past me. I throw out a foot. He trips, his head smacking against the wall.

Idly, I wonder if he was there—if he was one of the guards who beat me.

He thunks onto the cold stone floor.

The other guard calls his name. I keep silent, the tunnels like a crypt. He curses, then slides into the tunnel. I stay low, slashing the dagger against his ankle between the break of armor. He cries out, fumbling for his weapon. I yank it away before he can get a good grip.

There's more blood than I expected, and it covers my fingertips. I cut him deep. He clutches his leg, gasping as he squints around, unable to see.

But I am used to the dark.

Quietly gathering a large rock at the base of the tunnel, I bash it against his head. He slouches over. Palms shaking, I wipe the blood on his cloak, then clamber inside Illian's antechamber and slide the panel closed.

Anton blinks, and then his eyes widen. He mumbles something unintelligible until I stride over and rip the cloth from his mouth. He coughs like he's parched. My stomach climbs into my ribs at the sight. I cup his jaw in my palms, needing to see him, to gauge whether he's all right—

"Vas," he rasps. "You have to leave." But he doesn't understand—Illian will kill him. I'm surprised he hasn't yet.

"I'm going to free you," I say, studying his bindings.

"It might not look like it," comes his hoarse reply, "but truly, I can handle the situation on my own."

"You're practically an extension of the chandelier, attached to it like that!"

"Terrible choice on my part to put it there," he says.

"There has to be a way to free you." I want to tug at the chain that binds him to the chandelier, but it is fastened way higher than either of us can reach. Then I eye the rope holding the chandelier in place. It runs along the ceiling, down the wall, then winds around an ornate wheel—or crank, rather. "That crank. What's it for?"

"That allows us to light the thing. See that pin? It locks in place to prevent the chandelier from moving. The lever lifts the pin, allowing the chandelier to then be lowered by the crank. But even I can barely manage the crank despite the gear mechanism we built."

"But if I could break it somehow, maybe smash the lever?"

"That ah . . . would bring the whole thing down."

"I could find help for the crank, then," I try. "Where are your men? Basile? And Laurent, Gustav—"

"All enjoying a nice view of the ocean," he says, and I breathe a sigh until he adds, "through prison bars. We were ambushed by the general and his men in the dead of night. I believe they are being held in the Brisendali quarters."

Right. And aside from his personal guard, Miridran's army is one unit. They wouldn't have reported to Anton alone. If Illian gave them charge of something, they would have no choice but to obey, even before his so-called arrest.

It's my turn to curse. "It's my fault. I was caught in the tunnels—"

"Semantics, as of now."

Heaving a breath, I take stock of the room, searching for anything I might use to release the lock on his shackles. The desk is now empty, though I open every drawer, and the mantel on the hearth is swept free of decoration. There's a small bar built into the side wall, stacked with bottles but little else, then the double doors leading to Illian's room—which to my great displeasure are locked.

I spin about but find nothing else save for an open balcony, the balmy breeze wafting inside through softly billowing curtains. Nothing aside from the gaudy chandelier and the disgraced king chained to it, like a pig ready for roasting.

"Gustav is going to get an earful," Anton murmurs, giving his chains a pull. "He helped me design this blasted chandelier, though it was sadly my idea to dangle it in my brother's room like a trophy."

I drag a stool in front of Anton and climb atop it, reaching for his manacled hands. If I can free those bonds . . .

"I know you mean well, Minnow, but you are interrupting my perfectly planned . . . *plans*. Really, you need to—"

"I'm not leaving."

I set down my dagger and tug at the pins holding my crown in place. If I could use one of them to pick the locks . . .

"Vasalie," Anton says again. "As much as I appreciate the view—and truly, I do—I wonder if perhaps you might want to reconsider your rescue attire, being that it's little more than a negligée . . ."

"A negligée not unlike the slip of a thing you had me wear in Philam," I point out.

"Hardly counts when I didn't get to examine it properly. Speaking of, how was the gown?"

The performance, then King Illian's announcement . . . Anton doesn't know. I consider where to begin, how to convey the enormity of it, but his eyes widen at the sound of steps. "Vasalie, there's a pendant around my neck. Take it off, quickly. Look for the nearest source of light—"

The door flies open, rattling on its hinges.

I startle, the pin slipping from my grasp as guards spill into the room—far more than I can count. I'm wrenched away from Anton. He yells my name, pulling against his fetters, but it's no use—

A guard lurches forward, plants a fist into Anton's side.

Another, another.

"He is a *Crown*," I rasp, thrashing against the hands now clamped on my arms. "You will regret the day you laid a hand on him!"

"Is that so?"

The voice is cool, unbothered. I know who it is before the guards force me around to meet his gaze.

Illian's crimson waistcoat reaches his knees, brushing against his boots as he strides into the room. Rubies glint from his crown, red like the blood staining my fingertips. His gaze sails over me and he clucks his tongue in distaste. "Filthy. We'll need you cleaned up for your next task."

Task? After what I did to the flags? Did the Crowns see, and not care? But the warning was clear. They couldn't have ignored it, and yet—

"Ah yes, the message you left us," Illian drawls. "Very clever, Vasalie. Unfortunately for you, my men removed the flags for safekeeping against the coming storm before the Crowns boarded their ships." His lips curl.

My throat tightens; it hurts to breathe. I will every ounce of fury into my voice. "If you think I'll do any more of your tasks, you might as well kill me now."

He lets out a bark of laughter. "Oh, but it's too easy, don't you see? Deny me, and my brother suffers for it. Perhaps I'll strap the blade to your hand and make you end him yourself." He bends, snatching my glass dagger from the floor, then levels his gaze on Anton. "It's poetic, really. To be killed with your own blade."

Cold fear seizes my chest. I strain against the vicelike grip on my arms, but Anton's voice cuts through my anger. "Very sinister, brother," he says brightly, as if a bead of blood isn't blooming from the split in his lip. "We are all so very impressed. And terrified, of course. Though if I were you, I would recommend a bit less condescension around the eyes if you're going for the 'careless, all-powerful' ensemble."

"Your tongue won't free you from this one, Anton."

"No, really? And here I thought I'd just lick myself free."

A strain of annoyance tightens Illian's face, but he dismisses the comment and approaches me. Like always, he halts but a breath away, hand poised as if to touch me, as if he longs to graze his knuckles along the soft skin of my cheek.

"Soon," he whispers, as if sharing a secret. "One last task, and this will all be over." The cold tip of his largest ring skims my cheekbone, but his fingers never do. "But the sun has not yet set on Morta's performance this evening."

He backs away, and the guard behind me releases his hold on my arms. Aemon foists a wad of dark fabric into my hands.

An outfit. My eyes shift to Illian's. "I don't understand."

"A little gift from Annais, for the return of her son." Illian draws something from his waistcoat, and I stiffen. "This," he says, "is the katar you will use to deliver King Rurik to Morta's Lair tomorrow night. What do you think, Vasalie? Your very last task."

A weapon, to kill King Rurik with.

A weapon, to go with the outfit.

That outfit.

"You want to frame Razam," I breathe. It's the garb the queen's sons wear, down to the sun emblem etched onto the shoulder.

Illian shrugs. "Someone has to take the blame."

"Vasalie, don't," Anton says, his mask faltering. "Whatever he says, he is lying. He cannot hurt me—"

"By the souls, can someone shove a cloth in his mouth?" Illian spits, and the guard closest to him forces a gag between his lips. I yank fruitlessly against the one holding me.

I shake with rage. "You want Rurik dead? Do it yourself." I try to thrust the fabric into his hands, but he backs away. I toss it on the floor. "You're a damned coward."

"Do this," Illian says, unbothered, "and upon completion, and full surrender, I will show my mercy once again. Instead of ending my brother's life, like I should, I will simply banish him to the deserts of Mor. He won't be able to return to Miridran, but he will live. Preferable to death, wouldn't you say?"

"How do I know you won't slit his throat the moment I return?"

"Because I do not wish for you to hate me for the rest of our days," he says, a sickening tenderness in his gaze. "I cared for you once, you know."

"Until you threw me away—"

"It's a generous offer, Vasalie. Two lives for the price of one. King Rurik for Anton. His freedom, and yours, to make up for the years you lost. Consider it a gift." He pauses. "Of course, if anything should happen to me, Aemon's first order is to kill him."

If I were my old self—that lonely, hopeful girl I once was, desperate for his approval, desperate to make something of myself—I might have believed him.

*Consumed by darkness, his heart a snare,
Those around Him will remain unaware.*

But I am not unaware.

My breath echoes in my ears.

If I do this, he wins. My father wins. And how many would later die at their hands? How many will he slaughter in a war? But if I refuse, Anton dies, along with Miridran's hope for a better king.

My father deserves every foul thing in this world. Every bit of pain and suffering he inflicted on me and Emilia. I should deny him what he wants most: a crown. Power—and not just over Brisendale, but the whole of the north. And Illian—I can't let him make me a murderer. I can't let him have this victory over me.

Because that's what he wants—victory. Leverage. He could have someone else play this role, but he's decided it must be *me* yet again.

Then there's the prophecy. Should I aid them in this, I might as well damn the world. I wouldn't just be complicit, I would be the catalyst.

I should let Anton die, and I should die with him.

"My patience wanes, Vasalie," Illian says.

Anton is yelling against his gag, inaudible as it is. But I know what he wants. He is telling me to refuse. He is telling me to sacrifice *him*.

Except, now that I watch him, I'm not so sure.

There's defiance in that green-gray gaze, but something else, too. The gleam of an idea. A spark of hope. And somehow, I think I understand.

He dips his head in a single nod, as if to reassure me. *Yes, Vasalie. You know what I ask.*

And I do. I sense it as if he's whispered it in my ear.

"Kill him," Illian says, patience discarded. "I'm done waiting."

"No," I concede. "Keep him alive, and I will do it."

Chapter Thirty-Five

I move in slow, lithe steps, the melody sickeningly sensual and soft.

This soirée, hosted by King Rurik's emissary the following evening, is a small, private affair, and the only way Illian could get me inside the Brisendali wing. He offered me up like a platter to the salivating older man, who watches me now with rheumy, bulbous eyes.

At least he's kept his distance, what with his nearby wife and the handful of courtiers lounged about.

King Rurik, however, is not in attendance. I knew he wouldn't be. So I bide my time, waiting until the courtiers are too deep in their cups, enough that they won't notice me when I sneak away. It shouldn't be long now. So with every bend and twist, I am careful not to reveal the katar strapped to my thigh.

The outfit, too, is secured like a bustle underneath my dark, fur-fringed skirt fashioned after traditional Brisendali garb. Despite that, my too-tight bustier manages to squeeze the breath from me every time I shift, sending spurts of pain through my ribs.

I ignore it, rehearsing the speech I'd practiced on the way here, because I will not be killing King Rurik tonight.

Not when I have the chance to warn him instead. I think that's what Anton was trying to tell me, that Illian provided me with a way to speak with him in private.

A fool's hope it might be, but he is still the king who rules the Beast of the North. And he might not listen to a lowly performer, but I am the daughter of his esteemed general.

So I will fall at his feet, beg if I must. I will expose Illian and my father both.

Illian chose the wrong person to do his dirty work. I might not like what happened to me—I might think it unfair—but I can make it so that he rues the day he selected me.

Until then, I count the hours, the minutes, until those, too, dwindle away. And when finally their attention wavers, a boisterous game of tablut afoot, I make my escape down a nearby hall, recounting my instructions. Around the corner should be a sitting room with a balcony directly in line with the king's private veranda, where Illian assured me Rurik will be—well in his cups this time of night, and alone. A ritual of his, it seems. I am to slip in, complete my task, and leave the katar behind, after which Illian promises to set us free.

I sense the lie as surely as I taste the salt in the sea.

Yet the moment I round the corner, I come face-to-face with a loose-haired, inebriated Princess Aesir. And I'm so surprised that words flee me, even as she rams me up against the wall, her nails at my throat.

"What a little waif of a thing you are," she says, towering over me as if to prove just how small I am in comparison. "And rather damaged, no? But I admit I see the appeal." She drags a single claw down and across my clavicle. "Do take excellent care of my father, will you?"

"You want his power," I say, my voice low. "There are other ways to get it—"

"Don't bother," she says, disgust curling her smudged-red lips. "You cannot appeal to me, little dancer. Fates know how you appealed to the Master of Revels."

"They will kill you," I try. "They—"

"Tell Father dearest I'll keep his seat warm." She pinches my left cheek, wriggling it between her fingers. "Off you go."

I stand there, heart thundering as she waltzes away. I don't know what she hoped to accomplish by that. Dominance, perhaps, when she has so little—and will have even less once my father claims her crown. She will never be queen in her own right. King consort or not, she will always be second to him.

I take no pleasure in that.

I slip into the sitting room. It's a small, unlit space, the balcony doors slung open to reveal a night sky tufted with clouds. Adjacent is yet another wing of the palace hovering above the water's edge, yellow torchlight rippling across the waves. Even from here, I can make out more figures scattered across distant balconies.

I slide out and into shadow, the hood of a balcony above veiling me under the stark, moonlit night. It allows me to change, invisible to nearby eyes.

And to King Rurik, lazing on a chaise on the sprawling balcony next to me.

For a moment, I merely watch as he gazes off into the sea, a coil of smoke unspooling from the cigar in his hand. Whisper-thin drapes quiver in a gentle wind. A servant passes through them, presenting a tray, and Rurik plucks from it a glass of amber liquid and a stem of grapes.

Attired in black silk as I am now, brisk ocean air seeps through, chilling me to the bone—an icy reminder that I'm an insult to its finely crafted threads, stitched with perfect precision in the Razami fashion.

I drink in the salt-tinged air in an attempt to calm the frantic beat of my heart. My body feels like marble, heavy and weighted, ready to crumble. But I cannot waver.

It doesn't escape me how easily I could use this chance to flee. The water isn't far below. I could dive, reach the rocks quickly, steal a boat, and disappear into Philam.

But care for my own well-being has diminished, leaving nothing but a flimsy frame holding together what remains of my body and soul. I intend to use it to right my wrongs. When I pass into Morta's judgment, I will not regret my final days.

The servant shuffles away.

The first night bell rings out, shattering the silence. It echoes into the sea's abyss, jolting me from my thoughts. It's midnight now, and the time to complete my order is vanishing. I climb onto the balustrade and leap.

The second bell tolls.

Air whooshes from my lungs as I land on King Rurik's balcony, the smooth stone like a slap against my stinging palms. I shake it off and rise to my knees, the churn of the ocean masking the sound.

The third.

I draw in a breath, readying myself. He's right there. I can do this.

The moment I move, the curtains part. I halt just in time to see yet another silhouette slinking between them, stepping out of the adjacent room and onto the balcony.

No, I breathe, as Illian clasps hands with King Rurik, a smile painting his lips as the bell tolls on. And my confusion gives way to sudden, harsh clarity. He does not trust me; of course he doesn't. He is here to ensure I do as he commanded.

My feet are like posts, nailed into the ground as the final bells toll.

And when the last one rings out, Illian tilts a gaze in my direction, knowing exactly where I'll be.

My hand teases the hilt of the katar.

I could kill him instead. Plunge the blade into the cavity of his chest, lead King Rurik to Anton, to the stolen seal—

But then I notice the dagger strapped inside Illian's coat, the glint of that golden hilt. A dagger to keep me in check. To ensure Rurik doesn't survive.

Illian and King Rurik lean over the balustrade now, conversing. There is nothing beneath us, save for the sea. Once more, Illian cants his head toward me, then up, deliberately. I follow his gaze to where a bevy of his guards keep watch from the window above.

Understanding burns in my gut like hot, scathing oil.

If anything should happen to me, Aemon's first order is to kill him.

It's Anton or Rurik. I can only have one.

My pulse speeds fast as the wind. I feel weightless, like it might toss me into the sea. I almost wish it would, because my next move is clear.

I unsheathe the katar, carefully brandishing its H-shaped hilt. I don't know how to wield it properly.

I think of Queen Sadira, of her knife-sharp gaze, the way she'll wish me dead for what I'm about to do in her name. In the name of Razam.

She will never forgive me. Neither will Anton.

Don't do it, Vasalie, he would say. *There's another way.* But I shoot back angrily, *I have to save you!*

I have to save you, and this is the only way I know how.

Miridran needs a king. A good one. In this moment, that feels more important than vengeance, more dire even than the prophecy. More important than me or any feelings I might have, when after this, I'll never deserve him. Because if anyone can stand up to the evils of this world, the men like my father and Illian, it's Anton. So I have to buy him time—even if I damn my soul in the process.

Boot to stone, my steps are weightless and sure. I dash across a pool of moonlight as Illian's eyes connect with mine. And when I reach the Northern King—the king I grew up reciting prayers for—I grab the back of his head.

And drag the blade across his neck.

A sickeningly wet sound bubbles from his lips. One hands flies across his throat, the other gripping the balustrade to keep himself from buckling. That's when I see his face.

And I can't turn away.

I will see this forever. This moment, seared in my mind like the ridges of a scar. The blood. The sapphire eye, unusually bright, and his other one, widened with shock.

Blood coats my now-sticky hands, the katar locked in my trembling grip. *Watch him suffer,* a voice inside me says. The voice that knows I deserve for this to haunt me until I take my last breath, and maybe after that. *Watch every second of it.* And I do, the breath still in my chest, the blood in my ears throbbing a vicious beat.

His knees hit the ground.

And now I am a murderer indeed.

I should die for this. There is no redemption for my soul now that I have killed him.

I *killed* him.

A cold hollowness sinks into me. As if whatever goodness, whatever lovely thing that fought to keep a remnant of my soul pure, has now abandoned it for good.

I sense Illian's gaze on mine, hot like the blood on my hands. Shuttering my eyes, I try to pull myself back, to feel what I know I should.

His boots come into my vision. The katar slips from my grip and clanks to the ground. I had forgotten I was still holding it.

I face Illian, and for the first time, I feel equal. We deserve each other, this king and I. He deserves my fate, and I deserve his.

Shouts echo from nearby balconies, the observers Illian knew we would have. Then from inside, too, a moment before a bevy of guards sweep onto the veranda.

"Guards!" Illian rasps in their direction, his hand fisting my cloak. "The killer is getting away!"

They race for us.

He smiles down at me.

"Thank you," he says, soft as the whistling wind, before tipping me over the rail.

Memories of my father and Emilia assail me as I plummet into the roaring waves.

Fighting to reach the surface, I gulp down mouthfuls of water. It stings my lungs, my vision murky and black. *I'm not going to make it. I don't deserve to make it.* The thought crowds my mind like the anthem of ghosts, but still I push, swinging my arms with every ounce of strength my limbs possess.

I break the surface long enough to hear Illian's shouts. "Hurry! He jumped! Just down there!"

The pain in my chest is like shards of ice, so cold it burns. So cold it drains the last of my grit. There is nothing left.

So I let go.

And sink.

And sink.

I know darkness intimately.

I know the bounds of it, the feel of it. There are types, I have learned. The darkness between stars, vast and eternal. The cold darkness of uncertainty, a slick clamor against your skin. The panic that comes with it.

Then there is the hollow dark. Suffocating, hopeless, like in my cell.

That's how I knew I was not dead when I first awoke. This is not the peaceful abyss or suffering torment of Morta's Lair. No, it is the emptiness of captivity.

Before I lost consciousness in the pitch-dark sea, two strong arms had taken hold of my shoulders and pulled me back into the world. I learned after that it was Aemon, sent to retrieve me. He had been waiting, had known exactly where to find me. Illian knew I was never in any danger from that fall.

So here I lie, curled beneath rough-spun sheets, my back aching from the cot. Thick curtains deprive me of any light. It's dark enough to be a prison, and it might as well be. I am in Illian's apartments, though I don't know where.

I don't know how much time has passed.

I feel as if I no longer inhabit my body.

I drink whatever they give me, eat whatever they shove between my teeth, swallow whatever tonic they spill down my throat until I'm a lifeless heap on a stiff mattress.

King Rurik of Brisendale is dead, and I'd dropped that katar. It was the proof Illian needed to show the world that Razam was behind the assassination, and I gave it to him.

I have brought destruction on two countries now. Perhaps *I* am the new Eremis—the bringer of death the prophecies foretold.

I am certainly the murderer Illian accused me of being, and even my two years in prison no longer feel like punishment enough.

I should not have taken Illian's deal all those months ago. I should have taken my last breath in that prison. I was well on my way, maybe weeks from accepting the Fate of Morta's hand and escaping this world forever. But as the hours pass, a single question still pokes my mind, like a pin left in an unfinished dress.

Why me?

Yes, I was desperate for freedom, but there's more to this. I can feel it. Did Illian sense the darkness in me? Did he know just how vile I would become with my freedom on the line? Anyone else would have betrayed Illian by now. Anyone else would have spared Laurent. Rurik.

Anyone with a soul.

More hours pass.

For the first time, I drag myself from my cot, parting the curtains with my fingers. Idle gossip drifts up from the garden and walkways below—gossip I strain to hear.

It seems Queen Aesir was crowned, though the formal ceremony will take place back in Brisendale.

She also announced her engagement to General Stova.

My stomach churns, rising into my ribs. I stay there until the sun recedes and night holds sway, thick and starless. Then, between two towers, an orange glow bleeds onto the distant sea.

The pyre, lit for Rurik's passing. I assume his body will be buried in Brisendale, but a traditional Miridranian funeral is being held in his honor, with all the Crowns in attendance.

All except two. Queen Sadira is said to have departed in a furious rage with the rest of her court upon Illian's announcement. They tried to hold her for a hearing before the Crowns' Syndicate, but between her sons and her guard, she was untouchable.

It doesn't matter. With the entire north against her, and the threat of war from the south at her back, Razam will not last long. Because of me.

A murderer.

I wonder if Anton knows. If he loathes me. If he even still draws breath.

But all I feel is cold.

Cold, and dead, and worthless, just like when Emilia died. I made the wrong choice again. I failed her once more. I am unredeemable, now.

The fire grows taller, a pillar of flame, and I watch it for almost an hour until it finally withers and winks out like my last spark of hope.

Chapter Thirty-Six

Someone prods me, startling me from the prison of my thoughts. "Get up!"

My eyes peel open to find Sana leaning over me. She grips my arm and hauls me from bed. "Your time for wallowing is over."

"What does he want now?" I ask flatly, though a jolt of fear pinches my chest. But she ignores me, leading me instead into a large bathing chamber with a pool that seems to float off into the sky, held only by a wall of glass. A miasma of steam sends my lungs into a spasm, but she pays no heed to that, either, her rough hands stripping me bare.

The water is hot, almost scalding, the sea-glass roof focusing sunlight into the pool below. Another of Anton's inventions. I grit my teeth, knowing I'm owed this pain, and wade in until I'm waist deep. I can't think about why I'm being prepped like a pig for a spit, so I let my mind go numb, empty, not allowing my thoughts to form anything solid.

I am nothing but air, water, and shadows, even as two servants glide in after me, scrubbing then anointing me with oils and perfumes until I'm as raw and primed as a fresh cut of meat. Then I'm pulled out and guided to a divan where they use fans to dry me so as not to smear the oils, my hair twisted up into pins to keep it off my neck. Why they are taking such care of me, I don't know, nor do I let myself care.

Once I am dry, I am wrapped in violet and crimson silks—a gown that loops around my neck and chest and waist before fanning out onto the floor. My hair is then laced with a ribbon of rubies and braided loosely into an intricate, pinned mass. My wrists are clamped with bejeweled cuffs on my lower and upper arms. Strings of garnets dangle from my ears. Again, a flash of curiosity lights in my mind, but I tamp it down until it's smothered by emptiness and silence.

After, they paint my face, and I look more like Vastianna Stova, the girl I once was. Young and fresh, devoid of kohl, only a faint smear of rouge atop my eyelids, my lips tinted with fresh roses. Vasalie Moran, the dancer—the temptress with wings—does not exist here. She is unrecognizable. She is dead.

When they are through, they tuck a small sack of millen into the folds of my skirt and tell me that, later tonight, I will perform for Illian alone—just like he'd told me, all those weeks ago.

Then I'm escorted back to Illian's antechamber.

"His Majesty will be along in a moment," Sana says more to the other guards than to me. I keep my head down, refusing to meet Illian's gaze whenever he strides through the opposing doors.

But then a familiar voice calls my name. A tender one, painfully gentle. It reminds me of the way Emilia used to say it. I squeeze my eyes shut, trying to picture her, trying to recall the sound of her voice ...

"Vasalie," Anton says again, and I snap from my reverie and meet his gaze. He's across the room, drawn inside by another guard, who then attaches him to the chain dangling from the chandelier once more. At least he has been scrubbed clean, dressed.

And he's still alive. Still in one piece. Vicious, cruel hope flares within me, but I don't dare entertain it—

"Vas, listen to me," he implores, those green eyes holding fast to mine. "Whatever it takes to survive, do it." Aemon advances, readying his fist, but Anton ignores him. "Trust me."

"Trust you?" Aemon lets out a single guffaw. "Look at you, you pathetic fool."

"Stunning, even in such vile circumstances—yes, I know," Anton returns.

It earns him a fist in his abdomen. He barely reacts, taking a beat to spit blood before propping his head up once more. "Survive," he says—*pleads*. "Whatever the cost."

All numbness flees me, and I choke out a sob. "I killed him, Anton. It's over because of me."

I brace myself for his judgment, his righteous indignation. His fury. And yet I find something else within his gaze, etched into the set of his brows.

It is a wild, frenzied sort of ferocity, and it steals my breath.

"This," he says softly, "is *far* from over."

"Indeed," croons Illian, a shadow now emerging from the threshold. "There is still much to celebrate."

My stomach plummets like it did when he shoved me from the balcony.

To my great disgust, he mirrors me in a sleeveless, russet ensemble that fits snugly to his chest, with garnets and rubies rimming the seams. Embellished leather bracers cuff his forearms, matching his boots. But it looks regal rather than martial, as do his styled tresses, one lock dripping across his forehead like a curl of ink.

He holds his arm in front of me, expectant. "Time to go."

I grind my molars. "*Where?*"

"I am certainly not attending such a prestigious event alone," he says. "And my, don't you look lovely. A fine escort indeed. Sana did well."

Sana approaches, and clutched between her fingers is a sheer red veil. She attaches it to the circlet at the crown of my head, then drapes it to cover my face. And I know, then, where we are about to go.

Because it's an honor veil, a traditional practice during a Brisendali wedding. Every woman wears one, save for the bride, so that her betrothed might not see anyone but her as she walks down the aisle.

More specifically, so that my father might not see anyone but the queen who will gift him his long-anticipated crown.

"Vasalie."

I glance at Anton. He seems to hold my gaze, even through the veil. "Remember what I said."

Survive. It's what Emilia told me, too. I swallow against the lump in my throat.

Sana takes my hand and places it atop the silver-etched leather bracer on Illian's forearm. And even through the leather, I feel the heat of his arm, the subtle movements as he adjusts his weight, and it strikes me how strange it is. I have never held on to him before, never so much as gripped his hand. He feels more human than ever now, a collection of bones and sinew and muscle.

He tilts his gaze down at me, his eyes touching my cheeks, my lips, the skin of my neck. A satisfied smile bends his lips, and he tugs me toward the door.

And as my dress flares out behind me, weighing down each step, and as the pins holding the circlet against my head pinch and prick at my scalp, I can't help but wonder if Illian does, in fact, know that the general is my father.

Another storm stirs the air, threading a train of leaves into the wind. We stand poised at the precipice of yet another enclosure, a bougainvillea-laced arcade palisading us on all sides. Ahead stands a line of Crowns, waiting between cathedral trellises sprawling with blooms for the announcer to signal our entrance.

I survey the scene through a red screen.

It isn't unlike the garden where I first saw my father, though much larger. Chaises are scattered across the grass as opposed to chairs, with courtiers strewn across them in all their finery. Petals whisk about, garnishing an aisle that runs toward the far outer wall. There, a flowering espalier spirals on the outer wall like a halo—a perfect backdrop before which a carpet is set, fringed by candles.

"One wrong move," Illian whispers against my hair, "and he will pay."

Anton, he means.

The Crowns are individually announced; we are last. The only small mercy is that the name of their escorts are not made known, sparing me from being exposed.

By the time we glide into the garden, all eyes turn to the man they believe is the sole King of Miridran.

I might not know everything that happened in my absence, but with no one to oppose him, Illian's reign is secure. And here I am, the decoration on his arm.

He guides me to a chaise at the front, mere feet from the carpet, before taking his place in the center of it like a priest. Sana and Aemon linger behind, ensuring I don't try anything.

A Brisendali man in a white and blue robe enters. I recognize him as Rurik's adviser—a prelate not dedicated to religion but to the culture and health of his people. The only man who may perform a binding marriage.

The sun hovers behind the clouds and a chill grips my skin, as if the Fate of Morta herself breathes the warning of death into the air.

The start of the Brisendali anthem carries through, weaving a mix of fear and dread around my lungs until I can scarcely breathe.

I don't turn as my father approaches, though I hear the squelch of his boots.

But when he steps onto that carpet, my gaze is pulled to him like a moth to rotten fruit. He stands there, those cold, soulless eyes pointed back down the aisle.

Does he see her like I do?

Does he remember Emilia standing in a courtyard much like this one, dressed in white fur and pearls as big as snowdrops? Does he remember the vows he spoke to her, the woman he promised to protect? Does he remember trapping her, stealing her away, and then stealing her life?

Is he haunted by her ghost?

I'm trembling, but I can't look away. Not as a flurry of cerulean silk sweeps by. Not as Queen Aesir stands before him and speaks her vows, led by the prelate. Not even when my father does the same, then leans to kiss her pert, pink lips.

Not even when he faces the crowd in triumph, a king ready to be crowned, cheers rolling over him in waves. I wonder how long before his official coronation.

Then, so subtly I almost miss it, his eyes flick over me before turning away. Almost as if he knew where to look. My only consolation is that he cannot see me under my crimson veil.

Applause crowds my ears, the air filling with nectar-sweet praise, adoration. I feel sick.

But he didn't recognize me. Because if he had, he wouldn't let me go, not when he murdered Emilia to try to find me.

An announcement is made for a celebratory reception in the Dome Hall. The courtyard empties. Once again, I'm tucked against Illian's side. His eyes roam over me as he wets his lips, and then, without a word, he shepherds me away, steering us at an unusually quick pace.

I tug against him, trying to slow him down. My effort is ignored.

"I hope you know what you've done," I hiss. "The general is a monster and you've just sharpened his teeth."

"Oh really," Illian says idly. "And how do you know that?"

"I—rumors," I say, though my voice quavers with the lie. "Everyone speaks of his bloodlust." Illian may be despicable, but if I could only make him realize my father is worse . . . "Whatever it is you are doing, he *will* betray you."

"I'm touched by your concern."

Again, I tug against him, but his thick-gloved grip is tight. "Why—why are you doing this?"

A muscle feathers in his jaw, but it isn't until we reach the Dome Hall's wide double doors that he says, "A wise man once told me that patience is the only road that leads to true power. I have earned this tenfold."

"Killing and conspiring isn't earning."

"You have no idea what I've earned, Vasalie. But worry not; I trust you'll find out soon."

He yanks me inside the Dome Hall.

It looks different than on the Welcoming night, five and a half short weeks ago that now feel like an eternity. Long tables fill its length, flush with flowers and votive candles, their small flames unwavering in the still air. The sky itself is pomegranate red, the sunset caught between layers of clouds.

The music is jaunty and light while appetizers are divvied about. At every columned interval stands a Brisendali guard, so many that even the courtiers have begun to take notice.

Yet Illian seems far from concerned. I still don't understand how he came to trust the general, or how they connected in the first place. Trepidation slithers underneath my skin, setting me even more on edge. There's a missing piece to this wretched puzzle, one I can't seem to solve.

Illian leans in. "When that veil comes off, you will smile, eat what is placed before you, greet anyone who speaks to you with a polite nod, and nothing more. You will leave the talking to me."

I merely grit my teeth. He ferries me to a long, curved table at the far end, where the stage divider used to be. It's even more ornamented than the others—a sprawling candelabra set between roses; scallops of silk that fall in waves to the floor.

My father and his queen have yet to arrive, but their chairs are marked by even more ribbons, right in the center. Next to ours.

Other Crowns are directed into the seats on either side of us, separated from their courts, oblivious to the string of events that led to this moment.

How I long to tell them, to shout the atrocities before the whole of the Gathering, and yet if I do . . .

One wrong move, and he will pay.

My father and Queen Aesir parade through the double doors. I study the new Brisendali queen in all her piles of blue silk and decadence and wonder how long she might survive.

When finally they take their seats, my father is, of course, placed directly on Illian's left.

One seat removed from me.

Everyone with a veil removes it. Hesitantly, I untwine the pins banding it to my circlet, tugging a few curls loose as I do so in hopes of hiding my eyes—eyes that he might recognize without glitter and kohl.

Slabs of lamb garnished with rosemary are delivered onto our plates, along with a hearty loaf of bread, cheese, and conserve—a common meal back home. Again, I can't help but sneak another glance at Aesir, hoping to find even a modicum of regret. Her father is dead, and yet she is as content as ever in her cerulean dress. Cerulean, just like her father's glass eye. Just like the diadem set into her crown—

That diadem. A large, glinting sapphire, but not *just* any sapphire, no.

The eye looks just the way it did that night under the light of a waning moon as Rurik gazed up at me, blood encircling his throat like a torque. Bile spills into my mouth and I grab my napkin to cover it, swallowing until the surge of nausea subsides.

"Eat," Illian says.

I glare. My place setting is bare of anything sharp, even a fork. "And how am I supposed to do that, exactly?"

"You have hands. Unless you would like me to feed it to you . . ."

Hot fury burns my cheeks. Even if I wanted to, I wouldn't be able to keep the food in my stomach for long. I'm tempted to eat too fast, then vomit it onto his lap.

But then, remembering Anton, I pry a piece of bread loose and slide it between my teeth, swallowing against a wave of revulsion. Satisfied, Illian angles away, his attention on the guests now offering gifts to the new queen. I scoop a few bites into my napkin and ball it up.

Desert is served soon after—plump peaches doused in cream—during which a small troupe dances, ribbons unspooling from their hands. No one pays them much heed; it is but an idle show with an idle tune, set dressing and no more. Even the torches dim ever so softly, a quilt of stars now visible.

The moon is the real spectacle, however, so large it fills an entire arch from my point of view.

I turn my attention toward the show nonetheless. Dancers bound in front of us, and when they pass, my eyes latch on a dark shape between the columns near the back of the room.

By the look of it, Copelan sees me, too. Recognizes me.

I wonder what he thinks.

He witnessed what became of me in those tunnels, heard every word. And here I am now, at the left-hand side of the very same king, dressed in his silks, flush in his jewels. Like a cosseted princess. An appointed concubine.

I try to read his expression, only to wish I hadn't.

Disgust. He flames with it.

Even so, I don't know why it hurts so badly when he turns his back on me and leaves.

I force my eyes down to my plate and fall into the trance of my own thoughts. Nobles flit by, wishing the queen and her husband long life and prosperity. Dishes are cleared, replaced with fresh, crystalline glasses glistening with champagne, but it all passes in a smudge of motion until finally the clink of a toast rattles me back to the present.

It takes me a moment to realize my father and Queen Aesir are standing.

Aesir, for her part, delivers her oration, thanking their guests before holding a moment of silence for the passing of her father. "This season has been more trying than we could have anticipated," she goes on. "Yet you have wept with us, mourned with us. You have raged with us over the injustices brought about by those who wish to disrupt our hard-won peace.

"But where there was once mourning, there shall be joy and triumph." She lifts her chin to my father, who lingers at her side. "My father, the honored King Rurik, was blessed to have such a trusted friend, adviser, and mentor as General Stova, and that blessing continues as we welcome him into our family. As such, the title of consort will never fit, and so I am pleased to announce his coronation upon our return to Brisendale."

Because it's the only way he was willing to help her dispose of her father.

Not king consort but king, with all a king's rights and power. The reins of the country, handed over like a scepter.

If the Crowns are surprised, they hide it well, offering a polite sweep of cheers. A smile forms on his lips, broader than I've ever seen. It doesn't suit him.

Or perhaps that's what bothers me—the genuineness of it.

He knows he's won.

I clench my fists, releasing a new promise under my breath.

If I cannot defeat him in life, I will find him in death.

The general drops a kiss on his bride's lips, knocks back his drink, and signals for another glass. And just when I think he's about to take a seat, he says, "Please rise, all, for we have one more cause to celebrate on this joyous evening."

Then he turns straight to me.

Chapter Thirty-Seven

Everything freezes—my breath, the beat of my heart, even the wind.

My father gazes down at me, and I see now that he knows exactly who I am.

He has known the entire time. For half a breath, his eyes soften almost imperceptibly, the way they did when I was little, when I would crawl into his arms after he returned from his post.

And like the fool that I am—the daughter who once loved and admired him even as she watched him grow cold—I *beg* him to see the cage I'm in. I will him to drop his cruelty, the demon who wears his skin, and draw his sword on Illian. *Help me, Father.*

Help me.

Devilry seeps into his gaze then, and as he turns it to Illian, something cool and slimy hooks around my ribs.

"My daughter, Vastianna Stova," he says, gesturing toward me. "Please, won't you rise?"

The sound of my name on his lips shakes me.

My legs feel like splintered glass, but I force myself to stand. A sheen of sweat gives a sickly pallor to my skin. Aside from Copelan,

I doubt anyone recognizes me—not after the way Sana prepared me. No kohl, no liner, no face paint or millen to hide behind. I look younger, more innocent.

My father smiles, then, and I know that whatever he plans to say next will break me.

"Twelve years ago," he declares, "I sent my beloved daughter to West Miridran in a show of good faith, as a part of a courtship agreement designed by King Rurik and myself, and His Majesty, King Illian."

My lungs feel as if they've collapsed, as if they refuse to take another breath.

Twelve years ago, when I turned thirteen.

When he announced I was to be sent away, wed to a man overseas who I did not know.

"It was meant to forge a deeper bond between our two countries. Their courtship would not only solidify trade agreements to usher in wealth and prosperity, but ensure a lasting, healthy relationship between both our lands."

My ears begin to ring.

"And while we bear the weight of the happenings of the past few days, it is my heart's greatest joy to finally announce the engagement between my daughter and my dear friend, Illian Orvere, thus bringing to completion the agreement made long ago."

It was Illian.

Illian, who I would have been sent to on my thirteenth birthday.

Illian, who Emilia tried to protect me from.

I was no toy. I was a product. A commodity, primed and plucked to sell.

Again, I remember the argument I overheard between Emilia and my father. Had she seen Illian at the Gathering she performed at? Is that where they made their plans?

My hands lose feeling. My sight blurs. Emilia knew. It's why she fought so hard to stop it. She *died* for it, died trying to hide me away, died trying to help me escape. My ears roar with the rush of understanding, a tidal wave thrashing against my skull.

The clattering of applause nearly topples me.

It isn't until I feel a palm against my shoulder that I return to myself.

My father. His gaze is as dead as the Brisendali alstrea blooms after a frost. Having come to stand behind me, he turns my shoulders so that I'm facing Illian, and his next words wrap around my throat, squeezing my breath until I can feel my heart pounding in my ears.

"Illian Orvere, I gladly give you my daughter, my greatest pride. She is yours in every way."

I feel the tender press of my father's lips, damp against my forehead.

"I hope Emilia is watching," he whispers into my ear. "I hope she sees how badly she failed."

Hot tears stab my eyes, but the rest of me is frozen, numb with terror.

How badly she failed.

Because I never escaped him.

He knew. Somehow, he found me. "How long?" I rasp. How long has he known where I was?

"You were *so* easy to keep track of, selling Emilia's ring to buy passage on that ship." He scoffs. "I admit we lost you for a time, once you took up residence in that theater—or so I am told. I suppose I should thank you for running *straight to him* thereafter."

Straight to him.

Because I had caught his eye. And not just because of my dancing.

"He recognized me," I breathe. Somehow. Though we hadn't met.

A shrug. "I knew you were in Miridran, that it was only a matter of time before we tracked you down. So we sent drawings, descriptions. He suspected the truth once he got a good look at you."

I think back to the way Illian climbed onto the stage at the Melune. How his brows leapt an increment—a hint of a surprise once we were face-to-face. I'd assumed it was because I had been younger than he had initially thought.

"And when he found Emilia's glove in your belongings, that cemented it."

Her glove, embroidered with her name.

Emilia's glove.

The one that had gone missing.

"As far as my acquaintances knew, I had already sent you to your suitor."

I sway, the ground tilting beneath me.

To anyone else, this must look like he's whispering his blessings; a doting father sad to lose his daughter but glad to gain a son.

All this time, and I had played right into their plans. I should have seen it. Should have put the pieces together here at the very least, when at every step my father was there.

And now Illian thinks to collect me like a tax collector would his coins.

My father takes my wrist, his thick fingers squeezing the fragile bones the way he had years ago. He nods at Illian, who removes his gloves.

Illian holds my gaze as my father presses my palm neatly into his. Flesh to flesh. A deal sealed.

We are touching, for the very first time.

I wait for time to stop. It feels like it should. Then, softly, Illian tacks a kiss to my knuckles before sliding a ring onto my finger. It's cold, small, and altogether too tight, just like my shackles.

And before I know what's happening, he takes my jaw and nudges my lips to his.

My mouth is slack, numb, but he makes up for my lack of response, plunging harder, tilting my head back. His lips are wet. Cold, like frost. Like his soul.

Then, with a shudder that feels like relief, he backs away and slides his mouth to my ear. "You have no idea what it's been like being unable to touch you."

Revulsion climbs up my throat. I blink, and he comes into focus. His eyes are dark, heavy, and I remember all the times he looked at me this way before and never acted on it. Until now.

Until now, when my father allowed it.

The woman he brought to his room, swathed in my costume. The times he reached for me but pulled away—I understand, now. *She is yours in every way.*

Only then do I hear the crowd, the music. Illian lifts our hands, displaying my ring before them. And when finally the cheers subside, he leans in, confirming my guess. "Yes, Vasalie. I made a vow to your father not to lay so much as a finger on you until he gave his permission. And I kept my word."

But it has nothing to do with his word, and everything to do with whatever bargain they struck after working together for so long. He didn't want to risk losing Maksim's help. Or maybe because Maksim knew his plans and could expose him at any moment.

And my father—he didn't want me tarnished. I was insurance.

Leverage.

Property.

I feel Illian's palm against my cheek, but I remove myself from my body. Distantly, my father calls for celebration, but his words sound as though they are underwater. Figures dance, warping in and out of sight. Music soaks the air like mist.

I'm being pulled to the dance floor.

"You really knew this whole time?" I hear myself ask dazedly. Flatly.

Illian leads me into a waltz, his hand crawling up my waist. When he leans in, his breath is a cool wisp against my neck. "It was meant to be, don't you see?"

Because I had fallen right into his lap.

"But why, why didn't you—"

"Wed you sooner? Honestly, Vastianna, you made it much harder on yourself. If you hadn't run off, you would have been welcomed into my palace instead of starving on the streets." He spins me around, then guides me back into his arms, and there's a possessiveness to the way he holds me. "I am not so cruel as he. Your father wanted you in my court right away—wanted the deal sealed. But I would not have married you until you were sixteen. You could have had three years of learning, pampering, and yet you chose to flee."

Was it really kindness, I wonder, or more because he needed to accomplish something, first?

"Nonetheless, the hand of fate stepped in. Guided you to me in that theater. And that is precisely the magic of it. It was destiny, as if written among the stars themselves."

He looks at me as if I should agree with him. As if I should thank him for it.

"Unfortunately, by the time I confirmed who you were—that it was *you* who were meant to be mine—our plans to unite Miridran while he took Rurik's place were delayed, as I had yet to prove that Estienne was unfit for the throne—a feat that took far longer than I had expected. And of course I still had to handle my headache of a younger brother."

Because Anton wouldn't just die.

"But I alerted your father, who agreed to honor our initial agreement—one we struck at the very Gathering where my despicable father split my country from beneath me. I was promised Miridran in its entirety, and I was given a paltry third. Rurik even denied me Aesir's hand because of it."

And my father saw his opportunity with a young, devastated prince.

"The general's offer was too good to pass up," he says, confirming my line of thoughts. "I would reclaim what I lost, he would be king. I would have my Brisendali princess along with a marriage that would bind our kingdoms in mutual prosperity. Of course you disappeared after that. But as much as I would have wanted us to wed once I finally found you, we couldn't until we had what we needed. My father had made it impossible to locate anyone who had witnessed Estienne's birth, which would prove he was illegitimate—a fact I had long since known, thanks to my mother. It was by fate alone that we finally located Annais."

"And in the meantime, you threw me into a cell," I spit. It could have been even longer, had he not found Annais. How long would he have left me there?

"It was not so simple," he says. "The night of Lord Sarden's wedding, during our promenade, I asked you a question. Do you remember what it was, Vastianna?"

I want to shove him away and damn the consequences.

But then—

Lord Sarden's wedding.

It had been one of the happiest nights of my life.

The wedding itself was pleasant, but it was only after the revelry turned rambunctious that Illian offered to escort me into the gardens for some air.

It returns to me now, the way moonlight cut swathes through the evening fog, setting a scene that felt like a dream as we drifted between hedgerows. Oh, how my heart had swelled to have a moment alone with him. He'd walked beside me, his hands clasped neatly behind his back, and I remember itching to free those hands. To grab them, cradle them within my own, if only to thank him for bringing me. For letting me accompany him, laugh with him, and for everything else, too—all the ways he had changed my life.

Then he had turned to face me, a solemnity to his gaze. *Is it better*, he had asked, *to suffer for a reward guaranteed, or gamble with the risk of losing it altogether?*

This reward, I had asked. *How great is it?*

Invaluable, he'd responded. *Beyond measure. One could equate it to happiness eternal.*

And the suffering before, I had hedged. *Would it end in death?*

Never, he'd said. *Nothing so final as that.*

Then losing such a reward would be unimaginable, no? Perhaps worth whatever torment might come, so long as that torment would end.

He'd plucked a rose from a nearby bush. Twirled it once.

Thank you, he had said, then handed it to me.

Oh, what a mistake I had made.

I had sealed my own fate. He had asked me plainly, yet I thought nothing of it; even after, I wouldn't have guessed he had been referring to me.

"Your imprisonment was part of our agreement," Illian says. "One I would have liked to spare you from. His amendment was that I punish you for running away. For causing him such grief. The terms of our agreement were nonnegotiable. I delayed it as long as I could, even at the threat of your father revoking our deal. But I had wanted to show you what all I could offer. You were pampered, doted on. In the end, however, I had to honor my end of our bargain. And as much as it pained me, Vasalie, I knew it would keep you safe. And, well, you were becoming so defiant. So bold and beguiling. With half the nobles roaming around you, ready to pounce . . ." He trails off, running his nose along my cheek. "Didn't you wonder why we kept you alive, well fed, and away from the rest?"

I don't believe for a second that was all it was. He wanted to control me. Wanted to manipulate me into needing him, obeying him . . .

I jerk away. Illian's eyes flash, and he tries to haul me back toward him, but I retreat another step. Others are beginning to watch, the tension between us palpable. Every action I take will have consequences, but I feel as if I barely inhabit my own body.

I am breaking—before everyone.

"I believe it's time for us to retire for the evening," Illian announces, forcing a smile at those around us. He inches his fingers around my ribs. "My wife-to-be needs her rest and is still grieved over the loss of her king. I think it best for both of us." He clamps a hand on my hip and turns to where my father stands, talking to some of the Serain court. He pauses when he notices us.

"This is the part where you bow and cast your well wishes upon the groom and his bride," Illian says lowly, his thumb digging into my waist.

A small spark flares within me.

I raise my chin, just slightly, and look upon my father. "May every deed you have bestowed upon others be returned to you tenfold." And then, to Queen Aesir, a woman not much older than I am, or even Emilia when she wed my father, I say, "Congratulations, Your Grace. It takes a bold woman to replace my stepmother. May he love you with the ferocity with which he loved her."

I hold their gaze, even as I dip into a short, irreverent bow.

And then I stride away.

Chapter Thirty-Eight

Illian keeps pace with me to save face; he won't yank me around with so many eyes. But the moment I plow through those double doors, I tear myself from his grip, then round on him. "When was it you sold your soul to the Fate of Morta? When did that come into play?" I feel like I've swallowed fire, like it's burning a path down my throat. Illian's guards move behind us, watching me, readying to pounce.

Illian snatches the hand I pulled loose. "The Fate of Morta? Vasalie, that prophecy is a farce, and those priests are little more than fearmongers. Traitors to their people. And they were arrested as such."

He has not, knowingly, sold his soul. Not that it isn't rotted down to his core. But . . . if he didn't make some connection or agreement with the Fate of Morta—

I shake my head, studying him again.

And then I see it, there in the hollows of those dark, deceiving eyes. "You arrested the prophets because you *know* the prophecy is about you. You didn't want anyone to find out."

Perhaps he wasn't a knowing participant. But that doesn't mean the prophecy isn't true. None of this was ever about the Fate of Morta; it was about their plan. The prophecy was merely a warning of the destruction that would follow.

Voices echo, courtiers emptying from the Dome Hall. Quickly, Illian pulls me down the arc pass and into a narrow hall, then shoves up against me, my back flattening against the wall.

"I've had enough of your tongue. If it were up to your father, you never would have been here. He thought to keep you in that wretched cell until our agreement was final. But I not only needed a dancer, I needed my *Jewel*. I knew that only you, with your Fates-given gifts and talent, could worm your way into certain areas of the Gathering I could not and charm those I needed you to charm. Besides, if I had to earn the throne, I'd give you the opportunity to do the same.

"So I defied him and brought you here, and even that cost me. I had to prove to him that I could use your talents for the greater good. And he could have turned to Estienne had I not convinced him. He could have given you to *him* instead."

What a fool Illian was to not see my father's true intentions. That he would give me to Estienne was a mere threat to ensure Illian's cooperation.

All of this was about my father gaining power over Miridran and Brisendale both. He approached Illian when Illian was desperate and distraught by King Junien's actions. And Illian was fool enough to not only help seat my father on the Brisendali throne but cooperate in full—because as much as he wanted the kingdom to himself, he also came to want *me*. More and more, as time went on.

And that wanting kept him on my father's leash.

I spit on him. "You are a coward. Little better than a dog begging at his *feet*." My chest heaves with my rage. "And you lied to me. Your offer—you were never going to set me free."

Slowly, he wipes away the spray on his jaw. "I would have made you another offer when the Gathering was finished—one you couldn't refuse. All of this . . . I would have made it worth your while," he says—so like the question he posed to me that night.

Is it better to suffer for a reward guaranteed, or gamble with the risk of losing it altogether?

The reward, I realize, was the life he would have offered me after the suffering *he* put me through—at my father's behest or not.

He curls his hand around the back of my neck, thumb resting on my pulse. "But you've tested and tried me one too many times, Vastianna. First, back at my palace; then, at my brother's banquet. And every task since, you have pushed against me, but I remain patient. Have I not protected you all these years? From the eyes of the court, from poverty, even from your father? I took precautions to guard you during every task. You have been watched, shielded, from all sides. And should someone have caught you, I would have stepped in."

Just how many had he bribed? Paid off? All those times I felt like I was being watched . . .

The maid. The guards. The one from the docks. Who else? How many?

I open my mouth, but he prattles on. "Have I not given you everything you ever wanted? Riches, jewels, favor, did you not amass them under my wing?" He pauses, jaw working. "Oh, the things I could have done to you, Vastianna; the things I *should* have done to you. Then, after everything, I discover you've been with my brother, giving away my secrets and Fates know what else."

"Then kill me," I choke out. "The Gathering might not know me as your former Jewel, but in East Miridran, someone will eventually recognize me. This charade won't last forever."

"So what? I am the doting fiancé who let you pursue your passions at the Gathering, who then kept you guarded and safe."

"Safe? You let them charge me, beat me, throw me away—"

"Again, your father's terms," he says. "As I said, he wanted you punished. But I also had to keep your tenancy in that cell a secret. I couldn't have my future queen be tainted with the charge of murder, could I?"

No, he needed a way to bridle me, keep me compliant while all his plans came to fruition.

He had manipulated me, lied to me, broken me so thoroughly I had begged the Fate of Morta for death. I will not absolve him of it. I will not let him justify his choice.

My father's words come back to taunt me once again. *You'll never be more than a man's plaything.*

How right he was. Emilia never escaped my father. What made me think I could?

The last of my strength crumbles, and I slide down the length of the wall until I hit the floor.

Two large hands come under my arms and haul me up. I sag against them.

"Cooperate, Vastianna. The night isn't over yet," Illian says. "And you still have much to lose."

Anton finds my gaze when we return to Illian's antechamber. He frowns, checking me over, and when he finds no damage, he seems to breathe a sigh of relief.

But no relief swells within me. Illian was right. I have more to lose, and he didn't just mean Anton or my friends. I hug my arms around myself, eyeing the door set ajar, cracked to reveal the four-poster bed beyond.

Beside me, Illian waltzes in, his smile thin. "Glad to see you alert, little brother. I am eager to share my news."

"Don't tell me you have something interesting to say for once."

Illian doesn't take the bait; instead, he brandishes my wrist, displaying the blood-red diamond glittering from my finger. "Divine, isn't it? Just like my bride-to-be." He runs a cold knuckle along my cheek. And as subtle as it might be, he doesn't miss the twitch of Anton's lips. "So you *do* have more than a passing interest in her."

"I have an interest in not imprisoning women and being a complete maggot every second of every day," Anton shoots back.

I give him an exasperated look, as if to say, *Do you have a death wish?*

"Oh, I think it's more than that." Illian circles behind me, grazing his lips along the crescent of my neck, and when Anton's jaw tightens, I feel Illian smile against the curve of my shoulder. I jerk away, but I don't get far. He uses a ribbon on my gown to pull me back.

"You said you'd set him free if I played my part. And I did," I hiss. "If you wish me to have even a shred of respect for you when this is all over, you *will* let him go."

If my words affect him, he doesn't show it, letting his fingers skim my ribs. Anton follows them with his gaze, jaw working, until Illian pauses at the jeweled button on my skirt. "See, that's just it, my Jewel. Your role is not yet over."

He yanks it off.

Fabric comes loose, the skirt fluttering down my legs. Anton thrusts forward, but the chandelier rattles, forcing him to stop lest it fall.

"What was it I told you all those months ago?" Illian trudges on, his fingers edging toward my throat, and it takes everything in me not to lose control of my bladder. "Ah, yes. I told you your last evening would be spent with me. You still owe me a performance, Vastianna, and you just said you wish me to keep to my word."

With that, he tugs a ribbon on my back, and another layer of silk sinks to the floor.

Cold air grazes my shoulders, my collarbone. I'm left in nothing but a minuscule bustier and a wide sash hugging my hips like a skirt shorn high on my thighs.

"Turns out," he says to Anton, "you're not the only one who can construct a gown."

"Piss-poor job if it's falling apart."

Illian's laugh is caustic. "You always had that souls-awful sense of humor."

"It must vex you," Anton says, "that she would never have chosen you of her own free will."

Illian merely shrugs. "I have her, all the same."

"You do realize you can pay someone to fist the grapes. Less hassle, more willingness."

"Hatred does not last forever. In time, she will learn that I can please her as well as any."

"What, you think your extra limb is the size of a gourd or something? You can't overcompensate your way into her favor when you're the very definition of a *rectum*."

"Jealousy suits you well, Anton."

This is what Illian wanted all along. It wasn't just me he was after. He wanted power, yes, but that wasn't enough. He tried to have Anton assassinated time and again, and so it never would have been enough for him to win. No, he wanted to flaunt his prize in front of the brother he loathes. It might be the only reason Anton is still alive.

Illian doesn't intend to let him go. He brought him here so that he might watch *this*, and then he will no doubt finish what he failed to do before.

He might even make *me* do it.

I grab Illian's sleeve. "Please—I will dance for you, if that's what you want. And anything else."

Because two can play at Anton's game. Two can race to seize Illian's attention and deter him from the other.

"Vas, you are not his possession—"

"I want to," I cut in. Because he's right. I am not Illian's possession, nor his plaything.

I am a performer.

So I turn to Illian and place my palms softly against his chest.

"We can find a way to be happy," I tell him, "so let us strike an arrangement. Make a bargain with me, Illian. If I promise to give you my nights, will you give me my days? As your wife?" The words are so sour they curl my tongue, but I cage it between my teeth.

"I am not letting you out of my sight."

"I'm not asking for that. I wish only for the freedom to dance during the days. To have people to spend time with." I think of Laurent. Marian. Brigitte. If I can get him to release them, I can find a way to get them far away. "Let me choose companions. Show me the mercy you once did, and every night, when the stars light the sky, I will come to you happily."

Illian pulls me in by the waist, his cold fingers digging into my hips. "And I suppose you also want my brother to go free."

"You were my savior, once," I say, carefully plucking the same strings he had earlier, when he'd tried to sway *me*. "You said as much, and you were right. You were my protector. You were my *everything*."

The words are true. I had idolized him, respected him, and I let that sincerity show in my gaze. "Be that once more," I whisper. "Let me look upon you with gratitude and admiration as I once did. Keep your word. Let him go and have me instead. Willingly, and forever."

"Release him, and have your gratitude?" he asks, tilting his head. The feline smile he gives me unsettles me to my core. "Will you beg me for it?"

I glance at Anton—at those defiant, emerald eyes, the fierce, unwavering set of his jaw—and all over again, I return to the Sky Garden, curtained under the branches of a flowering willow, where Anton is telling me that Copelan doesn't deserve me. I recall that plush red and violet room, his heat on top of me, and instead of pulling away after the danger was gone, he instead set a tender kiss upon my lips. Then I am in the rowboat, breathing in gulps of sea mist when he is calling me strong, and after, in his quarters, his heartbeat the only thing tethering me to reality, his voice in my ear telling me I am art. The fire that sparked between us in his chamber, forbidden as it was, before Basile interrupted us.

And now, now he's pleading with me, protesting what I might do, no matter what it would cost him.

Time. I just need to buy us time.

"I will beg you with all that I have," I say, cupping Illian's face. His eyes flutter shut, chest rising and falling. The scent of clove and leather pervades my senses.

Say yes. Focus on me.

Opening his eyes, Illian nods at Aemon, who pulls a key from his pocket. He then slides it into the metal block attached to Anton's chains.

Anton falls, his knees hitting the carpet. He gives me a look, then examines his wrists, still bound in manacles, before Aemon releases those, too. I shoot my gaze toward Illian, my disbelief clear.

He pinches my bottom lip between his thumb and forefinger. "I do love anything that comes from these lush, rosy lips—even if they're lies."

Casually, he paces to the bar and pours himself a drink. "I did make a promise to set you free," he says, angling his chin toward Anton. He empties his glass in few quick gulps, then clanks it down. "It's one I intend to keep."

When he turns, he offers me a careless grin.

Too late, I see the intent in his eyes.

In one swift motion, Illian yanks the halberd from Aemon's hands and smashes the lever holding the pin on the crank. The chain holding the chandelier in place whips free, unspooling in a blink—

—and the chandelier drops onto Anton like a thousand spears, impaling him onto the carpet below.

Chapter Thirty-Nine

A scream tears from my lips, so loud and agonized that my vision flashes white.

I throw myself down next to Anton. He is pinned on his back, legs protruding at odd angles, shards staking his ribs, the soft flesh of his stomach. A large one pierces his right arm. Blood wells, running in rivulets into the carpet, soaking its weft. It's everywhere. *Everywhere.*

Anton sputters, struggling to breathe. If I can *just* lift one side of the chandelier—but if I do, he will bleed out. "Anton," I hear myself sob. I feel so far from my body. This is a nightmare, sent from the Fate of Morta—worse than any time in any cell, worse than broken bones and stolen time.

"It's all right," he manages, his green eyes capturing mine. But I can't accept this, can't—

"Vas," he wheezes, eyes widening. "*Vas—*"

A hand grabs my hair, ripping me away. I crash into a wall, and then Illian looms over me, his arms caging me in like the bars of a cell. "*Never* will another man's name be on your lips," he growls.

Angry heat surges through my veins, and something inside me snaps.

Shatters.

Chars.

I am a wildfire, and I intend to burn.

He tears at my bodice, but he doesn't see my hands. I find the small sack attached to my side. He did always love my millen; he'd been anticipating a private performance when he built this gown.

I open it and fling millen into his face. It blinds him in an ash-gray cloud. As he cries out, I yank off a ribbon holding the sash around my waist, throw it around his neck, *squeeze*—

In a blink, the guards are upon me, Aemon included. They tear my hands away as Illian sputters and chokes, angry, red swathes patching his face. His gaze slices toward mine, aflame with fury.

Then his features warp into something unrecognizable.

And I know, then, that I will not survive this night.

Sana jerks me back, throwing my wrists into shackles. To my surprise, her hands are trembling as much as mine. She, too, had seen what he did. She has been witness to all of this.

"Sana, please," I breathe, knowing it's useless, but I have to try.

And then she does something I don't expect. Her eyes latch on to mine, deliberately, as she leaves the manacles unlocked.

"You will spend every day back in that decrepit cell," Illian hurls my way. "And every day, Aemon will visit you with his sword and his fists. And he will keep visiting until you are so thoroughly broken you no longer remember who you are or where you came from. Then, and only then, will I come for you!"

"The p-problem with that, b-brother," says a weak voice from the floor, "is that you haven't yet won."

I whirl.

A pained grin slides across Anton's face.

Then, perhaps by a strike of fate, something vibrates the walls—something that sounds an awful lot like an otherworldly *growl*.

The doors are thrown wide, and a roar like thunder bellows into the room. All the guards, Aemon and Sana included, whip around, swords out, but they are woefully outmatched against a massive jaw stacked with dagger-sharp teeth.

Ishu rips into the two guarding the entrance, Basile behind her. Shouts erupt. Blood bathes the walls, even the ceiling. Several guards race around Illian, barricading him, while the others fight a flurry of claws and steel. I stand frozen, slack, until Copelan's face appears in the doorway.

"Vasalie," he shouts, and behind him runs Gustav. *Gustav.* And others I recognize from Anton's court. They're free.

I fling the manacles from my wrists, dropping to Anton's side. His eyes are open. I call his name, then scream it, because he isn't looking at me, even though I'm *right in front of him.*

Blood snakes down his lips, leaking in trails.

No—*no.* I grab his cheeks, willing him to blink, to say my name. Everything swarms around me in a blur, but all I can see are his eyes, blank and unseeing. "Anton, please," I sob. "Look at me."

The man who woke me up. Who saw me. Who *armed* me. Who made me feel strong, empowered, worthy—because I *am* worthy. I am not *less,* even as I am. Even when my body fails me. I am not less . . .

"He's gone," Copelan says, grabbing my shoulder. I don't believe him. I can't believe him.

"Vasalie," he says urgently. "We have to flee. The palace is full of Brisendali soldiers. Any moment now, they will hear what's happening in here." He pulls me up with strong arms.

Tears clog my vision, but finally I look at Copelan. Copelan, who abandoned me in the Dome Hall. "How are you here?"

He pulls me along, but I can't seem to control my limbs. "Vas—Souls. I'm sorry," he says. "I saw what happened during the last performance, and then that wedding . . ." He mutters a curse, and I gulp a painful swallow. The disgust I saw wasn't at me, then. "I managed to sneak Laurent a key, and he escaped. He told me everything. We freed as many as we could, and now, we have to hurry." He urges me onward.

But Aemon barrels into him. Copelan staggers back and unsheathes his sword, clumsily throwing it up against an attack, but it's clear that he barely knows how to use it. Aemon swings his halberd—

I kick the back of his knees, breaking his balance. When he falters, Copelan plunges his sword deep into Aemon's gut.

More of Illian's men swarm into the room. The fury of Ishu's growling shakes my bones.

Panting, Copelan says, "Run, Vas! The balcony. Laurent is below."

Frantic, I nod, lurching toward the open terrace. Laurent's voice comes on the wind. "Vasalie!"

He's on an adjacent balcony several feet below ours. It's too far for him to jump up, but he holds a rope over his head. "Catch," he calls. "We can use it to esc—"

A hand wraps around my throat.

"This only ends one way," Illian says against my jaw. I feel the cold, sharp press of steel against my clavicle. "Or I will send you to Morta's Lair myself." He angles my chin toward Laurent's frantic eyes. "Tell him to throw the rope. Catch it, secure it, and together, we will escape down to the courtyard."

"The rope isn't long enough for that," I say, hoping to buy time. But no one's coming. Cold sea wind thrashes against the palace walls, a squall on its tail. Thunder snarls in the distance, echoing Ishu's fury and the clash of steel behind us. Everyone is locked in battle, even Basile, who stands swinging before the corpse of his king—a sight I know I'll never forget.

"Then rip off your sash and lengthen the rope." Illian removes the dagger from my neck, slicing at the fabric.

He expects me to be a lamb, to lay down for slaughter, but I've grown claws. Teeth. *Scales.*

I slam into him, wrestling him down, nails carving into the flesh of his arms. The dagger falls from his hands, clattering against stone and sliding a few inches away. I scramble toward it. Laurent is yelling my name.

A sharp pain pierces my thigh, and a cry dries my lungs.

Rough hands flip me onto my back. Illian hovers over me, my dagger in hand. The very one I used to slice his flag. "Thanks to you, I had a backup on hand." He kicks the other dagger off the balcony.

"You will die for this," Laurent bellows from below.

"Throw me the rope," Illian says simply, "or I will finish her off while you watch."

Lights wink through my peripheral vision; I fight to remain conscious. My stomach empties onto the stone. When I glance up, I find Illian banding the rope around the railing.

He knows I will not get far with the wound he inflicted.

The pain is blinding, burning, as if the dagger had been made of molten rock.

But my body is familiar with pain.

I drag myself up, using the balustrade for support. A strange sort of trepidation settles thickly in my lungs—an ominous feeling I've felt only once before, when Emilia died. It's like a shadow, cold and hollow, sickly sweet.

Breathing through the anguish of the hole in my leg, I say a silent prayer, knowing that, this time, the Fate of Morta is close enough to hear. *End this. Take us both.*

Enough blood has been spilled today; the floor is marbled in it. Surely she is satisfied—especially now that I offer her my life.

Illian whips toward me, his face stained pewter, a remnant of the millen I threw at him. He grazes my bustier with the glass dagger, then pockets it, knowing I'm too weak to run. "I am going to tie us together."

"I want you to know that someday, somehow, I will find a way to kill you," I tell him. "My life may be in your hands, but one day, I will break free. And I will drag you to the depths of Morta's hell myself."

He doesn't even flinch. "You fail to frighten me, Vastianna."

"I'm going to call your bluff, brother."

Brother?

I freeze, everything tunneling to that voice.

That voice.

It is both familiar and altogether impossible. I must be hallucinating. Losing blood.

The rope falls from Illian's hands.

And when I manage to lift my head, I see him.

He looks the way he did when I left him alone before an audience the first night of the Gathering—radiant, limned in the gold of a glowing, storm-wreathed moon.

Only, he isn't quite himself. There's something different, something ethereal, about him—almost as if he's absorbing the shadows around him.

His name falls from my lips in a whisper, maybe even a prayer.

And beside him is Basile, looking thoroughly put out.

"How?" Illian rasps, pale as a wraith. His eyes whip toward the chandelier. I follow his gaze, but the chandelier is there, unmoved. Except there is no corpse pinned beneath its spikes. "You are a ghost. An aberration. You must be . . ."

Anton's smirk is devilish. Devastating. "Come and find out. Though if Mount Carapet wasn't enough to convince you, nothing will be."

Mount Carapet. He had told me he hadn't died. Hadn't he? But then . . .

I woke on a jut of rocks along the mountainside.

He had woken.

Not from being rendered unconscious, but from death. He hadn't lied.

The rumors are true.

He came back to life.

He walked away, because . . . because he *cannot* die.

Whatever Illian says, he's lying. He cannot hurt me.

He can't hurt me.

"How?" Illian yells again. He yanks me against his chest, the sharp tip of his dagger digging into my sternum. "Tell me!"

"You want to know?" Anton says, edging closer, his gaze carefully tracking his brother. "Release her first."

"You think me a fool?"

"Look behind me," Anton says. Past him, the battle has died down, Anton's men barricading the doors against a barrage of soldiers trying to force their way inside. "The palace is yours. In minutes, your men will break through. Well done, Illian. But I stand between your victory and escape, and believe me when I tell you that you will not leave here alive if you do not let her go. Everyone in this room will make sure of it."

Basile lifts his sword in emphasis, veins of red running down its length.

Beside them, Copelan skids to a halt. Gustav joins, too. He pats Anton on the shoulder, seemingly unsurprised at the return of his king. "Good to have you back. Took you long enough, though."

I feel the vicious beat of Illian's heart against my back as he says, "All those times. What, did you seduce the Fate of Morta into letting you live?" He laughs, but it's dry. "I can't kill you, can I? So what makes you think I'll give her up only for you to strike me down?"

Anton eases forward, but the sharp tip of glass splits the skin above my heart. Stars spiral through me, rousing a flood of nausea that warps my vision. I don't hear myself cry out, but I feel it in my throat. A strange scent fills my nostrils. I try to open my mouth, to warn Anton about the rope—that Illian has an escape—but cannot.

"Illian!" Anton thunders. For the first time, his eyes catch mine, but I'm too hazy to latch on to them. "Bargain with me, if nothing else. Trade me for her. Lock me up. Leave me in a dungeon to rot. Whatever you want."

No.

"*Illian,*" I wheeze. It takes everything in me to push it out. "Understand this." My throat burns. My mouth feels as if it holds a bucket of steam. Still, I force my voice through. "Your jewels are not enough. Your power is not enough. You are rich in diamonds but poor in spirit. You are *lacking*." Another tight breath, and then, "He does not envy you. I do not want you. You are but dust in the wind, here and gone again."

I feel the spike of his pulse. I made my mark. The strange scent grows heavier, filling every pore on my skin like a coat of millen. He shifts the dagger lower, his hand trembling, the tip edging just under my ribs. Pain splices through me in a dizzying rush.

And I see it there, the want in his gaze. The outrage. He shakes with it—shakes with the need to push that dagger up and underneath my ribs, even as he refuses to do it. For all he would hurt me, I am a belonging he will never release.

And he will stall until his men arrive or use me to escape. That, I cannot allow.

There's a whistling in the wind, a howling. A soughing that I feel in my soul. The sky is dark as dried blood, ready to devour.

I spin and hook my arms around Illian's neck like a noose.

Today, I claim him.

Today, I take his hand.

I am no longer his victim.

I will be the Fate of Morta and *I* will bring him death.

Anton's shouts come on the wind. "Vasalie, no—"

I tip us both over the balustrade.

Let my weight plummet backward.

And pull him over with me.

Chapter Forty

Pain.

The world is blinding, endless pain.

I choke for air.

I gaze at the balcony several stories up, see the way they shout for me.

"Vastianna," someone says—not below but inside my mind. The voice is lovely and feminine, soft as a drop of rain. But I can't talk to her yet. It takes all the strength, all the willpower I have left, to tilt my head just so.

I have to know if it worked.

Illian lies a few yards away, his body broken and bent at odd angles, his face pancaked into stone. Blood runs from him like thinned-out paint, soaking the nearby grass.

It offers me the modicum of peace I needed, even as I feel myself fade away.

I no longer try to hold on.

Letting go feels like a relief.

Breath leaves me.

Pain leaves me.

And I feel myself die.

Chapter Forty-One

My spirit slips free of this world like a snake shedding its skin. I am weightless, eternal. I feel as if I could inhabit the stars.

Below, my body is a smear of gore on the ground. Wholly broken, the way I always thought I was, when in fact I was far from it. I know that now. Then my gaze fixes on the husk beside me, blood collecting beneath a mass of leather and velvet.

I wonder if he is like me, hovering above the scene like a wraith.

I wonder if I will see him again.

Everything that happens next is in slow motion, even as figures spill onto the courtyard, forming a radius around us both.

Even as Anton kneels before me, gathering my corpse into his arms.

I want to tell him that it's all right. This was my choice.

A voice slides into my thoughts like water.

I know it instantly. I have heard her in my dreams, after all.

All my fears, my concerns, drop away when I turn.

Emilia is there, lovely and pure, a halo of golden curls framing her iridescent face. Oh, how I have missed her. How I long for her, even as she drifts before me.

She stretches out her hand to welcome me home.

Willingly, *eagerly*, I take it.

Chapter Forty-Two

Time feels infinite here.
    Boundless. Shapeless.
I don't know how much of it has passed.

The world is black like sludge. Like murk. I can see nothing beyond faint blurs of light, there and gone again. My own consciousness hangs by a thread, though I cannot reach it. I try to lift my hands, wriggle my fingers, but my body—if it can be called that—does not move at my command.

I always hoped death would feel like freedom, but it is no such thing.

Then a voice comes to me, a voice I recognize. Emilia's, but not. "This is her, no?"

Just then, a scene materializes before me, a whir of dark shapes and colors, but I can focus on nothing aside from the woman before me.

Silver, translucent skin gleams under the azure, iridescent glow of this place. She eases down her hood, and blue hair spirals about her neck, her gown floating in weightless ribbons. And when she looks at me, her sheer loveliness brings a pang to my heart.

Except I think perhaps I no longer have a heart.

The Fate of Morta.

I realize, then, that she holds me suspended. I am a few feet above the ground, weightless, pliant to her command. She twists her fingers, and I rotate before coming to face her again.

I try to move my lips but find that I cannot. It's as if I'm in the throes of a nightmare, except it's all too real.

Then I see the figure beside her, stepping into my line of focus.

Recognition is swift, like a jolt to my nonexistent heart. And when the Fate speaks again, I know I'm not dreaming.

"You can stop causing a ruckus in my cavern and scaring the wits out of my souls now, Anton."

Green eyes. Royal garb.

The glint of rings.

He is here. How is he here?

Then I see the lifeless body draped in his arms, broken and bruised, almost beyond recognition.

Carefully, he places my corpse before the Fate of Morta, and then his gaze latches on to mine. I wonder what I look like to him. A wisp, or a wraith? But try as I might, I cannot breathe his name—

A single stride brings him to me, except that he bounces back, as if there's a pane of glass between us.

"What in the souls have you done to her? Moranya, I thought you better than this."

Moranya. That must be her name now that she's no longer Mercy.

And how are they so familiar? But then I recall, dimly, that he's been here before. I wonder how many times.

How had he refused her hand?

"Anton, please. She is a new soul. I must determine her virtue before I can release my hold," Moranya says, gliding closer to me, examining me as if through a mirror. "Interesting, that despite her lovely sheen, I see blood, too. She has brought me not one but three souls."

Mine.

King Rurik's.

Illian's.

"A shame she can't stay with you," Anton says.

"Why bother with her to begin with? This is unlike you."

"She is a hero."

"Very admirable, little king. But does she know your truth?" Moranya whirls to face me. "Do you know the reason Anton has been able to return from my lair time and again?"

"Moranya—"

"Ah, I see she does not." To me, she says, "You see, he never took my hand because he has never loved anyone. Not even a single soul. I have worn many faces, and yet he has always refused me."

So that's how Anton did it.

Eremis loved himself, and so he took his *own* hand.

Anton loves . . . no one. He never has. And despite whatever feelings I have toward him, it only makes my heart break.

He loves no one, and I wonder if it's because no one has ever truly loved *him*. Because he hides his true self, keeps everyone at an arm's length.

I wish I could tell him that her efforts to turn me against him will not work.

I hope he can see it in my eyes.

But he merely dons his usual arrogance, a mask of surety that pulls his lips into an ever so slight grin. "A compelling yet pointless argument, Moranya, when I will not allow you to keep her here, all the same."

"You think you have the power to stop me?"

"Souls, no," he says, barking a laugh. "But I do happen to have a bit of . . . leverage." He draws a long chain from his tunic, a small, circular pendant attached. He flips it open to reveal a sphere of prismatic glass.

"My turn to tell a story."

The pendant—I remember it. He had tried to get me to take it when he was hanging from the chandelier, moments before Illian barged in. *Find the nearest source of light.*

He lets it fall, then twirls the chain in his hand so the pendant twists round and round. "You see, I found it interesting that the first time I died, I appeared before you exactly as I had been before my death, all my belongings in tow. That meant others would, too. Of course, I was never compelled to take your hand, even despite your allure, being that there was no one I loved enough to want to join. And so I saw you as your true self.

"But I knew better, my dearest Moranya, than to make Eremis's mistake in assuming you would not find a way to outsmart me one day. I decided I wanted my own version of immortality beyond whatever emotion I might feel. So I studied every tale I could find about you and Eremis both."

Once more, he palms the pendant, then tosses it upward a few times like an apple. "My favorite version of Eremis's story was the one where you turned his reflection back on him. Not by holding up a mirror but becoming his reflection yourself. I realized, then, that the answer was simple. All I needed was a way to see through your disguise when you inevitably found one to compel me.

"But that begs the question: How could I accomplish such a feat? Then I remembered the Temple of Zur, where some claimed the fragments of the mirror used in most versions of your tale were kept. And while you never used the mirror in the way most people believed, the mirror wasn't contrived, now was it? There was indeed a mirror, only it wasn't originally yours. It belonged to the Fate you seduced—and the temple priests claimed a fates-touched object always holds a remnant of its power. Like a thumbprint.

"All it took was a single fragment of that mirror, and two years in a workshop with Gustav Bayard—the son of a glass smith and inventor like myself—to create our prototype. A lens, we called it," he says, observing it once more. "Of course I couldn't be certain whether it would work unless I tested it out myself. And you see," he says, looking to Moranya, "I did, only you did not notice. It was a nice try, using Vasalie's face. And perhaps I might have taken your hand, had it not been for this; I suppose now we will never know. Didn't you wonder why I was fiddling with my jewelry? Oh, right—I make it such a regular habit with you, you were bound not to notice."

A sob builds in my chest, though I can't release it. He had tried to give me the lens, tried to explain how to use it, only he was cut off. He wanted to give me a way to return to life, all while potentially risking his own.

Perhaps I might have taken your hand, had it not been for this.

Because she appeared as me. I can't—can't—think about what that means, or what would have happened if I had taken that necklace from him.

Moranya's eyes widen, almost imperceptibly. She takes a step closer, observing the lens. "A marvel," she finally says, clucking her tongue. "Truly, I admire your efforts. But there is one problem, see. If I accept your little trinket, how do I know you won't create more?"

"Oh, I most certainly will, and I'll hand one to every member of my court if you do not bargain with me."

"Ah, but you gave yourself away, Anton, when you told me you might have fallen for a face such as hers. Replicate your lens, and you'll never see her again. Risk it, if you want. But we can settle this much more easily than that."

Anton fists his palms. "Name your price."

"You, of course."

He gives her a knowing look. "Try again."

"A piece of you, then." She straightens to her full height until she is as tall as he is. "I want a piece of your soul. The goodness of it. The warmth and comfort, for here, I am so very cold. That is my price, little king. For that, I will give you the girl."

I try and fail to shake my head. *No.* I might not fully understand, but a piece of his soul, his goodness . . .

I will him to look at me. To let me go—

"Anton," she says, pacing to him. She brackets his cheeks with her hands. A warm, cerulean glow radiates from her palms. Her voice softens like a lover as she says, "Would you not wish to give me something of yourself?"

I don't understand what she's doing. Some kind of power, and to my horror, his eyes flutter shut. He sways on his feet, as if he might lean into her. As if she has some hold over him, some allure he's barely resisting. "I would," he breathes, his hand inching upward toward her own. "Of course I would."

Anton! Voicelessly, I scream his name, over and over—

His eyelids fly open, as if jolting from a trance, and fury lights her gaze. She dashes a hand in my direction. A sleepy fog whisks over me then, but I fight to stay here. To listen, observe, even if I can do nothing...

"What, then?" Anton says. "You plan to turn her into soul sludge if I don't agree?"

"I will not offer twice." With that, she curls her fingers. A gathering of air coils around me like a chain.

"Wait."

Moranya pauses, the hint of a smirk curling her lips. She does not lower her hand. "Do we have a deal, then? A piece of you, for her?"

"Would I still be myself?" he asks.

"Yes or no, Anton?"

"My brother," he says. "Did you make a deal with him?"

"There is nothing in Illian Orvere that I desire."

"What are you planning then? Are you bringing Eremis back?"

Eremis.

The prophecy.

From Beauty foretold, a trap unfolds,
A return to the living, a plight of souls.

Moranya's brows notch in confusion. "Why would I do that?"

"Come now, we know each other better than this," Anton prods.

"You dislike the Fates. You would prefer us all under your dominion, would you not?"

"As much as I love our exchanges, and truly I do," she says, "I tire of your interrogation. The deal, Anton. Yes or no. Accept now, or lose her."

A jewel in His palm, a path divine.

"Wait—"

"Going once," she says, and I feel myself being squeezed, constricted . . .

"Moranya—"

With the Fate of Morta, He will align.

"Twice."

"All right," he cuts in, his gaze traveling back over me. I try to shake my head, jerk every muscle to no avail. Without his goodness—

The prophecy.

It isn't about Illian, or even my father.

It's about Anton.

Anton.

"Give me one day," he relents, and my heart seizes. "One day with my court, before you claim that piece of me for yourself. Then we have a deal."

No, I try once more. *No—*

Her smile is a wicked, lovely thing. "How long I have waited for you."

A blink, and then I feel myself fall.

Chapter Forty-Three

I open my eyes to starlight.

I must be in the heavens, nothingness swept around by the winds of an open void, because there is no pain.

Except my body responds, and the pain returns slowly, like the stitch of a needle. I lift my hand to eye level, turning it slowly. It isn't transparent; it's flesh and bone. And I am not floating. I'm lying in a bed. Curtains quiver in a balmy breeze.

I ease up, hands digging into a white nightdress, memory coalescing in my mind.

My soul, adrift.

The Fate of Morta.

Green eyes between blurry blinks, low murmurs breathing my name. *Vasalie. Wake up.*

Anton.

Had I dreamed it? It must have been a dream.

But then, I remember dying. The feel of falling, breaking, yet my bones aren't shattered. I feel like I always had before, familiar aches lancing my nerves.

I scramble from bed, not knowing where I am. I totter forward until I reach a wide window on the far wall. Leaning my weight on the sill, my eyes widen at the view.

Miles of sand ripple before me. Not the sand of the Miridranian beaches but yellow thick-grained sand, eddying across tempered dunes. My heart speeds. I turn, examining my surroundings. Sand-colored walls encompass a white bed, and underneath, a vibrant rug depicts jungle cats threading between jewel-colored trees. Otherwise, the room is empty, save for an arching door.

I stagger into the adjoining room. It's darker, a scattering of tasseled pillows strewn across a heavy rug. A table hitches against a wide window, complete with a pot of tea and two stoneware cups. Then a figure, perched on a chair—

"Vas?"

I jump, crashing into the potted plant next to me.

With a hearty laugh, the figure rises from his chair and bounds toward me, scooping me into a hug. "Vasalie, souls above. You're awake!"

Laurent. The sound of his voice pulls a sob from my chest. I squeeze him into a hug then ask, "What's happened? I remember dying. And I saw her, Laurent—"

"I know," he says, but he doesn't understand.

"Anton. Where is he—"

"Come," he says, gently taking hold of my arm. "I know you want answers, but this story isn't mine to tell. I will take you to someone who can."

I follow on unsteady feet. "At least tell me where we are?"

He pauses, looking back at me. And when he answers, his smile lights up the room. "Vasalie, welcome to Razam."

The door swings open, and I lose my breath.

It's similar to the room I'd found in the tunnel all those weeks ago, though larger. Several paintings—impossibly realistic, imposed on some sort of glass—hang along the sandstone walls, lit from behind. And yet the images look familiar. There's some of my father, of Illian. His room, his desk.

And then, *then* there's one I recognize, as if a memory had been plucked from my mind.

It's of Illian and my father meeting in the brothel in Philam, exactly as they had been, frozen in time. This is not artwork. It wasn't brushed with paint or oil.

Images, trapped in glass.

"We call them *stills* for now, though nothing quite fits," comes another voice.

Gustav.

And there he is, his smile broad. I hadn't even noticed him. Or Copelan next to him, both swathed in loose, silken clothes. They are by the window, hovering over a map alongside Prince Sundar.

"I don't understand," I say.

"I didn't either at first." Laurent gives my hand a squeeze; it feels so small cupped by his own. "But this," he says, gesturing around, "is Miridran's salvation."

"We've been working on it for years, Anton and I," Gustav says, approaching. He pauses before the image of my father and Illian. "We can capture reality with a device we call a Lensgraph—name pending. This is one of many reasons the recent tunnel additions in the Palace of Anell were built. We've been trying to gather proof of Illian's schemes for some time."

The invention Gustav helped build.

The proof Anton promised he would deliver.

The development Basile had referenced.

My feet move of their own accord. There, on the far wall, are *stills* of the banquet night. Everyone gathered at the table. The show of light on the walls. Then me, gazing into the looking glass after Anton pulled me away. I shake my head, words trapped in my throat.

"Of course by the time we had enough proof to bring before the Crowns' Syndicate, it was too late. The last image Anton caught took time to develop, and by then . . ."

The tunnels had been discovered, and Anton had been captured.

My eyes catch on a familiar *still* on the wall. It's the one I saw when I'd discovered the room in the tunnel, where Anton seemed to be looking right at me with that infuriating, all-knowing smirk. I touch a finger against the glass, leaving a thumbprint on his bottom lip.

Anton.

"I saw him," I say. And perhaps it had been a dream, but I swear, swear that it was real—

"Vasalie, your sacrifice that night has not gone unnoticed," Gustav says. "However, once . . ." He trails off, swallowing. "We had to flee Miridran. The Crowns' Syndicate will not allow Anton to rule after Illian's accusations—not without intervention."

Copelan meets my gaze for the first time, but he quickly glances down. Ashamed, I realize. Turns out I can't look at him, either.

"So Miridran doesn't have a king," I whisper, "with Illian dead."

Dead, by my hands. But Anton . . .

"The Crowns' Syndicate holds Razam responsible for King Rurik's death. And Illian's, now. The new king of Brisendale is calling for war," Prince Sundar answers. "He's camped a portion of his army in the Karithian archipelago, on an island just north of Miridran."

The new king. The Beast of the North. My *father*.

When Crowns divide, and nations collide,
Blood will run, high as tides.

"It's a war we cannot win," Prince Sundar continues. "However, once Anton went missing on the night of your final performance, my mother had the foresight to escape with these," he says, gesturing at the *stills*.

She didn't abandon us.

"It means we can now petition an audience with the Crowns' Syndicate on neutral ground and lay out our proof," Laurent says.

Proof—of everything my father and Illian did. Because Anton got that proof. He had been gathering it all along.

He'd kept his word to me. I press my hands to my chest.

"The general will not relinquish his throne easily," says a new voice—powerful yet feminine. Queen Sadira whisks into the room then, her sharp eyes taking me in. "But he will not garner support once the Syndicate sees this. Especially if you, his daughter, are the one to present it."

I blow out a breath.

Anton. He's given me everything I need to show the world who my father truly is. My revenge, Emilia's justice, it sits in my lap, wrapped with a bow. A rush of emotions surges through me and I have a hard time keeping it in. Everything I'd fought for is here, within my grasp.

I am *free.*

I can take my father down.

Except . . .

"Please tell me where he is," I rasp. My heart races, stutters. I pull against my nightdress, chest tight. "I saw him. He made a bargain and—"

"Breathe, Vastianna Stova," Queen Sadira says, approaching me. She skims her knuckles across my cheek, her expression so similar to how Emilia used to look at me that I almost crumble beneath her touch. "I will take you to him. But first, we must talk."

After our talk, Queen Sadira leads me into a secluded wing of her palace, the halls empty and mostly unlit. She dismisses the four guards standing watch at yet another archway, save for the one I recognize.

Basile.

Only his expression is blank as ever, and he merely nods at the queen, who then leaves me at the threshold.

"You will need to keep your distance, Princess," Basile says.

Princess. Because my father is now a king. I shudder, but when I peer into the moonlit room beyond, I feel like a carpet has been yanked from under my feet, and the world is dropping beneath me.

Anton stands by the window, but he does not see me.

He looks different. His hair is shorter, styled rather than waving around his shoulders. He wears a dark, buttoned vest that shows off his toned arms and matching silk pants.

The sight of him steals my breath.

It's been a week since I died—or so Her Majesty informed me. He brought me from the depths of Morta's Lair. Carried me himself. And I had slept through it all: the trip here, our arrival.

Give me one day with my court.

And I had missed it.

I watch him now, my heart disintegrating inside my chest, until finally, I muster the will to speak.

"I saw everything." My voice breaks apart like a cluster of sand.

Anton doesn't move, doesn't even stir. My pulse thunders, but I tread toward him until he has no choice but to acknowledge my presence.

When he turns, his lovely emerald eyes skim mine, and everything we've been through catches up to me like a tide, threatening to buckle my knees. A tear eases down my cheek, followed by several more. I grab his face—his sharp, arresting face. Beautiful, just as Eremis once was.

From Beauty foretold, a trap unfolds,
A return to the living, a plight of souls.

"Anton," I cry. "What you did . . ."

He is not the Anton you remember, Queen Sadira had warned me. *It's as though he remembers the Gathering differently.*

Because of the bargain, the deal he made, he had been himself for a day. One day, where he told Sadira what had happened in Morta's Lair. The lens. All of it.

That's what she told me.

He set provisions in place for Miridran. Wrote a decree making Gustav the King Regent to rule in his stead. Gustav, who is also of royal blood, his mother a cousin to the late Queen Saskia, his father a relation of King Junien's. In a few days, he will return to Ansa.

And now Anton is all but lost.

He was meant for so much more, yet he sacrificed it all. For *me*. And I had been so wary of him, so afraid he was like his brother. Another man who would use and discard me in the end.

It wasn't until he'd told us the whole story that we understood that he was the fulfillment of the prophecy, the queen had told me. He hadn't known, either. Not until the very end.

And I had watched it happen.

I am the *reason* it happened.

He looks at me with a growing . . . *interest? Amusement?*

"Anton," I try again.

"My," he says softly, his eyes roaming over me, "what little treat did they send me now? But even a treat as delectable as you won't satiate me enough to keep me here. Tell Sadira that I do not appreciate this betrayal of hers, especially after all I did for her."

"You . . ." I frown. "You don't know who I am."

"Should I? I do apologize if we've spent a night together; you understand. I do that often. It's rather difficult to keep it straight."

My heart drops.

He doesn't know me at all. And yet he remembers Sadira. His other memories are intact, muddled or not . . .

No—no. If I could just snap him out of it, get through to him—

"Of course," he says, eyeing my lips, "you are welcome to spark my memory . . ."

I don't even blink. Angry, resolute, I pull his mouth determinedly to mine.

It sends a jolt through us both. And when I ease back, I swear—*swear*—I see a hint of recognition. Hope stirs within me. I cling to it, fisting his shirt.

His breath fans my cheeks, my nose.

Then he's guiding me back, back until my shoulder blades press into the wall—

His lips find my throat.

It saps the strength from my legs. But he catches me, holds me, and when he kisses me, his teeth are there, pulling at my bottom lip—

I come undone. And together we sink, twin ships with a single anchor, and I forget the queen is just outside the door. Her warning. All I know is I need him. I *need* him.

My heart was just beginning to blossom at his touch. Unfold, like the first ray of sun on a Brisendali aster after a long winter. These were our first chapters, the very beginning of our story, if I dared hope for more—

He pulls back suddenly, running his tongue over his swollen lips.

"Who *are* you?" he breathes.

Emboldened, I step toward him, taking his hands in mine, but something stirs in his eyes. They flash, darken. *No.* I clutch him tighter. "Come back to me," I beg him. But it's as if he doesn't even hear me.

Eyes of shadows, glazed like mist,
Whose touch will kill, and lips will kiss.

"It seems the goodness Moranya took from him was *you*, Vastianna," I hear the queen say from behind me.

The goodness of it, Moranya had said. *The warmth and comfort.*

We all have our comforts, Minnow. I wonder if you might be mine.

"Anton," I breathe again. *The performances. Philam. Illian,* I try to say, but my throat tightens, squeezing around the words. I wrap a hand around it, and only just manage, "You remember the Gathering, don't you? You must—"

My windpipe cinches until I can no longer speak.

"I remember *enough*," he says, turning a sharp glare on Sadira.

"And now that my kingdom has been stolen from me, I am held hostage by the woman I thought a *friend*. A nice distraction this one is, Sadira, but I've had enough."

He remembers the Gathering differently, she had said. *And no matter how hard we try, our words never seem to reach his ears. We even tried to show him the stills. He sees nothing but a blank pane of glass.*

My pulse storms through my veins. "We need you. *I* need you."

*Consumed by darkness, his heart a snare,
Those around Him will remain unaware.*

Heat burns through my blood. "I don't care what Moranya did. Anton—"

"You *dare* speak ill of my Fate," he says, swinging back toward me. One step, and he's cornered me against the wall—

Soldiers in black swarm the room, Basile along with them.

"Leave him alone!" I beg, but they don't. They shove him until his back hits the opposite wall. Basile pins his arms above him. "Get her out of here!" he shouts.

"Vastianna," calls the queen.

I whirl around. "Why is he in here, hidden away like some kind of common convict? He is a *Crown!*"

He is stronger than this, stronger than what was done to him. I can reach him—somehow. I believe in him. Why don't they?

Queen Sadira sighs. "His first request was for us to imprison him. Lock him up. But I refused, and even now, I wonder if I made the right choice. If he reclaims the Miridranian throne, child, he could become a monster. You know the prophecy. The second Eremis will crave blood. He'll wash the lands with it in service to her."

*When Crowns divide, and nations collide,
Blood will run, high as tides.*

And I had seen it, hadn't I? She had some kind of hold on him, even before the bargain. He'd leaned into her touch, there for a moment, as if he were drawn to her somehow. And the stories of her—it wasn't just who she appeared as. She had a power beyond that. An allure of some kind.

"There has to be a way to undo this," I say.

"Maybe," says the queen. "But for now, it's time to go."

But I won't. I can't. I march toward him, resolute. "Take me to Moranya," I demand. "I want to speak with her."

"You can't," Sadira interjects. "Only in death. And to try to arrange that, Vastianna, would be an insult to what he did."

"But he found a way into her lair without dying." He'd carried my body there. "Surely I can, too." I eye him, see the pendant—the lens—still hanging around his neck.

"Even if I knew how he accomplished such a thing, he forbade it," she says.

"But we need him. Miridran *needs* him."

"Yes, we do. Like you, I do not intend to abandon him so easily, prophecy or not. We of Razam are loyal to our friends."

"Then I will find another way," I say, my eyes locked on his. "I will save you, Anton, like you saved me. This is my vow." I throw my hand around his neck and pull him down, pressing my promise onto his smirking lips.

He doesn't notice the way I unhook the chain, the way the pendant falls into my free, open palm.

If he could cheat death, I can certainly cheat a deal.

For my immortal king, I will find a way.

Acknowledgments

ACKNOWLEDGMENTS

ABOUT THE AUTHOR

BRITTNEY ARENA is a passionate storyteller, crafting emotional and immersive fantasy for all kinds of readers. With a background in both brand and visual design, she has always found solace in art. However, after a challenging health journey, she turned to writing, and what began as a coping mechanism evolved into a journey of exploration, allowing her to traverse new worlds from wherever she might be. When she's not penning tales, Brittney spends her time obsessing over k-dramas, playing with her camera, and waging war against ungodly amounts of pet hair. She currently resides in North Carolina with her husband and two pups and is always ready for the next adventure, whether it be on page or in real life. *A Dance of Lies* is her debut novel.

brittneyarena.com
Instagram: @reverieandink
Threads: @reverieandink
TikTok: @brittneyarena

ABOUT THE TYPE

This book was set in Caslon, a typeface first designed in 1722 by William Caslon (1692–1766). Its widespread use by most English printers in the early eighteenth century soon supplanted the Dutch typefaces that had formerly prevailed. The roman is considered a "workhorse" typeface due to its pleasant, open appearance, while the italic is exceedingly decorative.